Famous Monsters

Famous Monsters

Kim Newman

POCKET BOOKS

LONDON · SYDNEY · NEW YORK · TOKYO · SINGAPORE · TORONTO

First published in Great Britain by Pocket Books, 1995
An imprint of Simon & Schuster Ltd
A Paramount Communications Company

Copyright © Kim Newman, 1995

Simon & Schuster Ltd
West Garden Place
Kendal Street
London W2 2AQ

Simon & Schuster of Australia Pty Ltd
Sydney

A CIP catalogue record for this book is available from the
British Library
ISBN 0-671-85300-7

Typeset in Goudy Old Style 11/13pt
Hewer Text Composition Services, Edinburgh
Printed and bound in Great Britain by
HarperCollinsManufacturing, Glasgow

Thanks to my editors: Peter Crowther, David Garnett, John Gilbert, Maxim Jakubowski, Stephen Jones, Roz Kaveney, Maria Lexton, David Pringle, Alex Stewart. David S. Sutton. Also: Eugene Byrne, Ramsey Campbell, Gardner Dozois, Gary Potter, Karl Edward Wagner.

For Pat Cadigan

Contents

Foreword

The Author on the Autopsy Table *or*
Here Comes Everyone at the Cross-Genre
Jaunters' Ball

by

Paul J. McAuley

Kim Newman spends a lot of his professional life in the dark, closely watching other people's dreams.

I'm talking about his work as a film critic, of course; despite the waistcoat, whiskers and pocket watch, he is neither a reincarnation of Sigmund Freud nor of the White Rabbit. He writes regular reviews for a slew of magazines, has produced two comprehensive books of genre criticism (one about horror movies, of course; the other about westerns), and is a major contributor to the Horror volume of the *Aurum Film Encyclopedia*.

Despite all the time he spends in the dark, Kim is also a relentlessly, prolifically, productive author – this is his second short story collection* to be published in less than a year – of *noir* fictions, many of which are deeply informed by movie lore. *Where the Bodies are Buried* and its sequel, for instance, exhibit an intimate knowledge of every aspect of the horror movie business, from fanboy obsessions to the heart-breaking negotiations and Faustian pacts by which vision is cut down to fit the rack of genre preconceptions. Despite his love of movies – or because of it – Kim knows that Hollywood isn't where dreams are made: it's where they die a little, day by day. As the Martian in *Famous Monsters* has it, most movies turn out to be pieces of shit, but what the hell, it's show business.

Kim's ability to run two careers in parallel, with such intense productivity, is unnerving to some. A few envious conspiracy theorists hint that Kim gets so much published because he *knows* stuff about editors. There's even one loony tune hypothesis that 'Kim Newman' is an androgynous house-name adopted by a cabal of writers in a cynical bid to capture the post-feminist audience.

Could be that these people just can't stand success.

In fact, the secret of Kim's success is simple: he works damn hard. A lot of would-be writers get hung up on this simple fact, preferring instead to blether on about word processing programs, laser printers, stapling versus paper clipping, and the right colour folder in which to 'present' your work. But when it comes down to it, the advice of American writer Joe Lansdale ('Put ass to chair in front of

---

* The first is, of course, *The Original Dr Shade and Other Stories*.

typewriter') can't be beat. When Kim isn't sipping warm white wine in the plush womb of the preview theatre, daring Hollywood to do its worst, as like as not he is writing. (He uses a trusty Stone-Age Amstrad PCW with Babylonian Locoscript, hackers. Lord knows how many volumes would be needed to contain all his short fiction, and how many times I would have had to rewrite this introduction if he got hold of some up-to-date technology.)

Kim works so hard, in fact, that his output of fiction has split into two: as Jack Yeovil he has written a slew of tie-in novels that transcended their role-playing game origins, and a horror novel, *Orgy of the Blood Parasites*,[*] that for some reason was published first in Germany. It used to be that you could recognise whether Kim was Kim or Kim was Jack by whether he was drinking white wine or whisky; you could spot the flutter in his gaze a moment before he made his choice, as the appropriate persona clicked in. These days Kim and Jack increasingly reside under the same Panama hat.

Kim's frightening productivity isn't new in genre fiction, where writers traditionally have stayed above water by taking on any job that comes their way, especially at the beginning of their careers (Neil Gaiman completists should ask him about his *Duran Duran* instant book, a commission which Kim passed on, thereby demonstrating that even he has limits[†]). But Kim is unique

---

[*] Published in the UK by Pocket Books.
[†] Actually, the Neil Gaiman book I passed on doing was his enormously successful *Don't Panic: The Official Hitchhiker's Guide to the Galaxy Companion*. [KN]

in that, no matter what market it is aimed at, all his fiction has the same recognisable tone, informed by an intense fascination with the iconography of movies and pulp fiction. The result is that everything, even the Jack Yeovil tie-ins, forms a single œuvre which he is polishing towards some final masterwork we can't even glimpse yet – perhaps the œuvre in its entirety will be his monument, made luminous by his inordinate sensitivity towards signifiers buried in the genre products of popular culture, inextricably tangled together by sly cross-references.

Many of his characters, for instance, turn up in different roles in different stories, much as movie stars retain their own personae from film to film. Geneviève Dieudonné, who has a walk-on part in *The Big Fish*, first appeared as a vampire in Jack Yeovil's tie-in novel *Drachenfels*, and again as a vampire, in very different circumstances, in the alternate history novel *Anno Dracula*. The sinister media mogul Derek Leech, shadowy underwriter of the charming exploitative movie outfit New Frontier Pictures, featured in *Where the Bodies are Buried II: Sequel Hook* and in *Out of the Night, When the Full Moon is Bright*, has a fuller role in Kim's mainstream novel, *The Quorum*.

Alternate histories, in which historical characters take on new roles, are particularly suited to Kim's encyclopedic knowledge of twentieth century popular culture. *The Pierce Arrow Stalled And . . .* shifts the world's timeline on to a new track before the first sentence is completed, launching Hollywood Babylon on a rising curve of sleaze unrestrained by any Hays Code. In *Three on a Match*, alternate histories spiral out from the quantum spark of a match flame, collapsing when it is snuffed out. Not all of his stories are as overtly alternate as these – or *The Snow Sculptures of Xanadu*, *Übermensch*, and *Famous Monsters* – but if you are sensitive enough, many of Kim's stories contain traces, elements, little *hints*, that suggest we are no longer in Kansas.

Although Kim is primarily known as a horror writer, it's increasingly difficult to locate precisely a place for Kim's fiction within the Horror, SF or Fantasy genres from which he draws and reworks much of his imagery. Most of the stories collected here are never straightforward enough to be considered pure horror. Kim admits as much. He isn't comfortable with the excess for excess's sake of such modern exponents of horror as the splatterpunks, with their relentless sex'n'drugs'n'rock'n'roll'n'blood'n'guts riffs. The body count in some of his stories may be high, but the bloodwork is never dwelt on in loving close-up, and even the truly ultraviolent excesses of *Pitbull Brittan* are guyed by a fierce moral sense. The story gets its bite not only from the premise that everything the *Daily Mail* wrote about the miners' strike was the literal truth, but also from a conflation of Kim's contempt for the political stance from which those fantasies arose, with the redundant cliches of the thirties patriotic potboilers he parodies in every sentence. No wonder Mrs T gets to make the ultimate sacrifice in the end: Kim demands nothing less. There are plenty of monsters in the stories collected here, but, from the Martian bit-actor in *Famous Monsters* to the werewolf as hero in *Out of the Night*,

When the Full Moon is Bright, they are mostly victims of circumstance. The true monsters are the moguls and politicians who run the system which traps and manipulates everyone else.

The simple fact is that Kim has never written a straightforward story in his life. He sprawls across boundaries with a careless insouciance. In the stories collected here, genres bleed into each other just as the artifacts and mores of our culture bleed into the lives of the True People in *The Pale Spirit People*. *The Big Fish* is an homage to both the private eye and the horror pulp fiction of the 1940's. *Out of the Night, When the Full Moon is Bright* (down whose mean streets I chauffeured Mr Newman, who never seemed to mind when we got lost in the blighted suburbs of South Central LA, and now you see why) mixes the meticulously researched mythos of Zorro with werewolf lore, to sublime effect. And so on. This kind of genre cross-dressing spills over into Kim's own life. He is perhaps the last surviving fan of the weirdest detective series ever to grace British TV, *Adam Adamant* (now out on video for all you fans of bad sixties TV), and the only writer I know who dresses like someone from a steampunk novel, although these days he looks more like the young G.K. Chesterton than Adam Adamant, if G.K. Chesterton had taken to wearing a two feet long ponytail.

Whether horror, alternate history or fantasy, there's a unique, identifiable thread which runs through all of Kim's fiction, like the metal foil in a bank note. It may shine with the silver light of the movie screen, or it may be twisted and frayed with the branchpoints of alternate history, or it may be steeped in the deep, bloody dark of horror, but as long as it's there, you know you can trust the story. Trust me. I'm a doctor. But that's another story . . .

Famous Monsters

You know, I wouldn't be doing this picture if it wasn't for Chaney Junior's liver. They said it was a heart attack, but anyone who knew Lon knows better. Doing all these interviews with the old-timers, you must have heard the stories. They don't tell the half of it. I didn't get to work with Lon till well past his prime. Past my prime too, come to that. It was some Abbott and Costello piece of shit in the fifties. Already, he looked less human than I do. Wattles, gut, nose, the whole fright mask. And the stink. Hell, but he was a good old bastard. Him and me and Brod Crawford used to hit all the bars on the Strip Friday and Saturday nights. We used to scare up a commotion, I can tell you. I guess we were a disgrace. I quit all that after I got a tentacle shortened in a brawl with some hophead beatniks over on Hollywood Boulevard. I leaked ichor all over Arthur Kennedy's star. That's all gone now, anyway. There aren't any bars left I can use. It's not that they won't serve me – the Second War of the Worlds was, like, twenty-five years ago now, and that's all forgotten – but no one stocks the stuff any more. It's easy enough to get. Abattoirs sell off their leavings for five cents a gallon. But this California heat makes it go rancid and rubbery inside a day.

Anyway, just before Lon conked out – half-way through a bottle of Wild Turkey, natch – he signed up with Al to do this picture. It was called *The Mutilation Machine* back then. It's *Blood of the Cannibal Creature* now. Al will change it. He always does. The footage with Scott Brady and the bike gang is from some dodo Al never got finished in the sixties. *Something a-Go-Go*, that's it. Lousy title. *Cycle Sadists a-Go-Go*. It must be great being a film historian, huh? What with all this confusion and crapola. Do you know how they were paying Lon? Bottles. When Al wanted him to walk across a room in a scene, he'd have the assistant director hold up a bottle of hooch off-camera and shake it. Lon would careen across the set, knocking things and people over, and go for the booze, and Al would get his shot. I don't suppose I'm all that much better off. One of the backers is a wholesale butcher, and he's kicking in my fee in pig blood. I know you think that sounds disgusting, but don't knock it until you've tried it.

For a while, it looked like Lon would last out the picture. Al got the scene where he's supposed to pull this kootch-kootch dancer's guts out. He was playing Groton the Mad Zombie, by the way. So it's not Chekhov. Al has already cut the scene together. Okay, so there's some scratching on the neg. Al can fix it. He's going to put on some more scratches, and make them look like sparks flying out of Lon. Groton is supposed to be electric. Or atomic. One or the other. The girl keeps laughing while Lon gets his mitts inside her sweater, but they can dub some screams in, and music and growling and it'll be okay. At least, it'll be as okay as anything ever is in Al's movies. Did you catch *Five Bloody Graves*? It was a piece of shit. After this, he wants to do a picture with Georgina Spelvin and The Ritz Brothers called *The Fucking Stewardesses*. You can bet he'll change *that* title.

But one scene is all there is of Lon. So, when he buys the farm Al calls me up. I don't have an agent any more, although I used to be with the William Morris crowd. I do all my deals myself. I couldn't do a *worse* job than some of the people in this business. I used to be handled by a guy called Dickie Nixon, a real sleazo scumbag. He was the one who landed me in *Orbit Jocks*, and screwed me out of my TV residuals. Anyway, I know Al. I worked for him once before, on *Johnny Blood Rides Roughshod*. That was the horror western that was supposed to put James Dean back on the top. What a joke. The fat freak kept falling off his horse. It turned out to be a piece of shit. Al and me worked something out on this one, and so here I am in Bronson Caverns again, playing Groton the Mad Zombie. They've rewritten the script so I can be Lon in all the early scenes. I know it sounds ridiculous, what with the shape and everything. But, hell, I can cram myself into a pair and a half of jeans and a double-size poncho. In the new script, my character is a Martian – I mean, I can't play an Eskimo, can I? – but when John Carradine zaps me with the Mutilation Machine I turn into a human being. Well, into Groton the Mad

Zombie. It's the most challenging part that's come my way in years, even if the film is going to be a total piece of shit. I'm hoping my performance will be a tribute to Lon. I've got the voice down. 'George, lookit duh rabbits, George.' Now, I'm working on the walk. That's difficult. You people walk all weird. No matter how long I hang around you, I still can't figure out how you manage with just the two legs.

I'm an American citizen, by the way. I was hatched in Los Angeles. Put it down to the Melting Pot. Mom flopped down in the twenties, when the Old World political situation started going to hell. She'd been through WWI and couldn't face that again. It's in the culture, I guess. When your head of government is called the High War Victor you know you're in trouble. I'm not that way. I'm mellow. A typical native Californian, like my twenty-eight brood siblings. I'm the only one of us left now. The rest all died off or went back to the skies. I can't let go. It's showbiz, you know. It's in the ichor. You must understand that if you do all these interviews. What do you call it, oral history? It's important, I suppose. Someone should take all this down before we all die out. Did you get to Rathbone? There was a guy with some stories. I never got on with him though, despite all those pictures we did together. He lost some relatives in the First War of the Worlds, and never got around to accepting that not all non-terrestrials were vicious thugs.

I suppose you'll want to know how I got into the movies? Well, I'm that one in a million who started as an extra. It was in the late thirties, when I'd barely brushed the eggshell out of my slime. Four bucks a day just for hanging around cardboard nightclubs or walking up and down that street where the buildings are just frontages. In *Swing Time*, I'm in the background when Fred and Ginger do their 'Pick Yourself Up' routine. They were swell, although Rogers put my name down on some list of communist sympathisers in the fifties and I nearly had to go before HUAC. Do I look like a commie? Hell, how many other Americans can blush red, white and blue? I didn't stay an extra long. I suppose I'm noticeable. There were very few of us in Hollywood, and so I started getting bit parts. Typically, I'd be a heavy in a saloon fight, or an underworld hanger-on. If you catch *The Roaring Twenties* on a re-run, look out for me during the massacre in the Italian restaurant. Cagney gets me in the back. It's one of my best deaths. I've always been good at dying.

My big break came when Twentieth Century Fox did the Willie K'ssth films. Remember? Rathbone played Inspector Willie K'ssth of the Selenite Police Force. *Willie K'ssth Takes Over*, *Willie K'ssth and the Co-Eds*, *Willie K'ssth On Broadway*, and so on. There were more than twenty of them. I was Jimbo, Willie's big, dumb Martian sidekick. I did all the comedy relief scenes – going into a tentacle-flapping fright in haunted houses, getting hit on the head and seeing animated stars in fight sequences. The films don't play much now, because of the Selenite pressure groups. They hate the idea of a human actor in the role. And when Earl Derr Biggers was writing the books in the twenties, the Grand Lunar had them banned on the Moon. I don't see what they were bothered about. Willie always spots the killer and comes out on top. He usually gets to make a bunch of human beings look ridiculous as well. In not one of the books or movies did Jimbo *ever* guess who the murderer was, even when it was blatantly obvious. And it usually was. For a while, I was typed as the dumb, scared Martie. Some of my siblings said I was projecting a negative image of the race, but there was a Depression on and I was the only one of the brood in regular work. I've got nothing against Selenites, by the way, although the Grand Lunar has always had a rotten Sapient Rights record. It's no wonder so many of them headed for the Earth.

After the New York Singe, I was quickly dropped from the series. We were half-way through *Willie K'ssth On Coney Island* when the studio quietly pulled my contract. They rewrote Jimbo as a black chauffeur called Wilbur Wolverhampton and got Stepin Fetchit to do the role. They still put out the film under its original title, even though there wasn't a Coney Island any more. I'd have sued, but there was a wave of virulent Anti-Martian feeling sweeping the country. That was understandable, I guess. I had relatives in New York, too. Suddenly, forty years of cultural exchange was out of the porthole and we were back to interspecial hatred. Nobody cared that Mom was a refugee from High War Victor Uszthay in the first place, and that since his purges most of her brood siblings were clogging up the canals. I was pulled out of my apartment by the Beverly Hills cops and roughed up in a basement. They really did use rubber hoses. I'll never forget that. I ended up in an internment camp, and the studio annexed my earnings. The hate mail was really nasty. We were out in the desert, which wasn't so bad. I guess we're built for deserts. But at night people in hoods would come and have bonfires just outside the perimeter. They burned scarecrows made to look like Martians and chanted lots of blood and guts slogans. That was disturbing. And the guards were a bit free with the cattle prods. It was a shameful chapter in the planet's history, but no one's researched it properly yet. The last interview I did was with some Martian-American professor doing a thesis on Roosevelt's treatment of so-called 'enemy aliens'. He was practically a hatchling, and didn't really understand what we had to go through. I bet his thesis will be a piece of shit. There were rumours about this camp in Nevada where the guards stood back and let a mob raze the place to the ground with the Marties still in it. And who knows what happened in Europe and Asia?

Then the cylinders started falling, and the war effort got going. Uszthay must have been a bigger fool than we took him for. With Mars's limited resources, he couldn't possibly keep the attack going for more than six months. And Earth had cavorite, while he was still using Nineteenth century rocket cannons. Do you know how many cylinders landed in the sea and sunk? So, Roosevelt got together with the world leaders in Iceland – Hitler, Stalin, Oswald Cabal - and they geared up for Earth's counter-invasion. Finally, I got all the hassles with my citizenship sorted out, and the authorities reluctantly admitted I had as much right to be called an American as any other second generation immigrant. I had to carry a wad of documentation the size of a phone book, but I could walk the streets freely. Of course, if I did I was still likely to get stoned. I did most of my travelling in a curtained car. According to what was left of my contract, I owed Twentieth a couple of movies. I assumed they'd pay me off and I'd wind up in an armaments factory, but no, as soon as I was on the lot I was handed a stack of scripts. Suddenly, everyone was making war pictures.

The first was *Mars Force*, which I did for Howard Hawks. I was loaned to Warners for that. It was supposed to be a true story. I don't know if you remember, but the week after the Singe a handful of foolhardy volunteers climbed into their Cavor Balls and buzzed the red planet. They didn't do much damage, but it was Earth's first retaliative strike. In the movie, they were after the factories where the elements for the heat rays were being synthesised. In real life, they just flattened a couple of retirement nests and got rayed down. In *Mars Force*, I played the tyrannical Security Victor at the factories. I spent most of the film gloating over a crystalscope, looking at stock footage of the smoking plains where New York used to be. I also got to drool over a skinny terrestrial missionary, snivel in fear as the brave Earthmen flew over in their Christmas tree ornaments and be machine-gunned to death by John Garfield. It was typical propaganda shit, but it was a pretty good picture. It stands up a lot better than most of the other things I did back then.

I was typecast for the rest of the war. I've raped more nurses than any actor alive – although what I was supposed to see in you sandpaper-skinned bipeds is beyond me. And I did a lot of plotting, scheming, saluting, backstabbing, bombing, blasting, cackling, betraying, sneering and strutting. I saw more action than Patton and Rommel put together, and without ever stepping off the backlots. The furthest I ever went for a battle was Griffith Park. I had a whole set of shiny, slimy uniforms. I played every rank we had going. In *Heat Ray!*, I even got to play Uszthay, although that's like asking Mickey Mouse to play John the Baptist. I soon lost count of the number of times I had to swear to crush the puny planet Earth in my lesser tentacles. I got killed a lot. I was shot by Errol Flynn in *Desperate Journey*, bombed by Spencer Tracy in *Thirty Seconds Over Krba-Gnsk*, and John Wayne got me in *Soaring Tigers*, *The Sands of Grlshnk* and *The Fighting Seabees*. In *Lunaria*, Bogart plugs me as I reach for the crystalphone on the launchfield. Remember that one? Everyone says it's a classic. It got the Academy Award that year. Claude Rains asks Bogart why he came to Lunaria, and Bogart says he came for the atmosphere. 'But there's no atmosphere on the Moon,' says Rains. 'I was misinformed.' I wanted the role of the freedom fighter who floats off to Earth with Ingrid Bergman at the end, but Jack Warner chickened out of depicting a sympathetic Martie and they made the character into a Selenite. Paul Henried could never keep his antennae straight. I had to make do with being another Inferior War Victor. No one believed there were any Anti-Uszthay Martians. That's typical earthbound thinking.

Then the war ended, and suddenly there were no more Martian roles. In fact, suddenly there were no more Martians period. The allies did a pretty fair job of depopulating the old planet. Since then, we've been a dying race. We're feeble, really. Every time the 'flu goes round, I have to go to funerals. There was a rash of anti-war movies. There always is after the zapping is over. Remember *A Walk in the Dust* or *Terrestrial Invaders?* I didn't get work in those. All you ever saw of the Martian troops were bodies. There were plenty of newsreel scenes of big-eyed orphans waving their tentacles at the camera in front of the sludging ruins of their nests. Those movies didn't do any business. The whole solar system was tired of war. They started making musicals. I can't do what you people call dancing, so those were lean years. I did a bit of investing, and set up my own business. I thought I'd hit on the ideal combination. I opened a Martian bar and a kosher butcher's shop back-to-back. The Jews got the meat, and the Marties got the drainings. It was a good idea, and we did okay until the riots. I lost everything then, and went back to acting.

I did some dinner theatre. Small roles. I thought my best performance was as Dr Chasuble in *The Importance of Being Earnest*, but there weren't many managements willing to cast me in spite of, rather than because of, my race. I tried to get the backing to put on *Othello* in modern dress with the Moor as a Martian, but no one was interested. When Stanley Kramer bought up *Worlds Apart*, the hot best-seller about the persecution of Martians on Earth, I put in a bid for the lead, but Stanley had to say no. By then, I was too associated with the stereotype Jimbo Martie. He said audiences wouldn't take me seriously. Maybe he was right, but I'd have liked to take a shot at it. As you must know, Ptyehshdneh got the part and went on to be the first non-terrestrial to walk off with the Best Actor statuette on Oscar night. I'm not bitter, but I can't help thinking that my career in the last twenty years would have been very different if Kramer had taken the chance. Ptyeh' is such a *pretty* Martie, if you know what I mean. Not much slime on his hide.

Of course, Willie K'ssth came back on television in the early fifties. They made twenty-six half-hour episodes with Tom Conway under the beak and me back as dumb Jimbo. The series is still in syndication on graveyard shift TV. I get fan mail from nostalgia-buff insomniacs and night watchmen all over the country. It's nice to know people notice you. I saw one of those episodes recently. It was a piece of shit. But at the time it was a job, right? It didn't last long, and I was more or less on the skids for a couple of years. I was on relief between guest spots. I'm in a classic *Sergeant Bilko*, where they're trying to make a movie about the canal Bilko is supposed to have taken in the war. Doberman wins a Dream Date With a Movie Star in a contest and all the platoon try to get the ticket off him. Finally, Bilko gets the ticket and turns up at the Hollywood nightspot, and I turn out to be the Dream Date Star. Phil Silvers has a terrific talent, and it was nice just to be funny for a change. We worked out a good little routine with the drinks and the cocktail umbrellas. I'd like to have done more comedy, but when you've got tentacles producers don't think you can milk a laugh. I popped out of a box on *Laugh-In* once.

The sixties were rough, I guess. I had a little bit of

a drink problem, but you must have heard about that. You've done your research, right? Well, skipping the messy parts of the story, I ended up in jail. It was only a couple of cows all told, but I exsanguinated them all right. No excuses. Inside, I got involved in the protest movement. I was in with lots of draft evaders. They gave me some LSD, and I wound up signing a lot of petitions and, outside, going on plenty of marches. Hell, everybody now thinks the War on Mercury was a waste of time, but the planet was gung-ho about it back then. Those little jelly-breathers never did anyone any harm, but you'd creamed one planet and got a taste for it. That's what I think. I did a bit of organisational work for the Aliens' League, and spoke on campuses. I was on President Kissinger's enemies list. I'm still proud of that.

I had a few film roles while all this was going on. Nothing spectacular, but I kept my face on the screen. I was the priest in *The Miracle of Mare Nostrum*, Elvis' partner in the spear-fishing business in *She Ain't Human*, and Doris Day's old boyfriend in *With Six You Get Eggroll*. The films were mostly pieces of shit. I'm unbilled in a couple of Sinatra-Martin movies because I knocked around with the Rat Pack for a couple of summers before I got politics. I get a tentacle down Angie Dickinson's *decolleté* in *Ocean's 11*. I know you're going to ask me about *Orbit Jocks*. I was just naive. Again, no excuses. When I shot my scenes, I thought it was a documentary. They had a whole fake script and everything. I took the job because of the trip to Mars. I'd never been before, and I wanted to discover my roots. I stood in front of landmarks reading out stuff about history. Then the producers spliced in all the hardcore stuff later. I don't know if you've seen the film, but the Martian in all the sex scenes is not me. It's hard to tell with a steel cowl, but he's got all his tentacles.

I'm not retired. I won't retire until they plough me under. But I'm being more selective. I'll take a picture if I can pal around with any of the other old-timers. I was in something called *Vampire Coyotes* last year, with Leslie Howard, Jean Harlow and Sidney Greenstreet. I don't mind working on low-budget horror movies. It's more like the old days. The big studios these days are just cranking out bland television crap. I was asked to be a guest villain on *Columbo*, but I turned it down and they got Robert Culp instead. I went to a science fiction film convention last year. Forrest J. Ackerman interviewed me on stage. He's a great guy. When I finally turn tentacles-up, I'm having it in my will that I be stuffed and put in his basement with the Creature From the Black Lagoon and all that other neat stuff. Lon would have gone for that too, but humans are prejudiced against auto-icons. It's a pity. I hope Forry can make do with just Lon's liver. It was the heart and soul of the man anyway.

After this, I've got a three-picture deal with Al. That's not as big a thing as it sounds, since he'll shoot them simultaneously. *Blood of the Brain Eaters*, *Jessie's Girls* and *Martian Exorcist*. Then, I might go to the Philippines and make this movie they want me to do with Nancy Kwan. Okay, so it'll be a piece of shit . . .

If I had it all over again, do you know what? I'd
do everything different. For a start, I'd take dancing
lessons . . .

When I wrote this, I thought nobody would be interested
enough in film arcana to publish it. But after David
Pringle put it in *Interzone*, it was the first piece of
mine to be picked (by Gardner Dozois) for a 'Year's
Best' anthology. Recently, it was selected for inclusion
with other stories about Mars on a computer disc being
sent to the Angry Red Planet. Given that enough people
on Earth found the mix of literary alternate history and
movie trivia baffling, it is interesting to wonder what
Martians, if any, will make of it.

I originally hesitated because 'Famous Monsters' is not
a story but a monologue. (If really suicidal, I'd have gone
the Robert Browning route and done the whole thing in
verse). Its (selective) acceptance has encouraged me to
play faster and looser with the form and content of what
I write. This may not entirely be a good thing, though it
puts me in a corner with one of my favourite moderns,
Howard Waldrop. I read Howard's 'Night of the Cooters'
and 'The Passing of the Western' *after* writing 'Famous
Monsters'; a good thing, since 'Cooters' tackles related
subject matter while 'Western' has a similar solution to
the problem of telling its story. H.G. Wells is, of course,
one of my major influences, witness the cameos for a
Martian War Machine and Dr Moreau in *Jago* and *Anno
Dracula*. This was one of my first attempts to come to
terms with his legacy.

Intended as a 'fun' piece, there is (as usual) a seam of seriousness in the rescrambling of actual attitudes in Hollywood and Society at Large to various types of differentness, ranging from the patronising to the hysterical. I wondered how it felt to be Peter Lorre or Conrad Veidt, escaping Hitler only to wind up wearing Nazi uniforms in war movies. Also, it struck me as an interesting omission, in *War of the Worlds* and most subsequent alien invasion stories, that writers rarely speculate on what would happen *after* the bug-eyed monsters had been defeated.

The Terminus

They had me spend my first month out of training
processing statements. It was more like public relations
than police work. Nobody the desk sergeant passed
on to me was ever going to see any action arising
from their complaint. It was my job to give them
a polystyrene cup of coffee and politely explain that
playing in a public playground was not an offence. The
desk sergeant didn't approve of the Metropolitan Police
Graduate Entry scheme which had given me the rank of
Inspector over him; so I had to deal with all the nutters
in Holborn. They felt more comfortable surrounded by
blue serge and had vintage stories about Martians in the
plumbing. Most were satisfied just to get their loony
notions on police notepaper. I filed all the statements,
but they might as well have been shredded.

By the time Judyth Staines was sent to my strip-lit
cubicle, the novelty had gone. I'd learned all the
pigeon holes: she was an Overly Nervous Missing Persons Reporter. She wore her hair in purple tentacles,

insisted on the 'y' in her name, and had a cheery *Kill a Pig Today* patch on her jump suit. The disappearee was Robert Webb, the bass guitarist of a band called Slug Death. Ms Staines had last seen Webb in Goodge Street underground station at about quarter past ten the previous night. He had bought (I wrote 'purchased' in the statement) a ticket for Belsize Park and vanished into the lifts. Ms Staines had stayed in town to 'see someone' (cockney rhyming slang for 'buy drugs') and had later taken the tube to Belsize Park herself. She'd arrived at eleven and found the rest of Slug Death, still waiting for Webb. 'And since then he hasn't been back to our place, or rung up, or anything.'

Ms Staines had been up all night. Her charcoal eyeshadow had trickled, giving her that zombie look. She was not happy in a police station. She kept looking around nervously, like the leading lady of a psycho movie exploring an old dark house where, fifteen years before, an entire girls' basketball team had been fed into a giant kitchen blender by a family of demented fast food freaks. I gave her the Telly Savalas speech about calming down, waiting a few days, and not being too worried because although people sometimes disappear they usually turn up with a perfectly logical explanation.

'It's hard to explain without you knowing him. Bobby wasn't just about to disappear. We were going to a party. He had the bottle. He wasn't strung out, or hung up, or anything. He was just normal.'

I asked if she could give a description.

'You can't miss him. He has blue horns.'

I thought of a funny remark, but kept it to myself.

'He had most of his hair off, and the rest shaped like horns. He dyed them blue.'

After another month of statement processing I would have let Webb disappear on his own, but I still had a perverse feeling that being a policeman was all about kicking doors in and getting results. During the next Martian ceasefire I asked around, and ended up at New Scotland Yard. I found Eric Verdon, the liason between the Metropolitan Police and the London Transport Police, in the smaller of his two offices. The other was filled with eighteen tons of documentation, all the way back to horse-drawn trams.

'Oh yes,' Verdon told me, 'disapperances from the underground are not uncommon. Every once in a while some unfortunate wanders off where he shouldn't and meets with an accident. Sometimes our staff doesn't come across the remains for years. Some people never do turn up. Those are the most interesting, I think. This pile.'

It was an impressive stack of manila folders. On the night of 9 October 1872 (which I like to think of as appropriately foggy) Mr Julian Selwyn-Pitt, a landscape painter, walked into Oxford Street station and was never seen again. Since 1872, fifteen thousand, eight hundred and twenty-four people had followed Mr Selwyn-Pitt into Verdon's files. The figure was exclusive of all those whose disappearance was not reported and those, like Robert Webb, whose folders had not yet drifted down to settle in Verdon's office.

'So there are nearly sixteen thousand people lying around the tube somewhere?'

'Presumably. Over the years whole sections have been closed off, reopened, caved-in or forgotten. Even our maps are nowhere near complete. There are plenty of nooks and crannies that could comfortably accomodate a missing person. I often think of sardines.'

'Pardon?'

'The game. You must have played it as a child. It's like hide-and-seek, only when you find someone you have to hide with them. I always found it unnerving somehow. You'd start with a house full of children, and then one by one they'd vanish. Finally, you'd pull back the curtain and there they all would be, packed in like sardines, waiting for you. I'm sure it's like that down there. Somewhere there's a hidey-hole full of all those people.'

All my deductive prowess could make of that was that Verdon had been filed away for too long and faded out himself. The Singular Case of the Blue-Horned Vanisher remained unsolved. The traditional next step was an inspection of the scene of the crime. After the evening shift I had a couple of shorts to nerve me for my first foray into independent detection.

Goodge Street tube station is one of the deepest in London. It has polite robot lifts whose vocabulary is limited to 'please stand clear of the doors', and a rude night-watchman whose speech is limited to an incomprehensible Jamaican patois. I used my police identification to borrow a lantern, but the night-watchman's presence was required elsewhere for some important swearing and snoozing. I suspected that he did not want to slip into Verdon's fifteen thousand, eight hundred and

20

twenty-seventh manila folder. The lifts had shut off for the night. I had to go down a spiral staircase, lit by off-white Christmas tree bulbs.

I was conducting my search on the Winnie-the-Pooh principle of looking for a thing lost by losing myself and thus ending up next to the original object. When I passed the third PUBLIC NOT ALLOWED BEYOND THIS POINT notice I decided to chuck it in. Ms Staines would finally wash her hair and marry an accountant anyway.

I was a couple of levels below the actual railway tunnel and had succeeded in getting lost. Here were the catacombs where broken spades, long-handled brooms, buckets of sand, mops, antiquated ticket machines, lost uniform caps, and stray umbrellas drag themselves to die.

I found a locker full of tin hats and gas masks. A rusted 1930s sandwich box, complete with a green hairy lunch wrapped in pre-cellophane tracing paper. And quiet, no rumbling trains at night. Only the inevitable underground ear-cracking drip. It was a standing tap steadily leaking on to a bale of the *Chronicle*. Prams, bedsteads, army blankets, enamel basins, a rocking horse. After the public lavatory tiling gave way to bare bricks there wasn't even any Persian graffiti or football propaganda. Everything terminated here.

The damp kept the air clean. Verdon's files had been musty, but here the chilly air had a sweet afterscent. I sucked in a lungful, drawing the wind over my tongue, but couldn't catch the taste. I meandered without urgency in search of an exit. The drip was gone. The corridors were smooth and empty. The calm of a sea-bed during a storm. Nothing mattered. Through tunnels, down corkscrew stairs, past uninteresting junctions, at random into empty storerooms. I opened a brassbound door.

The hall was lit blue. The sweetness was stronger, soft yet slowing. There were more of them than I could count. Some pale faces turned without interest. An old man in a frock coat and a wing collar, a stocky type in a khaki sergeant's uniform, a girl in a mini-skirt and stiletto heels. Ulsters, bustles, Norfolk jackets, overalls, flat caps, pinstripes, kaftans, black leather jackets, denims. They weren't dead or alive. Just waiting.

This is the earliest story here; hence Telly Savalas, the punk haircut and seventies slang. Written during my 'wilderness years' of supplementary benefit queues and bedsittery, it first appeared in 1981 in *Sheep Worrying*, one of the fanzines Greg Daniels worked for in 'The Original Dr Shade'. Very lightly rewritten, it appeared in its definitive version in *Fantasy Tales* in 1985. The character names were taken from signatures on letters turning down my job applications.

The Big Fish

The Bay City cops were rousting enemy aliens. As I drove through the nasty coast town, uniforms hauled an old couple out of a grocery store. The Taraki family's neighbours huddled in thin rain howling asthmatically for bloody revenge. Pearl Harbour had struck a lot of people that way. With the Tarakis on the bus for Manzanar, neighbours descended on the store like bedraggled vultures. Produce vanished instantly, then destruction started. Caught at a sleepy stop light, I got a good look. The Tarakis had lived over the store; now, their furniture was thrown out of the second-storey window. Fine china shattered on the sidewalk, spilling white chips like teeth into the gutter. It was inspirational, the forces of democracy rallying round to protect the United States from vicious oriental grocers, fiendishly intent on selling eggplant to a hapless civilian population.

Meanwhile my appointment was with a gent who kept three pictures on his mantelpiece, grouped in a triangle around a statue of the Virgin Mary. At the apex was his white-haired mama, to the left Charles Luciano, and to the right, Benito Mussolini. The Tarakis, American-born and registered Democrats, were headed to a dustbowl concentration camp for the duration, while Gianni Pastore, Sicilian-born and highly unregistered *capo* of the Family Business, would spend his war in a marble-fronted mansion paid for by nickels and dimes dropped on the numbers game, into slot machines, or exchanged for the favours of nice girls from the old country. I'd seen his mansion before and so far been able to resist the temptation to bean one of his twelve muse statues with a bourbon bottle.

Money can buy you love but can't even put down a deposit on good taste.

The palace was up in the hills, a little way down the boulevard from Tyrone Power. But now, Pastore was hanging his mink-banded fedora in a Bay City beachfront motel complex, which was a real estate agent's term for a bunch of horrible shacks shoved together for the convenience of people who like sand on their carpets.

I always take a lungful of fresh air before entering a confined space with someone in Pastore's business, so I parked the Chrysler a few blocks from the Seaview Inn and walked the rest of the way, sucking on a Camel to keep warm in the wet. They say it doesn't rain in Southern California, but they also say the U.S. Navy could never be taken by surprise. This February, three months into a war the rest of the world had been fighting since 1936 or 1939 depending on whether you were Chinese or Polish, it was raining almost constantly, varying between a light fall of misty drizzle in the dreary daytimes to spectacular storms, complete with De Mille lighting effects, in our fear-filled nights. Those trusty Boy Scouts scanning the horizons for Jap subs and Nazi U-Boats were filling up influenza wards and manufacturers of raincoats and umbrellas who'd not yet converted their plants to defense production were making a killing. I didn't mind the rain. At least rainwater is clean, unlike most other things in Bay City.

A small boy with a wooden gun leaped out of a bush and sprayed me with sound effects, interrupting his onomatopoeic chirruping with a shout of 'die you slant-eyed Jap!' I clutched my heart, staggered back, and he finished me off with a quick burst. I died for the Emperor and tipped the kid a dime to go away. If this went on long enough, maybe little Johnny would get a chance to march off and do real killing, then maybe come home in a box or with the shakes or a taste for blood. Meanwhile, especially since someone spotted a Jap submarine off Santa Barbara, California was gearing up for the War Effort. Aside from interning grocers, our best brains were writing songs like 'To Be Specific, It's Our Pacific', 'So Long Momma, I'm Off to Yokahama', 'We're Gonna Slap the Jap Right Off the Map' and 'When Those Little Yellow Bellies Meet the Cohens and the Kellys'. Zanuck had donated his string of Argentine polo ponies to West Point and got himself measured for a comic opera Colonel's uniform so he could join the Signal Corps and defeat the Axis by posing for publicity photographs.

I'd tried to join up two days after Pearl Harbour but they kicked me back on to the streets. Too many concussions. Apparently, I get hit on the head too often and have a tendency to black out. When they came to mention it, they were right.

The Seaview Inn was shuttered, one of the first casualties of war. It had its own jetty, and by it were a few canvas-covered motor launches shifting with the waves. In the late afternoon gloom, I saw the silhouette of the *Montecito*, anchored strategically outside the three-mile limit. That was one good thing about the Japanese; on the downside, they might have sunk most of the US fleet, but on the up, they'd put Laird Brunette's gambling ship out of business. Nobody was enthusiastic about losing their shirt-buttons on a rigged roulette wheel if they imagined they were going to be torpedoed any moment. I'd have thought that would add an extra thrill to the whole gay, delirious business of giving Brunette money, but I'm just a poor, twenty-five-dollars-a-day detective.

The Seaview Inn was supposed to be a stopping-off point on the way to the *Monty* and now its trade was stopped off. The main building was sculpted out of dusty ice-cream and looked like a three-storey radiogram with wave-scallop friezes. I pushed through double-doors and entered the lobby. The floor was decorated with a mosaic in which Neptune, looking like an angry Santa Claus in a swimsuit, was sticking it to a sea-nymph who shared a hairdresser with Hedy Lamarr. The nymph was naked except for some strategic shells. It was very artistic.

There was nobody at the desk and thumping the bell

didn't improve matters. Water ran down the outside of the green-tinted windows. There were a few steady drips somewhere. I lit up another Camel and went exploring. The office was locked and the desk register didn't have any entries after 7 December 1941. My raincoat dripped and began to dry out, sticking my jacket and shirt to my shoulders. I shrugged, trying to get some air into my clothes. I noticed Neptune's face quivering. A thin layer of water had pooled over the mosaic and various anemone-like fronds attached to the sea god were apparently getting excited. Looking at the nymph, I could understand that. Actually, I realised, only the hair was from Hedy. The face and the body were strictly Janey Wilde.

I go to the movies a lot but I'd missed most of Janey's credits: *She-Strangler of Shanghai, Tarzan and the Tiger Girl, Perils of Jungle Jillian*. I'd seen her in the newspapers though, often in unnervingly close proximity with Pastore or Brunette. She'd started as an Olympic swimmer, picking up medals in Berlin, then followed Weissmuller and Crabbe to Hollywood. She would never get an Academy Award but her legs were in a lot of cheesecake stills publicising no particular movie. Air-brushed and made-up like a good-looking corpse, she was a fine commercial for sex. In person she was as bubbly as domestic champagne, though now running to flat. Things were slow in the detecting business, since people were more worried about imminent invasion than missing daughters or misplaced love letters. So when Janey Wilde called on me in my office in the Cahuenga Building and asked me to look up one of her ill-chosen men friends, I checked the pile of old envelopes I use as a desk diary and informed her that I was available to make inquiries into the current whereabouts of a certain big fish.

Wherever Laird Brunette was, he wasn't here. I was beginning to figure Gianni Pastore, the gambler's partner, wasn't here either. Which meant I'd wasted an afternoon. Outside it rained harder, driving against the walls with a drumlike tattoo. Either there were hailstones mixed in with the water or the Jap air force was hurling fistfuls of pebbles at Bay City to demoralise the population. I don't know why they bothered. All Hirohito had to do was slip a thick envelope to the Bay City cops and the city's finest would hand over the whole community to the Japanese Empire with a ribbon around it and a bow on top.

There were more puddles in the lobby, little streams running from one to the other. I was reminded of the episode of *The Perils of Jungle Jillian* I had seen while tailing a child molester to a Saturday matinee. At the end, Janey Wilde had been caught by the Panther Princess and trapped in a room which slowly filled with water. That room had been a lot smaller than the lobby of the Seaview Inn and the water had come in a lot faster.

Behind the desk were framed photographs of pretty people in pretty clothes having a pretty time. Pastore was there, and Brunette, grinning like tiger cats, mingling with showfolk: Xavier Cugat, Janey Wilde, Charles Coburn. Janice Marsh, the pop-eyed beauty rumoured to have replaced Jungle Jillian in Brunette's affections, was well represented in artistic poses.

28

On the phone, Pastore had promised faithfully to be here. He hadn't wanted to bother with a small-timer like me but Janey Wilde's name opened a door. I had a feeling Papa Pastore was relieved to be shaken down about Brunette, as if he wanted to talk about something. He must be busy because there were several wars on. The big one overseas and a few little ones at home. Maxie Rothko, bar owner and junior partner in the *Monty*, had been found drifting in the seaweed around the Santa Monica pier without much of a head to speak of. And Phil Isinglass, man-about-town lawyer and Brunette frontman, had turned up in the storm drains, lungs full of sandy mud. Disappearing was the latest craze in Brunette's organisation. That didn't sound good for Janey Wilde, though Pastore had talked about the Laird as if he knew Brunette was alive. But now Papa wasn't around. I was getting annoyed with someone it wasn't sensible to be annoyed with.

Pastore wouldn't be in any of the beach shacks but there should be an apartment for his convenience in the main building. I decided to explore further. Jungle Jillian would expect no less. She'd hired me for five days in advance – a good thing, since I'm unduly reliant on eating and drinking and other expensive diversions of the monied and idle.

The corridor that led past the office ended in a walk-up staircase. As soon as I put my size nines on the first step, it squelched. I realised something was more than usually wrong. The steps were a quiet little waterfall, seeping rather than cascading. It wasn't just water; there was unpleasant, slimy stuff mixed in.

Someone had left the bath running. My first thought was that Pastore had been distracted by a bullet. I was wrong. In the long run, he might have been happier if I'd been right.

I climbed the soggy stairs and found the the apartment door unlocked but shut. Bracing myself, I pushed the door in. It encountered resistance but then sliced open, allowing a gush of water to shoot around my ankles, soaking my dark blue socks. Along with water was a three-weeks-dead-in-the-water-with-rotten-fish smell that wrapped around me like a blanket. Holding my breath, I stepped into the room. The waterfall flowed faster now. I heard a faucet running. A radio played, with funny little gurgles mixed in. A crooner was doing his best with 'Life is Just a Bowl of Cherries', but he sounded as if he were drowned full fathom five. I followed the music and found the bathroom.

Pastore was face down in the overflowing tub, the song coming from under him. He wore a silk lounging robe that had been pulled away from his back, his wrists tied behind him with the robe's cord. In the end he'd been drowned. But before that hands had been laid on him, either in anger or with cold, professional skill. I'm not a coroner, so I couldn't tell how long the Family Man had been in the water. The radio still playing and the water still running suggested Gianni had met his end recently but the stench felt older than sin.

I have a bad habit of finding bodies in Bay City and the most profit-minded police force in the country have a bad habit of trying to make connections between me and a wide variety of deceased persons. The obvious solution in this case was to make a friendly phone call, absent-mindedly forgetting to mention my name while giving the flatfeet directions to the late Mr Pastore. Who knows, I might accidentally talk to someone honest.

That is exactly what I would have done if, just then, the man with the gun hadn't come through the door . . .

I had Janey Wilde to blame. She'd arrived without an appointment, having picked me on a recommendation. Oddly, Laird Brunette had once said something not entirely uncomplimentary about me. We'd met. We hadn't seriously tried to kill each other in a while. That was as good a basis for a relationship as any.

Out of her sarong, Jungle Jillian favoured sharp shoulders and a veiled pill-box. The kiddies at the matinee had liked her fine, especially when she was wrestling stuffed snakes, and dutiful Daddies took no exception to her either, especially when she was tied down and her sarong rode up a few inches. Her lips were four red grapes plumped together. When she crossed her legs you saw swimmer's smooth muscle under her hose.

'He's very sweet, really,' she explained, meaning Mr Brunette never killed anyone within ten miles of her without apologising afterwards, 'not at all like they say in those dreadful scandal sheets.'

The gambler had been strange recently, especially since the war shut him down. Actually the *Montecito* had been out of commission for nearly a year, supposedly for a refit although as far as Janey Wilde knew no workmen had been sent out to the ship. At about the time

Brunette suspended his crooked wheels, he came down with a common California complaint, a dose of crackpot religion. He'd been tangentially mixed up a few years ago with a psychic racket run by a bird named Amthor, but had apparently shifted from the mostly harmless bunco cults on to the hard stuff. Spiritualism, orgiastic rites, chanting, incense, the whole deal.

Janey blamed this sudden interest in matters occult on Janice Marsh, who had coincidentally made her name as the Panther Princess in *The Perils of Jungle Jillian*, a role which required her to torture Janey Wilde at least once every chapter. My employer didn't mention that her own career had hardly soared between *Jungle Jillian* and *She-Strangler of Shanghai*, while the erstwhile Panther Princess had gone from Republic to Metro and was being built up as an exotic in the Dietrich-Garbo vein. Say what you like about Janice Marsh's *Nefertiti*, she still looked like Peter Lorre to me. And according to Janey, the star had more peculiar tastes than a seafood buffet.

Brunette had apparently joined a series of fringe organisations and become quite involved, to the extent of neglecting his business and thereby irking his long-time partner, Gianni Pastore. Perhaps that was why person or persons unknown had decided the Laird wouldn't mind if his associates died one by one. I couldn't figure it out. The cults I'd come across mostly stayed in business by selling sex, drugs, power or reassurance to rich, stupid people. The Laird hardly fell into the category. He was too big a fish for that particular bowl.

•   •   •

The man with the gun was English, with a Ronald Colman accent and a white aviator's scarf. He was not alone. The quiet, truck-sized bruiser I made as a Fed went through my wallet while the dapper foreigner kept his automatic pointed casually at my middle.

'Peeper,' the Fed snarled, showing the photostat of my licence and my supposedly impressive deputy's badge.

'Interesting,' said the Britisher, slipping his gun into the pocket of his camel coat. Immaculate, he must have been umbrella-protected between car and building because there wasn't a spot of rain on him. 'I'm Winthrop. Edwin Winthrop.'

We shook hands. His other companion, the interesting one, was going through the deceased's papers. She looked up, smiled with sharp white teeth, and got back to work.

'This is Mademoiselle Dieudonné.'

'Geneviève,' she said. She pronounced it 'Zhe-ne-vyev', suggesting Paris, France. She was wearing something white with silver in it and had quantities of pale blonde hair.

'And the gentleman from your Federal Bureau of Investigation is Finlay.'

The Fed grunted. He looked as if he'd been brought to life by Willis H. O'Brien.

'You are interested in a Mr Brunette,' Winthrop said. It was not a question, so there was no point in answering him. 'So are we.'

'Call in a Russian and we could be the Allies,' I said.

Winthrop laughed. He was sharp. 'True. I am here

at the request of my government and working with the full co-operation of yours.'

One of the small detective-type details I noticed was that no one even suggested informing the police about Gianni Pastore was a good idea.

'Have you ever heard of a place called Innsmouth, Massachusetts?'

It didn't mean anything to me and I said so.

'Count yourself lucky. Special Agent Finlay's associates were called upon to dynamite certain unsafe structures in the sea off Innsmouth back in the twenties. It was a bad business.'

Geneviève said something sharp in French that sounded like swearing. She held up a photograph of Brunette dancing cheek to cheek with Janice Marsh.

'Do you know the lady?' Winthrop asked.

'Only in the movies. Some go for her in a big way but I think she looks like Mr Moto.'

'Very true. Does the Esoteric Order of Dagon mean anything to you?'

'Sounds like a Church-of-the-Month alternate. Otherwise, no.'

'Captain Obed Marsh?'

'Uh-huh.'

'The Deep Ones?'

'Are they those coloured singers?'

'What about Cthulhu, Y'ha-nthlei, R'lyeh?'

'*Gesundheit.*'

Winthrop grinned, sharp moustache pointing. 'No, not easy to say at all. Hard to fit into human mouths, you know.'

'He's just a bedroom creeper,' Finlay said, 'he don't know nothing.'

'His grammar could be better. Doesn't J. Edgar pay for elocution lessons?'

Finlay's big hands opened and closed as if he would rather there were a throat in them.

'Gené?' Winthrop said.

The woman looked up, red tongue absently flicking across her red lips, and thought a moment. She said something in a foreign language that I did understand.

'There's no need to kill him,' she said in French. Thank you very much, I thought.

Winthrop shrugged and said 'fine by me.' Finlay looked disappointed.

'You're free to go,' the Britisher told me. 'We shall take care of everything. I see no point in your continuing your current line of inquiry. Send in a chit to this address,' he handed me a card, 'and you'll be reimbursed for your expenses so far. Don't worry. We'll carry on until this is seen through. By the way, you might care not to discuss with anyone what you've seen here or anything I may have said. There's a War on, you know. Loose lips sink ships.'

I had a few clever answers but I swallowed them and left. Anyone who thought there was no need to kill me was all right in my book and I wasn't using my razor tongue on them. As I walked to the Chrysler, several ostentatiously unofficial cars cruised past me, headed for the Seaview Inn.

It was getting dark and lightning was striking down out at sea. A flash lit up the *Montecito* and I counted five seconds before the thunder boomed. I had the feeling there was something out there beyond the three-mile limit besides the floating former casino, and that it was angry.

I slipped into the Chrysler and drove away from Bay City, feeling better the further inland I got.

I take *Black Mask*. It's a long time since Hammett and the fellow who wrote the Ted Carmady stories were in it, but you occasionally get a good Cornell Woolrich or Erle Stanley Gardner. Back at my office, I saw the newsboy had been by and dropped off the *Times* and next month's pulp. But there'd been a mix-up. Instead of the *Mask*, there was something inside the folded newspaper called *Weird Tales*. On the cover, a man was being attacked by two green demons and a stereotype vampire with a widow's peak. '*Hell on Earth*', a Novelette of Satan in a Tuxedo by Robert Bloch' was blazed above the title. Also promised were 'A new Lovecraft series, '*Herbert West – Re-Animator*' and '*The Rat Master*' by Greye la Spina'. All for fifteen cents, kids. If I were a different type of detective, the brand who said *nom de something* and waxed a moustache whenever he found a mutilated corpse, I might have thought the substitution an omen.

In my office, I've always had five filing cabinets, three empty. I also had two bottles, only one empty. In a few hours, the situation would have changed by one bottle.

I found a glass without too much dust and wiped it with my clean handkerchief. I poured myself a generous slug and hit the back of my throat with it.

The radio didn't work but I could hear Glenn Miller from somewhere. I found my glass empty and dealt with that. Sitting behind my desk, I looked at the patterns of rain on the window. If I craned I could see traffic on Hollywood Boulevard. People who didn't spend their working days finding bodies in bathtubs were going home not to spend their evenings emptying a bottle.

After a day, I'd had some excitement but I hadn't done much for Janey Wilde. I was no nearer being able to explain the absence of Mr Brunette from his usual haunts than I had been when she left my office, leaving behind a tantalising whiff of *Essence de Chine*.

She'd given me some literature pertaining to Brunette's cult involvement. Now, the third slug warming me up inside, I looked over it, waiting for inspiration to strike. Interesting echoes came up in relation to Winthrop's shopping list of subjects of peculiar interest. I had no luck with the alphabet soup syllables he'd spat at me, mainly because 'Cthulhu' sounds more like a cough than a word. But the Esoteric Order of Dagon was a group Brunette had joined, and Innsmouth, Massachusetts, was the East Coast town where the organisation was registered. The Esoteric Order had a temple on the beachfront in Venice, and its mumbo-jumbo hand-outs promised 'ancient and intriguing rites to probe the mysteries of the Deep'. Slipped in with the recruitment bills was a studio biography of Janice Marsh, which helpfully revealed the movie star's place of birth as Innsmouth, Massachusetts, and that she could trace her family back to Captain Obed Marsh, the famous early nineteenth century explorer of whom I'd never heard. Obviously Winthrop, Geneviève and the FBI were well ahead of me in making connections. And I didn't really know who the Englishman and the French girl were.

I wondered if I wouldn't have been better off reading *Weird Tales*. I liked the sound of Satan in a Tuxedo. It wasn't Ted Carmady with an automatic and a dame, but it would do. There was a lot more thunder and lightning and I finished the bottle. I suppose I could have gone home to sleep but the chair was no more uncomfortable than my Murphy bed.

The empty bottle rolled and I settled down, tie loose, to forget the cares of the day.

Thanks to the War, Pastore only made page three of the *Times*. Apparently the noted gambler-entrepreneur had been shot to death. If that was true, it had happened after I'd left. Then, he'd only been tortured and drowned. Police Chief John Wax dished out his usual 'over by Christmas' quote about the investigation. There was no mention of the FBI, or of our allies, John Bull in a tux and Madamoiselle la Guillotine. In prison, you get papers with neat oblongs cut out to remove articles the censor feels provocative. They don't make any difference: all newspapers have invisible oblongs. Pastore's sterling work with underprivileged kids was mentioned but someone forgot to write about the junk he sold them when they grew into underpivileged adults. The obit photograph found him with Janey Wilde and Janice Marsh at the *premiére* of a George Raft movie.

The phantom Jap sub off Santa Barbara got more column inches. General John L. DeWitt, head of the Western Defense Command, called for more troops to guard the coastline, prophesying 'death and destruction are likely to come at any moment'. Everyone in California was looking out to sea.

After my regular morning conference with Mr Huggins and Mr Young, I placed a call to Janey Wilde's Malibu residence. Most screen idols are either at the studio or asleep if you telephone before ten o'clock in the morning, but Janey, with weeks to go before shooting started on *Bowery to Bataan*, was at home and awake, having done her thirty lengths. Unlike almost everyone else in the industry, she thought a swimming pool was for swimming in rather than lounging beside.

She remembered instantly who I was and asked for news. I gave her a *précis*.

'I've been politely asked to refrain from further investigations,' I explained. 'By some heavy hitters.'

'So you're quitting?'

I should have said yes, but 'Miss Wilde, only you can require me to quit. I thought you should know how the federal government feels.'

There was a pause.

'There's something I didn't tell you,' she told me. It was an expression common among my clients. 'Something important.'

I let dead air hang on the line.

'It's not so much Laird that I'm concerned about. It's that he has Franklin.'

'Franklin?'

'The baby,' she said. 'Our baby. My baby.'

'Laird Brunette has disappeared, taking a baby with him?'

'Yes.'

'Kidnapping is a crime. You might consider calling the cops.'

'A lot of things are crimes. Laird has done many of them and never spent a day in prison.'

That was true, which was why this development was strange. Kidnapping, whether personal or for profit, is the riskiest of crimes. As a rule, it's the province only of the stupidest criminals. Laird Brunette was not a stupid criminal.

'I can't afford bad publicity. Not when I'm so near to the roles I need.' *Bowery to Bataan* was going to put her among the screen immortals. 'Franklin is supposed to be Esther's boy. In a few years, I'll adopt him legally. Esther is my housekeeper. It'll work out. But I must have him back.'

'Laird is the father. He will have some rights.'

'He said he wasn't interested. He . . . um, moved on . . . to Janice Marsh while I was . . . before Franklin was born.'

'He's had a sudden attack of fatherhood and you're not convinced?'

'I'm worried to distraction. It's not Laird, it's *her*. Janice Marsh wants my baby for something vile. I want you to get Franklin back.'

'As I mentioned, kidnapping is a crime.'

'If there's a danger to the child, surely . . .'

'Do you have any proof that there is a danger?'

'Well, no.'

'Have Laird Brunette or Janice Marsh ever given you reason to believe they have ill-will for the baby?'

'Not exactly.'

I considered things.

'I'll continue with the job you hired me for, but you understand that's all I can do. If I find Brunette, I'll pass your worries on. Then it's between the two of you.'

She thanked me in a flood and I got off the phone feeling I'd taken a couple of strides further into the LaBrea tar pits and could feel sucking stickiness well above my knees.

I should have stayed out of the rain and concentrated on chess problems but I had another four days' worth of Jungle Jillian's retainer in my pocket and an address for the Esoteric Order of Dagon in a clipping from a lunatic scientific journal. So I drove out to Venice, reminding myself all the way that my wipers needed fixing.

Venice, California, is a fascinating idea that didn't work. Someone named Abbot Kinney had the notion of artificially creating a city like Venice, Italy, with canals and architecture. The canals mostly ran dry and the architecture never really caught on in a town where, in the twenties, Gloria Swanson's bathroom was considered an aesthetic triumph. All that was left was the beach and piles of rotting fish. Venice, Italy, is the Plague Capital of Europe, so Venice, California, got one thing right.

The Esoteric Order was up the coast from Muscle Beach, housed in a discreet yacht club building with its own small marina. From the exterior, I guessed the cult business had seen better days. Seaweed had tracked up the beach, swarmed around the jetty, and was licking the lower edges of the front wall. Everything had gone green: wood, plaster, copper ornaments. And it smelled like Pastore's bathroom, only worse. This kind of place made you wonder why the Japs were so keen on invading.

I looked at myself in the mirror and rolled my eyes. I tried to get that slap-happy, let-me-give-you-all-my-worldly-goods, gimme-some-mysteries-of-the-orient look that I imagined typical of a communicant at one of these bughouse congregations. After I'd stopped laughing, I remembered the marks on Pastore and tried to take detecting seriously. Taking in my unshaven, slept-upright-in-his-clothes, two-bottles-a-day lost soul look, I congratulated myself on my foresight in spending fifteen years developing the ideal cover for a job like this.

To get in the building, I had to go down to the marina and come at it from the beachside. There were green pillars of what looked like fungus-eaten cardboard either side of the impressive front door, which held a stained glass picture in shades of green and blue of a man with the head of a squid in a natty monk's number, waving his eyes for the artist. Dagon, I happened to know, was half-man, half-fish, and God of the Philistines. In this town, I guess a Philistine god blended in well. It's a great country: if you're half-fish, pay most of your taxes, eat babies and aren't Japanese, you have a wonderful future.

I rapped on the squid's head but nothing happened. I looked the squid in several of his eyes and felt squirmy inside. Somehow, up close, cephalopod-face didn't look that silly.

I pushed the door and found myself in the temple's waiting room. It was what I'd expected: subdued lighting, old but bad paintings, a few semi-pornographic statuettes, a strong smell of last night's incense to cover up the fish stink. It had as much religious atmosphere as a two-dollar bordello.

'Yoo-hoo,' I said, 'Dagon calling . . .'

My voice sounded less funny echoed back at me.

I prowled, sniffing for clues. I tried saying *nom de something* and twiddling a non-existent moustache but nothing came to me. Perhaps I ought to switch to a meerschaum of cocaine and a deerstalker, or maybe a monocle and an interest in incunabula.

Where you'd expect a portrait of George Washington or Jean Harlow's Mother, the Order had hung up an impressively ugly picture of 'Our Founder'. Capt. Obed Marsh, dressed up like Admiral Butler, stood on the shore of a Polynesian paradise, his good ship painted with no sense of perspective on the horizon as if it were about three feet tall. The Captain, surrounded by adoring if funny-faced native tomatoes, looked about as unhappy as Errol Flynn at a Girl Scout meeting. The painter had taken a lot of trouble with the native nudes. One of the dusky lovelies had hips that would make Lombard green and a face that put me in mind of Janice Marsh. She was probably the Panther Princess's great-great-great grandmother. In the background, just in front of the ship, was something like a squid emerging from the sea. Fumble-fingers with a brush had tripped

43

up again. It looked as if the tentacle-waving creature was about twice the size of Obed's clipper. The most upsetting detail was a robed and masked figure standing on the deck with a baby's ankle in each fist. He had apparently just wrenched the child apart like a wishbone and was emptying blood into the squid's eyes.

'Excuse me,' gargled a voice, 'can I help you?'

I turned around and got a noseful of the stooped and ancient Guardian of the Cult. His robe matched the ones worn by squid-features on the door and baby-ripper in the portrait. He kept his face shadowed, his voice sounded about as good as the radio in Pastore's bath and his breath smelled worse than Pastore after a week and a half of putrefaction.

'Good morning,' I said, letting a bird flutter in the higher ranges of my voice, 'my name is, er . . .'

I put together the first things that came to mind.

'My name is Herbert West Lovecraft. Uh, H.W. Lovecraft the Third. I'm simply fascinated by matters Ancient and Esoteric, don't ch'know.'

'Don't ch'know' I had picked up from the fellow with the monocle and the old books.

'You wouldn't happen to have an entry blank, would you? Or any incunabula?'

'Incunabula?' He wheezed.

'Books. Old books. Print books, published before 1500 *anno domini*, old sport.' See, I have a dictionary too.

'Books . . .'

The man was a monotonous conversationalist. He also moved like Laughton in *The Hunchback of Notre Dame* and the front of his robe, where the squidhead was embroidered, was wet with what I was disgusted to deduce was drool.

'Old books. Arcane mysteries, don't ch'know. Anything Cyclopean and doom-haunted is just up my old alley.'

'The *Necronomicon*?' He pronounced it with great respect, and great difficulty.

'Sounds just the ticket.'

Quasimodo shook his head under his hood and it lolled. I glimpsed greenish skin and large, moist eyes.

'I was recommended to come here by an old pal,' I said. 'Spiffing fellow. Laird Brunette. Ever hear of him?'

I'd pushed the wrong button. Quasi straightened out and grew about two feet. Those moist eyes flashed like razors.

'You'll have to see the Cap'n's Daughter.'

I didn't like the sound of that and stepped backwards, towards the door. Quasi laid a hand on my shoulder and held it fast. He was wearing mittens and I felt he had too many fingers inside them. His grip was like a gila monster's jaw.

'That will be fine,' I said, dropping the flutter.

As if arranged, curtains parted, and I was shoved through a door. Cracking my head on the low lintel, I could see why Quasi spent most of his time hunched over. I had to bend at the neck and knees to go down the corridor. The exterior might be rotten old wood but the heart of the place was solid stone. The walls were damp, bare and covered in suggestive carvings that gave primitive art a bad name. You'd have thought I'd be getting used to the smell by now, but nothing doing. I nearly gagged.

Quasi pushed me through another door. I was in a meeting room no larger than Union Station, with a stage, rows of comfortable armchairs and lots more squid-person statues. The centrepiece was very like the mosaic at the Seaview Inn, only the nymph had fewer shells and Neptune more tentacles.

Quasi vanished, slamming the door behind him. I strolled over to the stage and looked at a huge book perched on a straining lectern. The fellow with the monocle would have salivated, because this looked a lot older than 1500. It wasn't a Bible and didn't smell healthy. It was open to an illustration of something with tentacles and slime, facing a page written in several deservedly dead languages.

'The *Necronomicon*,' said a throaty female voice, 'of the mad Arab, Abdul Al-Hazred.'

'Mad, huh?' I turned to the speaker. 'Is he not getting his royalties?'

I recognised Janice Marsh straight away. The Panther Princess wore a turban and green silk lounging pajamas, with a floor-length housecoat that cost more than I make in a year. She had on jade earrings, a pearl cluster pendant and a ruby-eyed silver squid brooch. The lighting made her face look green and her round eyes shone. She still looked like Peter Lorre, but maybe if Lorre put his face on a body like Janice Marsh's, he'd be up for sex goddess roles too. Her silk thighs purred against each other as she walked down the temple aisle.

'Mr Lovecraft, isn't it?'

'Call me H.W. Everyone does.'

'Have I heard of you?'

'I doubt it.'

She was close now. A tall girl, she could look me in the eye. I had the feeling the eye-jewel in her turban was looking me in the brain. She let her fingers fall on the tentacle picture for a moment, allowed them to play around like a fun-loving spider, then removed them to my upper arm, delicately tugging me away from the book. I wasn't unhappy about that. Maybe I'm allergic to incunabula, or perhaps have an undiscovered prejudice against tentacled creatures, but I didn't like being near the *Necronomicon* one bit. Certainly the experience didn't compare with being near Janice Marsh.

'You're the Cap'n's Daughter?' I said.

'It's a honorific title. Obed Marsh was my ancestor. In the Esoteric Order, there is always a Cap'n's Daughter. Right now, I am she.'

'What exactly is this Dagon business about?'

She smiled, showing a row of little pearls. 'It's an alternative form of worship. It's not a racket, honestly.'

'I never said it was.'

She shrugged. 'Many people get the wrong idea.'

Outside, the wind was rising, driving rain against the temple. The sound effects were weird, like sickening whales calling out in the Bay.

'You were asking about Laird? Did Miss Wilde send you?'

It was my turn to shrug.

'Janey is what they call a sore loser, Mr Lovecraft.

47

It comes from taking all those bronze medals. Never the gold.'

'I don't think she wants him back,' I said, 'just to know where he is. He seems to have disappeared.'

'He's often out of town on business. He likes to be mysterious. I'm sure you understand.'

My eyes kept going to the squid-face brooch. As Janice Marsh breathed, it rose and fell and rubies winked at me.

'It's Polynesian,' she said, tapping the brooch. 'The Cap'n brought it back with him to Innsmouth.'

'Ah yes, your home town.'

'It's just a place by the sea. Like Los Angeles.'

I decided to go fishing, and hooked up some of the bait Winthrop had given me. 'Were you there when J. Edgar Hoover staged his fireworks display in the twenties?'

'Yes, I was a child. Something to do with rum-runners, I think. That was during Prohibition.'

'Good years for the Laird.'

'I suppose so. He's legitimate these days.'

'Yes. Although if he were as Scotch as he likes to pretend he is, you can be sure he'd have been deported by now.'

Janice Marsh's eyes were sea-green. Round or not, they were fascinating. 'Let me put your mind at rest, Mr Lovecraft or whatever your name is,' she said, 'the Esoteric Order of Dagon was never a front for bootlegging. In fact it has never been a front for anything. It is not a racket for duping rich widows out of inheritances. It is not an excuse for motion picture executives to gain carnal knowledge of teenage drug addicts. It is exactly what it claims to be, a church.'

'Father, Son and Holy Squid, eh?'

'I did not say we were a Christian church.'

Janice Marsh had been creeping up on me and was close enough to bite. Her active hands went to the back of my neck and angled my head down like an adjustable lamp. She put her lips on mine and squashed her face into me. I tasted lipstick, salt and caviar. Her fingers writhed up into my hair and pushed my hat off. She shut her eyes. After an hour or two of suffering in the line of duty, I put my hands on her hips and detached her body from mine. I had a fish taste in my mouth.

'That was interesting,' I said.

'An experiment,' she replied. 'Your name has such a ring to it. Love . . . craft. It suggests expertise in a certain direction.'

'Disappointed?'

She smiled. I wondered if she had several rows of teeth, like a shark.

'Anything but.'

'So do I get an invite to the back-row during your next Dagon hoe-down?'

She was businesslike again. 'I think you'd better report back to Janey. Tell her I'll have Laird call her when he's in town and put her mind at rest. She should pay you off. What with the War, it's a waste of manpower to have you spend your time looking for someone who isn't missing when you could be defending Lockheed from Fifth Columnists.'

'What about Franklin?'

'Franklin the President?'

'Franklin the baby.'

Her round eyes tried to widen. She was playing this scene innocent. The Panther Princess had been the same when telling the white hunter that Jungle Jillian had left the Tomb of the Jaguar hours ago.

'Miss Wilde seems to think Laird has borrowed a child of hers that she carelessly left in his care. She'd like Franklin back.'

'Janey hasn't got a baby. She can't have babies. It's why she's such a psycho-neurotic case. Her analyst is getting rich on her bewildering fantasies. She can't tell reality from the movies. She once accused me of human sacrifice.'

'Sounds like a square rap.'

'That was in a film, Mr Lovecraft. Cardboard knives and catsup blood.'

Usually at this stage in an investigation, I call my friend Bernie at the District Attorney's office and put out a few fishing lines. This time, he phoned me. When I got into my office, I had the feeling my telephone had been ringing for a long time.

'Don't make waves,' Bernie said.

'Pardon,' I snapped back, with my usual lightning-fast wit.

'Just don't. It's too cold to go for a swim this time of year.'

'Even in a bathtub.'

'Especially in a bathtub.'

'Does Mr District Attorney send his regards?'

Bernie laughed. I had been an investigator with the DA's office a few years back, but we'd been forced to part company.

'Forget him. I have some more impressive names on my list.'

'Let me guess. Howard Hughes?'

'Close.'

'General Stillwell?'

'Getting warmer. Try Mayor Fletcher Bowron, Governor Culbert Olson, and State Attorney General Earl Warren. Oh, and Wax, of course.'

I whistled. 'All interested in little me. Who'd 'a thunk it?'

'Look, I don't know much about this myself. They just gave me a message to pass on. In the building, they apparently think of me as your keeper.'

'Do a British gentleman, a French lady and a Fed the size of Mount Rushmore have anything to do with this?'

'I'll take the money I've won so far and you can pass that question on to the next sucker.'

'Fine, Bernie. Tell me, just how popular am I?'

'Tojo rates worse than you, and maybe Judas Iscariot.'

'Feels comfy. Any idea where Laird Brunette is these days?'

I heard a pause and some rumbling. Bernie was making sure his office was empty of all ears. I imagined him bringing the receiver up close and dropping his voice to a whisper.

'No one's seen him in three months. Confidentially, I don't miss him at all. But there are others . . .' Bernie coughed, a door opened, and he started talking normally or louder. '. . . of course, honey, I'll be home in time for Jack Benny.'

'See you later, sweetheart,' I said, 'your dinner is in the sink and I'm off to Tijuana with a professional pool player.'

'Love you,' he said, and hung up.

I'd picked up a coating of green slime on the soles of my shoes. I tried scraping them off on the edge of the desk and then used yesterday's *Times* to get the stuff off the desk. The gloop looked damned esoteric to me.

I poured myself a shot from the bottle I had picked up across the street and washed the taste of Janice Marsh off my teeth.

I thought of Polynesia in the early nineteenth century and of those fish-eyed native girls clustering around Captain Marsh. Somehow, tentacles kept getting in the way of my thoughts. In theory, the Capt. should have been an ideal subject for a Dorothy Lamour movie, perhaps with Janice Marsh in the role of her great-great-great and Jon Hall or Ray Milland as girl-chasing Obed. But I was picking up Bela Lugosi vibrations from the set-up. I couldn't help but think of bisected babies.

So far none of this running around had got me any closer to the Laird and his heir. In my mind, I drew up a list of Brunette's known associates. Then I mentally crossed off all the ones who were dead. That brought me up short. When people in Brunette's business die, nobody really takes much notice except maybe to join in a few drunken choruses of 'Ding-Dong, the Wicked Witch is Dead' before remembering there are plenty of other Wicked Witches in the sea. I'm just like everybody else: I don't keep a score of dead gambler-entrepreneurs. But, thinking of it, there'd been an awful lot recently, up to and including Gianni Pastore. Apart from Rothko and Isinglass, there'd been at least three other closed casket funerals in the profession. Obviously you couldn't blame that on the Japs. I wondered how many of the casualties had met their ends in bathtubs. The whole thing kept coming back to water. I decided I hated the stuff and swore not to let my bourbon get polluted with it.

Back out in the rain, I started hitting the bars. Brunette had a lot of friends. Maybe someone would know something.

By early evening, I'd propped up a succession of bars and leaned on a succession of losers. The only thing I'd come up with was the blatantly obvious information that everyone in town was scared. Most were wet, but all were scared.

Everyone was scared of two or three things at once. The Japs were high on everyone's list. You'd be surprised to discover the number of shaky citizens who'd turned overnight from chisellers who barely recognised the flag into true red-white-and-blue patriots prepared to shed their last drop of alcoholic blood for their country. Everywhere you went, someone sounded off against Hirohito, Tojo, the Mikado, *kabuki* and *origami*. The current rash of accidental deaths in the Pastore-Brunette circle were a much less popular subject for discussion and tended to turn loudmouths into closemouths at the drop of a question.

'Something fishy,' everyone said, before changing the subject.

I was beginning to wonder whether Janey Wilde wouldn't have done better spending her money on a radio commercial asking the Laird to give her a call. Then I found Curtis the Croupier in Maxie's. He usually wore the full soup and fish, as if borrowed from Astaire. Now he'd exchanged his carnation, starched shirtfront and pop-up top hat for an outfit in olive drab with bars on the shoulder and a cap under one epaulette.

'Heard the bugle call, Curtis?' I asked, pushing through a crowd of patriotic admirers who had been buying the soldier boy drinks.

Curtis grinned before he recognised me, then produced a supercilious sneer. We'd met before, on the *Montecito*. There was a rumour going around that during Prohibition he'd once got involved in an honest card game, but if pressed he'd energetically refute it.

'Hey cheapie,' he said.

I bought myself a drink but didn't offer him one. He had three or four lined up.

'This racket must pay,' I said. 'How much did the uniform cost? You rent it from Paramount?'

The croupier was offended. 'It's real,' he said. 'I've enlisted. I hope to be sent overseas.'

'Yeah, we ought to parachute you into Tokyo to introduce loaded dice and rickety roulette wheels.'

'You're cynical, cheapie.' He tossed back a drink.

'No, just a realist. How come you quit the *Monty*?'

'Poking around in the Laird's business?'

I raised my shoulders and dropped them again. 'Gambling has fallen off recently, along with leading figures in the industry. The original owner of this place, for instance. I bet paying for wreaths has thinned your bankroll.'

Curtis took two more drinks, quickly, and called for more. When I'd come in, there'd been a couple of chippies climbing into his hip pockets. Now he was on his own with me. He didn't appreciate the change of scenery and I can't say I blamed him.

'Look cheapie,' he said, his voice suddenly low, 'for your own good, just drop it. There are more important things now.'

'Like democracy?'

'You can call it that.'

'How far overseas do you want to be sent, Curtis?'

He looked at the door as if expecting five guys with tommy guns to come out of the rain for him. Then he gripped the bar to stop his hands shaking.

'As far as I can get, cheapie. The Philippines, Europe, Australia. I don't care.'

'Going to war is a hell of a way to escape.'

'Isn't it just? But wouldn't Papa Gianni have been safer on Wake Island than in the tub?'

'You heard the bathtime story, then?'

Curtis nodded and took another gulp. The juke box played 'Doodly-Acky-Sacky, Want Some Seafood, Mama' and it was scary. Nonsense, but scary.

'They all die in water. That's what I've heard. Sometimes, on the *Monty*, Laird would go up on deck and just look at the sea for hours. He was crazy, since he took up with that Marsh popsicle.'

'The Panther Princess?'

'You saw that one? Yeah, Janice Marsh. Pretty girl if you like clams. Laird claimed there was a sunken town in the bay. He used a lot of weird words, darkie bop or something. Jitterbug stuff. Cthul-whatever, Yog-Gimme-a-Break. He said things were going to come out of the water and sweep over the land, and he didn't mean U-Boats.'

Curtis was uncomfortable in his uniform. There were dark patches where the rain had soaked. He'd been drinking like W.C. Fields on a bender but he wasn't getting tight. Whatever was troubling him was too much even for Jack Daniel's.

I thought of the Laird of the *Monty*. And I thought of the painting of Capt. Marsh's clipper, with that out-of-proportion squid surfacing near it.

'He's on the boat, isn't he?'

Curtis didn't say anything.

'Alone,' I thought aloud. 'He's out there alone.'

I pushed my hat to the back of my head and tried to shake booze out of my mind. It was crazy. Nobody bobs up and down in the water with a sign round their neck saying 'Hey Tojo, Torpedo Me!' The *Monty* was a floating target.

'No,' Curtis said, grabbing my arm, jarring drink out of my glass.

'He's not out there?'

He shook his head.

'No, cheapie. He's not out there *alone*.'

All the water taxis were in dock, securely moored and covered until the storms settled. I'd never find a boatman to take me out to the *Montecito* tonight. Why, everyone knew the waters were infested with Japanese subs. But I knew someone who wouldn't care any more whether or not his boats were being treated properly. He was even past bothering if they were borrowed without his permission.

The Seaview Inn was still deserted, although there were police notices warning people away from the scene of the crime. It was dark, cold and wet, and nobody bothered me as I broke into the boathouse to find a ring of keys.

I took my pick of the taxis moored to the Seaview's jetty and gassed her up for a short voyage. I also got my .38 Colt Super Match out from the glove compartment of the Chrysler and slung it under my armpit. During all this, I got a thorough soaking and picked up the beginnings of influenza. I hoped Jungle Jillian would appreciate the effort.

The sea was swelling under the launch and making a lot of noise. I was grateful for the noise when it came to shooting the padlock off the mooring chain but the swell soon had my stomach sloshing about in my lower abdomen. I am not an especially competent seaman.

The *Monty* was out there on the horizon, still visible whenever the lightning lanced. It was hardly difficult to keep the small boat aimed at the bigger one.

Getting out on the water makes you feel small. Especially when the lights of Bay City are just a scatter in the dark behind you. I got the impression of large things moving just beyond my field of perception. The chill soaked through my clothes. My hat was a felt sponge, dripping down my neck. As the launch cut towards the *Monty*, rain and spray needled my face. I saw my hands white and bath-wrinkled on the wheel and wished I'd brought a bottle. Come to that, I wished I was at home in bed with a mug of cocoa and Claudette Colbert. Some things in life don't turn out the way you plan.

Three miles out, I felt the law change in my stomach. Gambling was legal and I emptied my belly over the side into the water. I stared at the remains of my toasted cheese sandwich as they floated off. I thought I saw the moon reflected greenly in the depths, but there was no moon that night.

I killed the engine and let waves wash the taxi against the side of the *Monty*. The small boat scraped along the hull of the gambling ship and I caught hold of a weed-furred rope ladder as it passed. I tethered the taxi and took a deep breath.

The ship sat low in the water, as if its lower cabins were flooded. Too much seaweed climbed up towards the decks. It'd never reopen for business, even if the war were over tomorrow.

I climbed the ladder, fighting the water-weight in my clothes, and heaved myself up on deck. It was good to have something more solid than a tiny boat under me but the deck pitched like an airplane wing. I grabbed a rail and hoped my internal organs would arrange themselves back into their familiar grouping.

'Brunette,' I shouted, my voice lost in the wind.

There was nothing. I'd have to go below decks.

A sheet flying flags of all nations had come loose, and was whipped around with the storm. Japan, Italy and Germany were still tactlessly represented, along with several European states that weren't really nations any more. The deck was covered in familiar slime.

I made my way around towards the ballroom doors. They'd blown in and rain splattered against the polished wood floors. I got inside and pulled the .38. It felt better in my hand than digging into my ribs.

Lightning struck nearby and I got a flash image of the abandoned ballroom, orchestra stands at one end painted with the name of a disbanded combo.

The casino was one deck down. It should be dark but I saw a glow under a walkway door. I pushed through and cautiously descended. It wasn't wet here but it was cold. The fish smell was strong.

'Brunette,' I shouted again.

I imagined something heavy shuffling nearby and slipped a few steps, banging my hip and arm against a bolted-down table. I kept hold of my gun, but only through superhuman strength.

The ship wasn't deserted. That much was obvious.

I could hear music. It wasn't Cab Calloway or Benny Goodman. There was a Hawaiian guitar in there but mainly it was a crazy choir of keening voices. I wasn't convinced the performers were human and wondered whether Brunette was working up some kind of act with singing seals. I couldn't make out the words but the familiar hawk-and-spit syllables of 'Cthulhu' cropped up a couple of times.

I wanted to get out and go back to nasty Bay City and forget all about this. But Jungle Jillian was counting on me.

I made my way along the passage, working towards the music. A hand fell on my shoulder and my heart banged against the backsides of my eyeballs.

A twisted face stared at me out of the gloom, thickly bearded, crater-cheeked. Laird Brunette was made up as Ben Gunn, skin shrunk onto his skull, eyes large as hen's eggs.

His hand went over my mouth.

'Do Not Disturb,' he said, voice high and cracked.

This wasn't the suave criminal I knew, the man with tartan cummerbunds and patent leather hair. This was some other Brunette, in the grips of a tough bout with dope or madness.

'The Deep Ones,' he said.

He let me go and I backed away.

'It is the time of the Surfacing.'

My case was over. I knew where the Laird was. All I had to do was tell Janey Wilde and give her her refund.

'There's very little time.'

The music was louder. I heard a great number of bodies shuffling around in the casino. They couldn't have been very agile, because they kept clumping into things and each other.

'They must be stopped. Dynamite, depth charges, torpedoes . . .'

'Who?' I asked. 'The Japs?'

'The Deep Ones. The Dwellers in the Sister City.'

He had lost me.

A nasty thought occurred to me. As a detective, I can't avoid making deductions. There were obviously a lot of people aboard the *Monty*, but mine was the only small boat in evidence. How had everyone else got out here? Surely they couldn't have swum?

'It's a war,' Brunette ranted, 'us and them. It has always been a war.'

I made a decision. I'd get the Laird off his boat and turn him over to Jungle Jillian. She could sort things out with the Panther Princess and her Esoteric Order. In his current state, Brunette would hand over any baby if you gave him a blanket.

I took Brunette's thin wrist and tugged him towards the staircase. But a hatch clanged down and I knew we were stuck.

A door opened and perfume drifted through the fish stink.

'Mr Lovecraft, wasn't it?' a silk-scaled voice said. Janice Marsh was wearing pendant squid earrings and a lady-sized gun. And nothing else.

That wasn't quite as nice as it sounds. The Panther Princess had no nipples, no navel and no pubic hair. She was lightly scaled between the legs and her wet skin shone like a shark's. I imagined that if you stroked her, your palm would come away bloody. She was wearing neither the turban she'd affected earlier nor the dark wig of her pictures. Her head was completely bald, skull swelling unnaturally. She didn't even have her eyebrows pencilled in.

'You evidently can't take good advice.'

61

As mermaids go, she was more scary than cute. In the crook of her left arm, she held a bundle from which a white baby face peered with unblinking eyes. Franklin looked more like Janice Marsh than his parents.

'A pity, really,' said a tiny ventriloquist voice through Franklin's mouth, 'but there are always complications.'

Brunette gibbered with fear, chewing his beard and huddling against me.

Janice Marsh set Franklin down and he sat up, an adult struggling with a baby's body.

'The Cap'n has come back,' she explained.

'Every generation must have a Cap'n,' said the thing in Franklin's mind. Dribble got in the way and he wiped his angel mouth with a fold of swaddle.

Janice Marsh clucked and pulled Laird away from me, stroking his face.

'Poor dear,' she said, flicking his chin with a long tongue. 'He got out of his depth.'

She put her hands either side of Brunette's head, pressing the butt of her gun into his cheek.

'He was talking about a Sister City,' I prompted.

She twisted the gambler's head around and dropped him on the floor. His tongue poked out and his eyes showed only white.

'Of course,' the baby said. 'The Cap'n founded two settlements. One beyond Devil Reef, off Massachusetts. And one here, under the sands of the Bay.'

We both had guns. I'd let her kill Brunette without trying to shoot her. It was the detective's fatal flaw; curiosity. Besides, the Laird was dead inside his head long before Janice snapped his neck.

'You can still join us,' she said, hips working like a snake in time to the chanting. 'There are raptures in the deeps.'

'Sister,' I said, 'you're not my type.'

Her nostrils flared in anger and slits opened in her neck, flashing liverish red lines in her white skin.

Her gun was pointed at me, safety off. Her long nails were lacquered green.

I thought I could shoot her before she shot me. But I didn't. Something about a naked woman, no matter how strange, prevents you from killing her. Her whole body was moving with the music. I'd been wrong. Despite everything, she was beautiful.

I put my gun down and waited for her to murder me. It never happened.

I don't really know the order things worked out. But first there was lightning, then, an instant later, thunder.

Light filled the passageway, hurting my eyes. Then, a rumble of noise which grew in a crescendo. The chanting was drowned.

Through the thunder cut a screech. It was a baby's cry. Franklin's eyes were screwed up and he was shrieking. I had a sense of the Cap'n drowning in the baby's mind, his purchase on the purloined body relaxing as the child cried out.

The floor beneath me shook and buckled and I heard a great straining of abused metal. A belch of hot wind surrounded me. A hole appeared. Janice Marsh moved fast and I think she fired her gun, but whether at me on purpose or at random in reflex

I couldn't say. Her body sliced towards me and I ducked.

There was another explosion, not of thunder, and thick smoke billowed through a rupture in the floor. I was on the floor, hugging the tilting deck. Franklin slid towards me and bumped, screaming, into my head. A half-ton of water fell on us and I knew the ship was breached. My guess was that the Japs had just saved my life with a torpedo. I was waist deep in saltwater. Janice Marsh darted away in a sinuous fish motion.

Then there were heavy bodies around me, pushing me against a bulkhead. In the darkness, I was scraped by something heavy, cold-skinned and foul smelling. There were barks and cries, some of which might have come from human throats.

Fires went out and hissed as the water rose. I had Franklin in my hands and tried to hold him above water. I remembered the peril of Jungle Jillian again and found my head floating against the hard ceiling.

The Cap'n cursed in vivid eighteenth century language, Franklin's little body squirming in my grasp. A toothless mouth tried to get a biter's grip on my chin but slipped off. My feet slid and I was off-balance, pulling the baby briefly underwater. I saw his startled eyes through a wobbling film. When I pulled him out again, the Cap'n was gone and Franklin was screaming on his own. Taking a double gulp of air, I plunged under the water and struggled towards the nearest door, a hand closed over the baby's face to keep water out of his mouth and nose.

The *Montecito* was going down fast enough to suggest

there were plenty of holes in it. I had to make it a priority to find one. I jammed my knee at a door and it flew open. I was poured, along with several hundred gallons of water, into a large room full of stored gambling equipment. Red and white chips floated like confetti.

I got my footing and waded towards a ladder. Something large reared out of the water and shambled at me, screeching like a seabird. I didn't get a good look at it. Which was a mercy. Heavy arms lashed me, flopping boneless against my face. With my free hand, I pushed back at the thing, fingers slipping against cold slime. Whatever it was was in a panic and squashed through the door.

There was another explosion and everything shook. Water splashed upwards and I fell over. I got upright and managed to get a one-handed grip on the ladder. Franklin was still struggling and bawling, which I took to be a good sign. Somewhere near, there was a lot of shouting.

I dragged us up rung by rung and slammed my head against a hatch. If it had been battened, I'd have smashed my skull and spilled my brains. It flipped upwards and a push of water from below shoved us through the hole like a ping-pong ball in a fountain.

The *Monty* was on fire and there were things in the water around it. I heard the drone of airplane engines and glimpsed nearby launches. Gunfire fought with the wind. It was a full-scale attack. I made it to the deck-rail and saw a boat fifty feet away. Men in yellow slickers angled tommy guns down and sprayed the water with bullets.

The gunfire whipped the sea into a foam. Kicking things died in the water. Someone brought up his gun and fired at me. I pushed myself aside, arching my body over Franklin and bullets spanged against the deck.

My borrowed taxi must have been dragged under by the bulk of the ship.

There were definitely lights in the sea. And the sky. Over the city, in the distance, I saw firecracker bursts. Something exploded a hundred yards away and a tower of water rose, bursting like a puffball. A depth charge.

The deck was angled down and water was creeping up at us. I held on to a rope webbing, wondering whether the gambling ship still had any lifeboats. Franklin spluttered and bawled.

A white body slid by, heading for the water. I instinctively grabbed at it. Hands took hold of me and I was looking into Janice Marsh's face. Her eyes blinked, membranes coming round from the sides, and she kissed me again. Her long tongue probed my mouth like an eel, then withdrew. She stood up, one leg bent so she was still vertical on the sloping deck. She drew air into her lungs – if she had lungs – and expelled it through her gills with a musical cry. She was slim and white in the darkness, water running off her body. Someone fired in her direction and she dived into the waves, knifing through the surface and disappearing towards the submarine lights. Bullets rippled the spot where she'd gone under.

I let go of the ropes and kicked at the deck, pushing myself away from the sinking ship. I held Franklin above the water and splashed with my legs and elbows. The

Monty was dragging a lot of things under with it, and I fought against the pull so I wouldn't be one of them. My shoulders ached and my clothes got in the way, but I kicked against the current.

The ship went down screaming, a chorus of bending steel and dying creatures. I had to make for a launch and hope not to be shot. I was lucky. Someone got a polehook into my jacket and landed us like fish. I lay on the deck, water running out of my clothes, swallowing as much air as I could breathe.

I heard Franklin yelling. His lungs were still in working order.

Someone big in a voluminous slicker, a sou'wester tied to his head, knelt by me, and slapped me in the face.

'Peeper,' he said.

'They're calling it the Great Los Angeles Air Raid,' Winthrop told me as he poured a mug of British tea. 'Some time last night a panic started, and everyone in Bay City shot at the sky for hours.'

'The Japs?' I said, taking a mouthful of welcome hot liquid.

'In theory. Actually, I doubt it. It'll be recorded as a fiasco, a lot of jumpy characters with guns. While it was all going on, we engaged the enemy and emerged victorious.'

He was still dressed up for an embassy ball and didn't look as if he'd been on deck all evening. Geneviève Dieudonné wore a fisherman's sweater and fatigue pants, her hair up in a scarf. She was looking at a lot of sounding equipment and noting down readings.

'You're not fighting the Japs, are you?'

Winthrop pursed his lips. 'An older war, my friend. We can't be distracted. After last night's action, our Deep Ones won't poke their scaly noses out for a while. Now I can do something to lick Hitler.'

'What really happened?'

'There was something dangerous in the sea, under Mr Brunette's boat. We have destroyed it and routed the . . . uh, the hostile forces. They wanted the boat as a surface station. That's why Mr Brunette's associates were eliminated.'

Geneviève gave a report in French, so fast that I couldn't follow.

'Total destruction,' Winthrop explained, 'a dreadful set-back for them. It'll put them in their place for years. Forever would be too much to hope for, but a few years will help.'

I lay back on the bunk, feeling my wounds. Already choking on phlegm, I would be lucky to escape pneumonia.

'And the little fellow is a decided dividend.'

Finlay glumly poked around, suggesting another dose of depth charges. He was cradling a mercifully sleep-struck Franklin, but didn't look terribly maternal.

'He seems quite unaffected by it all.'

'His name is Franklin,' I told Winthrop. 'On the boat, he was . . .'

'Not himself? I'm familiar with the condition. It's a filthy business, you understand.'

'He'll be all right,' Geneviève put in.

I wasn't sure whether the rest of the slicker crew were

feds or servicemen and I wasn't sure whether I wanted to know. I could tell a clandestine operation when I landed in the middle of one.

'Who knows about this?' I asked. 'Hoover? Roosevelt?'

Winthrop didn't answer.

'Someone must know,' I said.

'Yes,' the Englishman said, 'someone must. But this is a war the public would never believe exists. In the Bureau, Finlay's outfit are known as "the Unnameables", never mentioned by the press, never honoured or censured by the government, victories and defeats never recorded in the official history.'

The launch shifted with the waves, and I hugged myself, hoping for some warmth to creep over me. Finlay had promised to break out a bottle later but that made me resolve to stick to tea as a point of honour. I hated to fulfil his expectations.

'And America is a young country,' Winthrop explained. 'In Europe, we've known things a lot longer.'

On shore, I'd have to tell Janey Wilde about Brunette and hand over Franklin. Some flack at Metro would be thinking of an excuse for the Panther Princess's disappearance. Everything else – the depth charges, the sea battle, the sinking ship – would be swallowed up by the War.

All that would be left would be tales. Weird tales.

It occurred to me that Raymond Chandler and H.P. Lovecraft had a lot in common. Born in 1888 and 1890, they lived unhappily in America but dreamed of a lost and imaginary England. Awkward outsiders, they were often beset with financial troubles and began their writing careers in pulp magazines. Their visionary, challenging work was first presented alongside lurid dross, though they later came to be recognised as central to separate movements within their chosen genres, hard-boiled crime and weird horror. Married strangely to older wives, they distrusted and feared women, often presenting cruel, almost inhuman female characters. Some of their greatest work is set in seaside towns whose physical corruption has an almost philosophical dimension, and they used despised genres to make a genuine contribution to English and American letters. Since their deaths, they have become the most imitated and influential writers in their fields and are capable of inspiring entire collections devoted to their characters and themes, not to mention many of the best-selling novelists in their categories. Personally, I found the love of Chandler's prose which I developed in my late teens helped cure habits I'd picked up through an earlier interest in Lovecraft.

Here, I wanted to bring a touch of Lovecraft's Innsmouth to Chandler's Bay City, fusing elements from *The Shadow Over Innsmouth* and *Farewell, My Lovely*. If its narrator isn't quite Philip Marlowe, he certainly would like to be. I see him as more like Dick Powell than Bogart. The stylistic tangle the story can't resolve has something to do with the disparity between a Lovecraft protagonist, who is always overwhelmed by his hostile world, and a Chandler hero, who somehow shrugs it off. The other set of cross-generic twins of the period are Robert E. Howard and Cornell Woolrich, a pair of mother-dominated paranoid miseries whose vision of a hostile universe makes Lovecraft's cosmic horror seem quite sunny, but I can't envision a story in which Conan Wears Black, though a chance meeting in a diner with Bob and Cornell comparing photographs of their mothers has some horrific possibility.

A Quarter to Three

Sometimes the nights get to you, right? When there's no one pushing coins into it, the juke plays Peggy Lee over and over again. 'Fever'. The finger-click backing track gets into your skull. Like a heartbeat, you've got it in there for the rest of your life. And in the off-season, which when you're talking about the 'Mouth is – let's face it – all year round, sometimes you go from midnight til dawn with no takers at all. Who can blame them? We serve paint stripper *au lait* and reinforced concrete crullers. When I first took the graveyard shift at Cap'n Cod's Twenty-Four Hour Diner, I actually liked the idea of being paid (just) to stay up all night with no hassles. Maybe I'd get to finish *Moby Dick* before Professor Whipple could flunk me. Anyway, that's not the way it worked out.

Two o'clock and not a human face in sight. And in late November, the beachfront picture window rattles in the slightest breeze. The waves were shattered noisily on the damn useless shingles. The 'Mouth isn't a tourist spot, it's a town-sized morgue that smells of fish. All I'd got for company was a giant cardboard cut-out of the Cap'n, giving a scaly salute and a salty smile. He hasn't got much of a face left, because he used to stand outside and get a good sloshing whenever the surf was up. I don't know who he was in the first place – the current owner is a pop-eyed lardo called Murray Something who pays in smelly cash – but now he's just a cut-out ghost. I'd talk to *him*, only I'd be worried that some night he'd talk right back.

It's a theme diner, just like all the others up and down the coast. Nets on the ceiling, framed dead fish on the walls, formica on the tables, and more sand on the floor than along the seashore. And it's got a gurgling coffee machine that spits out the foulest brew you've ever tasted, and an array of food under glass that you'd swear doesn't change from one month to the next. I was stuck in a groove again, like Peggy if I forget to nudge the juke in the middle of that verse about Pocahontas. It's that damn chapter 'The Whiteness of the Whale'. I always trip over it, and it's supposed to be the heart of the book.

I didn't notice her until the music changed. Debbie Reynolds, singing 'It Must Have Been Moonglow'. Jesus. She must have come in during one of my twenty-minute 'blinks'. She was sitting up against the wall, by the juke, examining the counter. Young, maybe pretty, a few strands of blonde hair creeping out from under her scarf, and wearing a coat not designed for a pregnant woman. It had a belt that she probably couldn't fasten. I'm in Eng. Lit. at MU, not pre-med, but I

judged that she was just about ready to drop the kid.
Maybe quins.

'Can I help you, ma'am?' I asked. Murray likes me to
call the mugs 'sir' and 'ma'am' not 'buddy' and 'doll' or
'asshole' and 'drudge'. It's the only instruction he ever
dished out.

She looked at me – big hazel eyes with too much red in
them – but didn't say anything. She looked tired, which
isn't surprising since it was the middle of the night and
she was about to give birth to the Incredible Bulk.

'Coffee?' I suggested. 'If you're looking for a way to
end it all, you could do worse. Cheaper than strychnine.
Maybe you want ice-cream and pickles?'

'That's crap,' she said, and I realised that she really
was young. If she weren't pregnant, I'd have accused
her of being up after her bedtime. Sixteen or seventeen, I guessed. Cheerleader-pretty, but with a few
lines in there to show she had more to worry about
than who's dating Buddy-Bob Fullback these days or
how she'll get through the Home Ec. quiz next Friday. 'About cravings, that's crap. You don't want to
to eat weird stuff. Me, I don't want to eat at all,
ever again. But you gotta, or you disintegrate. It's
like having a tapeworm. You eat as much as you
can, but you still go hungry. The fo-etus gets all the
goodies.'

Fo-etus. That was how she pronounced it. I kind of
liked the sound of it.

'Well, what does your fo-etus fancy this morning?'

'A cheeseburger.'

'This is a fish place, ma'am. No burgers. I can

melt some cheese on a fishcake and give it to you in a bap.'

'Sounds like shit. I'll have one, for the mutant . . .'

Julie London was on now, 'Cry Me a River'. 'Cryyyyy me a river, cuh-ry me a river, I cried a reever over you.' That has one of the best rhymes in the English language in it; 'plebean' with 'through with me an' . . . now you say you're lonely . . .'

I slapped the frozen cake on the hotplate and dug out some not-too-senile cheese. We don't stock the kind that's better if it's got mould on it.

'Have you got liquor?'

'Have you got ID?'

'Shit, how come you can get knocked up five years before you can have a drink in this state?'

The ice in the cake popped and hissed. Julie sounded broken-hearted in the background. It must be a tough life.

'I don't make the rules.'

'I won't get drunk. The fo-etus will.'

'He's underage too, ma'am.'

'It's an it. They did tests.'

'Pardon?'

'Ginger ale . . .'

'Fine.'

'. . . and put a shot of something in it.'

I gave in and dug out the Scotch. Not much call for it. The highlander on the label had faded, a yellowing dribble down his face turning him leprous. I splashed the bottom of a glass, then added a full measure of soft drink. She had it down quickly and ordered another. I saw to it and flipped the cake over. I wish I could say it smelled appetising.

'I'm not married,' she said. 'I had to leave school. There goes my shot at college. Probably my only chance to get out of the 'Mouth. Oh well, that's another life on the rocks. You must get a lot of that.'

'Not really. I don't get much of anyone in here. I think the Cap'n will be dropping the Twenty-Four-Hour service next year. All his old customers drowned or something. It's entropy. Everything's winding down. You have to expect it.'

I melted the cheese and handed her her cheesefish bap. She didn't seem interested in it. I noticed she had a pile of quarters stacked in a little tower on the bar. She was feeding the juke regularly.

'This is my song,' she said. Rosemary Clooney, 'You Took Advantage of Me'. 'The bastard certainly did.'

She was a talker, I'd spotted that early. After midnight, you only get talkers and brooders. I didn't really have to say anything, but there'd be pauses if I didn't fill in the gaps.

'Your boyfriend?'

'Yeah. Fuckin' amphibian. He's supposed to be here. I'm meeting him.'

'What'll happen?'

'Who knows? Some folks ain't human.'

She pushed her plate around and prodded the bap. I had to agree with her. I wouldn't have eaten it, either. Murray never asked me if I could cook.

'Look, the lights . . .' She meant the sea lights. It's a localised phenomenon in the 'Mouth. A greenish glow just out beyond the shallows. Everyone freaks first time they see it. 'He'll be here soon. Another ginger ale plus.'

I gave her one. She took it slower. Captain Ahab looked insanely up from the broken-spined paperback on the counter, obsessed with his white whale. Crazy bastard. I'd love to see him on a talk show with one of those Greenpeace activists.

There was someone coming up from the beach. She shifted on her stool, uncomfortably keeping her pregnancy away from the rim of the counter. She didn't seem interested one way or the other. 'It's him.'

'He'll be wet.'

'Yeah. That he will.'

'It don't matter. I don't do the mopping up. That's the kid who gets the daytime haul.'

It was Sinatra now. The main man. 'It's a quarter to three . . .'

'No one in the place except you and me,' I said, over the Chairman of the Board. Her smile was cracked, lopsided, greenish. She had plaque.

The door was pushed inward, and in he waddled. As you might expect, he didn't look like much. It took him a long time to get across the diner, and he wasn't breathing easily. He moved a bit like Charles Laughton as Quasimodo, dragging wetly. It was easy to see what she had seen in him; it left a thin damp trail between his scuffed footprints. By the time he got to the counter, she had finished her drink.

He got up on to a stool with difficulty, his wet, leather-linked fingers scrabbling for a grip on the edge of the bar. The skin over his cheeks and neck puffed in and out as he tried to smile at her.

'. . . could tell you a lot,' sung Frankie, 'but you've got to be true to your code . . .'

She put down her glass, and looked me in the eye, smiling.

'Make it one for my baby, and one more for the *toad*.'

Like everyone in the field, I went through a period, at about thirteen, of reading H.P. Lovecraft. His 'Cthulhu Mythos' (actually worked into something systematic by August Derleth) is one of the pervasive ideas of horror and science fiction; and I've returned to it, in a Jack Yeovil-ish sort of mood, in 'The Big Fish' (a double pastiche), and the *Demon Download* cycle of novels, which incorporates Lovecraft lore into other mutant genre ideas. With a last line in the tradition of Lovecraft disciple Robert Bloch, this is a fond *hommage* to one of my favourite HPL stories, 'The Shadow Over Innsmouth'.

'One For My Baby (And One More for the Road)', by Johnny Mercer and Harold Arlen, was introduced in 1943, not by Sinatra (who sang it in 1958 on the *Only the Lonely* album) but by Fred Astaire in the otherwise forgettable movie *The Sky's the Limit*. I apologise for mutating the song.

Pitbull Brittan

To: Norman St John Stevas, Minister for Paranormal
    Resources

From: Department of Paranormal Resources
Date: December 9, 1982

ASSESSMENT OF SUITABILITY

Subject Name: Brittan, Richard Lionheart
Known Aliases: 'Pitbull'*
Date of Birth: 23 April 1947
Nationality: British, Caucasian
Status: Single
Current Occupation: Lieutenant, First Paratroop Regiment

*At school (Millfield), for obvious reasons, they called
him 'Dickhead'.

*   *   *

Talent: Subject's musculature is composed entirely of erectile tissue. When aroused, physically or emotionally, his heart pumps blood at an increased rate, producing pronounced turgidity of the surface flesh, extraordinary muscular strength, limited invulnerability and psychological capacity for feats of selfless heroism. Among the side effects of the process are a reddish flush over the entire body (most notable in the facial area), an expansion of size (necessitating the wearing of loose clothing), and an extreme, painful genital erection. When our boy gets a hard on, he goes into action like a pitbull terrier, and doesn't stop until the job's done.

Comments: Subject has been getting a lot of column inches (*sic*) since the yellow press latched on to his exploits in the South Atlantic during the late unpleasantness with Argentina. Subsequent to the Sheepdip Heights Incident, which resulted in his receipt of the Victoria Cross, it has been generally assumed by leader writers of the *Mail* and the *Express* that he will be joining us (see attached press cuttings) as 'a True-Blue British hero.' Given the fortuitous coincidence of his surname and his undoubted patriotic zeal, he is considered by the opinion formers to be exactly the type of high-profile Talent the DPR should be fostering as opposed to the 'colourless spoon-benders' most identified with the department. The Army has not yet concluded their investigation into Sheepdip Heights, but details will be 'forthcoming as soon as they are available'.

Thoughts: Subject is due soon to 'resign' his commission

and has been granted an 'honourable discharge' which should tell you something. Also, 34 is remarkably old for a lieutenant. Once it looked like he was going to get the VC, several of his files – most notably, the psychological evaluations – have mysteriously become unavailable to this department. My conclusion is that 1 Para want to pass Subject on to us, and I would tend to assume this is an oblatory equine situation, and we should employ the services of a veterinarian dentist before further considering recruitment.

Conclusion: It's hard to know whether to class this one as talented or disabled. In the short term, his prowess is doubtless remarkable – as that Argentine machine gun nest on Sheepdip Heights found out – but my impression is that there is a severe downside. Bluntly put, Subject can induce his bodily metamorphosis in all manner of ways – anger, sexual interest, fear, excitement, embarrassment – but can only reverse the process in the normal manner, by achieving a sexual climax. Note the references in the press accounts of Sheepdip Heights to Subject disappearing for a few minutes with 'a grateful shepherdess'. It has been suggested, but obviously not confirmed, that were Subject *not* to have some kind of emission within half an hour or so of arousal, the process would become irreversible, and the ever-increasing rush of blood into his tissues would lead, in rapid succession, to the explosion of Subject's genitalia, major veins and heart. The upshot is that if you want to deploy subject as a field agent, you would have to partner him with a trained prostitute or expect him to have a very short, messy career.

Suitability: F.

PS: I know the Suitability Rating might seem overly harsh considering the attached clippings (ref: PITBULL COMES THROUGH FOR BRITAIN, *Daily Mail*; BIG DICK STICKS IT TO ARGIES, *The Sun*; VC FOR VICTORY, *Daily Express*), but I have a bad feeling about this one, and after thirty years around Talents I've learned to trust my bad feelings. Subject is an unstable braggart, and, after our recent bad publicity, the DPR doesn't really need to be known as the employer of The Man Whose Dick Exploded.

Signed,

Raymond Noone, B.Sc., D.Parapsych (Oxon), OBE.

cc: Loric.

1

'Hang it all from the old oak tree, Slobotham, I'm bored!'

Richard Lionheart Brittan, 'Pitbull' to his friends, ground his teeth together mightily, handsome-ugly face contorted with mock agony. He clenched and unclenched ham-sized fists, wishing for an Argie or two within thumping reach. His veined marble knuckles needed a work-out.

'Bored, bored, bored!'

'Yes, sir,' agreed Slobotham, the quiet-spoken, ineffably deferential family retainer, passing him a deftly-mixed cocktail of saltpetre and valium.

'Don't want that filth, Slobbo,' he sneered, hurling the offending liquid, in its seventeenth-century cut glass goblet, at the wall. The glass shattered, and the medicine splattered, dribbling down the portrait of Brittan's great-great-grandfather, Sir Rodney Dangerfield Brittan, hero of the Mboto Uprising. The red-faced old fool looked even more angry than usual, with smoky cordial dribbling across his mutton-chops.

'Ahem,' reminded Slobotham, 'your problem, sir.'

'Rot my problem. Dosing myself with downers doesn't do a gnat's fart for my problem. What I need is some *action*!'

'Indubitably, sir.'

'Hah, yes, right! In-bloody-dubit-bloody-ably!'

Slobotham left the withdrawing room, as silently as he had come, leaving Brittan alone with his frustrations.

Since that spot of bother in the Falklands, there had been nothing worth doing for these beloved old islands. Peace bored him beyond all reason. Whipped out of the Paras on dodgy medical grounds, he was now cooped up in the family home like a trussed pig in a larder. Sometimes, he thought the quacks had been right: left alone, he might just explode.

He heard the blood thumping in his ears, and knew that was a danger signal.

Calming himself by thinking of potatoes, he strolled through the French windows, out on to the carefully manicured lawns of Brittan Hall, Herts. In the distance, on the croquet pitch, he could see two figures disconsolately knocking balls around, plainly as bored as he. At the sidelines, in a deckchair, a smaller man sat, his nose pressed into a large book.

This was not to be tolerated.

He surveyed his life. At thirty-six, he was at his physical and mental peak. He had a good private income, no close family ties, abilities above the average, and a heart that yearned for adventure, excitement, *action*.

Ideally, he would still be in the service of his country. Only the army didn't want him any more, the DPR didn't want him full stop. It seemed that lesser mortals found it hard to work alongside a Victoria Cross Man. The envious little oiks and spiteful desk jockeys had kept him out of his chosen profession.

He had his honour, but nothing else.

Apart from his VC. And his estates. And his friends.

'Jock,' he hollered, 'Basmo! Swell!'

The croquet players looked up, and saw him coming.

The tall Scot, bare knees between kilt and tartan socks thick with the black hairs that covered his entire body, bellowed with bagpipe lungs. 'Och, Dick-lad, 'tis gurrand tae sae yae,' the giant cried, his arms outstretched, suggesting a reach wider than the average man is tall, 'gurrand, gurrand!'

Brittan embraced his comrade, Jock McLochness, late of the 5th Highland Fusiliers. Playfully, they hugged with rib-cracking force, laughing in each other's faces. Brittan felt his friend's arms constricting, and saw the muscles cording in Jock's neck, shifting the swatches of hair that extended from his beard down into the hollows of his throat. He thrust out his craggy chin, and squeezed back, hearing the Scot's ribs grinding together.

'I say,' drawled the other croquet player, languidly leaning on his mallet, 'what are you two gorillas playin' at, what? Look like a couple of tarts dancin' the tango.'

Brittan broke the bearhug, and turned to his old schoolfriend, Basil Mapledurham (pronounced 'Mumm'). Basil adjusted the monocle in his right eye, and passed a hand over his patent-leather hair, his receding chin wobbling as he laughed.

'I could break you in two, Basmo!'

'Oh yes, but then who'd jolly well tell you left from right in the mornin'?'

Brittan laughed. 'Silly arse,' he said.

Basil took an elegant bow.

The reader took his prominent nose out of his book, and whined, 'Can't you apes keep quiet. It's hard to concentrate on higher mathematics with all this gibbering.'

Jock took hold of the reader's head, detaching the bottle-bottom glasses from it, and twisted the few remaining strands of hair on the egg-shaped dome.

'Knack, knack,' he said, 'anyone at hame?'

Sewell Head – Triple First in Romance Languages, Philosophy of Medicine and Particle Physics – writhed in the burly Scot's grasp, book dropping to the grass like a broken-backed bird.

'Leave old Swellhead alone,' Brittan said. 'He can't help being a brainbox freako.'

Jock dropped the genius, and Swellhead scrabbled for his glasses.

'Primate,' he sneered.

Brittan looked around at his friends, the three people closest to him in the world. Brawl and bicker they might, but these were men to take into the jungle. And each had a hidden side, a capability beyond the normal. Not a Talent in the sense that he was Talented, but certainly a lower case talent. Jock McLochness, the caber-tossing man mountain with arms as thick as a man's waist, was also – his deepest, darkest secret – Maude-Lynne Drevelle, pseudonymous author of over a hundred romantic novels. Basil Mapledurham, who played so well the part of the gadabout without a neuron to his brain, was a talented amateur actor, renowned for his ability to assume any role, any disguise, any face with total conviction, often improvising make-up and costuming on the spot. And Sewell Head, multi-disciplinary genius, was, should he have cared to compete, an Olympic-level boxer whose myopia belied his devastating left hook and ferocious attack.

With friends like these, Brittan couldn't understand why everything bored him so.

'I say,' said Basil, 'why don't we take a spin into Harpenford in the old motor, and have some jollies? We could rag the bally constabulary, all come home with police helmets and truncheons. We could scrump groceries from Old Mr Shapoor's emporium, just for a lark.'

It sounded dull to Brittan. Trivial mischief. The local coppers and officious tradespeople like Shapoor might be a thorn in the backside of every true Briton, but they were dimwit opponents, not worth the effort. A man who has faced Argie machine guns, felt bullets bouncing off his chest, can hardly be bothered with a bill-waving greengrocer or a parking-summons-issuing bobby.

'Purrhaps wae should gae tae London, oond vuzzit thae cullub, hae a wee dram or thurrety-eight, oond chase showgurrels araind thae West Aind.'

Brittan and his friends were all members of the Troy, London's oldest, most prestigious and least restrictive club for young gentlemen. They had spent many happy nights in the private rooms upstairs, feeding champagne and truffles to a succession of cockney chorus girls with funny names like Tracy, Sharon or Tina, then rogering the bints silly and sending them home in a minicab to somewhere horrible like Barnet. Now even that didn't appeal.

Tracys and Sharons and Tinas were all very well in their place, but lately Brittan – still single at an age when all his contemporaries at school, apart from this group of reprobates, were on their fifth or sixth brat and thinking of trading in the wife for a newer model – had started to wonder about women. Maybe he was due to become an old uncle, invited to his nieces' and nephews' homes for shooting or at Christmas, but never to know the comforts of a real family, the feel of a babe on his knee, the nightly kiss-and-cocoa of a wife . . .

Brittan sadly shook his head.

'Don't despair, Dick,' said Swellhead, 'we could always drop in on the Royal Society. There's a potentially fascinating lecture on tonight, about the parallel functions of Inuit Shamen and television newsreaders. Prof

Persimmons is bound to leave himself wide open to a thoroughgoing refutation in the subsequent debate.'

Jock picked Swellhead up, and dropped him again.

'Ouch,' Swellhead said, 'no need for that.'

'Och, yae melonbrained marauder, canna yae see that oor Dick-lad needs muir than a lecture on I-Knew-It Semen tae perk oop his spurrits?'

Brittan turned away, and looked across at Brittan Hall, its sixteenth-century towers nestled among ancient oaks and set in rolling, green English countryside. Slobotham, perfectly dressed down to his spats, was walking briskly across the lawns, a silver salver held up in front of him, catching the sunlight.

'A tenner says I can bean the butler with a croquet ball, haggis-breath,' said Basil, holding up a crisp note.

'Yurr on,' Jock growled, counting out ten pounds in small change from his sporran. The money was passed to Swellhead.

Basil dropped a wooden ball on the ground in front of him, and took careful aim with his mallet, holding it like a golf club.

Slobotham was ambling up the stairs by the rockery, weaving through the puzzle gardens, towards the ornamental bridge.

'Fore,' Basil shouted, thumping the ball a hefty whack, gouging a double-size divot out of the lawn.

The ball arced into the air, and lifted high over the lawn.

'She's lookin' damn fine,' Basil said.

Slobotham turned right at the summerhouse, stepping on to the boule court.

The ball bopped the butler squarely between the eyes, and bounced.

'There,' Basil snorted, 'right on the old noggin.'

'Och, yae jummy sassenach, a lucky toss,' grumbled Jock as Swellhead gave Basil the money.

'Bring the ball back, would you Slobbo,' shouted Basil.

Slobotham, who had wavered but not dropped the salver and its precious cargo, bowed, and picked up the ball. A red bump was growing on his high forehead.

'Haw haw haw,' Basil laughed. 'Bit of jolly, what?'

'Indubitably, Master Mapledurham,' Slobotham said.

The butler's salver bore a folded-over newspaper. *The Times*, of course. The *Telegraph* was for social climbers.

'It has gone in, sir,' Slobotham told Brittan.

He felt a surge of blood from his heart, and his chest expanded a little, stretching his vest.

'What's this?' Basil asked.

'I've placed an advertisement in the personals.'

'What? Lonely bachelor goat with lots of surplus cash and a jag needs popsy to pork, that sort of thing?'

'No.'

Brittan sorted through the paper, skipping the boring news pages – full of miners on strike, paranorms on the rampage and johnny foreigners scrapping with each other – and found the small ads. His was in a black-edged box, taking up a three-inch square of the journal of national record.

EX-SERVICEMAN SEEKS CURE FOR BOREDOM

> Stout-heart Briton, decorated, finding himself
> at loose end, interested in any legal adven-
> ture. 'Talented', healthy, independent means,
> own transport. Location, remuneration irrel-
> evant. Danger preferred. All replies considered.
> Damsels in distress a speciality. Harpenford
> 555

2

Phyllida Whemple's delicate lips trembled as she re-read
the boxed ad in *The Times*.

Damsels in distress a speciality.

At twenty-three, she supposed she counted as a damsel.
And distress was certainly somewhere in the region of
what she was in.

The telephone rang, jarringly loud, near her. Her heart
palpitated, and, with dread, she put the paper down and
reached out for the phone.

She knew what she would hear.

Trying to ignore the sudden temperature drop in her
backbone, she picked up the receiver, and recited Daddy's
town number.

'Hello,' she said, 'hello?'

The breathing was distant, as if beamed from a far-off
planet of asthmatic inverts with nothing better to do
than to frighten tender-hearted folks.

'Hello?'

The breathing was interrupted by something that could have been a cough or a spasm of mean-spirited laughter.

'Phyllida Whemple?' The voice, horribly familiar, croaked.

'Yes? Who is this?'

A pause. 'You know who this is. Scraggle, heh heh.'

'I warn you, this line is being tapped. The Metropolitan Police are tracing it even now. They have Talents with them, pinpointing your exact location through mental telepathy.'

The noise was definitely a chortle now.

'Nice girls shouldn't tell nasty lies, Phyllida. Not when they're dealing with Talented individuals.'

'Talented?'

'Very.'

It was what she had been afraid of, that Scraggle, the mystery caller who threatened Daddy, was a paranorm.

'Is your Dear Old Dad there?'

Daddy was in his study, going over business with the Chairman of the Coal Board and the Minister for Energy.

'No.'

'I've told you before about lying, heh heh. Don't make me tell you three times.'

'He can't be disturbed. He's in a meeting.'

'With the Chairman and the Minister, I know.'

Merciful Lord, they were watching the house! No one was safe.

'Just give him a message, pretty Phyllida. Tell him

93

he knows what the consequences will be if he insists on holding the union to the agreement. The consequences for him and, I regret, the consequences for you.'

'You . . .'

'Heh heh, you shouldn't think such language. Not a well-brought-up young lady like you. By the way, don't you think the blue-patterned hose are a little . . . um, provocative?'

The line went dead, but the whispered words hung in the air, sinking like little grapples into Phyllida's heart.

Involuntarily, she looked down. She was wearing blue tights. £79.99 a pair from Le Hose of Paris. Somehow, Scraggle had seen her.

It was what she had always feared, that someone would try to get to Daddy through her.

She replaced the telephone, carefully.

Last night, coming out of the Covent Garden bistro with Geraldine and Annabelle, she had been sure a black car, creeping down the street, was following them towards the taxi rank. And the calls had been going on for months. She had been getting them at home, at work, even at friends' houses. She knew she was being shadowed. Sometimes, she thought tramps in the street were dawdling after her. Sometimes, it was an unmarked grey van.

Two weeks ago, someone had sent her a dozen lillies and a condolence card. Two days ago, it had been a gift-wrapped dead duck, with her face Sellotaped to its stiff bill. The worst of it was that her father knew, and she could see it was preying on his mind, even when he should be concentrating on more important matters.

Like the union negotiations. This miners' strike was such a nuisance. If only that Arthur Scargill and his horde of horrible, unwashed pick-pushers could see how they were making Daddy suffer – why, he had hardly touched the '58 Chateau de Dieudonné with his honey-glazed lobster and Long Island lettuce at breakfast – she was sure they would all go back to their jobs at once in shame.

The inner doors opened, and the Chairman of the Coal Board – a tall American with a stetson hat – strode out, the Minister for Energy jogging alongside to keep up with him, Daddy remaining in the doorway.

'It's decided then, pardners,' the Chairman said. 'No goddamn compromises with the NUM.'

'Oh, absolutely,' purred the Minister.

'Damn straight.'

A valet helped the dignitaries with their topcoats. The Chairman turned to Daddy, and stabbed the air with a lit cigar.

'Remember, Walt, no compromise at all. It's Main Street and High Noon. We've got the NUM by the balls, and we don't let go until they sing soprano. Right?'

Daddy nodded, less sure than the Chairman.

'Of course,' he said. He was looking greyish and hollow-eyed, Phyllida thought, and, for the first time, a little old.

'Walter,' the Minister said, 'if there was anything . . . anything that might hinder you in the negotiations . . . you would tell us, wouldn't you?'

'Of course,' Daddy repeated.

'And there's nothing?'

'No,' he said, face falling, a glance shot at Phyllida, 'nothing at all.'

'Ride 'em, cowboy.' The Chairman made a fist. 'Remember, squeeze 'em like lemons.'

The Chairman and the Minister made their goodbyes, bowed to Phyllida, and left.

The telephone rang. This time, Daddy got to it.

Phyllida could tell from his face what was being said. Daddy was sweating, and looking shiftily at her.

'Until tonight,' she heard the familiar voice conclude.

Daddy hung up. 'Wrong number,' he said.

'Oh, Daddy,' she cried, slipping her arms around him, and hugging hard.

He kissed her on the forehead, and returned to the interior room without saying anything. He shut the doors behind him.

Phyllida felt excluded, left out of her father's world. He was trying to protect her, she knew. But he was taking the weight all upon himself, not confiding in his friends or colleagues, not calling in the police or the temps.

If he asked, she was sure the Prime Minister would lend him Corporal Punishment, her personal paranorm.

She wanted to cry. She was only a slip of a girl, and what could she do against the vast and sinister forces arrayed against Daddy and all he stood for? Delicately chewing the knuckle of her right forefinger – a childhood habit she had hung on to – she looked for inspiration to the framed photographs on the hall table.

There was Daddy with Joe Gormley, shaking hands. Daddy with Edward Heath (rather at the back of the collection). Daddy climbing a Yorkshire slagheap in bright green wellies. Daddy at a charity ball, with Princess Margaret on one arm and Barbara Cartland on the other. Daddy closing down a pit in Kent, waving to an idle and miserable-looking lot of shifty layabouts. Daddy at the negotiation table, tearing up a list of demands. Daddy with the Prime Minister, their fists raised in triumph.

Phyllida let her reflection fall upon the last picture, which was bigger than the others, and measured herself against Mrs T.

The PM had been just a girl once, and she hadn't cried, hadn't given in.

She tightened her tiny fists, and resolved not to crumple. Maybe Daddy was right. The police and the temps were too inefficient, too easy to infiltrate.

Perhaps there was another corner to which she could turn. She looked for the newspaper she had put down.

3

He had been answering the telephone all morning, and nothing promising had come up. Most of the callers were obvious crackpots, frustrated spinsters who thought their neighbours were white slavers with unspeakable intents, or train-spotting duffelcoats who alleged their parents were cannibal space aliens. One Northern-accented man had outlined an entirely admirable but essentially impractical scheme to assassinate Colonel Gadaffy, another soft-spoken lunatic wanted to establish a corps of crack paranorm soldiers to take over the United Kingdom after the coming nuclear holocaust. A Pakistani 'entrepreneur' had complained that Talented skinheads were mentally smashing the windows of his video shop in North London, and Brittan had snarled 'no tradesmen, no coloureds' at him. Several professional ladies had got in touch, offering themselves as damsels capable of giving or receiving various forms of distress. A couple of bored journalists had tried to pump him for his motives in placing the ad. A civil service milquetoast who purported to represent the Department of Paranormal Resources politely reminded him that, unlike heathen America, Great Britain had laws against vigilante activities.

'Hang it all by the bollocks from Nelson's Column,' Brittan swore.

The most promising inquiry before lunchtime came from Sandy Stewart, a Colchester schoolboy who complained that playground bullies habitually beat him up. Things were so desperate that Brittan was almost ready to persuade Jock, Swellhead and Basil – collectively, they

had decided to call themselves the Black Hat Gang –
to get in the XJ98 and head off to Colchestershire or
wherever Sandy lived to use all their powers of persuasion
on Gurt Git Gaiman and Nasty Roz Kaveny to get little
A. Stewart, 2B, back the three years of dinner money
that had been extorted with violence from him.

Then, *she* called.

'Did you put an ad in *The Times?*' she breathed, her
voice bell-like in its clarity, trembling slightly with
obvious distress.

'Yes, 'fraid so,' Brittan replied.

'And did you mean it?'

'Of course. A gentleman always means what he says
in *The Times.*'

'You don't mind danger?'

'Thrive on it, actually.'

'Ex-services? Decorated?'

'Brittan, Lieutenant Richard Lionheart, 1 Para,
Victoria Cross, at your service.'

'Victoria Cross?'

'You can call me Dick.'

'Dick. That sounds so . . . so strong, so firm, so
thrusting.'

He could hear the relief in her voice, the incipient
panic damped.

'Steady on, old girl. Whatever the trouble is, we've
got it covered. Pitbull Brittan is on the job now.'

'Pitbull?'

'Just a nickname.'

'I see.'

'Might I ask what the problem is?'

It came in a rush, but Brittan could sort it out as she went along.

'I'm Phyllida Whemple. I work in publicity, for Porcupine Publications. Well, that's what I'm doing now. It's just something to do until I get . . . um, well, married, or something . . . not that there's anything going on. I was engaged to a nice boy from the Guards, but that's all off now. Best thing, really. He wasn't very interested, I don't think. Anyway, my father is Walter Whemple. He's very high up in ACAS, you know, the industrial arbitration wallahs. He sorts out strikes and things, you know. The unions hate him. And he's been getting these telephone calls, and messages. Threats, Dick. I've been getting them too. There's this horrible man with a wheezy, whiny voice and a nasty laugh. He calls himself Scraggle. I think he's a Talent, you know. Anyway, I just heard him on the phone, really trying to frighten Daddy. He said something about seeing Daddy tonight, and I'm so worried this horrid creature plans to harm my father. He's a dear old thing, and tries to spare my feelings, but I know he's really worried. He's not looking well at all . . .'

'Phyllida,' Brittan interrupted, 'just tell me your town address, and you'll have nothing to fear. The Black Hat Gang will be right there.'

'The Black Hat Gang?'

'That's us. It's just a name. Swellhead thought of it. He's the brainy one.'

'Swellhead?'

'I'll explain later, when we meet.'

'Dick?'

'Yes?'

'Somehow, I think I can trust you. Thank you so much. Thank you so, so much.'

The girl hung up, and Brittan sat back, a warm feeling spreading out from his stomach. Phyllida's voice was still in his ears, her breathless, hurried tones resonating. He tried to imagine a face, a form, to go with the girl, but shut his thoughts off. If he tried too hard, he'd conjure up an angel, and Phyllida would turn out to weigh thirty stone and have a face like a relief map of Afghanistan.

The phone rang again. Dreamily, he picked it up.

'Dick,' said the familiar voice, 'I forgot to give you my address.'

So she had. She told him, and he wrote it down on the white edge of *The Times* crossword page.

When she was gone again, he told Slobotham to bring the rest of the Black Hats to the drawing room, so he could brief them on their mission.

The phone rang again.

'Phyllida, what did you forget now?' he asked.

'Nothing,' rasped an unpleasant voice. 'Nothing at all.'

'You're not Phyllida.'

'No, you're very observant, Lieutenant Brittan, very cunning, a very potent adversary.'

'Who are you?'

'I have many names. Some call me Scraggle.'

'Scraggle?'

'That's right. I understand you've just had telephonic intercourse with a Ms Phyllida Whemple?'

'How could you know that?'

Jock and Swellhead were in the room now. Brittan motioned to them to keep quiet.

'I have my Talents, Lieutenant. As you'll find if you persist unwisely in interfering in my affairs.'

'What do you mean by that, you swine?'

'Swine, eh? Testy this afternoon, aren't we?'

Basil was in the room too, alert, attentive.

'Lieutenant Brittan, I will advise you only once. Do not meddle with my business, do not associate with the Whemples, *père et fille*, and do not take an interest in industrial relations. Go help out poor little Sandy in Colchester. That's in Essex, by the way. Or maybe you should take a shy at Colonel Gadaffy. He's a personal friend, but he can take care of himself. At any rate, and by any means, cease and desist. The consequences, otherwise, could be extremely uncomfortable.'

The line went dead.

'Burn him up in blasted blazes,' blustered Brittan, his face red and bloated, 'I like his nerve. I like his ruddy nerve!'

4

Phyllida had taken the morning off work, and decided to do likewise with the afternoon. It wasn't like it was a *job* or anything. Porcupine could get along quite well enough without her for the day. She just went into the office for her pocket money. Anyway, she was too worried to be concerned with authors or books or horrid things like that. She hadn't read a book that wasn't by Jeffrey Archer since school, and didn't intend to start now.

While her father worked in his study, she fussed around

in the hall and the living room, occasionally looking in on Daddy to make sure he was all right.

She hoped this Dick Brittan would be the answer.

He had sounded so strong, so good-humoured, so confident. He had told her not to worry, and the situation didn't seem too bad now. Dick would see off Scraggle.

Every time a car passed in the street, she hoped it would be Dick and the Black Hat Gang, turning up to take over and make everything all right.

Peering through the net curtains and craning her head, she could see to the end of the mews, and watch the traffic passing. A grey van cruised by, too slowly. Then, a few minutes later, it passed back the other way.

Phyllida felt a clutch of terror. They were out there.

The doorbell rang, and her spirits rose. It was Dick, come to save them all.

Giddy, she opened the door, almost singing with relief . . .

And was confronted with a disgusting old woman, rattling a tin and shoving ratty heather at her. She was dressed in little better than rags, and had deep seams of dirt in her face. Her evil eyes glittered in a mask of filth, curtains of stringy brown hair framing her coarse features.

"Eather fur the norphans, missy?"

Phyllida backed away, trembling.

"Eather?"

She tried to slam the door, but the woman was on the welcome mat, shaking her heather.

She tried to tell her to go away, but words wouldn't come out of her mouth.

103

The crone looked around.

'Lurveley place,' she said, grinning to show off her yellow National Health teeth, 'lurveley.'

'Go away,' Phyllida said, quietly, trying to stand firm.

'Wot's 'at? I'm deaf, luvvy. Deef as a bat.'

The old woman stretched out a crooked finger, towards Phyllida's cheek. Phyllida was afraid the hag would *touch* her, pollute her . . .

The intruder was laughing now, dropping all pretence of deference. Phyllida knew this was one of Scraggle's agents.

'Lurveley,' she gargled.

A huge hand fell on the woman's shoulder.

'Wot?'

She was lifted out of the way, and put into the street, a square boot on her backside. She landed on the pavement, with a sharp crack, and ran off, clutching a bloody nose.

Healthy laughter followed her to the end of the mews.

A huge man came into the hall, and strong arms went around Phyllida. She had been feeling woozy in the head and trembly in the knees.

'Dick?'

The man nodded, radiating warmth and comfort.

'Phyllida?'

She smiled, and kept the embrace a moment longer than form demanded. Dick Brittan was a rough-faced, good-featured man, with a once-broken nose and laughing blue eyes with steely grey flecks in them. He wasn't exactly a *Face* model, but he was undeniably attractive in an earthy, British beef sort of way. His skin had a red-apple ripeness to it, tight and fleshy. Phyllida knew this was the kind of man she would have to be careful around.

'Don't worry,' he said. 'We're here.'

'We' must be the Black Hat Gang. There were three of them besides Dick, and none wore a black hat. One was a kilted bear of a man, bigger even than the fairly big Dick; the others, a reedy fop with no chin and an eyeglass and a funny little gnome with a huge and mainly hairless dome of a head and almost opaque glasses.

'Jock McLochness, Basil Mumm, Swellhead,' Dick said, introducing them.

Doors opened, and Daddy emerged from his study, horn-rims up on his forehead. 'What is this?'

He looked bewildered and baffled.

'Daddy,' she explained, 'I've called these people to help us.'

'Help? We don't need help.' Daddy looked disapprovingly at her.

'I don't mean any disrespect, but I think you do need help, sir,' said Dick, taking over. 'I know about Scraggle.'

'Scraggle?' Daddy's face lost all its colour, and he slumped into a chair.

'I'm Lieutenant Brittan, sir.'

'Pitbull,' said Jock.

'We understand you're expecting an unwelcome visitation tonight?'

Daddy slid his face into his cupped hands. His shoulders shook.

'It's true,' he sobbed. 'I didn't know who to call. If I'd told the Minister, I'd lose my position.'

Phyllida put an arm around Daddy, and consoled him.

'Oh, Daddy, she said. Don't be a silly. You're Mrs T's favourite. She was ever so grateful when you made the railwaymen cave in and accept those massive cuts.'

Swellhead was poking around the hall, looking at little objects. He picked up a shred of tatty heather, and tutted over it.

'Very interesting,' he said, producing a little cellophane packet and prodding the heather into it. 'I'll have to examine this in minute detail later.'

Dick was looking around too, checking windows and locks.

'It seems secure, defensible. I think we can surprise our visitors, Mr Whemple. They aren't expecting the Black Hat Gang.'

Daddy looked up, relief dawning in his face.

'Oh yes, we'll be ready for them. Jock, get the ordnance from the Range Rover. We can set up a few surprises in the hall.'

Dick seemed to expand as he took in a breath, filling out his marvellously cut £1,299.99 Bradstock & Whately of Savile Row suit. She had felt hard, solid muscle under his £149.99 Triple Q of Kensington hand-made shirt when they embraced. He seemed almost like a bronze statue, standing in her hallway. With him there, nothing could frighten her. Nothing would ever change for the worse.

'Phyllida,' he said, 'is there anyone you can stay with?'

'What?'

'There's no sense you being here, getting into danger. We can't risk that. Besides, things might get pretty dicey, pretty hairy. No sense in you being exposed to blood and guts and ruptured spleens and stuff like that. We have to spare your feminine sensibilities.'

'Oh yes,' she said, 'you're so thoughtful. I can call up Annabelle Krantzen, and stay with her in Bishop's Walk.'

'Fine. Weight off my mind. Now, Mr Whemple, let's start thinking tactics . . .'

Jock came into the hall, a couple of large iron mantraps slung on his back.

'Surrprise, surrprise,' he said, 'these'll snupp thae swaine in twain.'

'Rather,' said Basil. 'Ripping.'

Dick laughed, and clapped his friends on their shoulders. One of Jock's traps was sprung, and clanged in the air, leaping off his back.

'Dashed close thing, what,' Basil said.

'Nae harrum done, Dick-lad, nae harrum done.'

Dick took the trap, and with all the apparent effort of someone opening a ring-pull can, eased the pressure-spring trap wide open, and locked it in place, setting it down on the welcome mat.

'Let's see any gyppo get their heather through that,' he said.

5

With Phyllida safely installed in her chum's flat and out of the way, Brittan felt more secure. Whatever happened, the girl – an entrancingly slim brunette, more angelic than anything he could have imagined – wasn't going to get hurt. He was free to get rough with anyone who caused trouble.

They tried playing 'Twenty Questions' to pass the time, but Swellhead always got it within three questions, and Jock or Basil always hit him when he did.

The telephone rang once, and Brittan had tensed, waiting for the threat, but it was only the Minister for Energy, with some last minute pit closure demands to be worked into the agreement with the NUM.

Whemple was fidgety, expectant. Brittan felt sorry for him, and tried to keep him distracted by explaining how he had won the Victoria Cross.

'I could see the Argies levelling their guns at the column of civilian refugees, and there was only one thing to do. With all my men at my back, I ordered the charge. I felt bullets spanging off my chest as I went up that hill in bounds. There were thirty-one of us when we started off, and only I made it to the top.'

The others had heard this story too many times, and were snoozing, doing crosswords or reading.

'The gun nest was commanded by an officer they called the Green Gaucho, a paranorm who could spit venom. I went over the side, and laid about me, scattering Argies here and there. The Green Gaucho hissed, and I thumped my way towards him, squelching skulls . . .'

'Quiet,' said Swellhead, 'I heard something.'

Brittan shut up, and listened.

There were the usual small noises of the night. And the click of Jock priming his Thompson sub-machine gun.

'Thinkin' too much, brain-bean,' Basil scoffed.

'No, he's right,' Brittan said.

There was a soft hiss, like a slow puncture.

'Look,' Swellhead said, pointing at the lower edge of the door.

A curl of odourless white smoke was creeping in, and spreading like a pool of heavy liquid.

'Gas?' Jock asked.

'I don't think so.'

Brittan's heart was pumping iron, and his clothes were getting tight. There was a throbbing heat in his groin, and his John Thomas uncurled in his jockey shorts as it always did when he sensed danger. He knew he was about to go into action. The bloodbeat in his ears was a steady pounding now. The shoulderseams of his jacket strained, and bit into his bulging muscle.

The smoke was rising a little, taking shape.

Jock sighted on the man-sized column, and unloosed a brief burst of fire.

The wood behind the smoky form splintered as the bullets punched through.

'It was worruth a try,' Jock said.

The smoke was thick now, most concentrated about four feet off the floor, with trailing tendrils reaching out like the legs of an octopus. Brittan swore he could see eyes in the thing.

'Quick,' he said, 'the extractor fan.'

Whemple, who had been staring in amazement, was slapped out of his daze, and stabbed a button. A refreshing breeze pulled through the room, towards a whirling circle in the wall.

The smoke octopus was tugged towards the fan, and struggled in the air. It was getting more solid by the second.

Brittan grabbed the smoke, and pulled a fistful of it free. It came away, trailing tubers behind it, and whisped in the air.

'Everyone,' he said, 'before it becomes real.'

They all leaped on the smoke thing, and began fanning it into pieces, tearing candy-floss lumps loose and stamping on them. It was thicker than smoke, but could still be dispersed. It left scummy smears where it had been.

Out in the hallway, there was a wrenching clang, and a cry of high-pitched agony. Someone had tripped one of Jock's traps. Hooray.

The smoke thing was just a mess on the carpet. Then, the bullet-holed doors bent inwards as something heavy thudded against them. The lock shot out of the wood, and bodies forced themselves into Whemple's study.

The first one through the door was a wide-shouldered man in dusty overalls, with a miner's helmet on, a face-covering black visor extending underneath his lamp.

Jock got him in the upper torso with a machine-gun burst, and blood spat out of his wounds. His faceplate cracked, and he went down. But there were others, too many to shoot, pouring in. Jock was pushed back by two of them shooting at him with a rugby tackle, and slammed against a bookshelf, going down with leatherbound government reports bouncing on his head, his gun wrenched out of his hands.

Brittan's John Thomas stood straight out like an iron dowsing rod, tenting the front of his trousers. His belt was now cinched too tight, and his jacket had torn under the arms. He burst out of his shoes, his socks splitting like Turkish-made condoms.

One of the helmeted devils swung a gauntleted fist at him, and he caught the hand, crushing it like a sparrow. His assailant yelped, and went down on his knees. Brittan slammed his knee into the man's face, cracking the visor. He picked him up, fingers digging into flesh like vices, and tossed him at two more of the attack crew. They had yapping animals with them, dogs the size of pit ponies. Brittan saw Basil shoot one of these things, and heard it flop against the wall, a sack of shattered bones.

Brittan grabbed a helmeted head, and twisted it around on its neck, wrenching the faceplate around, relishing the grind and snap of vertebrae. Someone raised an automatic, and emptied a clip against his side, bullets flattening against his kidneys, bouncing off his rigid stomach muscles and slamming into another of the attackers, making him shudder and collapse. Brittan grabbed the automatic, and twisted it into a plasticine lump. Then he tugged the gunman's arm off, and tossed it away, leaving the one-armed man writhing on the floor as frothy blood jetted from his wound. He kicked the man, and jabbed a crushing elbow into the throat of another. Basil was taking care of a helmethead who was trying to set up some kind of apparatus, slamming his visored face into the workings of the machine. It exploded with a belch of white smoke, and Brittan guessed that was where the octopus thing had come from.

One of the helmetheads fiddled with a battery pack attched to his lamp, and a beam shot out. Green light, in a concentrated cylinder, painful to look at.

Jock waved at the light, trying to make it go away, and yelled out as the hair on his hand started to smoke. The smell of singeing flesh was heavy in the air.

Brittan ripped the remains of his jacket away, and took a deep breath, bursting all his shirt buttons, reducing the Triple Q to a few tatters of bandage around his chest and biceps, sleeveless cuffs like taut wristlets.

Jock screamed, as the green beam was shone in his face, and his skin began to pucker and boil.

Brittan stepped in the path of the light, and felt prickling pain in the centre of his chest. He looked down, and saw a circle of green between his round and reddening pectorals, focusing a painpoint on his sternum.

He set his teeth in a grimace and stepped forwards, ignoring the intensifying hurt.

The helmethead kept the beam steady, and held his ground.

Every inch was more agony. The light circle got smaller, more painful.

Behind him, Basil was shooting a dog thing in

the head. Swellhead was sparring with a helmethead, punishing his body with scientific blows.

Brittan's fists were swelling, fingers curved tubes like overstuffed sausages. He was just meat and bone, despite his Talent. He could be hurt. Sweat was pouring out of his armpits, trickling down his sides. He yelled his defiance.

The helmethead with the beam weapon was laughing behind his mask. For a moment, Brittan thought it was Scraggle, but then he realised the tone was higher-pitched, more rodentlike.

He was close enough now to reach out and hurt the man.

He laid a hand on the visor and squeezed, crumpling the steel-tempered plastic as if it were crêpe paper, catching quite a bit of nose and skin with it.

The helmethead's laughter turned to screams.

The beam was irritating his arm as he ground the mask shards into the man's face. With his other hand, he wrenched the lamp off the helmet. It didn't go out.

He pushed the man away, and turned his own lamp on him. His overalls began to smoulder, and then burst into flames. He screeched for a while, and the vile stench of overcooked human flesh rose from him. Whemple was there with the fire extinguisher, splurging white foam onto the fiery corpse.

The cries died down, and the night sounds came back.

Between them, the Black Hat Gang had seen off nine helmethead attackers, and two dog mutants. The study was a wreck, crowded with bodies and pieces of body. In the hallway, there was one more of the vermin, neatly snipped in two by the trap.

Brittan bellowed his triumph, the air roaring through his lungs. He was getting red spots in his vision now, and his John Thomas was a full foot of white hot poker, iron-turgid with excess blood. He could have bitten through a steel bar as if it were a stick of rock.

His arms were inflated like dirigibles, blue veins standing out like firehoses, and his neck was swollen until it was almost as large as his head. His face felt as if it were sculpted of fire.

'Well done, lads,' he said.

'It was nothin',' Basil drawled, 'just a spot of much-needed exercise. Not even very sportin' really.'

Whemple, shaken but unhurt, caught sight of Brittan.

'Lieutenant,' he blurted, 'your face . . .'

Brittan knew what he must look like. His face filled with blood became a snarling Japanese dragon mask, bulbous cheeks red, swollen forehead, lips pulled back in a terrifying snarl.

'Oh my lord, Pitbull,' Swellhead said, 'that was fast. Too fast. I'm afraid the process is accelerating.'

'What is it?' Whemple asked.

'Pitbull has a peculiar and unique metabolism, Mr Whemple,' Swellhead explained. 'In moments of need, it gives him strength, resilience and an unparalleled force of will. But, unless he achieves release, he could hurt himself permanently.'

'Permanently?'

Brittan's fly could stand no more, and his John Thomas knifed through the zip-stitching.

Whemple whistled.

Brittan's knob-end was the size of a velvety purple cooking apple, the connecting vein a pulsing, finger-thick tube, strained to capacity.

'Quickly,' Basil said, 'straws. You're in too, Whemple. It's your life he saved.'

'What's this?' the arbitrater mumbled.

Swellhead produced four straws, one shorter than the others, and held them in his fist.

'Choose,' he said to Whemple.

Brittan felt electric discharges of agony. The red spots in his vision were turning white, and the rapid pumping of his heart was up to ramming speed, assaulting his ears. The veins in his temples were near bursting point, and he could barely feel anything below the waist but agony.

Whemple's fingers fluttered over the straws.

'Nae, lads,' said Jock, staggering to his feet. His face was soot-black, and red weals peeled in his skin. His eyebrows were white ash, and his fresh burns glistened as if vaselined. 'I owe Dick-lad mae life, oond 'tis oop tae mae.'

Swellhead dropped the straws.

'Let's gae upstairs, Dick-lad,' said Jock, grimly.

6

Annabelle was trying to keep her mind off Daddy, prattling on about her new bloke, and how disgusting he was. Annabelle specialised in disgusting boyfriends, always choosing someone racially or physically grotesque just to have material for her monologues. Her last but two had been a Talent, fully registered with temps, and his code-name had been Mould Man. He could make things rot just by looking at them. *Uck!* Phyllida Whemple had been at school with Annabelle Krantzen, and the old windbag was her best pal, really, even if she did have a kraut name and a succession of nig-nog wastrel b.f.'s.

Phyllida divided her attention between Annabelle's meandering and the ITN news. Mrs T was making a statement about the miners, and how she didn't intend to give in to strike blackmail tactics. Good for her. Daddy's photograph was flashed up when they mentioned the arbitration talks, and the girls cheered him, raising their chilled white wine to the TV screen. Phyllida was pleased to hear that another 100,000 miners had gone cheerfully back to work. Then they were on to a report about a Colchester schoolboy who had been beaten to death by school bullies. 'If only Sandy had asked for help,' a headmaster said.

Annabelle turned the sound down, and poured herself another fluted glass of Moselle, dropping in a cherry.

'Anyway,' she said, fluffing a hand in her red meringue of hair, 'he's got a funny back, and laughs a lot while we're . . . you know . . . doing *it*. And he drools, repulsively.'

Phyllida shivered. She didn't look forward to meeting this one. Although, actually, Annabelle's repulso beaux usually turned out to be disappointingly ordinary, their faults magnified by her chattering imagination.

The doorbell chimed, the first line of 'Girls Just Wanna Have Fun', and Phyllida, more tense than she thought, jumped a little, spilling wine on a copy of *The Lady* she had been riffling through.

'It's Him,' Annabelle screeched with delight.

'Mr Drool?'

'Yurp, the very same. Don't breathe a word, and don't, on pain of unmarried pregnancy, giggle at his hump. He's very sensitive.'

She was on the entryphone, buzzing the boyfriend into the house.

'Watch his hands,' Annabelle advised, unlocking the flat door.

The light in the hallway went on, and Phyllida heard someone coming up.

'Coo-ee,' coo-eed Annabelle, and Phyllida heard squelchy kissing, as they met on the landing.

'Here,' said Annabelle, ushering her boyfriend in.

Phyllida was taken aback. Mr Drool really was a hunchback, albeit a very well-dressed one, with a malacca cane and an astrakhan-collared £999.99 Trubshaw & Colneyhurst camel-hair coat. He was older than Annabelle's usual tastes, with shocks of white hair above his ears and eyes and standing out of his beaked nose. He smiled, and his head oscillated from side to side.

'This is Scraggle,' Annabelle said.

A sliver of ice slipped down the back of Phyllida's dress,

117

slithering down her spine, weaving in and out of the vertebrae, and melting in the crack of her buttocks.

'Hello, Phyllida,' Scraggle said, wheezing in an awfully familiar manner.

Phyllida opened her mouth to scream, but nothing came.

7

Slobotham arrived within the hour, bearing a complete change of clothes, and Brittan, suitably dwindled and refreshed after a turn in Whemple's shower, was perfectly attired again, a fresh carnation in his dinner jacket, trouser seams perfectly aligned, purple cummerbund in place.

The crisis had passed.

'Thanks, Jock,' he said, patting his friend's shoulder as the doctor patched up his facial burns.

'Think nothing of it,' Jock said between clenched teeth. 'Yae'd hae dane the same furr mae.'

'Of course, my old Stone of Scone.'

The doctor, Whemple's own Harley Street man, was circumspect enough not to mention the state of the study as he worked on Jock.

Basil had a few scratches from one of the dog monsters, but otherwise the Black Hat Gang had come through unscathed.

Swellhead was in with the dead men, looking for clues.

Whemple was serving brandy snifters, fairly bubbling with relief.

The telephone rang, and Whemple picked it up, Brittan listening in on the hallway extension.

'Hello?'

'Whemple?'

'Scraggle?'

'Got it in one, heh heh.'

'You must be smarting, losing all those hired hooligans.'

'Not losing, sacrificing.'

There was a jostling at the other end of the line, and a feminine squeal, 'Daddy?'

'Phyllida,' Whemple and Brittan blurted out, together.

'Ah, Lieutenant Brittan, you are there,' wheezed Scraggle, 'I rather thought you might be.'

'Phyllida!'

'Yes, that's right. The attack on you was just a — how shall I put it — *divertissement*. My real purpose was the abduction of the lissome Ms Whemple, and very delightful she is too. A man in your condition would do well to have a Ms Whemple with you. So soft, so. . . um . . . pliant. And so much more congenial than some hairy haggis, wouldn't you say?'

'You foul-minded fiend, Scraggle!'

'Temper-temper.'

Jock appeared at the doorway, and delicately crossed the room on bow-legs, listening intently.

119

'What have you done to her?' Whemple demanded.

'Why, nothing . . . yet. Heh heh.'

'If you—'

'"Harm one hair on her head"? Lieutenant Brittan, you have an appallingly unimaginative grasp of metaphor, if I may say so. And you severely underestimate my own breadth of capabilities when it comes to harming Ms Whemple. Could you not think of a more apt expression? "If you pull one nail on her foot", "if you burst one eye in her head", "if you eat one vital organ in her innards"; "if you . . ."'

Brittan felt the blood hammering his skull, and his new underwear constricting.

'Getting it up, are we?' Scraggle chortled. 'Careful, don't get so excited. You might burst a blood vessel.'

'What do you want, Scraggle?' Whemple asked.

'It's not what I want, Mr Whemple, it's what the people want. Specifically, the miners. As you know, I represent the interests of the working men of this country, heh heh.'

Brittan felt as if he were about to sick up an undigested side of beef. To think that this piece of excrement in roughly human form claimed to be on the side of the working man, when all his kind ever did was pull down great industries, throwing millions on to the scrap-heap of unemployment, undoing the work of great men who laboured long and hard to run the corporations Scraggle and his filthy Trotskyist like were so incapable of appreciating! It was an obscenity!

'You are familiar with the demands of the National

Union of Mineworkers? No pit closures without consultation, increased safety precautions, shorter hours,
larger wage packets, earlier retirement, a dismantling
of all nuclear power stations, union representation on
the board, each miner to be allowed to poke the wife
of the pit manager every ten shifts, free cocaine and
whelks in the showers, that sort of thing.'

'You scum!'

'Come come, Mr Whemple. You're beginning to
sound like Lieutenant Dickhead here, heh heh.'

A current coursed through Brittan's urethra, and his
John Thomas twitched like a trod-on snake.

'At any rate, you will put up a spirited defence of the
government position - we wouldn't want Mrs T getting
suspicious and removing you, would we? – and then, at
the last minute, you will emotionally cave in and grant
all the concessions that nice Mr Scargill is demanding.
And everyone will be happy, no?'

'And Phyllida?'

'I imagine she'll be happy too. Well, at least *happier*.'

Brittan heard Phyllida's distant squealing and sobbing again.

'No, no, Greasy Eric,' Scraggle said to someone
at his end, 'that's not how you attach those live
wires.'

Brittan's shirt-seams began to pop, his cummerbund
stretched uncomfortably over his granite stomach.

'I must go now. It seems I have to do everything
around here. You just can't get hooligans like you used
to, heh heh. Abyssinia.'

Scraggle hung up. And Brittan swore that the Talent would die by his hand.

Whemple was crying again.

8

Brittan thumped his bowling-ball-like fist down on the polished table, imagining Scraggle's skull pulping under the force of the blow. Then he imagined fishing the fiend's eyeballs out with his thumbs, and shoving them as far up his foul nostrils as they would go, then getting a good grip on his lying tongue and pulling it out like a tape measure before tying it in a noose around his scrawny proletarian neck and pulling it as tight as a cat's arsehole and watching the union agitator's ugly face turn all the colours of the rainbow as the life leaked messily out of his verminous body. Jolted out of his reverie, he realised he had absent-mindedly picked up a Sung Dynasty vase and ground it to dust in his fists.

'Sorry, Whemple,' he said.

'Don't think of it,' the arbitrater said, waving the damage away. 'Ugly bit of crockery anyway.'

'Dash it to blistering blazes, I hate just sitting around here waiting for that monster's next call! I wish there were something we could *do* to save poor Phyllida from his lecherous horde of unwashed slackers!'

'Yes,' agreed Basil, cleaning his monocle on his ascot, 'it is rather distressin' to think of that poor, slim, virginal girl, slowly stripped of her flimsy underthings by buck niggers with gorilla brows and brawny forearms. To think of the horrible indignities that are doubtless this very minute bein' inflicted upon her helpless form, the ice baths and electrodes, the red-hot tongs and whippings, the caged rats pressed to her soft, white belly and encouraged to tuck in . . . I say, Whemple's off again. Never known such a man for blubbin'.'

The arbitrater was banging his head against the table, and bawling, his entire body wracked with heartbreaking sobs.

'Anyway,' Basil continued, 'what about the lighted cigarettes pressed to her quiverin' . . .'

Whemple howled.

'Shut up Basmo,' Brittan growled. 'You're being a silly arse again.'

'Sorry. Just tryin' to be realistic, what.'

''Tis turrible, turrible,' Jock agreed, gingerly squirming in his seat, trying to settle down comfortably on the three cushions he had piled under him, 'and tae think wae bae sae haelpless. If only wae ken wheere thae vullains haid taeken purr wee Phyllida. Thae must hae same kaind ae' haide-oot, whaire thae kin plot oond scheeme thair turrible, turrible deeds.'

Brittan thumped the table again, shaking everyone.

'Jock's right. We should find out where they've gone, and moustache them in their lair.'

'I believe, Pitbull, that the proper expression is "beard them in their lair",' Swellhead put in. 'The word "beard", in this case, meaning "to oppose face to face".'

Impatient, Brittan fetched his friend a gentle thump around the earhole, unloosing him from his chair and sending him sprawling across the floor. Jock and Basil laughed at this comical turn, but Brittan didn't feel any better.

Basil had been right. What Phyllida must be undergoing at this very moment was unthinkable, disgusting, infuriating . . .

In the space of the twenty minutes Brittan had spent in the company of Phyllida Whemple, he had realised that his bachelor days were over. If they both came out of this scrape alive and intact, he intended to marry the arbitrater's daughter, and keep her safe for ever from the designs of those who would wish to do her harm. His manly heart beat louder as he thought of her pale skin, bee-stung lips, lithe limbs, luxurious brown hair and appealing cloche hat.

Swellhead stumbled back to the table, righted his chair, and sat down. Brittan affectionately rubbed his friend's bald bonce, and Swellhead grinned, knowing that he had been an utter prig and that such abuse was all in good, masculine, comradely fun.

'Incinerate it in the lowest pit of the fiery furnace of Hell,' Brittan swore. 'We can't let Scraggle and his rabble win! We can't let down Mrs T and allow the unions to goose-step all over the country! Next thing you know, they'll be letting miners with dirt on their faces eat pie and chips at the Savoy! They'll lower the speed limit and have constables spend all their time bothering Jaguars and Porsches while nasty little Jap, wop and kraut cars crawl by and nab all the parking spots in the West End! They'll move into the Troy Club, the yids and the spades and the wogs and you won't be able to get near the bar or the billiards room for stinky louts in cloth caps with ferrets down their trousers and brown ale in their bellies!'

Together, they shook their heads sadly at the prospect of the end of civilisation.

Swellhead took a small packet out of his pocket and turned it over. It contained some sort of dried leaf.

'This is no time to blow reefer, egghead,' Brittan said, sternly.

Swellhead emptied the packet out.

'Obviously, these leaves are quite a different genus from *cannabis sativa*. As even an uneducated eye should note, these are from some peculiar subspecies of *calluna vulgaris*, commonly known as heather.'

'Typical of bloody old Swellhead, what,' said Basil, 'Poor old Phyllida's bein' mauled by mobsters, and he's sniffin' weeds. Deuced disgrace.'

'Shut up, Basil,' said Brittan, thinking he was only a few laps behind Swellhead mentally, and catching up fast as he got his second wind. 'He's talking about the gyppo.'

'That's right, the heather-seller who bothered Miss Whemple earlier. She's in the study now, with most of her head missing. Good work, Pitbull. It must have been a very tricky bit of thumping to whack her so properly. The maxilla was driven square up into the cranial matter, quite breaching the medulla oblongata. My guess would be that bone shards were distributed into the brain tissue as far as the fissure of Rolando. Anyway, my primary deduction is that quite a few of the other deceased types strewn about the place are her friends and relations. I found the quite distinctive puce and lemon yellow scarfs of the *Mazuke Grobbo* tribe of *tzigane*, noted for their interbreeding of Rottweiler and pit pony, and who are found, as you know, in only three places in Europe. The shunned village of Ostragrob in the Carpathians, the accursed Gronzelle Forest in the Loire, and the unemployment blackspot of County Durham, England.'

'That narrows it down,' Brittan said, slamming a fist into his open palm, 'Jock, you go to Romania, I'll take France and Basmo can go to Durham.'

'I say, I'd much rather I went to France, don't ch'know. Could drop in on that frightfully nice gel Monique Tour-du-Monde in Montmartre. Oh yes, like that, I would.'

Swellhead picked up the heather.

'Before you argue further, I have made some more deductions, with regards to this humble scrap of roadside vegetation. You'll note the yellow edging of the leaves, and the discolouration of the underside. This genus is common throughout the Midlands and the North of England, but I'd hazard a guess that this particular strain of heather-blight could only be found in one spot within these islands . . .'

Swellhead paused dramatically, waiting to be asked.

'And that spot, my friends, is the mining village of Thornley, in County Durham.'

At that moment, just as the Black Hat Gang were congratulating Swellhead for his braininess, Slobotham insinuated himself into the room.

'Sirs, if I might venture to add some information, I was just going through the pockets of those cadavers in

the study and I happened to find that each and every one
of them has in his or her possession a return ticket from
Thornley, County Durham, to London King's Cross.
Standard class.'

'And that, I think, proves my deductions beyond a
doubt,' Swellhead declared.

9

'Where am I,' Phyllida whimpered. 'Where am I?'.

She had come to in a dark place, and found her hands
cuffed behind her, and her legs tied together. She was
on a cot of some sort, strapped down. There was a most
nauseating smell nearby.

'Safe,' a familiar voice told her.

'Annabelle,' she cried, heart squeezing past her ton-
sils, 'so they got you too.'

'Not exactly.'

Phyllida's eyes fluttered, and she realised the room
was dimly lit. She turned around, wriggling in her
straps.

'Annabelle,' she gasped in horror, 'your clothes!'

Her best friend had, when Scraggle invaded the flat,
been wearing a quite fetching burnt orange shot silk
blouse and £750 slacks from Moritz of Swiss Cottage,
with heavy amber jade earrings and calf-hide pumps.
Now, she wore a greasy bandanna, crossed bandoliers of
bullets, a £2.50 Friedrich Engels T-Shirt and camouflage
pants tucked at the bottoms into army surplus size-eight
combat boots. She had ditched the earrings, and her

major accessory was a big ugly machine gun, slung around her shoulder.

'How could you do your make-up like that?'

Annabelle had green and brown tiger-stripes on her cheeks and hands, very sloppily applied, and no lipstick.

'It's awful.'

Annabelle prodded her with the business end of the gun.

'No,' she said, 'it's quite nice, really. Scraggle has pulled me out of my old useless, pointless life and shown me how to be a real woman, how to take charge of my destiny, how to realise my place in the revolutionary plan. You wouldn't believe it, but yesterday I actually washed up four used tea-mugs. Yes, me! I got my hands in soapy water, and managed to get those mugs clean. And I rinsed them! And dried! It was a mystical experience for me, to understand the nobility of labour, to feel yourself a part of the great proletarian mass which will sweep away like a tidal wave the artificial privilege of the pampered and pointless classes to which I used to belong.'

'Annie, you are talking such rot. If you could only hear yourself.'

'Capitalist bitch, pawn of the ruling classes, oppressor of the innocent, despoiler of babies . . .'

Annabelle was enthusiastically waving her gun. Phyllida hoped someone had explained about the safety catch. Her best friend always had been laughably inept with mechanical things.

'Babies,' Annabelle enthused, 'I want to have lots of

them, for the Revolution! I want to make babies with miners, to have them grow inside me, one after another, popping out. I always want to have two babies for each tit, and two or three more inside my womb. I'm an earth mother of the masses, Phyl. Scraggle has shown me the way.'

Phyllida turned her face to the wall, and cried.

10

Brittan's custom-made four-seater Jaguar XJ98 roared like a he-lion as it tore out of London, heading for the North-East. At the wheel, Brittan's mouth was set in a grim straight line. He ignored the blast of wind on his face as his machine, the physical extension of his eighth-of-a-ton of muscle and meat and bone, thrust into the darkness, eating up the throw of his headlights, driving lesser automobiles from its path. His hands were firm on the wheel and the gearshift, and his seatbelt hung unused beside him.

Seatbelts were for middle-class snails who cared whether they lived or died!

Brittan drew up close behind a slowcoach of the highways, an articulated lorry crawling along at 75 m.p.h., lazily clogging the road, and blocking his path to Phyllida.

He could read the legend on the back of the lorry: B.D. SMEDLEY & SONS, FINE PORCELAIN TOI-LETS AND INJECTION-MOULDED PLASTIC SEATS, EST. 1978.

'Scorch and cinder it to the very bowels of Pluto's dominion, toasting crumpets on a trident in the all-consuming brimstone burner of Abaddon and Phlegethon,' he swore.

No privvies would prevent him from saving Phyllida.

'Hold on tight, chums, this might be a touch gamey.'

The XJ98 swung out into the hard shoulder, crushing plastic cones under its grill, and nosed even with the articulated lorry. There were works up ahead, but Brittan knew he could ease back in front of B.D. SMEDLEY and leave the bogseat-bearing bounder in the dust before they hit the holes.

Swellhead had his pocket calculator out, and was measuring wind velocities and rate of acceleration.

'Thirty-eight seconds, Pitbull,' he concluded.

'Tchah,' Brittan spat. 'Hours to spare!'

Brittan looked the driver of the lorry – a porky mooncalf with a bewildered grin – and slammed his foot to the floor, sending more spurts of power into the perfectly-tuned engine of his majestic beast of the road.

As he brought the car around in front, Brittan playfully nudged the front bumper of the lorry, counting coup in this minor victory.

He roared his victory, feeling his powerful buttocks expand under him as the blood inflated his gluteal muscles.

The XJ98 left behind the honking horn of B.D. SMEDLEY's finest, and Brittan roundly condemned all toilets and seats to the abyss.

Jock laughed.

Behind them, the lorry skewed across the motorway a couple of times, and flipped over.

'Can't take the speed,' Brittan said, 'shouldn't be on the road.'

There were explosions as cars piled into the whale-size lorry, and a fine rain of porcelain fell. Burning petrol spilled across the asphalt.

Then, the lorry was lost behind them.

'Thornley, here we come,' Brittan said.

11

Thornley was Hell on Earth.

They had parked the XJ98 a few miles away, concealed in the undergrowth, then sauntered into the village. Basil had brought along his make-up kit and costume box, and now the four Black Hats were perfectly disguised as miners, so unrecognisable that they would have been refused entrance to the Troy Club. They wore cloth caps, mucky boots, and moleskin trousers with belts and elasticated braces, and their faces and hands were liberally dirtied with authentic-looking coaldust and machine grime. Just so long as they kept their mouths shut, they were as scurvy a crew of working class scum as Brittan could ever hope to scrape off his shoes.

As they approached the village, they heard the sounds of riotous revelry, clogs slapping concrete, conflicting brass bands playing 'On Ilkley Moor Bar Tat' and

'Danny Boy', darts thudding into boards, kegs emptying of beer, callused hands slapping wobbly bottoms, rifles being discharged in the air, glass breaking.

They kept close together, as they passed the 'WEL-COME TO THORNLEY' sign, which was daubed with 'NO SOUTHERN BASTARDS' and a skull and crossbones. Beyond, were rows of back-to-back miners' cottages, and lesser streets of squat prefabs with allotments out the back.

Hanging by a noose from the first streetlamp was a burning mannequin, with the Queen's smiling photograph pasted to the face.

Brittan could hardly contain his patriotic wrath, and felt a surging inside his furry britches. He knew there would be some action soon.

The next burning mannequin had Mrs T's face, and had had holes shot through its plastic torso.

Also massacred in effigy were the Archbishop of Canterbury, Corporal Punishment, the Princess of Wales, Rupert Murdoch, Steve Davis, Andrew Lloyd Webber, Loric and Michael Winner.

It was a horrifying spectacle.

Dancing around the lamppost from which the disembowelled Jeffrey Archer dangled, book-pages spilling gut of his violated stomach, was a ring of barefoot ragamuffin children, dust on their cheeks, holes in their dresses. They occasionally took time out of the ring to inhale aeroplane glue from plastic bags.

Brittan's braces were stretching, his fly buttons tugging at their holes.

The others were equally disgusted, and appalled.

Brittan could see the honest shock and disbelief on their disguised faces as they wandered closer to the heart of darkness that was Thornley, County Durham.

In his mind, Brittan heard again the retching laugh of Scraggle.

'Look,' Swellhead said, 'look . . .'

In the village square, surrounded by the brass bands, was a medieval five-person stocks, and heads were poking through the holes. Burly young men with beer bellies and fat cackling hags in floral print dresses were hurling rotten fruit at the unfortunates.

'Scabs,' they chanted as they threw the splattering projectiles. 'Bosses' lackeys, scabs . . .'

Brittan felt his fury expanding his chest. He sincerely admired the courage of those who stood up to the tyranny of the NUM, and stayed at work while the slackers, the scroungers and the slime skived off for their measly strike. These were the true Britons, the honest miners who knew their place, who didn't want to stuff their pay packets beyond all reason, who selflessly toiled in the dark to keep society on the rails. And Scraggle and his scum were making monkeys of them, subjecting them to awful humiliations.

He saluted the martyrs. But, in order to blend in with the crowd, the Black Hats picked up some fruit and took a couple of good shots. It set the disguise off perfectly.

The focus of all activity was a huge building in the square, with well-lit windows. The odour of gassy beer poured out of it in a poisonous cloud. Above the double-doors was a sign, THORNLEY WORKING MEN'S club. A neon noticeboard flashed SPECIAL VARIETY NITE, ALL WELCOME (EXCEPT SCABS).

Among the tin-helmeted miners, Brittan noticed others: swarthy Cubans in guerilla gear with sub-machine guns and berets, bearded Libyans in burnouses with scantily-dressed dancers on their arms, dour Russian plotters in ill-fitting suits with hammer-and-sickle tie-pins, garlic-smelling French terrorists in stripey jerseys and waxed moustaches, painted African savages with necklaces of knucklebones and seven-foot spears.

'This is obviously a nest of villains,' he concluded.

A little old man, his tatty jacket heavy with medal ribbons, advanced on his zimmer frame, and waved a gnarled fist at a smiling gold-toothed Cuban, shouting 'God bless the Queen!'

Bullets slammed into his bent body, and he was propelled half-way across the street, where he collapsed, coughing bloody foam. A team of clog dancers, their ribboned sticks waving, gathered around him, and started kicking viciously while singing 'When the Boat Comes In'. The crowd egged them on, crying 'give him another one, just like the other one . . .'

'We've got to get inside that club,' Brittan said. The others nodded in agreement.

Whistling Dvorak's Hovis Bread jingle, they strolled, hands deep in pockets, across the square, past the stocks, past the clog-killing mob, towards the doors of the club.

On the steps, they were pushed back when the doors were flung open and a thirteen-year-old girl, her clothes torn and her face bruised, was thrown out.

Brittan helped her up. The poor thing was crying.

A tall, wide Yorkshireman stood at the top of the stairs, laughing evilly. He had scratches on his face, and was slowly hitching his braces on to his shoulders. A badge pinned to his dirty shirt identified him as a shop steward.

'Please,' the girl whined, 'I did what you said, now please let my Daddy go back to work so he can feed me Mam and me twelve brothers and sisters, please, please!'

'Scab,' the shop steward spat.

Cowering in shame, the poor girl crept off into the night, whippets yapping at her heels.

'You strikers?' the steward asked.

'Oh aye,' said Basil, his Geordie accent exactly right. 'Way-hay.'

'Welcome to t'club,' said the shop steward, 'I'm Greasy Eric Braithwaite.'

He dug into his pockets and pulled out a fistful of ten-pound notes.

'Fresh from Tripoli' said Greasy Eric, 'with Colonel Gadaffy's blessings, brother. Feel free to take some.'

Brittan's fists were expanding, but Basil took the money, and managed to laugh like a genuine militant.

'Oh aye,' said Basil. 'Way-hay.'

'You'd best be in soon, brothers. T'comedian's nearly finished. It's Gladys and her balloon-tying next, and then t'big draw for t'raffle. Don't want to miss that. You got your raffle tickets?'

'Oh, er, aye,' Basil said. 'Way-hay.'

Greasy Eric pumped with his arm, and licked his lips.

'Don't want to miss t'raffle,' he said. 'There hasn't been so much interest in t'raffle since t'flying pickets nabbed that policewoman.'

They were admitted into the club, and found themselves in a thronging bar, with sawdust on the floor and overflowing spittoons.

Jock whispered to him. 'If wae're tae bae convincing in these dessguises, wae'd baist drink gallons ae yon beerr.'

Brittan nodded, and they squeezed up to the bar. A woman with three enormous breasts barely held back by an abused halter contraption and a foot-tall pile of mauve hair, was pulling quarts, and handing them over. There were buckets of pork scratchings on the drenched bar, and miners were stuffing handfuls into their mouths.

The Black Hat Gang got their drinks and sat by the stage.

A bowed old woman was making obscene shapes with balloons, while a young man sat at an organ playing 'Down at the Old Bull and Bush'.

The stench of beer and sweat and coal was overwhelming.

Brittan pulled the table closer, to cover the maypole straining the lap of his trousers.

'Not long now, Pitbull,' Swellhead said.

Gladys finished, burst her balloons, and left the stage.

Things quieted down a little, and the organist played an up-tempo introduction. A spotlight played on the curtains, and a man dressed in a gold and silver striped tuxedo, with a whirling red spangled bow-tie, stepped out. He was a hunchback, with a wig of slicked-back hair and circles of rouge on his cheeks.

The miners went wild, cheering and clapping. A Cuban at the next table emptied his machine-gun into the ceiling, causing a cloud of plaster dust to settle over the whole front row.

A stray bullet ricocheted off a light fitting and stung against Brittan's arm. He brushed it away.

He was intent on the compere.

He had never seen the man, but he knew who it was.

'Evenin' all,' said Scraggle, making flourishes with his hands, 'all evenin'.'

The crowd cheered again, and some of the tribesmen started banging bongos at the back.

'Settle down now, heh heh,' Scraggle said, 'don't get your braces in a twist. As we all know, it's raffle time. These raffles support the strike fund, and keep your union going. Last week, Brother Arkroyd won enough heroin to keep him zonkered for a year, providing he lasts that long. And before that, we all remember how Foggo Clegwittering won a Walther PPK with a full clip, and the chance to squeeze off eighteen shots at the scab of his choice. Well, this week's star prize is better than all those. Let's take a look shall we?'

The curtains parted, and the spotlights danced, focusing on a small figure strapped to a hospital cot.

'Lucky winner, this week's prize is yours to enjoy in any way you see fit,' Scraggle announced.

The miners were stamping their booted feet in unison

now, their bitter drool pooling around them on the floor and the tables.

Brittan's braces snapped as his shoulders heaved.

'Phyllida,' he breathed.

He could see her pale, frightened face in the shine of the lights, raised bravely, tear-tracks down her cheeks, hair out of place.

His belt burst, and his trousers split at the seams.

'Phyllida,' he bellowed, 'Phyllida!'

12

The follow-spot swung over the audience, and shone in Brittan's face. He had upset the table, and was exploding completely out of his disguise. The cloth cap shot off his head, his clothes fell away in pieces from his rippling muscles.

'Good evening, Lieutenant Dickhead,' Scraggle said, 'we were expecting you sooner.'

The crowd didn't seem so drunk any more. Brittan heard the rasp of drawn swords, the clicking of automatic weapon safety catches, the thump of clips being jammed into machine guns, and the revving of chainsaws.

Phyllida was squirming feebly. A girl in terrorist drag stood by her bed, gun pointed at her head.

Brittan's neck swelled, bursting his collar, the last of his disguise.

'Eee,' said someone common, 'look at the stiffy on that.'

He saw the red spots.

The miners had cleared a circle around the Black Hats. Jock broke his glass against the stage, and held up the jagged remains as a weapon. Swellhead had his fists up. Basil was holding a miner's pick.

'Really, I'm disappointed in you. That clue about the heather was so *obvious*. I'd have suspected a trap. But then again, I'm devious. Heh heh.'

Three hefties with whizzing chainsaws were surrounding the Black Hats, jabbing at the air.

'You've all heard about Dick Brittan, brothers, hero of Sheepdip Heights,' Scraggle announced. 'He killed thirty-two Argies with his bare hands, remember? *The Sun* had that picture of him with the "grateful shepherdess" who relieved him of the enormous all-over boner that was going to blow him up.'

Brittan saw white flares over the red spots, and heard the popping of his expanded veins as they threaded along his muscles, pumping adrenalin throughout his massive body.

'Actually, heh heh, they had to matte the girl into the picture . . .'

Brittan began to roar.

'. . . because after the Sheepdip Heights Incident, our True Blue British hero here really had to seek solace, not with a grateful shepherdess, but with a grateful *sheep*!'

The crowd began to laugh and make baaa-ing noises.

'Shut up,' Brittan shouted, a mighty gust of steamy anger escaping from his lungs. 'Shut up, you crook-back fiend!'

'Time for a jolly old work-out, I think,' said Basil, embedding his pick in the head of the nearest Libyan, neatly pinning his sunglasses to the bridge of his nose, and squelching into a scheming, foreign brain.

With his rock-hard forearm, Brittan parried the first of the chainsaws. It ground uselessly against his steel-tough skin, teeth spinning off like shrapnel, oily smoke belching out of the engine.

The miners came forward, and the fight was on.

Brittan took away a couple of the chainsaws, and whirled around, parting tattooed limbs from shoulders, fetching fat heads off necks, scooping yellow guts out of beerbellies.

The organist segued from 'Tie a Yellow Ribbon Round the Old Oak Tree' to 'You Don't Get Me, I'm Part of the Union'.

Swellhead boxed with a wiry whippet of a man, repeatedly breaking his nose.

Jock had two tables in his hands, and was squashing strikers between them. Blood ran around his feet.

Brittan's disguise had completely fallen off, and he stood, naked and erect, covered from head to foot in gore, downing slackers by the second, heel-crushing their chests with a single stamp.

A Cuban threaded an ammo belt into a hand-held heavy machine gun, and began to fire a burst at the Black Hats.

Brittan stepped in front of his comrades, and felt the familiar mosquito pinpricks of bullets bouncing off his iron muscles, spreading throughout the room.

It was just like Sheepdip Heights all over again, men falling all around him as bullets found other targets.

The Cuban found the gun too heavy, and angled

down, pointing his weapon at Brittan's crotch. Bullets flattened against his John Thomas and tickled his balls.

Brittan screamed at the pain, and threw his chainsaws like darts, one after the other.

Still buzzing, they cut through the air, and fell on the Cuban, carving him into five or six pieces, tossing his intestines high around him.

The triple-breasted barmaid vaulted the bar, and levelled a flamethrower, coughing a jet of fire.

His chest hair burned, but he deflected the blast. Sucking air into his lungs, he held his breath for a beat, then exhaled at speed.

The stream of fire broke against his breath and flowed backwards towards the barmaid. Her tank of fluid exploded, and she was cooked through instantly, tumbling down a hissing, smoking ruin with an ugly perm.

A sharp feedback whistle cut through the room, and everyone turned to the stage.

'Lieutenant Dickhead,' Scraggle wheezed into his microphone, 'before you do anything brave like fighting to the death, might I point out that Ms Whemple here isn't quite as bulletproof as some Talents we could mention. Heh heh.'

The guerilla girl still had her gun up, and it was slipped into Phyllida's heart-shaped mouth.

Brittan lowered his tree-branch arms, and stood down. He nodded to his friends, and they threw down their weapons.

Greasy Eric Braithwaite sniggered.

'That's better,' Scraggle said.

The organist was playing the 'Floral Dance', fiendishly fast.

'Go on,' Brittan shouted, 'you're very good at threatening helpless white women, aren't you? Shoot me in the head, why don't you? See what good that'll do you!'

Scraggle produced a Luger and aimed it point blank at Brittan's nose.

'I do believe I'll try,' he said, smiling.

The gun went off, and Brittan felt the bullet glance off the side of his nose, whizz along his cheek and spray off to the left somewhere.

'Gulp,' said Basil, a red hole appearing where his monocle had been, three pounds of grey gruel bursting out of the back of his skull, splattering against the framed picture on the wall behind him. It showed Gracie Fields simultaneously taking on George Formby and Ramsey MacDonald.

A manly surge of hatred hammered the insides of Brittan's ribs.

'You'll pay for that! Basmo was my fag at Millfield, you know!'

'I didn't bounce a bullet his way,' Scraggle said innocently, 'you did.'

Brittan swallowed a sob. 'Poor, brainless Basmo, never hurt anyone, always wrote to his mother once a week, let the younger boys have the pick of his stamp collection, fine useful winger, good off-spin bowler, and the best damned Poor Little Buttercup I've ever seen in my life.'

'Well,' said Scraggle, 'I think we can agree on "brainless". Someone take a dishcloth to that picture. It's historic.'

Basil Mapledurham grinned up from the floor, shattered eyeglass over the empty red socket.

Thinking about it, Brittan wondered whether the monocle and purple ascot quite went with the miner disguise.

'I wonder how many of your comrades at Sheepdip Heights went for a burton the same way, cut down by lead bouncing off you? You were the only one to make it to the top of the hill, weren't you?'

The floorboards were buckling under Brittan's huge feet, feeling the pressure of his curling toes.

'Still, I suppose those sixteen-year-old conscripts deserved what was coming to them, heh heh. It must have been easy for you to mistake that white flag they were waving for a death-ray aimed at the church school down below.'

Brittan snorted plumes of steam from his engorged nostrils. His brass balls beat like bull-hearts, pumping into his pig-iron rod.

'Enough of this conversation, heh heh,' Scraggle said, 'let's take them to the Pit.'

13

Brittan strained mightily at the manacles that pinned him to the wall of the coalface.

'Don't even bother, Lieutenant Dickhead,' Scraggle said, 'those were custom-made for you by our comrades in the British Steelworkers' Union. The tensile strength is incredible. Even more incredible than yours, heh heh.

You know, what with all that blood pumping around your body turning you into an upholstered Adonis, I still think that the hardest, heaviest muscle you have is the one between your ears.'

Brittan was getting near the end of it. His knob-end was pulsing and empurpled, sweating little drops of blood.

'A fascinating process. I'm surprised the DPR didn't scoop you in and dissect you to find out how you work. I'm sure there are industrial applications for your bizarro metabolism. Something for the lonely housewife.'

'Curse you, may you writhe in eternal torment with maggots squirming in and out of the pus-filled open sores on your lice-infested, leprous carcass as you scream for ever in the Domdaniel pits of Erebus and Acheron!'

'Tut tut tut, that temper really will be the death of you.'

Brittan rattled his chains. They were embedded into the rough coalface by three-foot-long pins.

'I believe that if you had time, you could probably pull those out.'

Scraggle was smoking a cigar in a long holder. With him was Greasy Eric Braithwaite, who could hardly contain his foul mirth, and the mad-eyed guerilla girl who turned out to be Annabelle Krantzen, Phyllida's treacherous friend. She should have known better than to trust a kraut, of course.

'Sadly, time is a commodity you don't have in abundance.'

The union leader consulted a gold pocketwatch.

Jock was unconscious in the corner, his head a mass

144

of blood-filled lumps. Swellhead was by him, mummified with a coil of thick rope. And Phyllida was shackled only a few feet away, just out of his reach, slumped decorously in a dead faint.

'First, of course, you'll have to tell me Walter Whemple's private telephone number at the Arbitration and Conciliation Service. That way I can tell him to cave in immediately.'

'You'll never get it from me,' Brittan said, jaws clamped around his tongue.

'Not even if I play a few little games with your friends?'

Scraggle stubbed out his cigar on Swellhead's bald dome. The genius yelped.

'Don't tell him, Pitbull,' Swellhead screeched, 'don't tell.'

Scraggle took out his cigar clipper, and clipped off the tip of Swellhead's nose.

'Don't tell. Don't mind me, just don't tell him anything.'

Scraggle bit off one of Swellhead's ears, and spat it out, daintily wiping his mouth with a lace doily.

'Just keep quiet. I can take anything.'

'Greasy Eric,' Scraggle said, 'do you have that rock drill about you?'

The shop steward chortled as he handed Scraggle the piece of heavy equipment. The union leader cradled it in his hands, and checked the connecting leads and the drill bit.

'I don't care what you do to me,' Swellhead shouted,

'I'd rather die than see your perfidious strike succeed! The forces of history are against you, you addle-pated socialist fool! The dark days of the early seventies when a miners' strike could bring down a democratically-elected government are defunct and departed!'

Scraggle blew on the bit of the rock-drill, and shoved it against Swellhead's rope-bandaged back.

He looked at Brittan. 'The telephone number?'

Brittan looked at his friend, who was silently pleading. Knowing he was doing the right thing, he shook his head.

Scraggle smiled and shrugged, and the drill whined through rope, cloth, bone, flesh, lungs, more bone, skin, more cloth, and more rope, poking out of Swellhead's chest, dripping red gobbets down his front.

'Don't tell,' Swellhead gurgled, coughing lumpy gore. 'Don't ever tell.'

The drill bit whirred, spraying bits of Swellhead's insides about. The genius' bald dome bobbed, and lolled lifeless.

'He didn't mind dying to foil your plans, union scum! You still don't have that number! Ha!'

Scraggle let the drill die down, and left it where it was.

'I suppose I'll have to go through directory enquiries then, heh heh. I was never sure whether it was 689 0543 or 689 0534.'

Swellhead's corpse fell over, and Greasy Eric laughed at the dead man.

Brittan's balls were the size of honeydew melons now, taut as overinflated balloons. His John Thomas was a full four inches longer than it had ever been, his knob-end a toadstool-shaped cannonball.

'I wish we could stay around to see that schlong explode,' Scraggle said, consulting his watch, 'but we have to be off now. We've got to be at the negotiating table tomorrow morning, early. A pity. It would have been fascinating to watch the veins all over your body popping like bangers, and to see your eyeballs bug out on six-inch stalks and your heart go off like a hand-grenade wrapped in semtex. Heh heh. My theory is that when you go boom, your bones will be turned to shrapnel, and we'll also get Ms Whemple and Mr McLochness here with the same blast. Bonus points, you might say. I could be wrong, of course. We'll be back sometime next week to check out the damage. By the way, watch out for the pit rats.'

Scraggle shut his watch, and, his vile cohorts with him, left. Greasy Eric was whistling 'Working in a Coal Mine'.

It was dim, but there was a single bare bulb hanging from the rock roof. Somewhere, water was dripping. They must be miles below ground.

Brittan looked down at himself. The veins on his John Thomas were a patriotic bright red and blue, the skin stretched thin over them.

'Goodbye old son,' he told his manhood, 'we've been through a lot together.'

There was nothing for it but to wait it out.

He looked at Phyllida, lovely in repose, chest rising and falling with faint breath, hair over her face.

'Goodbye, darling,' he said.

14

'Goodbye, darling . . .'

Phyllida was dreaming. She was on the Riviera with Dick, trying to decide between dresses in a couturier's. She liked the pink, but the mauve was appealing also. She nibbled the edge of her Amex goldcard, unable to make up her mind. She kept asking Dick what he thought.

And Dick kept saying, 'Goodbye, darling . . .'

Slowly, she swam towards the surface of consciousness, her head aching politely. She was weighted down with chains.

Suddenly she was awake, and shaking. Something furry had rubbed against her tights.

She had a ladder!

She hated having a ladder in her tights. It made her look so common. She couldn't stop shuddering at the thought.

'Phyllida?'

It was Dick, chained naked to the wall. She couldn't help staring. He was *enormous*.

She'd talked about her size preferences penis-wise with Annabelle and Geraldine, but never had she even considered something on this scale. Not even on her horses. It was almost *ridiculous*!

'My God, Dick, but you've got an absolutely *huge*—'

'Yes, yes,' he said impatiently.

She giggled. 'I mean, God, imagine . . .'

He looked up at the ceiling, his face bright red. The poor dear must be dreadfully embarassed. It was most cruel of Scraggle to humiliate him like this.

'Tell me, um, er, doesn't it . . . um, er . . . *hurt* or anything?'

Dick groaned, the arteries in his neck pulsing away like bicycle pumps. Veins stood out all over his immensely-muscled body.

'Oh, I see,' Phyllida said, 'it's your *Talent*. I wondered what it was. You turn into a Human Hunk, like that American fellow who's always in the Sunday supplements.'

'Ye dinnae understand, lassie,' groaned a voice from the dark. It was Jock McLochness.

Dick's head seemed to be swelling along with the rest of him, slabs of muscle under the skin blowing up like an inflatable cushion, mouth gaping open, eyes starting forwards like a fish's.

''Tis turrible, turrible. Puir wee Pitbull's done furr this taime. After all wae bain throo.'

'What is it?'

She had shifted her position, sitting up and edging nearer to Dick. If she leaned over in her chains, she could almost reach him.

'Dick's going tae gae boom.'

'I don't understand.'

'It's . . . the Talent . . .' Dick gasped. '. . . Unless I get some sort of, um, well, um, sexual relief, um, well, I'm . . . going . . . to explode . . . very messily.'

149

The enormous penis was right in front of her face, throbbing visibly, its veins stretched to breaking point.

Dick rattled his chains. It was obvious that, even if he had been a foreigner and accustomed to practise the un-British sin of Onan, he could do nothing with his hands.

'Well,' she gulped, 'there's only one thing to do then. Mr McLochness, if you'd be so kind as to look the other way for a moment.'

'Phyllida . . . darling . . . you don't have to . . . I didn't want . . . it to be like this.'

'Nonsense, I want to.'

'Somehow . . . I'd thought of flowers, and strawberries, and champagne, and silk sheets and things . . .'

'Don't be silly.'

Geraldine Leighton-Critchley had shown her how with an ice lolly when they were at school. She hoped her mouth could open wide enough.

'Remember,' he gasped, 'lots of spit . . . lots of tongue . . .'

15

Nine o' clock sharp.

Greasy Eric Braithwaite, crammed into a brown off-the-peg suit, handed him a fountain pen.

Scraggle looked across the table at Walter Whemple. The arbitrator hadn't slept, and his tie was fifteen degrees off the mark. He had cut himself shaving, and his hands were still shaking.

'How is your daughter, Mr Whemple?' he asked. 'Philippa, wasn't it? Heh heh.'

Whemple's eyes burned fury at him.

The agreement lay unsigned on the table, granting the NUM everything they wished for. Scraggle felt exultation, this close to the achievement of his purpose. A selective telepath, he could see in Whemple's mind that he was about to give in, much good it would do him.

Greasy Eric stifled a snigger. He was expecting three months' holiday with pay from now on, and a session every shift with Mr Entwhistle's daughter Ethel, and a cut of every miner's union dues, and the chance to kill anyone in the Pit he didn't get on with, and tax relief on his mortgage.

Scraggle swallowed his impatience. The miners were fools to think he really wanted their strike to succeed. His aim was nothing less than the destruction of British industry, and the dragging-down of the elected government. That consortium of South American dictators, Marxist idealogues, organised crime figures, Irish Republicans, hippie drug fiends, Japanese big businessmen, KGB hard-liners, French pastry-chefs, Middle-Eastern mullahs, Nazi mad scientists, shape-changing vampire paranorms, Labour Party politicians and anarchist agitators who paid him so handsomely would be delighted at the accomplishment of this mission.

Even if this gambit had failed, he still had Plan B.

He looked forwards to not having to mingle with brutish working class morons any longer.

'Well,' he said, 'no sense waiting.'

With a flourish, he put his signature on three copies of the agreement, and then pushed them across the table to Whemple.

'Do you want to borrow my pen?'

Whemple had his own out, and was fiddling with it. Scraggle had put pencil 'x' marks where the arbitrator was to sign.

Annabelle, in a plain black dress with seamed black stockings and a black leather shoulder holster, massaged his hunch and neck, soothing out the aches of the recent troubles.

Scraggle smiled, and waited for Whemple to sign. The arbitrator took the top off his pen.

Then scraggle shot a look at the gallery, sensing the minds beyond the mirrored window. Mrs T was up there, and the Chairman, and the Minister, and the media. He hoped Whemple could put on a proper show for them.

'Lovely girl, I remember, that Philippa. Heh heh.'

Swallowing hard, Whemple put pen to paper, squeezing a blot of ink from his nib.

Scraggle's chest tightened. Victory!

'Stop,' bellowed a voice, and there was the sound of breaking glass.

16

His body expanding inside his loose combat jacket, Brittan vaulted through the windows into the committee rooms.

Whemple looked around, startled. Scraggle screeched

fury, and Annabelle pulled out a Colt Police Python and squeezed off a shot.

Brittan caught the bullet in his huge fist, and squeezed it cold, tossing it back at the guerilla girl. It bounced off her and clanged against the glass table.

'How did you . . .'

'Escape?' Brittan asked, grinning. 'It was easy. A little ministration from a healing angel, and I was small enough to slip those manacles of yours.'

'Curses,' Scraggle swore.

Jock and Phyllida were right behind him, Schmeisser machine pistols primed and ready.

Three of Greasy Eric's miner goons, wearing those damned helmet deathrays, stepped forwards, hands going to their battery packs.

Phyllida and Jock sprayed them with hot lead, and they jitterbugged against the wall, spray-painting the radiators with blood.

Scraggle sat back in his chair, suddenly and sinisterly calm, and watched the fight.

'This one's mine,' Greasy Eric said, standing up. 'Come on, you Southeren bastid, let's see you try it on with a *real* man!' He growled like a Bradford grizzly bear, and leaped at Brittan.

The two giants locked in a wrestling hold, Greasy Eric's hands trying to get a purchase on Brittan's steel-tense muscles. Brittan tossed the shop steward at the table, and it shattered in a thousand pieces under him.

Spitting blood and teeth, Greasy Eric got up again and made a grab for Brittan's John Thomas, grasping it firmly through the camouflage trousers.

'Let's see if t'pole comes off.'

Brittan breathed hot air into Greasy Eric's face. 'Nobody does that,' he shouted, grabbing a bone-powdering hold on the shop steward's wrist, and wrenching off his hand.

'Bloody Nora!'

Brittan dropped the still-writhing hand and launched a straight piledriver right at Greasy Eric's blood pudding of a face.

The shop steward's neck snapped, and his head flopped down, the back of his head bumping against his spine, a split gaping in his throat.

'Die, capitalist exploiter of the proletariat!' shouted Annabelle, taking careful aim with her gun.

Phyllida stepped in, and pulled a fistful of her best friend's hair out, then went for her eyes with sharpened and polished nails.

Annabelle screeched, and Phyllida slapped her silly, pushing her down on to the floor, and kicking her properly.

'Phyllida!' Whemple gasped. 'You're safe!'

'Daddy!'

'Very touching,' said Scraggle, looking at his watch.

Brittan suddenly had a bad feeling about this hard-won victory of free enterprise democracy.

'I just thought you'd all like to know that, in about twenty seconds, my associates will put Plan B into effect.'

'Plan B?'

'Yes, my comrades in the service unions have been pumping coal gas into the London sewers all night. When the word comes through that this agreement

hasn't been ratified, they'll toss in a match, and it'll
be the Great Fire of London all over again.'

'You dirty dog!'

Scraggle laughed and stood up. He bowed to the
gallery.

'Madame Prime Minister, it's been a load of laughs,
but now's the time to go bye-bye.'

Brittan was at his full erection again, a mountain of
iron-threaded bone and engorged muscle ready to do
or die for his country, his Prime Minister, and his
woman.

A trapdoor was lifting up in the floor behind Scraggle.
He was applying a flame from his cigarette lighter to one
of his cigars.

Coal gas was odourless, but Brittan could hear it
seeping.

Scraggle turned, but Brittan moved with a speed that
belied his massive size and weight. Grasping Jock around
the waist, Brittan hurled his friend like a caber, pitching
him accurately at the manhole.

Scraggle gasped in horror as the kilted tornado landed
in the hole, plugging it up completely.

'Hah,' said Jock, 'yae cannae dae a thing aboot it.'

There was a rumble deep in the earth, and the floor
was shaking.

'One stray spark, heh heh,' Scraggle said.

It was like an earthquake, building up slowly.

A look of horror and surprise crossed Jock's bearded
face, and his eyes rolled upwards. Then, with a champagne cork pop, Jock shot out of the manhole at the
apex of a geyser of flame and slammed against the

roof, flattening the top of his head like a breakfast egg.

There were distant explosions, and bursts of flame came from everywhere. Jock hit the floor, a broken puppet.

Brittan reached for Scraggle, and his fists closed where the arch-fiend's throat had been an instant earlier. He saw Scraggle gingerly lowering himself through the manhole, ignoring the flames swarming around him. It was as if the man were made of asbestos.

He stood over the manhole, looking down at Scraggle. Their eyes met, and they understood each other perfectly, with a white hot purity. Hero and villain, linked by their struggle, they were the same, two sides of one coin. Scraggle's lips puckered in a kiss. He was having trouble getting his hunch through the manhole.

Brittan stamped on Scraggle's hands, and the union leader lost his grip. He looked up, panic on his ugly face, and was pulled down as if by a massive suction from below, disappearing into the inferno of the London sewers. Brittan thought there was a distant splash, and spat after Scraggle, hoping the world had heard the last of the monstrous mastermind. The echo of Scraggle's chesty laughter was in the flames.

Then, Brittan was being bustled out of the committee rooms, Phyllida pulled close to his side. There were policemen and firemen everywhere. Scotland Yard men were dragging Annabelle away. He saw Mrs T and the Minister of Energy being whisked off, surrounded by uniformed Talents. Brittan recognised Corporal Punishment, the PM's personal bodyguard and night-time avenger, in his distinctive black bodysuit, swinging his cane to clear the flames.

Phyllida was hugging him, arms not quite stretching around his chest.

'It's all over,' she said, as they got into the open air.

Parliament Square was lit up by the burning buildings on the other side of the Thames. The air was thick with the din of fire alarms and fire engines.

Brittan looked at the skyline of London, that ever-changing symbol of everything British and noble. Flames were sprouting everywhere. He thought he saw the Post Office Tower leaning like the one in Pisa. Helicopters buzzed over the city.

'Out of my way,' shouted a fireman, unrolling a length of hose.

Brittan tapped him on the chest. 'Ahem,' he said. 'Courtesy costs nothing.'

'Out of my way, *please*!'

'That's better.' He stepped aside, and the chastened public servant got on with the business of dousing the flames.

Brittan felt the warmth spreading from his groin.

'Phyllida,' he said, 'will you marry me?'

'Oh yes, Dick, yes, yes, yes.'

His John Thomas was aimed like one of the guns of Navarone.

Phyllida pressed herself against him, lifting her leg up and over his erection, kissing his chest, her hands in his hair.

'Let's find a quiet spot,' she said, 'before you explode.'

17

He wore his old uniform for the ceremony, feeling it stretched tight across his chest.

In the antechamber at Number 10, while the PM was busy with Loric, Corporal Punishment tried to keep Brittan talking to soothe his obvious nerves. The Corporal was talking about the Victory Over the Miners, and the collapse of the discredited NUM. The fires were under control now, and the damage wasn't as bad as had been feared. One good thing was, subsequent to this outrage, it looked as if Parliament would reinstate the death penalty. The Corporal whooshed his cane through the air at the thought.

Nothing had been heard of Scraggle, and he was presumed dead.

Finally, Loric emerged from the inner sanctum. The distinguished Talent raised an eyebrow at Brittan, and left without saying a word.

'The PM is ready to see you now,' Corporal Punishment said.

Brittan was admitted alone.

'Ahh, Lieutenant Brittan,' Mrs T exclaimed, rising and smiling, 'do come in . . .' The PM extended a limp hand to be held briefly.

Brittan felt awkward, but proud. Stiffly, uncomfortable in his starched trousers, he walked around the desk.

'You wore your Victoria Cross?'

Brittan nodded, and saluted.

The commendation lay on the desk, tied with a blue

ribbon. There was a huge portrait of Churchill over the fireplace.

Mrs T looked out of the window, the orange of the last of the fires reflected on her face.

'So many sacrifices,' she said.

Brittan thought of the Black Hat Gang. Basil Mapledurham, grey matter dripping off Gracie Fields' face. Sewell Head, drill sticking out of his tit. Jock McLochness, skull pulped against the ceiling.

'. . . but all worth while. We can't give in, you know. We can't.'

The PM was quite animated on the point.

'If it's not the miners, it's the railwaymen, the steelworkers, the TUC.' She made a fist in the air. 'We must not turn from our purpose, Lieutenant.'

Brittan agreed.

Of course, all the sacrifices were worth it. After all, he might have lost his three closest friends. But he had gained someone far more important – Phyllida. Already, she had left her position with the Porcupine people and was planning a big society wedding, picking out curtains for Brittan Hall, wondering who to replace Slobotham with, thinking of names for children.

At the thought of Phyllida, his John Thomas began to come to attention.

Mrs T picked up the decoration, and handed it to him.

'You have our thanks, Lieutenant. You are a British hero.'

He swelled with pride, his knob-end displacing the zip fastener, pushing it down and open.

'Lieutenant,' the PM gasped.

His muscles inflated, his heart pounded, his balls rumbled. Brittan felt the danger zone throbbing near, and knew there was only one thing for it.

'Ma'am,' he said, lifting the PM up by the hips, 'I hope you'll excuse me . . .'

This was written, in my Jack Yeovil hat, for *Temps*, a mainly-funny shared-world anthology devised by Midnight Rose (Neil Gaiman, Alex Stewart, Roz Kaveney, Mary Gentle) in which Britain has a tradition of bureaucratic superheroes. It proved problematic, exacerbating a strain between the Midnight Rose people and their publisher (Penguin/Roc). Though the editors were sensitive and enthusiastic, 'Pitbull Brittan' appeared in a slightly bowdlerised form. Surprisingly, objections were raised not to the gross sexual or violent content but to the politics; even more surprisingly, the objection was not to the piece's obvious, indeed vicious, left-wing attack, but to right-wing sentiments expressed ironically.

The effect of the trims was to mute the point of the story, which I thought of as proceeding from the fantastic premise that everything the *Daily Mail* implied about the miners' strike was the literal truth. I have restored most cuts, and thus made the story marginally less good-humoured. The reason for the nasty edge was that, conscious that Alf Garnett and Archie Bunker became heroes, I wanted the authorial voice to be as objectionable as possible. It's certainly not subtle.

Though *Temps* is a comic universe, Neil and Alex

felt obliged to bracket 'Pitbull Brittan' with a distancing text alleging it to be a fiction *within* the world of the rest of the collection, which deals with sensible, believable, down-to-earth characters like a man who turns into a giant frog but is afraid of the water. Neil wrote a witty introduction, covering the career of author Jack Yeovil within the *Temps* world, and listing various other adventures of the hero (*Pitbull Brittan Gives Them What For, Hurrah! For Pitbull Brittan*), but I feel this story needs to be grabbed by the throat rather than held at arms' length.

Having created enough monsters in my time, I have *no* intention of writing any further adventures for Lieutenant Dickhead and the Black Hat Gang.

The Snow Sculptures
of Xanadu

There had been a private zoo here once, but now only mosquitoes thrived. In the thick, sweaty heat, they pestered Welles. During his lifetime, Charles Foster Kane had decreed Xanadu insect-free, as if the force of his unstoppable will – the power that had shaped the destinies of nations – were able to hold back the swamplands surrounding his Florida fastness. The Pleasure Dome had begun to rot while Kane still lived, as his powers ebbed and history slowly crept past him, and, with his death twenty-five years ago, the decay had begun to accelerate. The walls were breached like those of a besieged city that has finally yielded, the stinking cages of the menagerie held only dead animals, forty-foot windows were patched over with boards. Welles thought that if the place were left to nature, it would inevitably sink like the House of Usher into the giant tarn surrounding it.

A fitting set for a ghost story.

The former Boy Wonder stood outside the gates of Xanadu, the shadow of their wrought iron K motif falling upon him, and was conscious of how much he had changed since his last visit. In 1941, with an RKO contract to make a ground-breaking documentary about the Great American, he had stolen miles of footage in Xanadu as the Kane functionaries dismantled and inventoried the fortress's infestation-like collection. Statues, books, paintings, furniture, uncategorisable mementoes, jigsaw puzzles, phonograph records, vehicles, tapestries: all boxed or burned. Welles had felt that there was no waste as long as the process was caught on film. No gesture or moment was insignificant once processed by Gregg Toland's camera. Of course, he could not have foreseen that all his footage would end up like Kane's collection, listed and buried in a vault.

Up in the eaves of Xanadu, something with wings squawked, its cry like a jaguar's snarl played backwards.

Then, Welles had been slim and promising; now he felt fat and thwarted. Charles Foster Kane Jr, a lifelong recluse crippled in the 1916 automobile accident that took his mother's life, had stirred the might of his inherited empire, and pressured RKO into abandoning *American*, just as they dissuaded *News on the March* from issuing its newsreel obituary. Junior, still nursing the hurt of his parents' divorce, acted as if he wanted the memory of Kane erased, working diligently at squashing biographies with all the zeal of an Egyptian priest wiping a dissolute pharaoh out of the history books. Now, in 1965, few people remembered whether Kane had been a real person or a made-up character. His name was sometimes good for newspaper sales – as when, in 1949, it had seemed probable that an American black marketeer found dead in a Viennese sewer was the old man's bastard son – but mainly, he was as shadowy a concept as his 'Rosebud', as forgotten a heap of detritus as his Xanadu.

Down the coast, a white spurt shot up. Part of the old Kane Estate was now leased to Cape Canaveral. Junior's passion was the sky, prompted by the cripple's hope that even if he could not walk he could fly. Welles remembered Junior's involvement with Howard Hughes' 'Spruce Goose' during the War, and his establishment of a Kane Aviation Company in the fifties, diversifying into jet engines and prototypical rockets. Kane components would go to the moon one day, or bear the payload of man's final war. And Kane papers and television programmes would bear the news of both events.

Welles wondered again if the summons he had received was a hoax. Xanadu seemed from the outside to be completely deserted. Sun-bleached walls crumbled invisibly, and there was no sign of habitation. He looked back at the limousine, but the driver – half his face hidden by goggle-like glasses - betrayed nothing.

As young men, Kane and Welles had been much alike, the sleek and dynamic Boy Wonders of 1894 and 1940, but they had aged differently, Kane becoming a shambling, bullet-headed mammoth, shunned by the rest of the tribe, while Welles buried himself in beard, bloat and B-movies, squandering his theatrical reputation on cameo appearances and cheap magic tricks. It all started with *American*, the dream movie, to combine fiction and documentary in unprecedented ways. The footage had never even been edited together, but still *American*, the masterpiece that never was, cast its shadow over all Welles's subsequent, tidily completed but lesser-than-expected works: *The Ambersons*, *Heart of Darkness*, *Don Quixote*, *The Trial*. If *American* had been finished, things would have been different. Welles would have been greater than Ford, than Hawks, than Hitchcock. Than Eisenstein, than Murneau, than Flaherty . . .

Finally, the gates were opened, and a thin, smiling man in a tropical suit led Welles to the house. The driveway was apparently unending, Xanadu growing larger with each step. Welles had heard of Dr John Montague before, had read his published account of his investigation into the notoriously haunted Hill House in Connecticut. That had ended in tragedy for one of Montague's researchers, but the scientist took care elaborately to exonerate himself in his book. Junior had commissioned the parapsychologist to look into his own family's haunted mansion, perhaps to prescribe a rite of exorcism. Welles wondered why Junior hadn't simply had Xanadu burned to the ground, and its ruins seeded with salt.

Montague chatted as they walked to Xanadu, mainly about magic and trickery. Welles was known as an expert, having once sawn Rita Hayworth in half and capped the trick by marrying the girl. He had hoaxed the world that the Martians were coming. Montague assumed that the master magician would recognise a trick if he saw one. Welles realised there was something lacking in Montague, a failure to understand that magic was what you could not explain. That was its beauty, its trick. Probing the works, finding the concealed mirrors and strings, was the most effective method of exorcism.

The K above the door was weathered, most of its circle fallen away, leaving only a rind between the topmost arms of the letter. It looked like an R.

'Rosebud,' Welles whispered.

Rosebud had proved the most overexplored false trail in American biography. The *News on the March* team had never found an explanation for Kane's last word, and neither had the would-be makers of *American*. Joe Mankiewicz, drunk, had suggested it was the mogul's private nickname for the private parts of his second wife, the former street-corner diva Susan Alexander. That had been as good a solution as any.

Welles saw Montague's team in the grounds, blending in with the overgrowth like camouflage birds, prodding directional mikes and anemometers into various apertures. Montague talked about cold spots and ectoplasm and resonances. In the parapsychology texts, Xanadu had overtaken Borley Rectory, the Loren Home, the Frieburg Tanz Akademie, the Overlook Hotel and the Belasco Mansion as the world's most haunted house; although Welles realised none of the rumours and reports that had filtered back to him had ever specified exactly *how* Xanadu was haunted.

Some excitement was caused among the psychic researchers by the sighting of a large bird flapping lazily out of the eaves of the West Wing; the thing Welles had heard earlier. It looked like a vast, leathery bat with a horned swordfish's head. Montague explained the creature was a living fossil, but that no one had got close enough to one to classify it. Welles remembered recreating some shots of Xanadu in miniature at RKO, reusing some of the back projection plates from *King Kong*. He wondered how the painted pterodactyl had migrated from Hollywood to Florida.

While Xanadu was decaying, the Kane Empire had been reshaping itself – Junior taking only a capricious interest, but capable men springing up from inside the business – and preparing for a war which, ultimately, would take it from the verge of bankruptcy to corporate heights to which Kane had never even aspired. Riding the tide of national purpose, Kane papers and magazines had re-established themselves as essentials in any American living room. In the fifties, Kane interests diversified: while Junior reached for the sky, his corporation crept into television, stealing a march on the competition as the new medium took hold on American life. Organisation Men in grey flannel prowled the executive suites, as the name of Kane came to mean a many-headed but single-minded beast, almost independent of Junior, infiltrating America's living rooms. Kane papers backed and then denounced Joseph McCarthy, as if the old man's ghost were still influencing editorial policies. Kane and Korea, Kane and Nixon, Kane and Kennedy, Kane and the astronauts: the old man would have loved the second half of the century more even than he had the first.

Montague listed the accomplishments of his team: trance mediums, physical mediums, psychometrists, psychotronics, psychokinetics; ghost breakers in grey flannel, punching a time-clock and tuning in to the beyond just as his old audience had tuned in to the *Mercury Theatre of the Air*.

Even in his lightweight suit, Welles was perspiring uncomfortably. He was surprised, then, when Montague, on a doorstep as wide as an interstate highway, handed him a parka. The scientist pulled on a thick coat himself, and flipped the fur-lined hood up over his head. He looked ready to strike for the South Pole. Perplexed, Welles followed suit, wrapping the cumbersome garment around himself. He waited for the punchline, but none came.

Montague threw open the great doors of Xanadu, and stepped in. Welles followed, and was embraced by an invisible blizzard. As the doors slammed to behind them, he felt as if he had left the valley of Shangri-La and returned to Tibetan wastes. The scientist looked smug, and Welles tried to conceal his astonishment. Outside was tropical heat. Here, within the walls of Xanadu, an arctic frost lay over everything. Welles asked if there was any scientific explanation. Montague didn't answer, but provided the information that Charles Foster Kane, born in 1864, spent his first years in a Colorado boarding house, coping with the fierce winters.

The statues and paintings were gone, but in their place were shaped blocks of ice. One of Montague's team was taking photographs of a swirling column that turned into a perfect Floradora Girl. The ice shifted and cracked as the girl performed a dance step with the grave dignity of a glacier.

The thick frost on the walls was shaped into dioramas. Welles was drawn to a screen-sized patch of sparkling ice.

Street scenes turned into stage sets. The view crept up over houses and in through roofs. Welles wished he had a film crew with him. The ice pictures were the images he had dreamed of when he first conceived *American*. They melted and re-formed in different configurations.

Montague stood back, and let Welles wander through the halls of Xanadu, constantly amazed, delighted and intrigued by the ice sculptures. The scientist was cool and cautious, not expressing an opinion. A lifelong measurer and tabulator, Montague was probably not even qualified to have an opinion.

Now Welles understood why the Kane people had sent for him. It was not that he could explain the ice sculptures, any more than he could explain 'Rosebud'. It was that he was the only one who could appreciate what was here.

The great staircase of Xanadu was thick with snow that came from nowhere and smoothed away the steps, fanning out around Welles' feet as it blanketed the parquet. The staircase was a slope suitable for skiing, for sledding. For an instant, as if a diamond bullet had pierced his brain, Welles thought he had an answer to the unanswerable. Then, like ice in the sun, it melted away.

This story happened because Jonathan Carroll put *Ego*, an Austrian magazine, in touch with me about writing something for the fifteith anniversary, in 1991, of *Citizen Kane*. I responded not with the think-piece they expected but with this ghost story, which is also a homage to

Shirley Jackson's *The Haunting of Hill House*, from which Dr Montague is borrowed. Jackson's book, of course, was effectively filmed as *The Haunting* by Robert Wise, the editor of *Kane*. 'The Snow Sculptures of Xanadu' is one of my attempts to combine historical people with famous fictional characters. I probably borrowed the practice from Philip José Farmer, along with David Thomson and Howard Waldrop. I find it irresistible, no matter how much it annoys some people.

Citizen Kane is a touchstone: 'The Pierce Arrow Stalled, And . . .' returns to the circumstances of its creation, while my collaborative 'Ten Days That Shook the World' (with Eugene Byrne) is an alternate world story in which Charles Foster Kane achieves the Presidency only to be unseated by a communist revolution. In an early script draft, Kane's son was to join an American fascist group and be killed while committing sabotage, but the sub-plot was dropped; it is *suggested*, but not quite stated, that the boy dies in the car crash with his mother. I decided to let him live.

Three on a Match

The army bastards had never let Adolf use his rifle. He'd been issued with a weapon, of course, but a useless relic tied together with string, functional only as a crutch, a shovel or crowbar. He was just an orderly, running errands along the trenches, and Willi Schanke was the great rifleman. 'Old Sharpeye', they called Schanke, remembering the Karl May novels they'd been raised on – the finest sniper in the Kaiser's army. But Old Sharpeye had been caught in the bombardment, and was Old No-Head now, a sheet of corrugated iron from the trench-wall having slid from the mud and messily decapitated him. The headless body was crammed into an undignified position, the prized rifle – barrel still gleaming through the mud spatters like a silver sword unearthed by an archaeologist – caught in a torso that was bent like an elbow. Adolf took the gun, and tugged. It came free easily.

The bombardment was over and all was quiet. The British positions were only a hundred yards away, well within range of Old Sharpeye's rifle. He was known – had been known – for his almost supernatural ability to pick off officers and men. Many swore Old Sharpeye could make a bullet change direction in the air, so it would shoot to a point directly over the trenches and then angle down into the tin-hatted skull of some pathetic tommy. He knew that was just superstition. Old Sharpeye had been just a workman, and this rifle was his secret, a superb tool.

Now Adolf was Old Sharpeye. Three quarters of the men in this stretch of trench had died in the bombardment. As a corporal, he was probably the highest rank alive. It was his duty to pursue the war as best he saw fit. He had no interest in rallying the bedraggled and wounded, in shoring up the exploded walls, in restoring lines of communication. He had a rifle in his hands, and that made him a sniper.

The tommies didn't know what was about to strike them down. They would be complacent, thinking they'd hammered their enemy earlier this night, and there would be no retaliation. They didn't know Old Sharpeye was here, crawling up through the mud, working his way into the blind like a duck hunter, gathering walls of earth around his position, rifle barrel always kept out of the filth of France.

Finally, he was in place, rifle aimed into the darkness, stock against his shoulder and cheek, eye in line with the sight. He could hear the tommies moving about, but sound was not enough to give him a bearing. He needed a light, just a simple spark. Then, he'd fire.

·   ·   ·

They'd pounded Jerry for two hours just after nightfall, and Owen had been expecting the order to go over the top. He was sure the German trenches had been soundly breached, and that there was an opening in the line. Ever since the shelling ceased, they'd been hearing the moans of the unattended wounded on the other side. He didn't want to go, of course, but since they had to sometime, why not now, when Jerry was less able to put up a fight? That, of course, was why the order wouldn't come. It would have made sense to attack now, and sense was not a strategy General Haig had much use for.

His hands were shaking, and he needed a smoke. He had the cigarettes – as an officer, he always had them – but his matches were gone somewhere. Matches were scarce, anyway. It was as if the allies needed all the fire they had for the war effort.

'Brewer,' he called to his sergeant, 'you got matches?'

The sergeant shook his head, but Corporal Shipman dug out a box from his flap-pocket. Owen offered the men cigarettes, and shook them out.

'One match left,' Shipman said, the box rattling hollow.

Brewer grinned.

They all knew about three on a match. It was the worst bad luck you could get.

If a black cat crossed your path, or you walked under a ladder, or thirteen turned up for dinner, or you spilled salt, your chances of incurring the wrath of the gods were much the same as they always were. But here, in the trenches, there was a good reason for the three on a match superstition.

The first flicker alerted the sniper.

The second gave him time to fix his aim.

The third . . . *pow!* Your brains were leaking into your tin hat, and your parents were getting a 'regret to inform you' letter.

'Who's it to be?' Brewer said, unlit smoke sagging from his wide mouth.

'Me,' Owen said.

Sometimes, he wondered if he wanted to die. He'd seen hundreds pass through his detachment, but he was still here. Maybe his scribblings were keeping him alive. Maybe a soldier god was watching over him, intent that the war be recorded in more than generals' memoirs.

Brewer saluted.

Shipman struck the match, and sucked fire into his cigarette, then exhaled smoke through the glow-worm . . .

The light flared, and Adolf swivelled the barrel, eyeline perfect down the sight, moving his shoulders.

He was cold and dirty, and he had been lying here as if dead for twenty minutes that seemed like twenty days. He would pot his tommy, and crawl home before dawn.

The light bobbed, and his aim was fixed.

The light held . . .

. . . *and he pulled the trigger. When they found what he'd done, Adolf was promoted. He was Old Sharpeye, the man who had single-handedly held back the British when the trench was breached and the enemy could have overwhelmed the line. The army rallied around, shored up the hole, thrust forwards. Defeat was no longer a certainty. He was decorated* by the Kaiser. He wasn't a stinking Corporal any more, he was a godlike Sergeant. Even officers nodded their heads in respect when he strode by, his long rifle on his shoulder like a frontiersman's flintlock. He shot many tommies, pulling off apparently impossible feats of marksmanship. He shot fliers out of the sky. He fired into the barrels of artillery emplacements, exploding the shells inside. He killed officers carrying vital dispatches. He became a legend. Even the British knew him. Feared him. A special shell was created, like a steel cape. With it, he could crawl into No Man's Land unhurt, and fire at will. He had many close scrapes. Newsreels filmed him in his shell, crawling into action. War was changing, and so were the men who fought it. He began to notice how others resented him. Those who had belittled him when he was a Corporal were exaggeratedly polite now. He would never rise above the rank of sergeant because he was an Austrian, because he was short, because of his accent, because he was not Jewish. Caricatures of him appeared in British newspapers, making him ridiculous with his brush of a moustache and his tortoise shell, a character from Lewis Carroll. He stepped up his private campaign. Baron von Richtofen, the air ace, had claimed a total of eighty men before he was shot down. Adolf would kill eight hundred before the war was over. He was no aristocrat, jousting in the skies. But he was a Teutonic Knight for all that, suitably armoured and with a shining bolt-action sword. He was given Theo von Kretschmar-Schuldorff as a squire. The aristocrat, an ex-officer broken in rank for some maverick action, looked after his rifles, polished his shell, answered the mail he received by the sackload from well-wishers throughout Germany and his homeland. The rumour was that the Kaiser intended to sue for an honourable peace soon. And, although the official estimate of his score put him in the hundreds, he knew he had only killed seventy-eight so far. Seventy-eight well-chosen targets. He must step things up. Von Richthofen had racked up his score by picking off unarmed spotter planes between missions. He must find a way to increase his total. The idea occurred to him while he was with one of the women who flocked to the hero. As his penis disappeared and re-emerged from the French girl's mouth, he reviewed his career. Thus far, each of his kills had served a strategic purpose. Each had materially affected the course of a battle, of the war. Now, he must do something different. The enemy must be demoralised, terrorised, battered. He must be more than a Lewis Carroll joke, he must be a terrifying creature of the night, not a turtle but a wolf, a vampire, a hawk. The girl finished, spat into a basin, and left him. She had looked Jewish. Inspired, he began killing chaplains, children if they could be found, civilians, the wounded, women. He got his score up to 158. Then, just after he had performed a daring daylight strike on a hospital position in which he neatly shot three nurses through their heads, his squire slipped a bayonet into his kidneys and fished around until internal organs dribbled down his thigh. It took him days to die, days without drugs, days without honour . . .

Shipman puffed in ecstasy on his fag, while Brewer lit up. Owen felt queasier now, less sure of his immortality. The matchlight made Brewer's face devilish and red in the dark, a Mephistopheles mask floating. Owen's mouth was dry, the paper of the cigarette stuck to his lips. Brewer held the match out to him.

. . . In 1919, the German High Command deposed the Kaiser, and insisted on an honourable peace. Germany could fight on, but would not. The Kaiser was tried and sentenced by his own people, a new constitution was agreed upon by all Germans, and a vast rebuilding programme – funded by an international coalition – did its best honourably to restore the countries most blighted by the war. Kerensky in Moscow and Darrow in Washington held back the might of their newborn empires while old Europe cleaned its houses. The royal scum of a dozen nations went into monied exile, and appeared only in the rotogravure sections of the more frivolous newspapers. In the USA, a ridiculous law against liquour was laughed out of Congress, and instead legislation was passed on the Russian Liberal model, allowing for the empowerment of the working men, of the coloured peoples, of women, of the marginalised. In the Russian Union, returning soldiers foreswore for ever the use of war, and Vladimir Ulianov oversaw the establishment of a workable agricultural plan which would feed not only the peoples formerly under the rule of the Tsar, but a good deal of India and Points East as well. The British Empire was peacefully dissolved by Prime Minister Herbert Wells, and the coal, steel, shipbuilding and cotton industries were success- fully nationalised by an edict signed symbolically in Jarrow, hitherto the scene of much of the dispute between capital and labour which was now abolished. Wells, Kerensky and Darrow met in Paris – with von Ludendorff and Feuillade, Gandhi and Zapata, and a score of others – and founded the League of Nations, a first step towards the establishment of Wells' beloved world state. Henceforth, all the resources of the globe would be alotted according to need, the entire human race made aware of its kinships rather than its enmities. An *age of wondrous inventions, amazing scientific breakthroughs, startling artistic achievements, astonishing philanthropies, and general good-humour dawned, and lasted longer than anyone believed possible . . .*

Owen looked into the matchflame, and saw visions . . .

. . . his head exploding around a German bullet; the still-burning match falling from his hand into a cracked-open box of shells; the resulting blast embedding Brewer and Shipman into the mud of the trenches; the rising column of flame a signal for the German attack he knew must come; Jerry pouring through the breech; the allies routed and retreating; all France under the boots of the hun; Germans in Paris, London, New York, Tokyo; the King hanging in chains, upstart Willy forcing his way to another throne; German navies filling the seas like giant black reptiles; German planes swarming in the skies like angry clouds; civilian populations raped and shot; the Imperial Eagle replacing the Union Jack in India, Africa, Canada, Australia; the whole world a kitchen to fill the bellies of Prussians; painters, musicians, artists, actors, poets executed; petty officals exalted as terrible tyrants; entire races lined up for extermination. A century of unrelieved horrors. All in the flame.

Owen blew out the match. No shot came.

The light went out, and Adolf, uncomfortable and bored, left Old Sharpeye's rifle to rust in the mud, scurrying back to the safety of the trenches.

'Turning superstitous?' Brewer asked.

Owen spat away his unlit cigarette.

'Just cautious,' he said.

This was written for Peter Crowther's anthology, *Narrow Houses*, on the theme of superstition. I tried not to write to the formula Karl Edward Wagner once described as: 'here's an old legend . . . *aaargh*, it got me!'

Ratting

'You know *Watership Down*,' Teddy said, hefting his .22 to his shoulder and tracking an invisible rabbit through muddy green grass. 'You've read the book, you've seen the film, you've bought the video, now . . .'

He made a *pow* sound and jerked his rifle as if he'd fired.

'. . . *eat the pie!*'

Terry grunted but didn't laugh. He hadn't read a book since *Janet and John* and only watched videos with exploding cars or big teats in them.

It was a waste, really. Only having Terry as an audience for his funnies.

'Weren't no rabbit in they ditch,' Terry said, missing the point.

Teddy's brother's gun scattered so much shot into anything he hit that it was useless for eating. To Terry, eating wasn't the point: shooting was the point, killing was the point.

It was another boring summer. No school, no work,

no nothing. Teddy wanted to hitch round the country on his own, but Dad insisted he hang around Alder with Terry. Dad had the idea he could keep his brother out of trouble.

Dad was daft.

They were walking on the B-road that snaked out across the moor. It had been wet and everything was a stark green. One of Teddy's boots was worn through at the sole; every time he put his foot in a puddle his sock got a soak.

A blue van drove along and the brothers had to edge into a lay-by to let it pass. Teddy recognised Goddard, the vet. Someone out this way had trouble. How animals managed to survive the millions of years before they invented vets was a puzzle. Of course, back in prehistoric ages they hadn't had Terry Gilpin to worry about.

It was another day of poking around the countryside in search of something for Terry to kill. And of Teddy cracking funnies his brother didn't understand.

'Youm hear about Sharon Coram's tattoos?' Teddy said.

Terry's interest almost perked. Sharon was the girl who shagged everyone in Alder. Actually, Teddy figured she shagged everyone except Terry, which was why his brother was so interested.

'Tattoos?'

'Yeah, got 'em done over Taunton way. One of they New Age Traveller blokes.'

'Sharon an't got no tattoos.'

'Not where you can see 'em. On her inner thighs, up under her skirts, so they rub together when she walks.

184

She'm got Prince Charles on one side and Lady Di on the other.'

'You'm shittin' me,' Terry said.

'Know what happened when she got home and showed 'em to Gary Chilcot?'

Gary was more or less Sharon's most regular boy-friend.

Terry shook his head.

'Gary takes off her jeans and her knickers and that and says, "Well, I don't recognise the face on the right or the one on the left . . ."'

Teddy paused, to punch up the laugh line.

'" . . . but the one in the middle's Terry Gilpin."'

There was a long pause. Teddy had meant to say the name of a teacher they didn't like or some old village git, but the last time he'd told the funny he got laughs using his brother's name.

Gears ground painfully in Terry's mind.

'You callin' I a cunt?' he said, making a fist around his shotgun.

'It's a funny, thicko,' Teddy said.

Terry took a grip on Teddy's shoulder and squeezed. Teddy's arm popped and sharp pains leaped across his back.

After the hurting stopped, things were even. Teddy was fed up with this. Every day, Terry would find some excuse to maul him. Usually he didn't even have to tell a funny or pull a stunt.

'Let's go rattin',' Terry said.

They were out near the Starkey farm anyway. It had once been one of the biggest in the county but bits had been sold off years ago, and now Jimmy Starkey just had a few fields with a couple of cows and an overgrown patch next to the house where all the rubbish of the village ended up. The yard, which was piled high with rotting junk, was the source of a smell famous throughout the village as the Starkey Stench. The pile was alive with rats and Starkey had been known to let village kids pop off guns at them. They were doing him a favour, really. The last time Teddy and Terry had freed the Starkey Stench of rats, Jimmy had given them a couple of fivers and a gallon of his home brew.

But since then, Terry had been found out as the one who cut up the tyres on Jimmy's car. He had been pissed on cider and didn't remember why he'd done it. A typical Terry stunt: useless, pointless and doomed.

Usually when you got near the Starkey farm, just about when the Stench hit the nostrils, your ears would be assaulted by yapping. Jimmy had a dog called Vindaloo, a mongrel old as Cliff Richard and noisier than a rusty chainsaw. If Vindaloo still had teeth, Jimmy wouldn't have to let kids shoot his rats. The dog had been a well-known biter of vermin. Newcomers always thought him a dangerous child-killer, though Vindaloo had never, so far as Teddy knew, laid claw or tooth on human flesh.

When they got to the Starkey yard, with the Stench all around them, Teddy saw Vindaloo in an old plastic laundry basket by the front door. He was breathing badly.

Teddy knelt by the dog and realised Vindaloo smelled badly too. He started a feeble whine. Teddy stroked and the dog leaked a gallon of spit from his loose mouth.

Terry stood in the yard, looking at the pile of rubbish. It seemed to seethe. Yesterday's rain had turned much of it to sludge. A rat poked its head out of a hole near the top and vanished again. The rodents had tunnelled extensively in the pile, like Vietnamese soldiers in a Chuck Norris video. There could be dozens of them, slipping in and out of secret entrances, carrying off food, spreading disease.

Something close to Teddy mooed, and he jumped. A cow plodded around the side of the house, wandering loose. Someone must have forgotten to close a gate. The milker shouldn't be this close to the house.

Jimmy Starkey didn't have many cows, so each was important. He was one of those farmers who treated animals better than anything else. He kept Vindaloo around long after he was any use and lavished such care on his livestock that they were always taking show prizes that bigger farmers, who simply spent money on theirs, tried all year to snaffle.

Teddy had the idea there was something wrong at the Starkey farm. Jimmy wasn't likely to leave a gate open. He practically brought his cows breakfast in bed. And Vindaloo was not the lovably obnoxious monster Teddy had known since he was a kid.

Even the Stench was different somehow.

'You go in an' ask 'en,' Terry said. He was just bright enough to realise Jimmy would still not be pleased to see him.

Teddy knocked on the door. His shoulder twinged again. Terry had really hurt him this time. Maybe dislocated something.

187

Inside the farmhouse, someone said something. The door was unlatched. It swung open.

Teddy stepped inside. Like a lot of old places, it had a low ceiling and he had to stoop.

'Mr Starkey?'

He found Jimmy in his front room, sat in an old chair. He was in a state, hair uncombed and eyes red. Afternoon telly was on with the sound down. Some soap serial with shaky walls and smiling Australians.

'Mind if we rat your pile?' Teddy asked.

'What?'

Jimmy looked up. He hadn't shaved in a couple of days.

'We're rattin'. Shootin' rats.'

Jimmy shook his head, understanding.

'Yurp, of course you can shoot rats.'

With a gulp of anxiety in his stomach, Teddy noticed Jimmy had a gun in his lap. It was an old pistol, almost an antique.

'Mr Starkey, you'm all right?'

Jimmy looked down at his gun and up at Teddy.

'No,' he said.

Teddy wanted to leave. He was worried about what Jimmy would do with the gun.

'Donal Goddard offered to put 'en to sleep,' Jimmy said. 'But I couldn't let 'en. It shouldn't be a stranger. I should do it myself. Too sick to be any use to hisself. All he'm got in front of 'en is pain.'

Jimmy held up the gun.

'But I can't do it. I just can't. I thought I could, but . . .'

Teddy understood. 'It's Vindaloo,' he said.

Jimmy nodded sadly. 'He'm has got to be put out of his misery. Teddy boy, please do it for me. Vindaloo always liked you.'

Teddy thought about it and agreed.

'Thank 'ee, boy,' Jimmy said. 'Rat any time you want.'

Teddy turned away, and left the front room. He held up his .22. It wasn't powerful but if he held it to Vindaloo's head it should do the job.

It wasn't pleasant but it had to be done.

As he stooped to go through the farmhouse's low door, another jolt of pain writhed up his back. And an idea for a stunt.

It was too good to miss. Terry would shit himself.

His brother was standing in the middle of the yard looking at the rubbish, drawing beads with his gun. The loose cow was near him, chewing a tuft of grass that grew out of a rotten cardboard box.

Teddy paused in the doorway to get worked up and came out muttering to himself.

'Rude old bugger,' he said, 'callin' me filth, callin' youm a tosser. He'm out of order completely. He'm got no cause to spit on us Gilpins. He'm no better'n us. No better 't all.'

Terry looked at him, jaw slack.

'We'm can't rat,' Teddy told him, pretending fury. 'Bloody Jimmy Starkey ordered us off his property pronto. Says he'll put a boot to your arse if'n he sees you again. He cuffed I round the earhole.'

Terry's face sagged as it sank in.

'Tell 'ee what,' Teddy said, sharply. 'He'm been so bloody rude, I'm gonna shoot his dog.'

Quickly, Teddy jammed the .22 barrel against the back of Vindaloo's skull and fired. The shot was muffled. The dog jerked and was cleanly dead.

Teddy looked up as his brother goggled. He'd been right: his brother was completely whacked, eyes wide, mouth open.

Slowly, horribly, a grin spread across Terry's face. His teeth and eyes gleamed.

'Yeah,' he said, raising his shotgun and aiming from the hip, pulling both triggers at once, 'and *I'm gonna shoot his cow.*'

Terry's shotgun made a noise Teddy would hear for months.

I heard somebody tell this story in a common room at the University of Sussex in the late seventies and assumed it was a modern legend, and that I'd hear endless variations of it along the lines of the dead-granny-on-the-roofrack story. Actually, it never has turned up, so I thought it worth recording for posterity. I used some left-over characters from my novel *Jago*, who turned out to fit their roles surprisingly well.

The Pierce-Arrow Stalled, And . . .

. . . rolled a dozen yards, then settled into dusty ruts. North of San Luis Obispo, the coast road was primitive, many sections still unpaved. As the wheel wrenched in his hands, Roscoe 'Fatty' Arbuckle felt the engine under the sleek hood choke and die. Long as a truck, the Pierce-Arrow was newly-delivered, a $25,000 custom-built toy with full bar and solid silver accessories. 'Of course the car's four times the size of anyone else's,' he'd explained, 'I'm four times as big as the average guy.'

The jolt woke up Lowell Sherman. In jauntily rude tones, the actor said 'These *special* jobs are *less* reliable than *factory* models. All the attention to *fripperies* means *essentials*, like *wheels* and *engines*, get *neglected*.'

The motor strangled again. 'She won't turn over,' Roscoe complained.

Fischbach, the other passenger, slumped gloomily against the thousand-dollar upholstery. The director, a last-minute addition to the expedition, had been fidgety ever since they'd left Los Angeles. 'There are no coyotes out here, are there?' he asked.

For a minute, they just sat. After four hours, the leather seats were hot and greasy as fresh-fried bacon. Roscoe felt a layer of gritty sweat between his bulk and his clothes; fat was his fortune, but it literally weighed him down. He tried again, turning the key with deliberate smoothness. The engine didn't even choke.

They were many miles from the nearest town. Here, where the desert met the sea, there was nothing. They hadn't seen another automobile for nearly an hour.

He opened his door and squeezed out. His belly hung like an anvil from his spine, pulling him towards the dirt as he bent over the hood. Fishbach and Sherman stood around. The metal catch seared Roscoe's fat fingers. As the hood sprang up, bad-tasting smoke belched. If this were one of his features, his face would now be blacked like a minstrel's.

'Looks like we *won't* be making the *party* in San *Francisco*,' said Sherman. Roscoe had to agree.

Fischbach muttered, as if he'd known the trip would end in disaster.

By 1921, Hollywood was generally conceded to be Sodom and Gomorrah re-erected among orange groves. Now America was dry, the attention of the professionally moral was drawn to the last bastion of sin: motion pictures. There was confusion in pulpit and editorial as to whether the vociferously condemned immorality was found on the screen in the heated embraces of Rudolph

Valentino and Agnes Ayres in *The Sheik*, or at wild parties hosted by the stars, where passions were reputed to be even more heated. The true cause of censorious ire was indeed the off-screen activities of young men and women who, thanks to a new-made art, were the idols of youth. But, short of reviving the ducking-stool and public stocks, little could be done to regulate the behaviour of private citizens in private pools and palaces. Thus the voice of anger was raised against the movies themselves; sermon and column inch insisted Hollywood must clean up its act. However, sixty million Americans liked their pictures just the way they were.

To the rapt masses, who violated the Volstead Act as regularly as they purchased picture show tickets, Nita Naldi could display as many inches of above-the-knee skin as she wished; Mr Hyde could be as horrible as it was possible for John Barrymore to make him; and Cecil B. De Mille would be remiss were his camera to stay outside the doors of the bedrooms and bathrooms where the most interesting moments of his films invariably took place. But even those who paid rapt attention to sheets slipping from the shoulders of the Talmadge sisters tutted over each fresh scandal: the suicide (in *Paris*!) of starlet Olive Thomas, reputedly in despair over her husband's devotion to cocaine; the marriage of Charlie Chaplin to a pregnant sixteen-year-old; the quickie divorce of Mary Pickford and her hasty remarriage to a more important leading man, Douglas Fairbanks. In 1917, Los Angeles passed an ordinance providing for the censorship of motion pictures according to the whims of a council appointed by the city's political machine. Though never enforced, this precedent raised the spectre, deeply feared by studio heads who knew outside regulation would hurt their wallets, of a national body constituted by federal government to pass judgment on the content of films. Costly scenes would have to be reshot, exciting storylines would have to be toned down, expensive footage would have to be jettisoned.

In the summer of 1921, Adolph Zukor, president of Paramount Pictures, convened a meeting attended by Jesse L. Lasky, Lewis Selznick, Louis B. Mayer, Marcus Loew, William Fox and Samuel Goldwyn. It was decided the solution was that the industry itself should fund and operate a self-regulatory body with an unimpeachably moral figurehead. Through attorney Charles Pettijohn, the moguls approached Will H. Hays, Postmaster General in the Administration of President Warren Gamaliel Harding, offering him upwards of $115,000 *per annum* to head an office which would oversee the output of all studios, insisting on rigid standards of on-screen morality. Pettijohn suggested Hays should serve as a twentiety-century Savonarola and preside over a bonfire of the vanities fuelled by the prints of corrupt films. The studio bosses did not understand his remark but, experienced with inflammable film stock, conceded such an event would provide a spectacular blaze. Hays declined the position, allowing that citizens' groups protesting immoral pictures had a legitimate concern but that 'all problems are of such a degree as to warrant no outside interference'. Privately, Hays told Pettijohn he would only take up the offer if there were one case, with nation-wide publicity calling attention to the situation in Hollywood, that would prompt the public, who at the time felt nothing either way, to call for censorship. The lawyer took Hays' refusal back to the moguls and, wrapped up in their endless byzantine plotting against each other, they quietly dropped the issue.

Catriona Kaye, *Libido in America:*
A Social History of Hollywood (1953)

'You said there'd be a *party*,' she complained.

Semnacher was fed up. If Virgie didn't pan out soon, he'd drop her from his roster. He'd been around show folk from the vaudeville days and knew a lot of 'saints', but she took the biscuit. Only a day ago, she was on an operating table getting rid of a baby. Now she wanted to go to a party and spree on bathtub hootch. In her twenty-five years, she had put out for at least a thousand men. If it were possible to sleep her way to stardom, she would manage it. Only she wouldn't.

She pouted, nickel-size red dots on her china doll cheeks. Her full lower lip was out. Semnacher looked about the lobby of the St Francis. Mr Arbuckle was expected, he'd been told, but had not yet arrived. He was overdue. The agent suspected the Labor Day party was off. Virgie, who'd painted herself to impress the big shots, was going to be disappointed. She'd celebrate by going out and giving somebody gonorrhea. Probably get knocked up and be back at the Wakefield Sanatorium. She was getting to be a regular client of the best known – if not the best, to judge by the look of Virgie – abortionist in San Francisco.

'Let's skedaddle to a speak,' she said. 'This is the dregs.'

She turned to stomp off, just in time to collide with a bellhop's cart. Semnacher heard his client go 'oof' as a brass-cornered trunk sunk into her abdomen. He didn't reach her in time to keep her on her feet. Blood spotted her dress over the crotch. She clamped her teeth in pain. The hop goggled, trying to apologise. There was no need, it wasn't his fault. Semnacher told the kid to go get a doctor.

A week later, Virginia Rappé was dead. Dr Melville Rumwell, her attending physician, listed cause of death as complications from a ruptured bladder, notably peritonitis. He omitted to report the true cause was most likely a botched abortion which he himself had performed.

Garbo is *The Temptress* (1926).

In a minor panic over the smoke-trails of scandal that escaped after the mysterious, and little-reported, death of director William Desmond Taylor in 1922, Zukor again entreated Pettijohn to approach his old friend. Will H. Hays had other concerns and definitively refused the renewed offer. Besieged by the successive breaking waves of the Teapot Dome Affair, President Harding was asked if he could point to *anyone* in his cabinet whose reputation was spotless. Wearily, he singled out his Postmaster. Hays was not as pure as the press believed; he had accepted a $75,000 'gift' and a $185,000 'loan' from oilman Harry Sinclair, the architect of Teapot Dome, as a reward for chairing the Republican National Committee that had secured the nomination for Harding. Nevertheless Hays emerged as the 'clean man' of the Administration; he can be credited with persuading Harding to serve out his term quietly, and regulating his colleagues by serving as Hatchet Man in the Anti-Trust Drive of '23. In 1924, Hays became Vice-President, serving under the almost silent Calvin Coolidge for four years; in his every spare moment, he conspired to put himself in the White House. He barely had time to go to the movies, much less consider going to Hollywood to take up a dead-end sinecure.

Catriona Kaye, *Libido in America:*
A Social History of Hollywood (1953)

Garbo in *Love* (1927).

At the 1928 Republican Convention, Hays bid successfully for the nomination and gracefully accepted the defeated Herbert Hoover on to his ticket. The election was fought on a single issue; whether or not to repeal the Volstead Act. So public a moralist as Will H. Hays could not conceivably come out in favour of drink. The Democratic candidate, inescapably wet, thus garnered the liquid vote, forcefully arguing that a law which made criminals of nine tenths of the population should not remain in force.

The Democrat and Gloria Swanson (with whom he was never linked in the Hearst press lest Pulitzer papers link William Randolph Hearst with Marion Davies) hosted a lavish pre-election party at which bootleg booze flowed so freely even the lax Los Angeles police had to take note. Hays tried to make capital of the candidate's arrest, but the public noted that, along with the jovial Boston Irishman, charges were levelled against all their favourite screen personalities: Douglas Fairbanks, Richard Barthelmess, Mary Miles Minter, Lon Chaney, Buster Keaton, 'Fatty' Arbuckle, Mae Murray. When the case came to trial, the distinguished defendants, many of whom engaged in pleasant banter with starstruck officers of the court, were each fined the sum of one dollar and dismissed.

After a third recount, Hays conceded the election. Joseph Patrick Kennedy was duly sworn in as the thirty-first President of the United States of America.

Catriona Kaye, *Libido in America: A Social History of Hollywood* (1953)

Garbo Talks! *Anna Christie* (1930).

During the second half of the twenties and well into the talkie era, there was considerable competition among female stars in regard to nudity. The game seemed to be who could get naked soonest, stay naked longest. Gloria Swanson, Pola Negri, Barbara La Marr and Clara Bow were regularly in states that made Theda Bara, sex siren of the 'teens, blanch. The true contest was between directors; fans followed the bitter feud of Cecil B. De Mille and Erich von Stroheim as each pushed back the limits of what was acceptable. While De Mille presided over a succession of screen-filling orgies, intent on cramming more naked people into one huge set than were ever assembled in the most depraved potentate's harem, von

Stroheim would constantly one-up his rival by staging bedroom scenes of startling intimacy and conviction. De Mille was obsessed with mere scale, the martinet genius sneered, but was a provincial with no imagination. With a curl of the lip, Von Stroheim conceded the only director worthy of sharing his podium as the Master of Sin was Ernst Lubitsch, of the famed 'touch that means so much'.

During von Stroheim's *Salammbô*, audiences were unable to believe Valentino and Swanson were not actually engaged in vigorous intercourse. *Justine and Juliette*, von Stroheim's first talking picture, offered Janet Gaynor as Justine and Louise Brooks as Juliette, with George Arliss as the Marquis de Sade and von Stroheim as Satan. It would have been banned in nineteen states were it not for a federal ruling overturning the power of local authorities to 'suppress works of proven artistic merit'. Despite Kennedy's much-resented intervention on behalf of his pet industry, which led to the burning of movie palaces in Boston and Birmingham, *Justine and Juliette* became the most successful film of all time, breaking the fifteen-year-old record of *Birth of a Nation*. It swept the third Academy Awards ceremony, taking Oscar statuettes for the production, direction, Arliss, Gaynor and Brooks (sharing Best Actress), Interior Decoration and Sound Recording. When Great Britain and Germany banned the import of *Justine and Juliette* and other 'immoral' pictures, there were protests by intellectuals angered at the silencing of a voice as great as von Stroheim's and by film fans infuriated by the loss of a chance to see a fabled 'hot' movie.

In both countries the film was shown by special licence; a print was later discovered in Hermann Göring's personal archive.

For all the attention garnered by the erect nipples of Mae Clarke in *Waterloo Bridge* and the lush posterior of Miriam Hopkins in *Dr Jekyll and Mr Hyde*, not to mention an oiled Myrna Loy horse-whipping a victim to ecstasy in *Mask of Fu Manchu* and Charles Laughton kissing Jackie Cooper on the mouth in *Sign of the Cross*, there were still limits. The areas of the human anatomy observable in movies were as rigidly defined and patrolled as the frontiers laid down by a Balkan peace treaty. However, as history had shown, frontiers were always on the move and, in time of emergency, liable to disappear entirely. 1932, the movies' most licentious year, saw the President's federal aid programmes in collapse, a second Wall Street crash and the growth of William Dudley Pelley's Silver Shirts. Unthinkably, movie attendances were falling. Many people stayed at home and listened to talking boxes.

It was time for the last taboo to be tested, and in *King Kong* the fig leaves finally came off. In the jungles of Skull Island, Kong clutched the heroine in his huge paw and, delicately as a smaller character might peel a grape, divested her of her already-tattered dress. Then, in the most often-reproduced image in thirties' cinema, the hairy fist opened, presenting on a palm-platter the totally naked girl, legs slightly apart, eyes wide in surprised ecstasy.

Catriona Kaye, *Libido in America: A Social History of Hollywood* (1953)

Garbo Strips! *The Painted Veil* (1934).

Melvin Purvis stood at the back of the auditorium, by the main exit. DA William Powell was prosecuting gambler Clark Gable. The girl, who had slept with both of them and probably the court ushers besides, was pretty upset about things. Movies were dumber than ever.

The G-Man concentrated on the audience, not the picture. Dillinger was in the crowd somewhere. And with him Anna Sage, a Rumanian madame who'd agreed to finger him in return for leniency in her deportation hearing. Also Polly Hamilton, a waitress rumoured to be Johnny's girl of the week.

Sage was wearing a red dress. As the show let out, she would pass Purvis. Then he was supposed to light a cigar to signal the agents staking out the Biograph. In a precise move which would give that fairy J. Edgar a hard-on, the G-Men would close on their man and take him down. If Johnny wanted to shoot it out, Purvis would oblige. None of the men on the Dillinger Squad expected the outlaw to face trial. Purvis also reckoned the Sage deal was phony; Hoover would have her packed off to Cluj before she could blab her part in the downfall of Public Enemy Number One. This was a Bureau pinch, credit would not be shared. There was a war on between Hoover's Bureau of Investigation and Ness's FSF; and since Ness, the President's blue-eyed Mr Law, brought in Capone, Hoover, lagging behind, wanted to claim this score for himself.

Gable was in prison, prowling behind bars, spitting defiance. Powell knew the homicide for which Gable was convicted was justified, but he was obliged to call for the chair. Any DA that pally with a mobster was dirty, Purvis knew. A few years back, the movie would have hushed it up, but an earlier scene had shown Powell taking a bribe from his friend, fixing a concealed weapon beef.

The movie was nearly through. Although clocked at ninety-three minutes, *Manhattan Melodrama* seemed to run longer than the Ring Cycle. The con threatened Powell, promising to spill the dirt in a last-minute confession. The DA took out a phial and poured it down Gable's throat. He called for guards, claiming the hood was trying to kill himself with acid. Gable wouldn't be singing now, his vocal cords were eaten out. Purvis was impressed: the curl of smoke from the dripping ruin that had been a mouth was authentic. He'd once seen a frail acid-sloshed by Charlie Floyd; the movie effect was identical. The warders dragged Gable down the Last Mile to the Death House.

All around, people were readying to leave, gathering coats and hats. Purvis's hand was in his jacket, fingering the cigar. A girl, complaining that this movie was too rough, pushed out early, bewildered date in tow.

The finish was a kicker, Gable's eyeballs cooking as they hit him with the juice. He jittered against the straps, moustache aflame. A scream scratched and Gable's head exploded in a shower of grey sludge. Purvis had never seen anyone get the chair, but guessed this was an exaggeration.

The end title rolled and the house lights went up. His hands were sweat-slick. The next minutes would make him the most famous lawman in America after J.

Edgar Fruitbowl and the Gang-Busting Ness Monster. He stepped into the foyer, surveying the emerging crowds. Women were shaken, the men nervously laughing. Finally a red dress appeared, with Anna Sage inside it. She was alone, her face a study in conflicting agonies.

'It vas Polly,' she explained, 'she vas upset . . . by the thing vith the acid . . . she valk out . . . she drag Johnny out . . .'

Purvis wheeled about, pulling his automatic. All around, agents did the same. In the crowds, they could not see the Public Enemy. People scattered in panic. A lot of G-Men would be posted to Alaska.

'Johnny,' Sage whined, 'he is gone, no . . . ?'

Purvis took his cigar, bit it, and spat out the end, spattering wet tobacco over a poster. A brown stain obliterated Gable's grin.

Following *King Kong*, complete nudity and bizarre sex were linked with a certain genre, a cross-breed of pulp adventure, monster fantasy, primitive eroticism and dark poetry. The first male member in mainstream movies belonged to Johnny Weissmuller, who removed his loincloth for a healthy underwater embrace in *Tarzan and His Mate*. Among the highlights of the 'Jungle Jiggle' cycle were Victor Fleming's *Red Dust*, with Gable joined in a muddy monsoon threesome by Harlow and Mary Astor; James Whale's *She*, with Louise Brooks, greatest star of the age, as the ancient princess whose embrace reduces Randolph Scott to a smoking skeleton; and von Sternberg's *The Rape of Helen*, with Marlene Dietrich extensively abused by Ronald Colman at the outset but slowly emasculating him into her self-destructive slave. When Harry Cohn insisted Frank Capra shoot scenes of the tantric rites of Shangri-La for *Lost Horizon*, James Hilton unsuccessfully sued Columbia for besmirching his novel. A consequence of the popularity of these pictures was a polarisation of public taste. More sophisticated audiences responded less to the films than to satire at the expense of their absurdities in Busby Berkeley's *Roman Scandals*, *Dinosaur Dames* and *Ziegfeld Cavegirl*. In 1939 Hal Roach produced *One Million B.C.*, the most elaborate of its genre since *King Kong*. He neglected to provide much in the way of special effects monsters, knowing fans would mainly be attracted by an artistic recreation of the times before clothes were invented, with superb specimens Victor Mature and Carole Landis demonstrating the rough-and-tumble lovemaking of Piltdown Man. While receipts for Roach's movie in the cities were slightly disappointing, the appetite for *exotica* held up in suburban and rural theatres, prompting the much-quoted *Variety* headline 'Nabes Crave Cave Babes'.

Catriona Kaye, *Libido in America:*
A Social History of Hollywood (1953)

After shooting the President, Bruno Richard Hauptmann, an unemployed carpenter who'd recently broken with the Silver Shirts, took refuge in a New Jersey picture house. Jack Warner was perversely proud the assassin chose a double bill of Warner Brothers' reissues, *I Am a Fugitive From a Chain Gang* and *Wild Boys of the Road*. Warner deemed his studio's output a force for change and debate, on a par with the New York and Washington press.

Orson Welles listened to the sales pitch. Warner strolled about his office, which was the size of the Union Station Men's Room and smelled about the same, pausing under framed posters for notable releases, commenting on each like a Long Island host introducing his ancestors to a social-climbing guest.

'After *Fugitive*, Robert Burns was granted an unconditional pardon and chain gangs were abolished throughout the South. After *Little Caesar* and *Public Enemy*, the President – God rest him, the sonofabitch – appointed Elliot Ness head of the Federal Strike Force. That means Capone got nailed because we made a picture. After *Waiting For Lefty*, membership of the American Federation of Labor almost doubled . . .'

That might be true but Warner would rather cut his throat than let a union get real power on his lot. An ex-bootlegger who knew the underworld score, Kennedy had helped keep IATSE off the moguls' necks by having Ness indict Benjamin Siegel and the other mugs who tried to muscle in. Some said that was why the President had been knocked off. That was what Howard Hawks was rumoured to be alleging in *JPK*, the hush-hush project he and Howard Hughes had shooting at RKO, with Cary Grant as Ness and Karloff as Hauptmann.

'President Coughlin has personally asked us to make a picture about the way they're treating priests in Mexico,' Warner declared. 'We've got Curtiz on it, with Muni as the pastor shot by Pancho Villa. If we go to war, movies will take us there.'

Welles wondered if that was a good idea, but the thought of a medium with such *power* was intoxicating.

'Writers fight to work here, ever since we let Fitzgerald make *Tender is Night* the way he wanted. All them books they said couldn't be done, we did: *Sun Also Rises*, *Lady Chatterley*, *Postman Always Dings Twice*. And we didn't clean 'em up neither. We got the full set: Bill Faulkner, Ben Hecht, Cliff Odets. We let Fonda make that picture about hoboes on motorcycles with all the crazy music and the weird ending the kids went wild for. Let the rest of the town serve up tits and ass, we're the studio with balls.'

Welles was intriged. Broadway was sewed up by old farts who thought Arthur Wing Pinero a dangerous radical, and even radio was too small for what he wanted to do. Hollywood hadn't really changed; the studios still stumbled in the dark for something that would sell. Even the greats weren't immune: von Stroheim couldn't get a job since *Cimarron*, the epic Western that lost more money than any other movie since *Intolerance*. But the *potential* was there. Hawks showed that, and Jack Ford and a couple of others. And it was a hell of a train set.

'So, Boy Wonder, what do you want to make? Name any book, and I'll buy it. Name a star, I'll get him. Name anything.'

He was tempted to suggest *Dr Faustus*, using split-screen to play both Faustus and Mephistopheles. Then he pondered *Heart of Darkness*. No, there was only one choice. Like everyone else, he'd read it that year.

'What'll it be?' Warner asked. 'What's your dream movie?'

'*Gone With the Wind*, Jack.'

Warner stuck out his hand and flexed his fingers for the shake.

'Deal.'

The institution in 1937, at the insistence of President Charles Coughlin, of a Ratings Board was intended to curb an industry even advocates insisted had got wildly out of hand. Actually the Board served to sanction even more excess: pictures awarded an 'A' certificate, which barred children under sixteen, were effectively allowed, under the constitutional right to freedom of speech, to represent anything short of real-life murder and bestiality. Those who had gone as far as they thought possible went further; in Technicolor and on giant screens, Hollywood productions were able to show what had hitherto only been seen in 8 mm at firehouse smokers. The most celebrated scene of the late thirties came in Michael Curtiz and William Keighley's *The Adventures of Casanova* when Mae West demonstrated her throat capacity by swallowing to the root Errol Flynn's justly legendary attribute.

Catriona Kaye, *Libido in America:*
A Social History of Hollywood (1953)

'Are you really Dillinger?' the kid asked.

Johnny nodded. 'The same.'

'And you've been hiding out here for . . . how long?'

'Since before everybody got the same idea, son.'

The kid beamed and shook his head. He was a handsome pug, this long-legged hobo. He'd have done good in the movies before they went to hell. Not really a kid, either. His name was Jimmy Stewart.

They were up around the fire that burned most nights in the middle of Agry. It'd been a ghost town five years ago, when Johnny came to get away from the G-Men. Now its population was up to gold rush numbers.

As American servicemen were poured into the so-called Holy War in Mexico, more and more kids drifted in. Inverting W.C. Fields' catchphrase, the draft-protestors cried 'give this fucker an even break'. Nearly a million young men disappeared from the record books. They aped Henry Fonda and Woody Guthrie in *Blowin' Down This Road*, gathering in abandoned railroad sidings and backwoods towns. Several states had chosen to tolerate these shadow communities, but there were still Sheriff's Deputies with baseball bats.

'Don't you want to be a soldier-boy, son?'

'Not in this war, Mr Dillinger. I don't mind what Cárdenas does in his own country. It's not the fight I care for. That one's in Europe and the Pacific.'

Most Americans felt that way. The war was Coughlin's crusade and plenty, of all political persuasions, wanted out of it. The President was just a jumped-up radio preacher filling the shoes of a martyr. Some wanted America to tend its own garden and win back its lost children; some thought it'd need all its armies for the big war that seemed more likely every day.

In the firelight, Stewart's face was set. Johnny thought he looked a little like a hero. Hollywood had missed something.

Garbo Fucks! *Ninotchka* (1939).

The climax couldn't top the scene where Rhett laid

Scarlett down on the red stairs, ripped open her clothes and rutted with her for a full five minutes. The King reputedly wanted his crown back and insisted he be allowed to go better than Flynn. Since that steamy interlude, the audience had been getting restless as tragedy piled upon tragedy. The plantation burned as the Jayhawkers encroached. The guerillas were played by Hollywood Mexicans.

It boiled down to whether you were interested in the love or the war, Roscoe supposed. The love stuff was over in the plot, but the war went on. It was supposed to be the Civil War but he knew better. When a city burned or a wounded soldier limped, he thought not of Atlanta in 1864, but Tijuana in 1940. This was the movie that summed it up, the feelings of a whole generation. A new generation.

Roscoe, a jolly relic from an innocent age, was bewildered, and a little blue. His films had been for children; even the grown-ups of 1922 were children next to the hard-eyed youngsters scattered through the auditorium of Grauman's Chinese.

Orson Welles was the new von Stroheim, Keaton claimed. As powerfully as he felt assaulted by *Gone With the Wind*, Roscoe agreed. On his best days, he had never been one-fourth the director this kid – another fatty, they said - was. If he grew a heart as he got older, he might be better than Griffith, than Chaplin.

Tears welled in Leigh's eyes and the music swelled. She was too thin to be really beautiful. Her face was expressive and angular rather than plumply lovely the way Mabel Normand or Mary Miles Minter had been.

Still, she was radiant. And she had a voice. Roscoe felt uninvited tears in his own eyes.

Gable strode away from Tara, orange skies outlining him. Movies were in colour now, too. They roared and they blazed. Roscoe missed Nickelodeons, gingham dresses, candy canes. He missed being young and a star too.

'How shall I fight on without you?' Leigh asked. 'What about the war?'

Turning, flashing the famous grin, Gable said, 'Frankly my dear, I don't give a fuck.'

All around, the audience cheered. The commotion was so loud that the closing narration was inaudible. Roscoe, skilled from years in silent pictures, tried to read Leigh's lips, but the camera pulled away and she turned into a black silhouette.

I write about film for the same reason Arthur C. Clarke writes about space exploration. As a writer of non-fiction, I've spent a great deal of time thinking about the cinema, and ideas just come along by association. I've also written quite a few alternate histories; and, dealing with twentieth-century America, the cinema often comes to mind. This story throws a small pebble into the past and watches ripples spread . . .

In the real world, Roscoe made it to that party, Virgie died in the same way upstairs rather than in the lobby, blame was unjustly accorded, though a jury later aquitted Arbuckle, Hays took the job as 'Czar of the Rushes', Shirley Temple replaced Mae West as a Top Box Office attraction in 1933, John Dillinger (probably) saw the end of *Manhattan Melodrama*, Father Coughlin's call for War with Mexico was ignored, Jimmy Stewart got work in the movies, Hauptmann was executed for other crimes, Welles' dream project was *Citizen Kane* and David O. Selznick made *Gone with the Wind*. The Arbuckle case affected the evolution of an art form and entertainment industry, though the real clamp-down did not come until nearly ten years afterwards.

The Hays Code, and the mindset that created and enforced it, was not an unambiguously bad thing, as scores of outstanding films made under its strictures show, but there was a notable hobbling of certain types of movie. Compare the freshness and sensuality of a pre-code film like the 1932 *Dr Jekyll and Mr Hyde* with the stifling obfuscations of the 1941 remake, which would desperately like to be steamily sophisticated but just comes across as stodgy and silly. There certainly were personalities (Louise Brooks is a good example) for whom there was no space in thirties films; I'd exchange the entire filmography of Marie Dressler (a major star at the time) for just one more Brooks vehicle on a par with *Pandora's Box*. Imagine *Apocalypse Now* redone in accordance with the Hays Code ('Saigon, heck!'), but balance that by wondering how *To Have and Have Not* could be any better freed from censor restrictions (When they turned down the ending of Hemingway's novel, Howard Hawks asked the censors to suggest a finish they *would* approve of.) If Roscoe had missed the party, movies might not have been better but they would have been different.

Übermensch!

On the way from the aeroport, the cab driver asked him if he had ever been to Metropolis before.

'I was born here,' Avram said, German unfamiliar in his mouth. So many years of English in America, then Hebrew in Israel. In the last forty years, he'd used Portuguese more than his native tongue. He had never been a German in his heart, no more than he was now an Israeli. That was one thing Hitler, and his grandparents, had been right about.

He had been – he *was* – a Jew.

This was not the Metropolis he remembered. Gleaming skycrapers still rose to the clouds, aircars flitting awkwardly between them, but on this grey early spring day, their facades were shabby, uncleaned. The robotrix on traffic duty outside the aeroport had been limping, dysfunctional, sparks pouring from her burnished copper thigh. Standing on the tarmac, Avram had realised that the pounding in the ground was stilled. The subterranean factories and power plants had been destroyed or shut down during the War.

'That's where the wall was,' the driver said as they passed a hundred yards of wasteland which ran through the city of the future as if one of Mr Reagan's orbital lasers had accidentally cut a swath across Germany. The satellite weapons were just so much more junk now, Avram supposed. The world that needed the orbital laser was gone.

Just like the world which needed his crusade.

Perhaps, after today, he could spend his remaining years playing chess with a death-diminished circle of old friends, then die from the strain of playing competitive video games with his quick-fingered grandchildren.

'That used to be East Metropolis,' the driver said.

Avram tried to superimpose the city of his memory on these faceless streets. So much of Metropolis was post-war construction, now dilapidated. The *cafés* and gymnasia of his youth were twice forgotten. There wasn't a McDonald's on every corner yet, but that would come. A boarded-up shack near the wall, once a security checkpoint, was covered in graffiti. Amid the anti-Russian, pro-democracy slogans, Avram saw a tiny red swastika. He had been seeing posters for the forthcoming elections, and could not help but remember who had taken office the last time a united Germany held a democratic election.

He thanked the driver, explaining 'I just wanted to see where it was.'

'Where now, sir?'

Avram got the words out, 'Spandau Prison.'

The man clammed up, and Avram felt guilty. The driver was a child, born and raised with the now never-to-be-germinated seeds of World War Three. Avram's crusade was just an embarassing old reminder. When these people talked about the bad old days, they meant when the city was divided by concrete. Not when it was the shining flame of fascism.

The prison was ahead, a black mediaeval castle among plain concrete block buildings. The force field shone faintly emerald. Apparently the effect was more noticable from outer space. John Glenn had mentioned it, a fog lantern in the cloud cover over Europe.

The cab could go no further than the perimeter, but he was expected. From the main gate, he was escorted by a young officer – an American – from the Allied detachment that had guarded the man in the fortress for forty-five years.

Avram thought of the Allies, FDR embracing Uncle Joe at Yalta. Old allies, and now – thanks to the baldpate with the blotch – allies anew. If old alliances were being resumed, old evils – old enmities – could stir too.

Captain Siegel called himself Jewish, and babbled sincere admiration. 'As a child, you were my hero, sir. That's why I'm here. When you caught Eichmann, Mengele, the Red Skull—'

'Don't trust heroes, young man,' he said, hating the pomposity in his voice, 'that's the lesson of this green lantern.'

Siegel was shut up, like the cab driver had been. Avram was instantly sorry, but could not apologise. He wondered when he had turned into his old professor, too scholarly to care for his pupils' feelings, too unbending to see the value of ignorant enthusiasm.

Probably, it had started with the tattoo on his arm. The bland clerk with the bodkin was the face that, more than any other, stayed with him as the image of National Socialism. These days, almost all young men looked like the tattooist to Avram. The cab driver had, and now so did Captain Siegel. So did most of the guards who patrolled the corridors and grounds of this prison.

Not since Napoleon had a single prisoner warranted such careful attention.

'Jerome,' Siegel said, summoning a sergeant. 'Show Mr Blumenthal your rifle.'

The soldier held out his weapon for inspection. Avram knew little about guns, but saw this was out of the ordinary, with its bulky breech and surprisingly slender barrel. A green LED in the stock showed that it was fully charged.

'The beam-gun is just for *him*,' Siegel said.

'Ahh, the green stuff.'

Siegel smiled. 'Yes, the green stuff. I'm not a scientist . . .'

'Neither am I, any more.'

'It has something to do with the element's instability. The weapon directs particles. Even a glancing hit would kill him in a flash.'

Avram remembered Rotwang – one of 'our' Germans in the fifties – toiling over the cyclotron, trying to wrestle free the secrets of the extra-terrestrial element. Rotwang, with his metal hand and shock of hair, was dead of leukaemia, another man of tomorrow raging against his imprisonment in yesterday.

Jerome took the rifle back, and resumed his post.

'There've been no escape attempts,' Avram commented.

'There couldn't be.'

Avram nearly laughed. 'He surrendered, Captain. Green stuff or not, this place couldn't hold him if he wanted to leave.'

Siegel – born when the prisoner had already been in his cell twenty years - was shocked. 'Mr Blumenthal, careful . . .'

Avram realised what it was that frightened the boy in uniform, what made every soldier in this place nervous twenty-four hours a day.

'He can hear us, can't he? Even through the lead shields?'

Siegel nodded minutely, as if he were the prisoner, trying to pass an unseen signal to a comrade in the exercise yard.

'You live with the knowledge all your life,' Avram said, tapping his temple, 'but you never think what it means. That's science, Captain. Taking knowledge you've always had, and *thinking what it means* . . .'

After the War, he had been at Oak Ridge, working with the green stuff. Then the crusade called him away. Others had fathered the K-Bomb. Teller and Rotwang built bigger and better Doomsday Devices – while Oppie went into internal exile and the Rosenbergs to the electric chair – thrusting into a future so bright you could only look at it through protective goggles. Meanwhile, Avram Blumenthal had been cleaning up the last garbage of the past. So many names, so many Nazis. He had spent more time in Paraguay and Brazil than in New York and Tel Aviv.

But it had been worth it. His tattoo would not stop hurting until the last of the monsters was gone. If monsters they were.

'Through here, sir,' Siegel said, ushering him into a bare office. There was a desk, with chairs either side of it.

'You have one hour.'

'That should be enough. Thank you.'

Siegel left the room. Even after so short a time on his legs, Avram felt better sitting down. Nobody lives forever.

Almost nobody.

When they brought him in, he filled the room. His chest was a solid slab under his prison fatigues, and the jaw was an iron horseshoe. Not the faintest trace of grey in his blue-black hair, the kiss-curl still a jaunty comma. The horn-rimmed glasses couldn't disguise him.

Avram did not get up.

'Curt Kessler?' he asked, redundantly.

Grinning, the prisoner sat down. 'You thought perhaps they had the wrong man all these years?'

'No,' he admitted, fussing with the cigarette case, taking out one of his strong roll-ups. 'Do you mind if I smoke?'

'Can't hurt me. I used to warn the children against tobacco, though.'

Avram lit up, and sucked bitter smoke into his lungs. The habit couldn't hurt him either, not any more.

'Avram the Avenger,' Kessler said, not without

admiration. 'I was wondering when they'd let you get to see me.'

'My request has been in for many years, but with the changes . . .'

The changes did not need to be explained.

'I confess,' Kessler said, 'I've no idea why you wanted this interview.'

Avram had no easy answer. 'You consented to it.'

'Of course. I talk to so few people these days. The guards are superstitious about me.'

Avram could understand that. Across the table, he could feel Kessler's strength. He remembered the old uniform, so familiar in the thirties. The light brown body-stocking, with black trunks, boots and cloak. A black swastika in the red circle on the chest. He'd grinned down from a hundred propaganda posters like an Aryan demi-god, strode through the walkways of Metropolis as Siegfried reborn with X-ray eyes.

Avram felt he owed Kessler an explanation. 'You're the last.'

Kessler's mouth flashed amusement. 'Am I? What about Ivan the Terrible?'

'A guard. Just a geriatric thug. Barely worth the bullet it'd take to finish him.'

'"Barely worth the bullet." I heard things like that so many times, Avram. And what of the *Führer*? I understand he could be regrown from tissue samples. In '45, Mengele—'

Avram laughed. 'There's no tissue left, Kessler. I burned Mengele's jungle paradise. The skin-scraps he had were of dubious provenance.'

'I understand genetic patterns can be reproduced exactly. I try to follow science, you know. If you keep an ear out, you pick things up. In Japan, they're doing fascinating work.'

'Not my field.'

'Of course. You're an atom man. You should have stayed with Rotwang. The Master Engineer needed your input. He could have overcome his distaste for your racial origins if you'd given him a few good suggestions. Without you, the K-Bomb was ultimately a dead end.'

'So?'

Kessler laughed. 'You are right. So what? It's hard to remember how excited you all were in the fifties about the remains of my home planet. Anything radioactive was highly stimulating to the Americans. To the Russians too.'

Avram couldn't believe this man was older than him. But, as a child, he had seen the brown streak in the skies, had watched the newsreels, had read the breathless reports in the *Tages Welt*.

'If things had been otherwise, I might have been Russian,' Kessler said. 'The Soviet Union is the largest country on the planet. If you threw a dart at a map of the world, you'd most likely hit it. Strange to think what it'd have been like if my little dart had missed Bavaria. Of course, I'd have been superfluous. The USSR already had its "man of steel". Maybe my dart should have struck the wheatfields of Kansas, or the jungles of Africa. I could have done worse than be raised by apes.'

'You admit, then, that you are him?'

220

Kessler took off his glasses, showing clear blue eyes. 'Has there ever really been any doubt?'

'Not when you didn't grow old.'

'Do you want me to prove myself? You have a lump of coal for me to squeeze?'

It hit Avram that this young-seeming man, conversing in un-accented German, was hardly even human. If Hitler hadn't got in the way, humanity might have found a champion in him. Or learned more of the stars than Willy Ley imagined.

'Why weren't you in the army? In some SS elite division?'

'Curt Kessler was – what is the American expression? – 4F. A weakling who wouldn't be accepted, even in the last days when dotards and children were being slapped in uniform and tossed against the juggernaut. I believe I did my best for my *Führer*.'

'You were curiously inactive during the war.'

Kessler shrugged. 'I admit my great days were behind me. The thirties were my time. Then, there seemed to be struggles worth fighting, enemies worth besting.'

'Only "seemed to be"?'

'It was long ago. Do you remember my enemies? Dr Mabuse? His criminal empire was like a spider's web. The *Führer* himself asked me to root it out and destroy it. He poisoned young Germans with drugs and spiritualism. Was I wrong to persecute him? And the others? Graf von Orlok, the *nosferatu*? Dr Caligari, and his somnambulist killers? The child-slayer they called "M"? Stephen Orlac, the pianist with the murderer's hands.'

Avram remembered, the names bringing back *Tages*

Welt headlines. Most of the stories had born the Curt Kessler byline. Everyone had wondered how the reporter knew so many details. Germany's criminals had been symptomatic creatures then, twisted and stunted in soul and body, almost an embodiment of the national sickness. And Kessler, no less than the straight-limbed blonds trotted out as exemplars of National Socialism, made the pop-eyed, needle-fingered, crook-backed fiends seem like walking piles of filth. As a child, Avram's nightmares had been of the whistling "M" and taloned *nosferatu*, not handsome tattooists and smart-uniformed bureaucrats. It was possible for a whole country to be wrong.

'They're all gone,' Kessler said, 'but they'll never go away really. I understand Mabuse's nightclub is due to re-open. The Westerners who've been flooding in since the wall came down like to remember the decadent days. They have the order of history wrong, and associate the cabarets with us, forgetting that we were pure in mind and body, that we closed down the pornographic spectacles. They'll have their doomrock rather than jazz, but the rot will creep back. Mabuse was like the hydra. I'd think he was dead or hopelessly mad, but he'd always come back, always with new devilry. Perhaps he'll return again. They never found the body.'

'And if he returns, will others come back?'

Kessler shrugged again, huge shoulders straining his fatigues. 'You were right. Adolf Hitler is dead, National Socialism with him. You don't need X-ray vision to see that.'

Avram knew Kessler could never get tired as he had got tired, but he wondered whether this man of steel was truly world-weary. Forty-five years of knowing everything and doing nothing could be as brutally ache-making as the infirmities visited upon any other old man.

'Tell me about your childhood.'

Kessler was amused by the new tack. 'Caligari always used to harp on about that, too. He was a strange kind of medieval Freudian, I suppose, digging into men's minds in search of power. He wanted to get me into his asylum, and pick me apart. We *are* shaped by our early lives, of course. But there's more to it than that. Believe me, I should know. I have a unique perspective.'

'There are no new questions for us, Kessler. We must always turn back to the old ones.'

'Very well, it's your hour. You have so few left, and I have so many. If you want old stories, I shall give you them. You know about my real parents. Everybody does. I wish I could say I remember my birthplace but I can't, any more than anyone remembers the first days of their life. The dart was my father's semen, the Earth my mother's womb. I was conceived when the dart ejaculated me into the forest. That is my first memory, the overwhelming of my senses. I could hear, see, smell and taste everything. Birds miles away, blades of grass close to, icy streams running, a wolf's dung attracting flies. I screamed. That was my first reaction to this Earth. My screams brought people to me.'

'Your parents?'

'Johann and Marte. They lived in the woods just outside Kleinberg. Berchtesgarten was barely an arrow's-reach away.'

'How were you raised?'

'There was a war. Johann and Marte had lost four true sons. So they kept the baby they found.'

'When did you realise you were different?'

'When my father beat me and I felt nothing. I knew then I was privileged. Later, when I joined the Party, I felt much the same. Sometimes, I would ask to be beaten, to show I could withstand it. There were those among us too glad to oblige me. I wore out whips with my back.'

'You left Kleinberg as a young man?'

'Everyone wanted to go to the big city. Metropolis was the world of the future. We would put a woman on the moon one day soon, and robots would do all our work. There would be floating platforms in the seas for refuelling aeroplanes, a transatlantic tunnel linking continents. It was a glorious vision. We were obsessed not with where we were going, but with how fast we would get there.'

'You – I mean, Curt – you became a reporter?'

'Poor, fumbling Curt. What a big oaf he was. I miss him very much. Reporters could be heroes in the thirties. I was on the *Tages Welt* when Per Weiss made it a Party paper. It's hard to remember when it was a struggle, when the Mabuses and the Orloks were in control and we were the revolutionaries. That was when it became exciting, when we knew we could make a difference.'

'When did you start . . .'

'My other career? An accident. Johann always tried to make me ashamed of what I was, insisted I keep myself hidden. That was the reason for the eyeglasses, for the fumbling idiocy. But "M" was at large, and I knew – knew with my eyes and ears – who he was. I could not catch him as Curt Kessler and the police would not listen to me, so the man inside came out.'

The man named "M" had been turned over to the police, eventually. There had been little left of him. He had spent the rest of his life in Caligari's asylum, in the cell next to the often-vacant room they reserved for Dr Mabuse. He never killed again, and he would have been unable to rape even if the opportunity arose.

'Why the uniform?'

Kessler smiled again, teeth gleaming ivory. 'We all loved uniforms, then. All Germans did. The cloak might have been excessive, but those were excessive times. Theatre commissionaires looked like Field Marshals. I was at the rallies, flying in with my torch, standing behind the *Führer*, making the speeches Luise wrote for me. All men want to be heroes.'

'You were a Party member? A Nazi?'

'Yes. Even before I came to Metropolis. We prided ourselves in Bavaria on seeing the future well before the decadents of the cities.'

'They say it was the woman who brought you into the Party?'

'Luise? No, if anything, she followed me. The real me, that is. Not Curt. She always despised Curt Kessler.'

'Was that difficult for you?'

'It was impossible,' Kessler smiled. 'Poor Luise. She was born to be a heroine, Avram. She might not have been blonde, but she had everything else. The eyes, the face, the limbs, the hips. She was born to make babies for the *Führer*. Goebbels was fond of her. She wrote many of his scripts before she began broadcasting herself. She was our Valkyrie then, an inspiration to the nation. She committed suicide in 1945. When the Russians were coming. Like many German women.'

'Luise Lang would have faced a War Crimes tribunal.'

'True. Her other Aryan quality was that she wasn't very bright. She was too silly to refuse the corruptions that came with privilege. She didn't mean any of the things she did, because she never thought them through.'

'Unlike you?'

'By then, I was thinking too much. We stopped speaking during the War. I could foresee thousands of differing futures, and was not inclined to do anything to make any of them come to pass. Goering asked me to forestall the Allies in Normandy, you know.'

'Your failure to comply was extensively documented at your own trial.'

'I could have done it. I could have changed the course of history. But I didn't.'

Avram applauded, slowly.

'You are right to be cynical, Avram. It's easier to do nothing than to change history. You could have given Truman the K-Bomb, but you went ghost-hunting in Paraguay.'

'I'm not like you,' he said, surprised by his own vehemence.

'No one is.'

'Don't be so sure.'

Kessler looked surprised. 'There've been other visitors? No, of course not. I'd have known. I scan the skies. Sometimes things move, but galaxies away. There were no other darts, no tests with dogs or little girls. Since

226

Professor Ten Brincken passed away, no one has even tried to duplicate me as a *homunculus*. That, I admit, was a battle. The distorted, bottle-grown image of me wore me out more than any of the others. More than Mackie Messer's green knives, more than Nosferatu's rat hordes, more even than Ten Brincken's artificial whore Alraune.'

Ten Brincken had been second only to Rotwang as the premier scientific genius of Metropolis. Either could have been the equal of Einstein if they had had the heart to go with their minds.

'I am reminded more and more of the twenties and thirties,' Kessler said. 'I understand they want to get the underground factories working again. Microchip technology could revive Rotwang's robots. *Vorsprung durch Technik*, as they say. The future is finally arriving. Fifty years too late.'

'You could be released to see it.'

The suggestion gave the prisoner pause. 'These glowing walls don't keep me in, Avram, they keep you out. I need my shell. I couldn't soar into the air any more. A missile would stop me as an arrow downs a hawk. The little men who rule the world wouldn't like me as competition.'

Avram had no doubt this man could make the world his own. If he chose to lead instead of follow.

'I've seen swastikas in this city,' Avram said. 'I've heard Germans say Hitler was right about the Jewish problem. I've seen Israelis invoke Hitler's holocaust to excuse their own exterminations. The world could be ready for you again.'

'Strength, Purity and the Aryan Way?'

'It could happen again.'

Kessler shook his head. 'No one eats worms twice, Avram. I was at the torchlight processions, and the pogroms. I wrestled the *nosferatu* beyond the sunrise, and I saw shopkeepers machine-gunned by Stormtroopers. I was at Berchtesgarten, and Auschwitz. I lost my taste for National Socialism when the stench of ovens was all I could smell. Even if I went to China or Saturn, I could still taste the human smoke. I surrendered, remember? To Eisenhower personally. And I've shut myself up here. Buried myself. Even the human race has learned its lesson.'

Avram understood how out of date the man of tomorrow's understanding was. 'You're an old man, Kessler. Like me. Only old men remember. In America, seventy-five percent of high school children don't know Russia and the United States fought on the same side in the Second World War. The lesson has faded. Germany is whole again, and Germans are grumbling about the Jews, the gypsies, the Japanese even. It's not just Germany. In Hungary, in Russia, in the Moslem countries, in America and Britain, in *Israel*, I see the same things happening. There's a terrible glamour to it. And *you're* that glamour. The children who chalk swastikas don't know what the symbol means. They don't remember the swastika from the flag, but from your chest. They make television mini-series about you.'

Kessler sat back, still as a steel statue. He could not read minds, but he could understand.

'When I was a boy, a little Jewish boy in Metropolis, I too looked up at the skies. I didn't know you hated me because of my religion, because of the religion my parents practised no more than I did. I wore a black blanket as a cloak, and wished I could fly, wished I could outrace a streamlined train, wished I could catch Mackie Messer. Do you remember the *golem*?'

Kessler did. 'Your rabbi Judah ben Bezalel raised the creature from clay in Prague, then brought it to Metropolis to kill the *Führer*. I smashed it.'

The echo of that blow still sounded in Avram's head.

'I saw you do it. I cheered you, and my playmates beat me. The *golem* was the monster, and you were the hero. Later, I learned different.'

He rolled up his shirtsleeve, to show the tattoo.

'I had already seen that,' Kessler said, tapping his eyes. 'I can see through clothing. It was always an amusing pastime. It was useful at the cabarets. I saw the singer, Lola—'

'After you killed the *golem*,' Avram continued, 'all the children took fragments of the clay. They became our totems. And the brownshirts came into the Jewish quarter and burned us out. They were looking for monsters, and found only us. My parents, my sisters, my friends. They're all dead. You had gone on to Nuremberg, to present Hitler with the scroll you snatched from the monster's chest.'

'I won't insult you by apologising.'

Avram's heart was beating twice its normal pace. Kessler looked concerned for him. He could look into another's chest, of course.

'There's nothing I could do to make reparation. Your

229

family is dead, but so is *my whole planet*. I have to live with the guilt. That's why I'm here.'

'But you are here, and as long as you remain, you're a living swastika. The fools out there who don't remember raise your image high, venerate you. I know you've been offered freedom by the Allies on six separate occasions. You could have flown out of here if you'd consented to topple Chairman Mao or Saddam Hussein, or become a living weather satellite, flitting here and there to avert floods and hurricanes. Some say the world needs its heroes. I say they're wrong.'

Kessler sat still for a long time, then finally admitted, 'As do I.'

Avram took the heavy metal slug from his cigarette case, and set it on the table between them.

'I've had this since I was at Oak Ridge. You wouldn't believe how much of the stuff Rotwang collected, even before they found a way to synthesise it. The shell is lead.'

The prisoner played with his glasses. His face was too open, too honest. His thoughts were never guarded. Sometimes, for all his intelligence, he could seem simple-minded.

'You can bite through lead,' Avram said.

'Bullets can't hurt me,' Kessler replied, a little of the old spark in his eyes.

'So you have a way out.'

Kessler picked up the slug, and rolled it in his hand.

'Without you in the world, maybe the fire won't start again.'

'But maybe it will. It started without me last time.'

'I admit that. That's why it's your decision, Curt.'

Kessler nodded, and popped the slug into his mouth. It distended his cheek like a boiled sweet.

'Was I really your hero?'

Avram nodded. 'You were.'

'I'm sorry,' Kessler said, biting through the lead, swallowing.

He did not fade away to mist like the *nosferatu*, nor fragment into shards like the *golem*. He did not even grow old and wither to a skeleton. He just died.

Guards rushed in, confused and concerned. There must have been a monitor in the room. They pointed guns at Avram, even though their beams couldn't hurt him. Doctors were summoned, with enough bizarre machinery to revive a broken doll or resurrect a *homunculus* from the chemical stew. They could do nothing.

Avram remembered the destruction of the *golem*. Afterwards, the brown streak had paused to wave at the children before leaping up, up and away into the skies of Metropolis. They had all been young then, and expected to live forever.

Captain Siegel was upset, and couldn't understand. Doubtless, his career would be wrecked because this thing had happened during his watch. The Russians would insist an American take the blame. Siegel kept asking questions.

'How did he die?'

'He died like a man,' Avram said. 'Which, all considered, was quite an achievement.'

The Blitz Spirit

The Shelter was already crowded when he arrived. A wedge of queue stood topside. Men in hats and wide-shouldered two-breasteds and women with cellophane raincoats over Austerity creations clustered and craned around the entrance. The ARP man on the door lifted the red velvet rope for Frankham without checking his clip-board. The queue muttered but he gave a familiar wave. Most of the civvies recognised him. They wouldn't be here if it weren't for his write-ups.

A barrage balloon caught the searchlight overhead, a low-lying and heavy cloud in December skies. From the depths, band music poured. Three shrills swung 'Don't Sit Under the Apple Tree'. He stood alone in the bare cage lift as it descended. He was always given elbow room. It was a sign of respect.

Peter Frankham saw himself in the burnished metal of the cage, looking Nigel Patrickish, with thin 'tache and slouch hat, gabardine draped over his shoulders, double-length of watchchain in his waistcoat and ballooning bags. He'd had the look for three months and it wasn't yet through.

The cage rattled open and a commissionaire let him into the Shelter proper.

'There was another bomb in Oxford Street,' someone said. 'Shut down the tube for hours.'

'Don't go on an' on an' on,' he said back.

The dance-floor thronged. Surplus bods huddled in the dark by the walls, tucking into plates of snoek, drinking bombers. Noise was all around: chatter, swing, clatter, siren whines, shrills.

He had passed a stretch of rubble in Oxford Street. It might have been the His Master's Voice shop. The wardens had it roped off and sludgy piles of debris gave off steam where fires had been put out. The whole street was blacked out, Christmas tat turned to sinister black shapes strung from lamp-posts.

Many in the crowd, men and women, wore uniform. Dancers had jackets undone, sweat-ringed as they jived and jitterbugged, knowing they could die any second. Chippies and touts worked the Shelter on a professional basis. Frankham could spot them a mile off. *Time Out* called him 'Caesar of the Spivs'.

He had no business here. Once he had written a place up, everyone else would go and his actual attendence would be surplus to schedule. But he liked to make snap inspections. Sometimes, he'd pick apart a hole he had built up. These were ephemeral times; nothing stood long. The music got faster.

The band – a young man in a flying helmet surrounded by his instrument panel, flicking switches – pin-balled through 'Coming In on a Wing and a Prayer' and the three shrills were off, replaced by a geezer with a painted tie that hung to his knees, an hour-glass-shaped purple coat and a cigar twice the size of the Old Man's.

The dancers collapsed exhausted and crowds surged in to fill their space. The band went oom-pah and the geezer wheezed through impersonations of Benito and Adolf, topping off his sound-bite of an act with 'Der Führer's Face'. The audience knew the routine, and joined in the chorus.

'When der Führer says, "We iss der master race",
We HEIL—'
An enormous collective oral wet fart resounded.
'HEIL—'
Again.
'Right in der Führer's face . . .'

The Shelter was on its last legs, Frankham thought. Retro was all very well, but it shaded too easily into camp.

He left without even sampling his complimentary drink. Outside, as the doors opened, an all-clear sounded.

About eleven, he stopped by Monty's for a coffee-shock. He wrapped a five-pound note in his ration coupon and got the real stuff. Black market, with five sugars. The brush-moustached orderly gave Frankham a smart salute and stumped off on a shrapnel-stiff leg.

'Bit of a prang last month,' he had explained as he plonked down Frankham's mug, sloshing a bit too much in the saucer.

Monty's was in the warrens of Soho, just across from the Windmill. From his place at the counter, Frankham could see the frontage. An audience disgorged from all exits, having just seen *Tonight and Every Night*. Many were whistling the hit, 'Seeing It Through'. The revue was doing better business than *Hello Playmates!* at the Dominion. There was a quote from Frankham on the marquee: 'It's tickety-boo!'

A child-sized figure in a gas mask, trailing a filthy foot of grown-up coat, crept in behind a punter and started rooting around in the neglected corners. The orderly gave an 'oi, you' and shooed the creature out.

'Kids,' he said, 'bless 'em.'

A professorial foreigner was mouthing off at a corner table, surrounded by nodding acolytes as he dipped biscuits in his tea. He had a Viennese beard and a dubious accent.

'Looking backwards is a comprehensible but perilous reaction to the chaos of the present,' Johnny Foreign declaimed. 'Faced with the direst circumstances, it is sometimes natural to wish to return to a time when similar hardships were endured only to be overcome . . .'

Frankham couldn't help but smile. Johnny Foreign was the spit and image of the sinister, sneaky figures on the framed posters behind the bar. CARELESS TALK COSTS LIVES. LOOSE LIPS SINK SHIPS. A definite morale-breaker and no mistake.

A bald little man sidled up to Frankham at the counter and opened his ratty Bud Flanagan coat. His many inside pockets were distended with compact 78s and wire-tape cassettes.

'Slightly bomb-damaged stock,' he whispered out of a corner of his mouth. 'Coupon or cash.'

He had all the sounds: George Formby, Hutch, Gracie Fields, Madonna's *Blitzkrieg*, the yank crooners, Hoagy.

Frankham waved the looter away. His wares still had gummy circles where price-stickers had been. He went to tap Johnny Foreign's table and made an exchange with one of the acolytes for an Artie Shore bootleg.

A family of refugees were holding up foot traffic on Wardour Street. The police were checking papers with trouble. None of the adults spoke any English, and a sullen, bone-weary schoolgirl was having to translate to her three apparent parents, converting terse British sentences into lengthy Mittel Europa circumlocutions.

The street was blocked off by a check-point. Frankham shivered in his gabardine and slipped on his phones, adjusting the wire cassette until swing plugged directly into his brain. The Glenn Miller remix fed his jumping synapses. 'Pennsylvania 6–5,000,000'.

'Pass on, please,' said a constable, waving pedestrians by. Soldiers in berets that seemed black in the night shoved the refugees against a wall and patted their pockets for contraband. The *Herald* had run an exposé, indicting bogus refugees as the worst of the black marketeers.

Somewhere, far away, perhaps across the river, was the crump of a big explosion. Another one.

Frankham strode on. He was behind schedule.

The War Room wasn't as overpopulated as the Shelter.

It was more expensive and coupons were short since the bank freeze. But after his write-up, it would be the Next Place.

Frankham sipped a reasonable cocktail and leant backwards on the bar-rail with proprietorial insouciance. The dance floor was a map of the European theatre. Hostesses with pointers shoved toy ships and model troop dispositions about. They wore khaki skirts and had their hair done up under peaked caps. They all had sex appeal in buckets.

The Old Man himself, or rather a working simulacrum thereof, sat on the band-stand, bulging his boiler-suit like a giant baby, puffing on a jutting cigar, and sampling famous sayings into non-stop swing.

'We shall fight them . . . fight them . . . fight them . . .'

A black couple in US army uniform combined acrobatically, the man standing on Belgium and lifting his scissor-legged partner over his head, vaulting her from Normandy Beach to Peenemunde. Her skirts divided and closed like a snapping trap.

'. . . on the beaches . . . the beaches . . . the beaches . . .'

The dancers were probably with the management. They were too good to be civvies.

Everyone was given a cigar as they came in. Frankham had dumped his in a bucket of sand, but plenty lit up, adding to the smoke-filled room fug that hung under the ceiling, obscuring the lights.

The speciality dancers reached a frenzied climax, dry-humping and rolling across France like the 8th

Army. The Old Man turned a blubbery cartwheel on the band-stand, padding wriggling. Dresden exploded in a three-foot flame which whooshed around the legs of dancers, blowing up skirts to reveal suspenders and cami-knickers. Harmless miniature fire-bursts sparked all around, singeing a few, producing squeals of drunken delight.

'Never before . . . I said *before*,' the Old Man rumbled like a public school Foghorn Leghorn, 'in the field of human conf . . . I said, human conflict has so much, and I mean *sooooo* much, been owed . . .'

In a sense, Frankham reflected, it was all owed to him.

Frankham had seen it coming a year or so back, when the first big band tracks leaked into the clubs just as the PM was denying plans had been laid to reintroduce rationing. He had written about it in cutting edge zines, then the overground press. The Blitz Spirit was returning in style. When the Austerity line of fashions hit shops just as the bombing campaign shifted from public transport to department stores, the battle to stay in fashion racked up its first casualties and more eager recruits enlisted. 'Theme Museums' offering realistic simulacra of the darkest hours opened, bombarding the civvies with special effects. Hair salons became barber's shops, and stylists became skilled in straight-razoring 'taches to pencil lines. De Havilland sound systems swept from the East End into the city, reproducing stuttering swing and syrup sentiment. The British film industry, with Ministry of Information funding, turned out cheap but successful remakes of *The Foreman Went to France*, . . . *one of our planes is missing* . . . and *The Goose Steps Out*. When the BBC repeated *Allo Allo* and *Dad's Army* to higher viewing figures than the soaps, bombs fell on Albert Square and Brookside Close in retaliation. Euro-talks in Hamburg ground to an unresolvable deadlock, with ambassadors constantly on the point of recall. The spiv look alternated with the uniform style and there was much confusion over just who was entitled to wear British Army combat fatigues. Every West End theatre had its wartime revue running; Andrew Lloyd Webber turned *The Colditz Story* into a musical smash while Cameron Mackintosh produced *Every Night Something Awful*. Frankham had already signed for a coffee table book on the movement. It was to be called *The Finest Hour*.

As he emerged into Cavendish Square, a knot of SS skins were being turned away from the War Room. The skinhead *Grüppenführer* spat abuse at the tommy on the door, biting down on harsh German phrases like cyanide-filled teeth. The tommy stood his ground.

There'd been a brief shooting war on Remembrance Sunday, Nouveau Nazis skirmishing with flight-uniformed young men who called themselves the Few. It had been blown up in the papers, but the factions had chased each other up and down Charing Cross Road and St Martin's Lane, trading wild shots and smashing windows.

It was hard to get a cab. Frankham ambled along Margaret Street towards Regent Street and found a corner he could hail from. Standing on the pavement, he was aware of shapes crouched in the alley behind. Three sexless figures lay, their lower bodies swaddled in dirty sleeping bags. Blank insectile eyes stood out in black-snouted faces. Gas masks.

There was a rush of noise and a whisk of air and Frankham dropped to the ground. Then came the flash and a scatter of hot ashes.

It had been close, maybe a street away. He turned and stood, and saw thin but giant flames shooting up above All Souls Langham Place and Broadcasting House. That one must have been an incendiary. It had fallen somewhere up on Great Portland Street, near the Post Office.

Fire-engines clanked and people were running towards and away from the explosion. Just standing, he was jostled. He patted the dust from his gabardine and stung his palm on a hot spark.

'. . . mumble, mumble,' said a gas mask.

'Pardon?' he said, involuntarily.

'Mustn't grumble,' the gas mask repeated.

'Worse things happen at sea,' another mask confirmed.

In the Troy Club, a Boffin, hand fused with a tumbler of Glenfiddich, tried to explain the nature of ghosts and time.

'. . . a collective wish can summon aspects of the past, *invoke* them if you will, actually bring into being objects or persons long gone . . .'

Frankham ignored the bespectacled loon and ordered a stiff-ish gin and it from the barman, who had patent leather hair, hooded eyes and a white dinner jacket.

'Close scrape, I've just had,' he said.

'If it's got your name on it, not much you can do, sir.'

Frankham threw the drink at the back of his throat. The stinging behind his eyes calmed him.

'Shook me up, I must say.'

The Troy always had the wireless on. A clubman spun the dial on the waist-high laminated cabinet, trying to find *ITMA*. He could only get purred news announcements about the latest raids, and spun on at random. The wireless coughed out a sample of ranting Adolf, passed John Peel introducing Ambrose, then scratched into 'The Lambeth Walk'.

'Bloody bad show, this,' snorted a Blimp who was having his ear bent by the Boffin. 'Young turks have done for us well and proper. Too many green hands on the tiller, you know. All the good men pensioned off and put out to pasture.'

An airman, barely old enough to raise a 'tache, drank quietly and seriously at the bar, ignoring the Blimp and the Boffin. His hands were shaking almost unnoticably.

'I should be up there,' he said, thumbing toward the ceiling. 'I was due aloft tonight, but they cancelled the scramble. Bomb or something. Fifth columnists, they say.'

'Very nasty business, sir,' said the barman. 'The enemy within.'

'It's deuced frustrating,' the airman declared, looking at his hands. 'Just sitting here. Not being able to fight back. I'd just like to get one of the bogeys in my sights.'

'Not a man from the Last War on the General Staff,' blustered the Blimp. 'All babies and boyos, with their *computer* planes and *ballistic* what-have-you. Don't know the words to "God Save the King" and jitterbug to yank bands on their leave . . .'

'As a society turns in on its insides,' said the Boffin, 'loses forward momentum in nostalgia, the patterns of time and space itself may bend and bow, and even break. Nobody seems to notice . . .'

'Bloody yanks. Bet they come in when it's all over, grinning and dispensing chocolate and nylons like bloody manna from Heaven. Heaven, Arizona.'

'We continually try to rethink, to reimagine, the past. It's possible that we actually unpick our destinies, change the situation. Look at all the books: *Fatherland*, *When Adolf Came*, *SS/GB*, *The Man in the High Castle*, *The Sound of His Horn*. We can wish it otherwise, and otherwise it could very well become . . .'

Frankham looked at his empty glass.

'Another drinkie, sir?' asked the barman.

Frankham ordered one and sprung for another for the airman. He was out of coupons but they knew him at the Troy. The barman could get anything, rationed or not, if slipped a little folded green.

'Think it'll ever end?' the airman asked. 'The War?'

'What war?' Frankham asked, missing something.

The airman didn't answer, just drank. The Troy shuddered, framed pictures of Churchill and the Princesses rattling on the walls. A distant thunder shook the windows. A blind rolled up with a snap, and a voice from below shouted 'put that light out'.

To judge from the streaks of angry red in the three o'clock skies, fires had spread. Narrow winding Hanway Street was unaffected by the actual bombardment, but the air was tangy with traces of smoke, the gutters heavy with the run-off from nearby firehoses.

Frankham and the airman, whose name was Somerton, had left the Boffin and the Blimp to their fractured conversation in the Club and ventured out in search of a livelier place. Somerton suggested a dance hall Frankham had already written up and written off. Since he was in a ginnily generous mood, he acceded. Who knows, the hole might be looking up. Everything comes around again eventually.

In the sky, dark shapes wheeled and swooped. Somerton looked up, almost with longing. There was a distorted burst of fire, and a patter of spent shell-cases sounded a dozen yards away. After a fireburst, something with a comet-tail of flame plunged downwards.

'Score one for some lucky blighter,' Somerton said.

Oxford Street was still barred to vehicle traffic, but gangs of soot-faced rubble-shifters were swarming over an extensive spill of debris. The fires were dying down and workmen were rooting through for hapless bods who might be trapped. A few disgraceful souls were getting in a spot of Christmas looting, pulling prizes – video recorders, Aga stoves, gramophones – out of the wreckage. Most wore gas-masks and were fast on their feet, no matter how weighted down they were.

The plane, with swastika markings, had come down in the fountain at the base of Centre Point. Its bent black fuselage was propped in the steaming shallow waters, hot chunks of wing-metal spread down into Charing Cross Road.

'A bogey,' spat Somerton. 'Messerschmitt.'

Frankham's head was hurting. Behind his skull, things were shifting. He needed more gins. Or fewer.

A souvenir stall opposite Centre Point was squashed flat by a sheared-off aeroplane wheel. Union jack bunting was turned to muddied scraps, and cellophane-wrapped ARP helmets and beefeater models congealed into crinkling pools of melted plastic. A pair of Japanese tourists – enemy axis aliens - snapped photographs of the stall from every angle, and were apprehended by a couple of constables. Frankham supposed they would be shot as spies.

Somerton wanted a look at the smashed plane. It was some new design, incorporating aerodynamic advances the Air Ministry was not yet aware of. In the empty cockpit, a bank of computer consoles shorted and sparked. The pilot must have hit the silk and come down somewhere nearby.

From the direction of Holborn came the sharp crack of gunfire. Rifle-shots. Then, a burst of machine-gun. Men in uniform trousers and braces broke away from the rescue gangs and siezed weapons from a jeep stalled by Claude Gill's.

Somerton crouched down, hauling Frankham out of the line of fire. At a run, Stormtroopers charged down New Oxford Street and were greeted by accurate fire.

Pinned down between the tommies entrenched in the Virgin Megastore and an armed policeman who had been hiding in the entrance to Forbidden Planet, the Nazis were cut up properly. They hooted and heiled as bullets hit home.

The air was thick with flying lead. Frankham felt a stab in his upper arm and a hot damp seeping inside his jacket-sleeve.

'Rats,' he said, 'I've been shot.'

'So you have,' Somerton commented.

It was over swiftly. When the last goose-stepping goon was halted, knocked to his knees by a head-shot, some of the civvies gave out a cheer. In the open air, it sounded like the farting response in 'Der Führer's Face'. Only the enemy seemed to have sustained casualties.

Frankham tried to get up and became awkwardly aware of the numbness in his upper chest.

'After you, Claude,' he said to Somerton, waving at the airman to stand.

'No,' said Somerton, helping Frankham up, 'after you, Cecil.'

A Red Cross nurse came over and had a look at him. Her hair was pinned up under her cap. Frankham took a deep breath and it didn't hurt too much. The nurse poked a finger into the blackened dot-like hole in his gabardine, and felt through his jacket and shirt.

'Just a graze, sweetheart,' he said.

'Keep smiling through,' she told him, and left. There was a row of civilian casualties by Top Man, all with neatly-bloodied bandages around their heads.

'Proper little angel,' Somerton commented.

'Sometimes, I think it's harder on the women,' Frankham said. 'Yet they complain so little.'

Enough rubble had been shifted to let tanks into Oxford Street. Three of them had been held in reserve near Marble Arch and now they rumbled placidly towards the downed *Messerschmitt*. Frankham and Somerton gave the Victory V sign as they passed, and a tank officer, bundled up in thick jumpers, returned the gesture.

'Makes a feller proud,' Somerton said. 'To see everyone doing their bit.'

He woke up with a fearful gin head in some chippie's single bed. He remembered a name – Dottie – and the dance hall, and vaguely supposed he was as far out as Camden or Islington. His arm was stiff and cold, and there was a shifting and uncomfortable girl next to him, face smeared with last night's make-up.

He didn't know what had happened to Somerton or to the girl – Hettie? – he had been dancing with.

Frankham rolled off the bed and hauled himself upright. Dottie – or was this Hettie? – was instantly relieved and filled out the space under the sheet, settling in for more sleep.

He dressed one-handed and managed everything but his cuff-links. The hole in his arm was a scabby red mark. He guessed there was still a lump of bullet inside him.

Outside, he didn't recognise the street. Half the buildings in the immediate area had been bombed out, either last night or within the last month. One completely-demolished site was flooded, a small reservoir in the city. The neat piles of fallen masonry were mainly bleached white as bones.

As he walked, his head hurt more and more. Around him, early morning people busied themselves, whistling cheerfully as they worked, restoring recent damage. There weren't many cars about, but a lot of people were nipping between the craters on bicycles.

There was a tube station nearby, the Angel. It was a part-time shelter, but the trains were running again. A policeman at the entrance was checking papers. Many of the bombed-out were being reassigned to vacant housing.

As he went down the escalator into the depths, Frankham passed framed advertisements for Ovaltine, a Googie Withers film, Lipton's Tea, powdered eggs, Bovril. Every third advertisement showed the Old Man giving the V sign, with a balloon inviting tourists to share the 'Blitz Experience'.

Suddenly, half-way down the escalator, Frankham had to sit, a shudder of cold pain wrenching his wounded arm. Passers-by stepped delicately around him, and the moving steps nudged him out at the bottom. He found a place to sit, and tried to will the throbbing in his forehead away.

A little girl with curls stepped into his field of vision. Her mother, with a calf-length swirl of skirts and precious nylons, tugged disapprovingly.

'Don't play with the poor man, dear.'

The little girl dumped something in his lap and was pulled away. Frankham looked down at the canvas-covered lump and, with his good hand, undid the bundle. A gas mask tumbled out. He lifted it up to his face and, fumbling with the straps, fitted it on, inhaling the smell of rubber and cotton. Somehow the pain was eased. He drew up his knees and hugged them.

It wouldn't be over by Christmas, Frankham knew. But that didn't matter. London could take it.

This was written for *The Time Out Book of London Short Stories*. London, where I was born but did not grow up and where I now live, is a city which contains overlapping layers of its own past, like a wall that has been fly-posted and stripped so many times that a crazy collage emerges.

Where the Bodies
Are Buried

In High Street, Robert Hackwill caught sight of his own name. It tugged the corner of his eye, drawing his attention. The elections were months past but his posters were still up in some places.

He stood in front of Valerie's Video, which he remembered as a junk and curio emporium. Ten years ago, it became a video rental shop, then spread to encompass premises on either side, becoming a video super-rental shop. The added-on shopfronts were boarded up and Valerie's was selling off used cassettes from £1.99. Only half the shop was devoted to videos, the rest boasting odd items from dusty fresh fruit to Nintendo cartridges. Video had been an eighties boom business.

The window was covered with glossy, saggy posters for films Hackwill wouldn't want Colin and Sammy to see. *Babes Bust Out*, with a pouting silicone freak in a shrunken T-shirt with prison arrows, brandishing a machine gun half her size, an out-of-focus exploding helicopter in the background. *Steam Heat II*, an 'erotic thriller' advertised by a buxom silhouette in a darkened bedroom raising a bloody trowel, the frightened eyes of the man beneath staring out from between the censor certificate and the credits block.

His election poster had been a nice black and white photograph of him, taken a year or so ago, before he got the slight flabbiness about his chin Helen was on at him to do something about. And 'VOTE HACKWILL'. No clever slogan, no promises: he was well enough known in town to stand on his reputation. Besides the Party had held this ward since before World War Two. He couldn't find the poster in Valerie's window, so he looked at the boarded-up shop next door. It had been fly-posted for jumble sales and discotheques. He was sure one of his posters had been up here, but it was either buried under more recent layers or shredded to strips.

He must have been mistaken. He felt silly, as if he'd been caught out. Then he looked back at the video posters and saw it. Bigger than the others and mainly black shadows with dripping red and green letters, it advertised a horror movie. Probably one of the video nasties he'd campaigned against a few years ago when everybody was worried about kiddies renting out snuff films. A single red eye, stark mad, stared out of the shadowed ruin of a face, a double-row of shining teeth clenched and exposed in a lipless mouth. A withered hand, fingers tipped with steel claws, seemed to reach out of the poster, each shiny claw containing the screaming face of a teenage boy or girl. Underneath was an abandoned graveyard, tombstones leaning at bizarre angles, weeds growing up around forgotten monuments.

At the top of the poster were the words 'Rob Hackwill Knows . . .', and, in bigger letters like razor-slashes in velvet, the title of the film, *Where the Bodies Are Buried*. He looked again, assuming he'd mistaken something similar for his name. Rod Bicknell, Don Treadwell, Jack Robwill? No, it was definitely 'Rob Hackwill'. Most people called him Robert. Only Helen and a few of his oldest friends, and enemies, called him Bob, even. But Rob Hackwill was unmistakably a variation of his name.

He detected, for the first time, the possibility of a cruel joke. And if cruel jokes were involved, the obvious suspect was the Independent. Reg Jessup, a sitting councillor, had left the Party and stood again on his own ticket, besting the official candidate to be returned as more of a nuisance than the actual opposition. Elaborate and pointless jokes were a hobby of his. Reg's entire political career was an elaborate and pointless joke.

He stormed into Valerie's, sounding the bell, and cringed. By the counter was a cardboard cut-out of a small blonde woman in karate pyjamas, aiming a kick somewhere in the vicinity of Hackwill's head, mouth open in an intimidating silent yell.

'Don't mind her,' said another blonde, a girl whose hair was bleached almost white. She sat on a high stool behind the counter, dressed all in black and reading a film magazine. 'She's just an ad for *Foxy Kickboxer*.'

The girl thumbed over her shoulder, indicating a

television high up on a shelf, sound turned low. The original of the cut-out, less imposing when shrunk into the tiny box, exploded out of a jacuzzi, pyjamas plastered over prominent nipples, and launched punches into a half-dozen Asians. They had swords but she saw them off with just her hands and feet, and, in one case, her breasts.

'Not exactly Wim Wenders,' said the girl, 'but there's a market for it.'

He didn't know the girl. She wasn't Valerie, whose real name was Jeanie Morris. Hackwill had met Jeanie when the council reprimanded her for renting 18 certificate films to sixteen-year-olds.

'I'm Robert Hackwill,' he announced.

The girl's dead-white brow wrinkled and she looked at him as if he had declared himself the Prime Minister or Ken Dodd.

'I want an explanation.'

'Rob Hackwill?'

'Robert. Mr Hackwill. Councillor Hackwill. And I want to know why you're defaming me in your window.'

The girl burst out laughing and covered her mouth with glossy black fingernails.

Dust from the building site drifted across Denbeigh Gardens along with the battering drone of pneumatic drills. When Hackwill found himself coughing, Reg gave him a matey back-thump, harder than necessary. He had to grip hard to keep hold of his briefcase.

'Get those lungs clear, Bob,' he said. 'I thought you'd kicked ciggies into touch, old thing.'

Hackwill coughed against his free fist, knowing his face was burning red. The man from the *Herald* was taking photographs. He was sure the paper would pick the worst-looking one of him, as usual, to go with the story.

Next to the grassy triangle of Denbeigh Gardens rose the skeleton of the Discount Development. It should've been finished six months ago, but there'd been cock-ups since Day One. Hackwill had worked closely with the McKinnell Brothers from the beginning. His firm was supplying many of the materials. It was a plank of his campaign that the Development would be an invigorating economic injection for the area. His family economy was certainly invigorated; the Brothers' generous 'consultation fees' were putting Sammy through junior school.

As Ben McKinnell, almost spherical in his shell-suit, explained to the reporter about the set-backs, Reg smirked at each lengthy anti-union aside. Reg said if you put a penny in the slot, any McKinnell Brother would give out a five-minute tirade about the tyranny of workshy yobs.

Lucia Howell, the Opposition leader, tottered on high heels, peering at neglected flower-beds as if she took this inspection lark seriously. One of her ever-present St Bernards rooted around somewhere, getting underfoot. Denbeigh Gardens was council property but nothing much had ever been done with it. The playground consisted of two lethal swings and a concrete lump supposedly in the shape of a whale, its flapping tail broken off by vandals. There was a shed, reputedly locked since the turn of the century, marked with a 'Council Property: Keep Out' notice. Denbeigh Gardens would be no loss. Hackwill could force the sale through but it would be easier if the decision were unanimous.

Ben McKinnell, questioned, admitted the original plans had underestimated the parking space necessary for the Development and that he was more than willing to pay a good price for the Gardens.

Hackwill looked across the area. Kids played tag around the mutilated whale. Their young mothers loitered by the shed, using it as a windbreak while they lit cigarettes. He wished he hadn't given up. Brickies on their tea-break whistled and called at the smoking girls, receiving only snooty looks and rude gestures. McKinnell joked that he wanted to send his builders on an Anti-Sexism Awareness course, and Jilly Kenner, Hackwill's militant deputy, commented that being arse-raped a couple of times might improve their attitude.

'Right on, Jilly,' said Reg. He always backed anything that made the Party look like loons.

'Excuse me, Councillor Hackwill?'

He turned and saw a tweedy young woman in glasses.

'I'm Ginger Dillon, from the Denbeigh Residents' Committee.'

Hackwill remembered the name. She'd written many letters, complaining. Mrs Dillon was a NIMBY; in favour of the Discount Development, but Not In My Back Yard.

'We're petitioning against the loss of this park area.'

Mrs Dillon handed him a substantial folder of signatures. Hackwill heard the click of the *Herald* man's camera and saw Reg's grin widen. He had suspicions that this had been stage-managed.

'There has been consultation with the residents at every stage of the Development,' said Ben McKinnell, waving a fat cigar. 'Mrs Dillon represents a minority opinion.'

Hackwill found himself with the petition in one hand and his briefcase in the other. Another cloud of dust whisked past and he coughed again, this time racked with convulsions. He dropped case and folder, and bent double. Reg hit his back again. Lucia scrambled to pick up the petition and huddled with Mrs Dillon. The NIMBY had been an Opposition candidate at the last election. Unsuccessful, thank Christ. Reg, Jilly and Lucia were quite enough.

Hackwill cleared his lungs and straightened up. Reg brushed his shoulders like a valet, solicitous for his health. The Independent had been the same in school thirty years ago. He had a way of seeming to be a friend while actually making you look bad. Sometimes, Hackwill wished they were back in Ash Grove Primary, where direct methods could end a dispute. District Councillors weren't allowed to give Chinese Burns.

Reg had Hackwill's briefcase, upside-down. As he handed it over, the catch broke and things fell out. He made a grab for the plain brown folder with his consultancy invoices, certain the *Herald* reporter would make a sudden grab for the evidence and Hackwill would find himself indicted, shamed and forced to resign. There was nothing illegal in being paid for a job well done, but he knew how it would look if it came out.

'What's this, Bob?' Reg asked, holding up the cassette box. 'Taking home a pervy video?'

He opened the black box and read the title.

'*Where the Bodies Are Buried*. Sounds gruesome. I had you down as more a *Chariots of Fire* sort of chap.'

Hackwill didn't want to explain why he'd rented the tape. It would make him look ridiculous.

'For the kids,' he said.

'But,' the grin infected Reg's entire face, 'this has an 18 certificate. I'm sure Colin isn't fourteen yet and Sammy is just a baby.'

Hackwill snatched the video and stuffed it into his case along with all the papers. The invoices were safely buried at the bottom.

'When can we expect the council's decision?' asked the reporter.

Hackwill had to concentrate.

'About the car park?' the man from the *Herald* prompted.

Mrs Dillon glared like a witch. Ben McKinnell exhaled smoke, which dissipated on the breeze.

'Next Tuesday,' Hackwill replied. 'We'll discuss it fully in council, and, if there's any disagreement, put it to a vote.'

'How did you like the film?' asked the neo-albino girl, whose name was Shelley.

Hackwill harrumphed about it being rubbish. Bloody rubbish, to be precise. Shelley had to bend down low to put the film back in the W section behind the counter and her short black skirt rode up.

'It's a popular rental,' she said.

When Colin had discovered his Dad had taken out *Where the Bodies Are Buried*, he wanted to be allowed to watch the video. All his friends had seen it and it was supposed to be wicked. Apparently, there was a scene where a boy's eyeballs crawled out of his head and strangled him with trails of optic nerve. Also, Colin helpfully informed his father, the baddie had their surname, Hackwill. He sent Colin and Sammy to bed and put the tape on. After the first five minutes, in which a girl was attacked in a graveyard by a monster with one red eye, Helen gave him a funny look and went upstairs too.

Shelley slipped the video in its place and stood up. She smoothed her skirt, giving him a shop assistant smile. She was the age of the girls in the film, the girls chased and killed by the monster, Rob Hackwill.

He'd watched most of *Where the Bodies Are Buried* on fast-forward, going to regular speed when anyone was murdered or, looking around to make sure Helen wasn't back, whenever a teenager took off her clothes. There was no story, just a series of freakish deaths. During one of the murders, the victim – a fat gangster with a cigar stub permanently in his mouth – shouted 'Get back, Hackwill' as the monster advanced. Then his cigar turned into dynamite and exploded, making a fireball of his head. Hackwill played it over twice, to make sure. The fat man definitely said 'Hackwill'.

While on fast-forward, he'd come to a scene without a murder or sex, when the heroine visited a middle-aged man played by someone he remembered as a Sheriff in a seventies TV show. He decided to watch properly, hoping there'd be an explanation. The Sheriff was a Judge in *Where the Bodies Are Buried*, and the heroine, a disturbingly mature schoolgirl named Tina, was his granddaughter. Her parents and most of her friends had been killed, and the Judge knew something.

'Rob Hackwill,' the Judge sighed, voice heavy with dread. 'He's come back.'

Hackwill had shivered. He didn't understand why people paid good money to be frightened.

'Rob Hackwill?' pouted Tina, who was unlikely to give Meryl Streep nightmares at Oscar-time. 'I've heard that name somewhere before.'

The Judge nodded and shook his head. 'You must have been very little when it happened, the suicides, the scandal . . .'

The picture went wavy and the Judge's voice continued to explain while pictures showed a mob chasing a one-eyed man into the graveyard.

'He was a blackmailer,' the Judge said. 'A vicious, evil blackmailer. He had an uncanny knack for ferreting out secrets, for inflating innuendoes into slanders, for discovering where the bodies were buried. For years, he preyed on the town, turning people against one another, ruining lives, wrecking marriages. Everyone came to dread the anonymous poison letters. Everyone with a secret.'

The mob, led by the fat gangster and the Judge, cornered the cringing man. He was the actor who played the monster, without make-up. He fell exhausted against a gravestone and begged for his life.

'We found out it was Rob Hackwill. He'd been a councilman until we indicted him for taking graft from the Mob. The letters had been his revenge. He hadn't done it for the money. It had all been to ruin the city.'

The gangster had a blowtorch. He advanced on the blackmailer, belly looming over the camera.

'That night,' the Judge said, 'we tortured him, trying to find where he had stashed the evidence he used against us. He wouldn't talk but we kept on torturing him until there was no point torturing him any more. We left him with the other dead things, thinking we had heard the last of Rob Hackwill. But now . . .'

The film came back to the Judge, who held his head in his hands. Tina was looking at him, disgusted.

'But now he's come back.'

The lights went out and when they came back the Judge's tongue inflated to the size of a watermelon, bursting his head like a pimple. Tina screamed as the Judge's head stretched and split. The camera whirled around, and standing in front of the french windows was the monster.

Rob Hackwill.

Hackwill froze the frame and looked at his namesake. The poison penman had made a bargain with the Devil, a dark woman in a black leather body-stocking. He could come back to life, providing he regularly delivered souls to his mistress in Hell. He lived in a cavern under the graveyard and had one red eye, shining bare teeth and steel claws. When he killed someone, he said something funny. Hackwill unfroze the frame.

'That was the trouble with the Judge,' the monster said, 'his tongue always wrote cheques his ass couldn't cash.'

He'd fast-forwarded through the rest of the film: Tina summoned up the Devil who, changing her mind, dragged the monster back to Hell, where he was torn apart by the ghosts of his victims. In the last scene, Tina was back in a depopulated school, shaken but a survivor. She went to the ladies for a smoke and a black shape with a glowing red eye burst out of a toilet bowl, filling the screen. Heavy metal played over the rising end credits.

'The sequel is supposed to be worse,' Shelley said.

'There's a sequel?'

She shrugged. 'There's always a sequel.'

'You've got it?'

He didn't want to rent the film, just look at the box. All morning, he hadn't been able to get the bits of *Where the Bodies Are Buried* he had seen out of his head.

'It's not on video yet. It's not even been at the Palace.'

Shelley dug through a pile behind the counter and found a film magazine. She paged through it until she came to an advert.

'Here,' she said.

It was a scrambling of the video poster, the same elements in a different order. The red eye, the claws, the graveyard, the jagged teeth, the screaming teenagers.

Where the Bodies Are Buried, Part II: Hackwill's Back!

'I'll bet you can't wait,' Shelley said. 'It must be fun having everybody be afraid of you.'

• • •

Because Reg and Jilly abstained, the Denbeigh Gardens vote was dead-locked. It was not a Party issue. One of the Opposition, who owned a delivery firm connected with the McKinnell Brothers, voted for the sale. But, under the influence of Mrs Dillon, Lucia had taken against it, so no decision could be made. There was nothing more to be done in this meeting. As chairman, he sat facing everyone. At the other end of the table, the Reg Jessup grin shone. Hackwill thought he heard Reg's suppressed chortle.

'Does anyone wish to change their vote?'

Hackwill looked at Jilly, hoping she'd turn around and toe the Party line for once. If Ben McKinnell hadn't made that joke about Anti-Sexism Awareness, he might have a better chance of getting a proper car park.

Reg was abstaining just to stir things up. He had been the one who delivered the McKinnell Brothers' proposition to him in the first place. As usual, he had set everything in motion and backed off.

No one wanted to change.

'We have to make a decision.'

'If it's an even split,' a clerk said, 'surely, the motion falls—'

'Perhaps we stay here until someone cracks,' Reg suggested.

Hackwill drummed his fingers on the table. Looking down, he noticed he'd scratched the veneer. His nails were too long. He must cut them.

He'd hoped he could just go into the Palace, buy a ticket and hide in the auditorium, but for the first time in years there was a queue. Hackwill had told Helen he'd be home late because of another committee meeting. There was a cut-out in the foyer. Rob Hackwill, the monster. The cut-out was about his size and the red eye lit up electrically. Hackwill couldn't look at his namesake.

The queue was mainly excited young people. He was sure most weren't old enough to see the film. They were blithely unaware that they were breaking the law, but he, well above the legal age for an 18 film, was the one skulking guiltily, hoping no one would notice him.

'Come to see yourself?' someone asked.

Bewildered, he turned, heart thumping. It was Shelley, in a floor-length black dress slit up the thighs. She was with a boy who wore eyeshadow.

'Chris, this is the real Rob Hackwill,' she told her boyfriend. 'Remember, I told you about him.'

The boy smiled, showing sharp eyeteeth.

'Robert,' he insisted. 'Not Rob.'

'You must be becoming a horror expert,' Shelley said. 'You'll be subscribing to *Fangoria* next.'

'Pardon?'

'He didn't think much of *Where the Bodies Are Buried*,' Shelley told Chris.

The boy shrugged. 'I thought it was overrated too,' he said. He had an educated voice, a bit posey. 'Allan Keyes betrayed his own story. His vision is way too weird to be hammered into a commercial package . . .'

'Keyes?'

'Allan Keyes is the director,' Shelley explained. 'He's better known as a writer. You must have seen his books. *Strange Segments*, *Busting a Gut*, *Cornworld* . . .'

'Did he make this too?' Hackwill asked, nodding at the poster for *Hackwill's Back*.

'No,' Chris said, 'he got shafted by Hollywood. Sold away the rights for a mess of Beverly Hills pottage.'

'It must be like being locked out of your own house,' Shelley said, 'having your life's work taken away from you.'

'This is directed by the woman who made the Putrid promos.'

The queue started moving and Hackwill got a ticket. He had to exchange an embarassed greeting with the cinema manager, whom he knew from some committee or other, before he was allowed into the auditorium. The manager was surprised to see him, but he didn't bother to find an excuse.

'Rob Hackwill?' said the manager. 'Funny, I'd never thought of it before. Odd coincidence, eh?'

He finally escaped into the dark and sat near the back. Shelley and Chris were down in the front row. As the lights went down for the trailers, he saw them kissing and imagined their tongues entwining like slithering snakes, knotting their heads together.

The main character of *Where the Bodies Are Buried, Part II* was Frankie, a teenage boy whose penis was cursed by Rob Hackwill and turned from time to time into a toothy snake. In one scene, the condition came upon him while he was screwing the school slut. The snake ate its way out of the girl, splattering Frankie with her insides.

Days later, Hackwill remembered the scene with a

chill. Knowing it was all special effects – rubber and ketchup and complicated electronic gadgets – did not help.

In the Town Hall Gents, he looked down at his own penis. He'd drunk several cups of tea and his bladder was uncomfortably full. He remembered Frankie's trouser snake and could not let his bladder go. It was agonising. Behind him, someone coughed. He turned, zipping up sharply, and smelled cigar smoke. Ben McKinnell stood by the hand-drier.

'Councillor Hackwill,' he said. 'About the vote . . .'

'No change, I'm afraid.'

The developer shrugged. 'We'll have to play a rougher game.'

Years ago, when the McKinnell Brothers were starting out, there were stories about a shop steward whose hands got broken.

Ben McKinnell gave him a large brown envelope. 'Councillor Howell might be persuaded to change her vote.'

'Lucia? Not likely.'

'Open the envelope.'

He did and slid out a sheaf of black and white photographs, eight by ten like film stills.

'Taken with a telephoto lens,' Ben McKinnell explained. 'That's why they're a bit grainy.'

Lucia Howell was an animal lover. With her husband Quentin, she was known for breeding show-dogs. Her mantelpiece was crowded with trophies and ribboned medals. They could be seen in the background of the photographs. Lucia and Quentin were recognisable, as were their prize-winning St Bernards: Courage, Missy and Big Brute. Hackwill had not realised how much of an animal lover the Opposition leader was, or how enthusiastically her husband, a gentleman farmer, joined her in her hobby.

Tea still sloshing inside him, Hackwill left the Gents. Ben McKinnell ducked out and left the Town Hall.

Lucia was in the corridor outside the committee room. She had Big Brute with her. His tongue flopped to the floor as she scratched his abundant neck-fur, cooing in his large ear.

'Lucia,' Hackwill began, 'could I have a word before the meeting? Something has come up.'

Mrs Dillon had found his home number and called dozens of times, leaving stinging messages with Helen and, in one case, Sammy. When he got in, he had to take one of her calls. It was surprisingly painless, since he was able to divert the NIMBY bile towards Lucia.

After the vote, he'd felt an enormous sense of release. For one thing, his bladder let go. For another, Lucia's change of vote encouraged several Opposition councillors to follow suit. The sale of Denbeigh Gardens went through. Then Reg lowered his voice to sound like the gravelly American who narrated horror film trailers and comically snarled 'Hackwill's Back!'

The Independent couldn't know exactly how he'd influenced Lucia, but Hackwill realised Reg did understand. They had known each other too long and could keep nothing hidden. At school Reg had been the look-out, watching for teachers while Hackwill snatched some snotnose's dinner money. He had got his jollies being part of it without getting his hands dirty.

Hackwill tucked into his bacon and beans with relish. Since the meeting, he'd not thought of *Where the Bodies Are Buried*, parts I or II. The monster had brushed his life and was now speeding back to Hell, never to be heard from again.

'Turn the telly off,' Helen told Colin, 'and come have your tea.'

Hackwill looked across the kitchen into the front room. Colin was squatting by the television set.

'After the bweak,' Jonathan Ross said, 'we'll be talking to the most fwightening man in the world . . .'

He knew what the chat-show host would say.

'Wob Hackwill.'

Mal Gariazzo, the actor under the Rob Hackwill rubberface, was a volatile little American who barely let Ross get out a question before getting into his flow. He talked about Rob Hackwill as a mythic archetype, as an aspect of the Jungian Unconscious, and movie monsters as the demons of the modern pantheon.

'In a very real sense, Jonathan,' Gariazzo concluded, 'our society *needs* Rob Hackwill.'

Helen clapped ironically. She'd heard about Rob Hackwill the movie monster somewhere, but not thought it interesting enough to discuss with her husband. Now her only comment was that she realised why he'd brought home that horrid video a few weeks ago.

It wasn't as if Robert Hackwill were a common name. He'd never come across another Hackwill to whom he was not related, let alone another *Robert* Hackwill.

Fascinated, he watched Gariazzo rattle on. In an open-necked striped shirt and leather trousers, the actor was very unlike the dead-faced monster, but he did the deep and scary Rob Hackwill voice when prompted.

The television showed a clip from *Part II*. Rob Hackwill spoke to Frankie from the cover of the Satanic Heavy Metal LP the teenager played backwards to bring the monster back from Hell. 'You and me, bro,' the monster said, 'we're gonna tear down this graveyard town and cover it with asphalt. Their lives will be our parking lot.'

Ross asked Gariazzo whether Allan Keyes, the creator of Rob Hackwill, would be participating in further sequels. The actor deftly skipped the question. Hackwill recognised the trick from meetings: it always came when someone didn't want to deal with a point raised by a report.

'We've already done *Where the Bodies Are Buried, Part III in 3–D*,' Gariazzo said. 'Rob Hackwill will be badder than ever. Straight from Hell to a Theatre Near You, he'll be slashing and snipping, getting close to your heart and deep into your pulsating brain.'

Ross shut the actor up and introduced a pop group. Five poofs with squeaky voices whom Sammy thought were outstanding.

'Excellent,' said Colin, 'My Dad From Hell.'

Without thinking, Hackwill cuffed his son. The blow landed harder than intended and Colin was knocked over. Helen drew in a sharp breath.

'Bob,' she said, 'he's bleeding.'

He looked at his fingers and saw drops of red at the points of his nails. Colin, frightened, scrambled away. Helen, shocked, extended her hands as if to protect herself. Hackwill hissed through bared teeth.

Hackwill dreamed he was in Hell, his face being stripped of skin and flesh by a white-haired girl demon.

When he woke up, his left eye wouldn't open. It was sleep-gummed and no amount of warm water would do anything for it. In the end, Helen shrugged and said it was bound to come unstuck eventually and that he shouldn't worry about it too much.

Looking at himself with one eye in the mirror, he thought his face was tighter, more shrunken. And his right eye was rimmed with red as if he were a heavy drinker.

'Since you stopped smoking, you've become a wreck, Rob,' Helen said.

'Bob,' he corrected.

'Pardon?'

'My name is Bob.'

'That's what I said, Bob.'

'No, you said Rob. Like the monster, Rob. Not Bob, like the husband.'

She left him in the bathroom, examining his face. His eye still wouldn't open.

'Get used to it, Rob,' he told himself.

Reg was in his office to give him the news about the Howells. Their Land Rover had gone off a bridge. They were both dead.

'Looks like they lost control,' Reg said, keeping the gloating to a minimum. 'But the police are puzzled by one detail.'

Reg let it dangle, until Hackwill snapped a question. 'What?'

'The dogs. There's no evidence of a break-in, so it looks like Lucia and Quentin did it themselves.'

'Did what?'

'Killed their dogs. With a carving knife. Those St Bernards were like their children, but . . .'

Hackwill was uncomfortable. The photographs Ben McKinnell had given him were locked in the filing cabinet. He'd have to destroy them.

'Bob, is there something wrong with your eye?'

He thought he should be there to see the ground broken. It was the first really hot day of the summer and the bulldozer driver's bare belly flopped over his jeans belt as he sat at the wheel, starting up his machine. A few stood at the perimeter of Denbeigh Gardens, watching. At least the NIMBYs weren't staging a human chain.

Hackwill could imagine Mrs Dillon going down under the blades, sliced up and redistributed like the dummies of the *Where the Bodies Are Buried* films, entrails spread like bright streamers in the marks of caterpillar tracks.

The bulldozer growled across the park, scraping away grass. The wedge-shovel ploughed against the concrete whale and broke it up, sweeping the chunks aside. The swings crumpled as if they were made from paper straws. On the return pass, the machine smashed down the ancient hut. It proved completely empty.

There was a brief pause when the driver saw something white in the earth and thought it might be a human thigh-bone. Ben McKinnell pronounced it a piece of a cow and tossed it away. The levelling of Denbeigh Gardens continued.

Underneath the grass, there was only soft earth.

He was late for the meeting. As he entered the room, someone growled 'Hackwill's Back' in a horror film accent. Reg didn't even have to do it himself now. It was a standing joke.

There had been a snap election to fill the empty place on the council and somehow Ginger Dillon had been selected by the Opposition. She was a one-issue councillor and her pet peeve was the Discount Development. Every time Hackwill sat in his chair at the head of the table, Mrs Dillon pulled out more press cuttings and statistics, coming perilously close to libelling everyone concerned with the Development from the McKinnell Brothers down to the site tea-boy.

Even before the minutes of the last meeting could be read, Mrs Dillon was waving documents that proved Douggie McKinnell had been fined for bribing a borough surveyor in the next county.

'These people are no better than gangsters, Mr Chairman, and we've let them have the run of town.'

Hackwill was tired. His sleep had been troubled recently. Helen and the kids were treating him strangely. Also, he knew that sooner or later he would sit down in council and Mrs Dillon would raise the matter of consultancy fees.

'The Development is nearly a year overdue, with no end in sight. I propose we suspend our relationship with the McKinnells and reassess our whole position.'

Hackwill looked at Mrs Dillon with his one red eye and tried by sheer force of will to shut her up. A sound started in his stomach and vibrated up through his teeth.

Somewhat alarmed, the woman paused in mid-rant and cringed back into her seat. Everyone else was similarly stunned. Good. It was time he reaffirmed his control over the situation.

'That's better,' Hackwill hissed. 'Any other business?'

The publicity for *Where the Bodies Are Buried, Part III in 3–D* began months before the film came to the cinemas. Little boxes in every newspaper and magazine Hackwill picked up bore messages: 'He Knows, Be Scared', 'In Your Face, Rob Hackwill' and 'The Hack is Comin' Back!' Rob Hackwill was everywhere: posters, pop records, T-shirts, comics, paperback books, Halloween masks, Christmas Tree ornaments. The monster was impossible to escape. Hackwill understood from Shelley that each film made more money than the last and that each new sequel boosted video rental of earlier titles.

Every once in a while, he would drop in to Valerie's Video to check up on the snowballing Rob Hackwill craze. Shelley, the only person in town who didn't show either fear or contempt in his presence, was helpful, and collected articles from horror film magazines for him. She'd had a row with Chris, and the project filled her suddenly-available free time.

When Jeanie Morris judged one of the rental cassettes

of the original *Where the Bodies Are Buried* battered enough to be sold off to make room for new stock, Shelley kept it back for Hackwill. He felt obliged to cough up the £1.99 for the film that had somehow become a piece of his life. The only other videos he owned were a collection of his own appearances on the local news, taped off the television, and Elvis and Ann-Margaret in *Viva Las Vegas*, which Colin had given him for his birthday last year.

Shelley sorted through her stack of papers and cuttings, searching out something for him. She was taking time off between college and university, and hoped to study film at East Anglia. She subscribed to a raft of film magazines, as interested in the ones with pictures of a grinning Rob Hackwill on the cover and disgusting colour stills of mutilated bodies inside as she was in the ones with no illustrations and huge wedges of incomprehensible text littered with footnotes and references. Personally, she preferred black and white films, which Hackwill thought might be why she dressed only in black – down to her lipstick – and had such white skin and hair. He could not imagine Shelley with a suntan.

There were Rob Hackwill cut-outs all over Valerie's Video. He caught sight of his reflection in the glass of the window. Among the Rob Hackwill shapes, he lurked, his red eye and bared teeth matching their rictus expressions. He had developed the habit of drawing his lips away from his teeth and hissing. His hand was given to locking into a clenched claw too. He supposed it must be psychosomatic.

All over town, his old election posters were reappearing,

surgically altered to overlay the characteristics of the monster on his face. Usually, one eye was obscured and the other coloured red, and a gash of teeth was drawn over his smile. Written across 'VOTE HACKWILL' was the scrawl 'or he'll kill you!'

'Here's the piece I was telling you about,' Shelley said, handing over several photocopied sheets clipped together. 'It's by that bloke who used to be on Channel 4. An analysis of the whole Rob Hackwill phenomenon. It gets woolly towards the conclusion, but there's meat in the text.'

The Channel 4 fellow began by dissecting the name 'Rob Hackwill' – '"Rob": to steal, a crime; "Hack": to maim, a lowlife; "Will": the force of determination, a power of the mind' – then followed the changes Keyes had made between 'A Trickle of Shame', his original short story, and *Where the Bodies Are Buried*, the first film. The author suggested Rob Hackwill had escaped from Allan Keyes, growing into a different kind of character. In the story, the monster, who didn't even have a name, was simply an incarnation of the guilts that prey on the characters. In *Where the Bodies Are Buried*, Rob Hackwill, thanks to Mal Gariazzo and some touches of black humour, had somehow become an engaging personality for the film's predominantly teenage audience. Rob Hackwill was 'at once the true face of evil behind the hypocrisy of his older generation and the anarchic troublemaker who brings down the corrupt figures – fathers, judges, policemen, mob bosses – who represent the small-town setting.'

Hackwill had to struggle to weed out the meaning of the article, and felt he knew no more at the end than at the start. The point seemed to be that there were many Rob Hackwills. He supposed he was one of them.

'Rob,' Reg said – everyone called him Rob now – hovering over his desk, 'have you noticed that no matter how hot it gets, Mrs Dillon doesn't wear short-sleeved blouses? But you can see blue marks through her sleeves. What do you make of them? D'you reckon hubby gives her a bit of a belt?'

He shook his head. No, Mr Dillon didn't hit his wife. There was no Mr Dillon any more. He had left the bitch last year, and Hackwill knew why. He couldn't take her Problem any longer.

Her Surprising Problem.

He hadn't needed a McKinnell to find out. He'd managed on his own. He'd discovered he was good at finding things out. Sometimes, Reg hinted at things to help him, but mainly he did things on his own.

'One thing about Ginger,' Hackwill said, 'she's certainly been a shot in the arm.'

Reg laughed out loud but Hackwill could tell he was scared as well as pleased. He must have a Secret too. Everybody did.

Allan Keyes didn't give many interviews, but he had made an exception for the leading American horror film magazine. Shelley left Hackwill a message on his ansaphone telling him she was photocopying the piece for him.

When he played the message back, Reg was still hanging around his office.

'Allan Keyes, eh?' he said. 'Who'd have thought it?'

'What?'

'I suppose it must be the same Allan Keyes.'

Hackwill looked at Reg, and felt his eye burning under the patch. Reg was being especially infuriating.

'We were all kids together. Now he's in Hollywood and we're still stuck here in the old town.'

'Do you mean to say we knew this Keyes?'

Reg laughed.

'More you than me, Robbo.'

Most of the interview was about Allan Keyes's reconciliation with New Frontier, the company that made the *Where the Bodies Are Buried* films. He had signed away all rights to the story and characters in exchange for the chance to direct and rumours had been circulating that he was unhappy with the way the sequels had been handled. He said Rob Hackwill had become too clownish, too obvious. He wasn't scary any more, and there was too much Heavy Metal in the films. Now, after the stalling of a big studio project, Keyes was returning to the series, providing an original storyline for *The Redevelopment: Where the Bodies Are Buried IV*.

Hackwill looked at the photocopied photograph of Keyes inset into the text. The face was bleached to white, the eyes holes in the picture, a razor-cut fringe of black hair indistinguishable from the background. Nothing in the reproduced and degraded image reminded him of anyone he could consciously remember. The article was entitled 'The Man Who Created Rob Hackwill', and illustrated with scratchy sketches, by Keyes himself, of his early ideas of the character.

Mal Gariazzo, whose death-by-hanging had been ruled 'due to sexual adventure' by the Hollywood coroner, would obviously have to be replaced. Keyes, who was fulsome in his praise for the late actor, promised that a new face would mean a new Rob Hackwill, a more serious monster for the nineties. 'No crappy jokes,' he promised, 'just no-frills scares.' The new film would 'explore the Rob Hackwill mythos', and finally explain that the whole curse was due to the fact that the town's founders had built on an Indian burial ground. 'Rob Hackwill is white America, the parasite,' Keyes explained, 'the cancer on the virgin land, the epitome of the twentieth-century nightmare.'

At the end, the interviewer asked the question Hackwill had been waiting for. 'Where did the name come from?'

'It's kind of silly,' Keyes said. 'When I was a kid in England, there was a bully in my playground . . .'

'Remember when you made him drink water from the toilet?' Reg said. 'And the time you hung his shorts from the climbing frame after PE? You were a right little monster, Robbo.'

Hackwill still could remember almost nothing.

Ben McKinnell told him there was another set-back, and no more capital was available for the Discount Development. Hackwill fixed the developer with his eye and made demands. McKinnell countered with threats. Certain deals could be made public. He chewed his cigar stub and Hackwill was reminded of the gangster in *Where the Bodies Are Buried*, the one whose head catches fire.

McKinnell inhaled and began to cough. Hackwill made no move to help him. The cigar fell, and smouldered on the carpet. McKinnell's face was red, and his hands were around his own throat. He looked as if he were throttling himself.

Hackwill hissed through his teeth.

The developer fell off his chair and crawled a few feet before turning on his back, eyes staring up. Ben McKinnell had swallowed his own tongue and choked on it.

Hackwill made and unmade a clawed fist.

Who'd have believed it? He chortled to himself, his nails rapping the table.

Ginger Dillon was a heroin addict, nearly bankrupt because of her habit. Jilly Kenner, the feminist, had paid for her university tuition as a nude model. The publisher of the *Herald* had a taste for underage girls and had stopped running editorials making 'Rob Hackwill' jokes. Jeanie Morris kept a selection of hard-core pornography under the counter for special customers and was willing to turn over her client list to keep the secret safe. His own secretary had had two abortions before her sixteenth birthday and another one on the way. The chair of the housing committee had three bank accounts under assumed names. Douggie McKinnell had killed a business rival with a cricket bat. The manager of the Palace was bent as a nine-bob note and HIV Positive. Chris, Shelley's ex-boyfriend, was Mrs Dillon's dope delivery boy. Helen had slept with Sammy's art teacher three times. Colin had a dirty magazine hidden under his comics.

He sat in the darkened room, in his seat at the head of the table. He felt as if he were the dark heart of the town. He could see the glowing lines that connected everything. He knew everything there was to be known. But he still couldn't remember the child who'd grown up to be a writer.

Shelley was leaving for East Anglia. He gave her an envelope full of fifty-pound notes to supplement her grant. She was the only one he had any time for. He hoped Sammy would grow up to be like Shelley, but there was not much chance of that now, the kids being with their mother, raised to be mini-Helens.

'Good-bye, monster,' Shelley said, kissing his cold cheek.

She walked away, her long, black coat outlining her sleek figure. She reminded Hackwill of the actress who played the Devil in the *Where the Bodies Are Buried* films. Before she was out of sight, she turned and gave him an encouraging wave.

The bulldozers were still there, under tarpaulins. Work was supposed to resume any day, as soon as the surviving McKinnell Brothers had sorted out their complicated tangle of affairs. Ben McKinnell had been heavily insured and the cash injection would keep the Development going. Hackwill thought it would never be finished:

the Development would drag on forever, spreading across Denbeigh Gardens to swamp the close where Mrs Dillon lived, then sprawling through the town, ripping up the roads and parks and houses, replacing asphalt with mud.

He stood where the Gardens had been, soil clogging the soles of his shoes. Holes were excavated all around like mass graves. He'd been spending a lot of time here, loitering, thinking. He walked carefully across the bare earth. It was dark and the ground was treacherous.

There was a bright moon to guide him, but he knew where the chasms were anyway. This was his country, for he was a monster. That was something he accepted. He had scraped bare this scar on the town map. Everything that got in his way, he had removed.

He wondered when he'd he become a monster. When he saw the poster for *Where the Bodies Are Buried* in Valerie's Video? When Allan Keyes first turned on his word processor and dredged up a name from his own past for a made-up character? When he had accepted his first consultancy fee? Or back in the playground, when Reg and he had picked out a solitary little boy and made a mark on his mind?

'It was here,' a voice said.

Reg stood by the bulldozer, wrapped up warm in an anorak. Hackwill had noticed him hanging around on the fringes of his one-eyed vision for days now.

'We used to play here, remember?'

Hackwill realised it was true. Ash Grove, closed down years ago, was a few streets away. Denbeigh Gardens had been on the way to and from school.

'Allan used to make up stories about a monster in the shed,' he said, remembering at last. 'It ate eyes.'

'Found his vocation,' Reg said. 'If you hadn't made him drink loo-water, he wouldn't be in Beverly Hills porking popsies in bikinis and shovelling half Colombia up his nose.'

Hackwill remembered the screwed-up child-face, leaking tears. The face was close, because he was holding the kid's shoulders, shaking them. Reg egged him on, making suggestions, darting about like an ape, grinning and laughing.

'The little shit *owes* you, Robbo,' Reg said.

Hackwill found a pick-axe in his hands. It had been stuck into a pile of rubble like the sword in the stone. His long-nailed fingers gripped the wooden handle.

'He shouldn't have done what he did, made you a laughing-stock.'

'Allan didn't mean anything, Reg,' Hackwill said, swinging. 'Rob Hackwill just came to life and got away from him.'

Allan Keyes had picked the wrong name for his playground demon. Like everybody, he hadn't remembered properly. Hackwill would never have chosen Allan if it hadn't been for Reg. Yet again, he'd let Hackwill take the consequences.

The pick-point sank into Reg's breast-bone and came out from between his back-ribs. The Independent emptied his lungs in a reverse gulp and blood burst from his mouth. Hackwill pulled the implement free and Reg tottered.

He growled, 'Get the point?'

282

Reg extended his arms as black blood squirted from his mouth and the hole in his chest. Every time he'd ever been in trouble, Reg had been there, guilty and chuckling and safe. Hackwill reached out a claw-hand and took a patch out of the Independent's face. He crumpled it in his fist like a slimy leaf, then dropped it.

'What's the matter,' he snarled, wiping his hand on Reg's anorak, 'why the fallen face?'

It wasn't fair, but he had to accept it: he was Rob Hackwill, the monster.

Reg stood at the lip of one of the excavations. With a prodding finger, Hackwill toppled him backwards. The grave-darkness swallowed him.

Hackwill looked up at the night sky and laughed, a red film on his vision turning the moon into a blood-eye. As far as anyone was concerned, he was *the* Rob Hackwill.

He stood on the brink, kicking in earth on top of the dead man. Reg's white and red face disappeared under black clods.

Looking up from the hole, a gust of wind hit his frozen face. His shut eye shocked open and he saw figures where the swings had been. A small child on the ground; another, bigger one on top of him, holding his face into earth; and one standing by, looking out for adults, chuckling.

The wind passed and his eye closed again, shutting out the children. His face was set. He saw only the place that was his home now, a playground turned to a graveyard. Rob Hackwill squatted in the shadows between piles of earth, a night-creature hiding from the dawn.

· · ·

Vary rarely, it's possible to trace the spark which led to a particular story. In this case, it was a line in an essay by Dennis Fischer in his book *Horror Film Directors: 1930–1990*, discussing Wes Craven, writer-director of *A Nightmare on Elm Street*. Of Freddy Krueger, Fischer wrote 'Craven named his creation after a child who tormented him as a kid'. The bully must have made a lasting impression because the villain of Craven's first film *Last House on the Left*, who is even more repulsive than Ol' Pizza Face, was called Krug. My first thought was that there must be some middle-aged hardware store manager in Ohio who is really fed up with all the jokes about his name. Then, I gave some thought to the 'franchise' horror characters who became prominent in the eighties and 'Where the Bodies Are Buried' crept out of my head, oddly in parallel with Alan Bleasdale's TV serial *GBH*, which also features a councillor whose twitches and involuntary arm-movements reflect personal and political corruption. Just in case you were wondering, I borrowed the name 'Rob Hackwill' from a friend who never did me any harm.

I finished *Nightmare Movies*, my non-fiction book about horror films, before franchise characters became dominant. It strikes me as interesting that almost all the *Fangoria* cover boys have been promoted from the ranks: Jason isn't even the murderer in the first *Friday the 13th*, and doesn't put on his trademark hockey mask until *Part III* (in 3–D); Leatherface is just one of the killers in *The Texas Chain Saw Massacre*, and his would-be franchise status isn't obvious until *Leatherface: Texas Chainsaw*

Massacre III; Pinhead is billed (as 'Lead Cenobite') very low down the cast of *Hellraiser* and has only a bit part, but – thanks to his appearance on the poster – became the series' signature character and star; and John Carpenter tried a *Halloween* (*Halloween III: Season of the Witch*) without Michael Myers and made an interesting picture which the fans rejected, then sold off the rights to others who churned out far less interesting retreads of the original with Michael back in the lead.

Robert Englund, who plays Freddy Krueger, is billed *ninth* in *A Nightmare on Elm Street* but rises to before-the-title status in the sequels. Originally, Krueger was a child molester, but this seamy side – which hardly sits with kiddie merchandising – has been expunged to the point when, as I was told by Nancy Collins, a submission to an *Elm Street* comic exploring this aspect of the killer's activities was rejected with extreme prejudice. Franchise characters cannot be manufactured (Craven tried with 'Horace Pinker' of *Shocker* to pull the trick off again and didn't manage it). They get away from their creators and establish identities shaped by their merchandising-happy corporate owners and their free-associating fans. A genre climate which can produce series starring the Toxic Avenger or the transexual killer from *Sleepaway Camp* hardly strikes me as conducive to much interesting work, and I find it depressing that Sam Raimi should be stuck in the rut his *Evil Dead* films have become, or that Clive Barker and Wes Craven should be constantly flirting with the possibility of returning to series they originated and which have been bled dry by flashily unrewarding sequels.

Where the Bodies Are Buried II: Sequel Hook

The deal was on the table and, though his American agent told him he was insane, Allan Keyes was going to take it.

It's not like you're signing your soul away for nothing, the voice said silently, *you have a percentage of the gross.*

Ray Calme, President of New Frontier Pictures, had the script in one hand, the contract in the other. The contract was thicker than the script and word-processed to a higher standard. According to Whit Pulsford, Allan's agent, it was also more frightening.

Where the Bodies Are Buried would be *An Allan Keyes Film.*

'Allan,' Calme said, 'I like you. I like you oh so much. We're going to make pots o' money.'

What do you mean 'we', kimosabe?

Allan shifted in his chrome and leather s-m chair while Calme weighed the documents as if he were a

Scale of Justice. New Frontier, despite the Hollywood address, wasn't a studio but a suite of offices above a loan company. They rented facilities on a film-by-film basis and were strictly non-union.

'You Brits, you're like visionaries. Look at Alan Parker, Adrian Lyne . . .'

Neither of whom have ever made a film that was any good, actually.

'Tony Scott, Roland Joffé!'

Good grief.

'And Renaissance men! To have a real, live novelist who can also direct a film . . .'

That's a moot point . . .

'Forget *Karnage*,' Calme said, 'it's in the used-tapes-from-$2.99 bin. The theatrical prints are guitar plectrums.'

Allan was uncomfortable. After all this sweet talk, he expected to get royally screwed.

'This is a chance for you to start over.'

Last year, Allan had made it into the Top Ten of *Film Threat*'s 'Frigid Fifty', a list of the people least likely to get another job in Hollywood not involving parking cars or asking 'still or sparkling?' all day. Having seen most of *Karnage*, the film with his name on it, Allan thought the magazine overestimated his career prospects.

'*Where the Bodies Are Buried* is going to change industry perception of you,' Calme continued, happily lining up script and contract on his teakwood desk. 'And it'll get New Frontier some respect. Trust me.'

The air conditioner buzzed like a meat-grinder, reminding Allan of New Frontier movies: *Hacksaw*

Hookers, *The Cincinatti Flamethrower Holocaust*, *Gross*.
Surprisingly few were in-house productions. Calme preferred to pick up cheapies made in Europe or by semi-
amateurs in Nowhere America, splice in tits 'n' gore,
and slap on a high concept title. Calme had titles in
his drawer he'd not yet been able to find films to fit.
They had first met when Calme tried to buy up *Chitinous
Splinters*, his student film, and rename it *Bug Bomb*.

'This monster, this Rob Hackwill, he's gonna be
like Frankenstein for the eighties, for the *nineties*. Just
from reading the script and looking at the sketches
the make-up goons have worked up, I can't sleep for
thinking about the son-of-a-bitch.'

Calme made a snarly monster face and claw-gestured,
impersonating Rob Hackwill.

Maybe you should play the part, Ray-Ban.

'It's a dynamite scary idea, Allan. The blackmailer
who knows everything and can't be killed. The monster who knows *where the bodies are buried* and won't
ever let up.'

*un film de Allan Keyes . . . for best achievement in
direction, the nominees are . . .*

'By the time New Frontier does the sequel, we won't
be able to afford you.'

'There can't be a sequel,' Allan said quietly. 'At the
end, I'm killing him forever. It's part of the ritual.'

'You'll be at Pyramid or Warners, making *mucho
dinero*,' Calme said, rubbing his thumb against his
fingers. 'You know who used to get coffee for me?'

Roger Rabbit?

'Oliver Stone. Now he won't talk to me in the

street. I can't get him on the phone. Next year, that's you.'

This year, this month, this day, Allan Keyes had precisely one American screen credit. That was only because his deal had been worded so he couldn't take his name off *Karnage*. His directorial career consisted of *Chitinous Splinters*, a piece of student surrealism that sometimes turned up after midnight on public television, the werewolf episodes of *Emmerdale Farm*, and two weeks fighting to preserve his script for *Karnage*, only to find himself unceremoniously booted off set in favour of his producer's college room-mate. In interviews, the *Karnage* krew claimed he was a dilettante who didn't know how to take a lens cap off. Ray Calme was his only chance to become an official director. A *writer*-director.

'You and Ollie,' Calme said, letting one hand savagely attack the other. 'Like this.'

The deal was that Calme would let Allan make *Where the Bodies Are Buried* in return for a fifth of the fee. Even New Frontier would pay for the script if a writer weren't attached to it as director.

The crazy thing was that Allan, alone in a city of table-waiting Hitchcocks and valet-parking Antonionis, didn't *want* to be a director. He had always been more interested in prose, and had gone to film school almost on a whim. The *Emmerdale* assignment, coming in the middle of a decade of scribbling underemployment, had been a surprise and an ordeal, crawling along because someone somewhere had happy memories of how stoned he was during the brief festival run of *Chitinous Splinters*.

Allan didn't even want to be in the Big Parking Lot

of Lo-Cal, USA. Like Lesley, his long-term live-in, he *preferred* the British climate. He had constant twinges that he should get back to Somerset and just be a writer. But the movie thing bit deep: after watching *Karnage* aborted under other hands, what he wanted was to protect his baby.

It's the world's most powerful natural instinct, after all.

Calme, smiling his professorial drug dealer's smile, patted the script gently, and hugged the contract (*his* baby) to the *Hacksaw Hookers* T-shirt he wore under a Savile Row suitcoat. Allan had been surprised to learn, from a New Frontier hand-out, that Ray Calme had a degree in industrial chemistry.

'Theatre owners are going to hate you, Allan, because *Bodies* is going to make people shit with fright. No kidding, they'll have to replace seat-covers every performance.'

Allan knew that, compared with Ray Calme, the idiot who mutilated *Karnage* was liable to have his life's work preserved by the Museum of Modern Art. The New Frontier formula was 95% tits 'n' gore, plus 5% crappy jokes. Allan, still deep down the underage horror fan who had sneaked into the Palace to see the X-certificated *Devil Daughter of Dracula*, had never been able to get to the end of a New Frontier movie without pain.

'Allan,' Calme said, 'I know we can do real business.'

The step was taken and he was committed, for better or flamethrower holocaust. Allan relaxed.

'I have notes,' Calme said, indicating the script.

Allan was prepared to be reasonable, to take advice

on board and weigh it up, then shoot what he wanted anyway.

Most of the agony was in the past. When reworking 'A Trickle of Shame' as a screenplay, Allan had switched the story's West Country setting into an American Mid-West that owed more to movies than experience. The middle-aged teacher heroine became a teenage high-schooler and the dead serious monster grew a nastily twisted sense of humour. Still, the heart of the piece was untouched; the story retained its integrity, its subtext. There was a seriously scary point to it all.

'I love the scene where the bimbo's boobs come to life and slap her around,' Calme said, chuckling. 'Don't change a word of the script.'

Except, he means, to limit the action to as few sets as possible to save on carpentry.

Allan had been trying to wrap personal concerns in a commercial package. He was, so far, pleased to come up with something which appealed to Ray Calme but wouldn't disappoint his readers. In the end, he was doing this deal because he couldn't stand to go to another convention and have to explain how other people had turned a perfectly-formed story like *Karnage* into celluloid sludge.

Calme leafed through the script, amusing himself.

'The guy's tongue exploding his head? Outstanding.'

The effect would cost more than the actor. But it would be worth it.

Calme came to the end.

'Here's my problem,' he said.

Allan's heart froze.

'After the monster is torn apart by the ghosts of his victims, you have Tina, the tits girl, shut the scrapbook on him, and there's a flaming "End" title?'

Allan nodded. That was how he saw *Where the Bodies Are Buried* finishing.

'It's like the Hammer Films,' Allan explained. 'You leave with the dust of Dracula blowing in the wind. I'm fed up with the non-endings films have these days. It's all over and then you see there's one monster still under the floorboards. It cheats the audience.'

'Yeah, yeah, good stuff, Allan, right enough. But, for $15,000 and a shot at director, you've got to give me a sequel hook.'

At one o'clock in the morning, Allan got home to the rented house he had left twenty hours earlier. The first day of shooting was done, and he wanted to shove his head through a plate-glass door.

Lesley had stayed up, and made Ovaltine and sandwiches for him as he sat in the cramped kitchen and wound down. They had been together for so long he didn't even need to tell her what he wanted in his sandwiches. She didn't ask him what it had been like.

His nerves were still singing. He could still hear the clatter and chatter of the set.

'I don't know,' he said.

Heh heh heh . . .

'Maybe there's a way this can work . . .'

Lesley put an arm around him and helped him to bed.

* * *

Two middle-aged couples walked out in the first fifteen minutes, shaking their heads and complaining about the noise. A blast of Heavy Metal followed them from the auditorium. Calme said that was good; he'd be ashamed to make a horror film parents liked.

Suddenly, it's Ray-Ban who 'makes' the films, isn't it?

Before anyone outside an edit suite had seen an assembly of *Where the Bodies Are Buried*, Allan had signed, for over five times the money, to direct *City Hammer*, an action script by a British comics creator. He knew he'd have to rewrite, without credit. Not as personal a project as his own film, it would show he could explode a helicopter with the best of them. It was a step out of the gutter, away from New Frontier; not to a Major, but to a high-profile Independent, Mojacar. Also, as Whit told him, it got him taken seriously. In this town, people judged worth by asking price. It was better to have directed a schlocky flop for $80,000 than a sleeper hit for $15,000. It was especially useful, Whit now conceded, to have leaped from $15,000 to $80,000; that curve should land Allan $400,000 for his first studio project (probably a big budget sequel) and, if that hit, settle him in the $2,000,000 club until he had a monster that edged in with the Spielbergs and John Hugheses in the *Variety* Top Ten Grossers, whereupon his asking price entered the Twilight Zone.

Getting ahead of ourselves, aren't we?

Calme had driven Allan, and a couple of New Frontier suits who hadn't showed their faces during the actual shooting, out to Westwood for a sneak preview of *Where the Bodies Are Buried*. Lesley, who'd lived with the traumas of creation but never seen footage, had gone inside to find out what the agony was about, but Allan, along with the New Frontier brass, kept to the foyer.

A scattering of cast and crew also turned up, including Mal Gariazzo, the tinily energetic Italian-American who seemed possessed by the wicked spirit of Rob Hackwill. His screen time was limited and he was billed eleventh but his snakily crazed performance would elevate him from 'who is . . . ?' to 'get me . . . !' Before landing the part, for which he'd campaigned intensively, he'd been in New Frontier beach bimbo films as the hero's geeky friend who didn't get laid and threw up on the wet T-shirt queen. Now he'd be up for the British villain's sadistic sidekick in action blockbusters.

As the film unspooled, Gariazzo, in a much-strapped leather jumpsuit, nervously stalked the foyer, chain-munching popcorn. Without the glowing red eye, mangled face, exposed teeth and steel claws, he was unrecognisable as the monster, but occasionally he gave out horribly unmistakable Rob Hackwill laughs.

Mal-de-merde thinks he's Rob Hackwill, does he?

Where the Bodies Are Buried was being shown after a Christian Slater film; the theatre was packed with teenage couples and gaggles of girls. From the foyer, Allan could tell exactly where the movie was by the pitch of the screams. He knew the film to the shot, to the *second*, and he could feel in his stomach an excitement that corresponded with the crescendos of tension and the pay-offs of shock.

'It's the tongue next,' he said.

He could have sworn the auditorium doors swelled

outwards with the rush of audible fear. Then came a ripple of relieved laughter and a settling-down as the scene changed.

Gariazzo chortled and clawed the air in triumph. He took his power personally. The monster's crazy-funny streak came directly from the actor. Allan couldn't help but look at Gariazzo sometimes as if he were his daughter's first boyfriend.

Remember, you signed the paper, Daddy. You don't own Rob Hackwill. New Frontier does.

After about an hour, during the flashback when Hackwill was taken to Hell and given his mission of vengeance by the Devil Princess, a girl in her early teens was helped out of the cinema by a clutch of her friends. She was sobbing silently and unsteady on her ankles.

'We should get a pub shot of that,' Calme chortled.

'Wow,' said one of the girls, '*intense!*'

'Can I get the door for you?' Gariazzo asked, a Hackwill croak in his voice.

The hysterical teenager looked at the innocently-smiling actor and went cross-eyed as she fainted. Gariazzo laughed his normal laugh. Calme was suddenly concerned, thinking of lawsuits. The audience screamed again. Allan Keyes had arrived.

'As adults, we forget the wonders and terrors of childhood,' Allan told Turner Mockridge, the withered kid from *Fangoria*. 'Children are permanently afraid. Me, I was besieged by this vast, formless, black wall of fear. It's the flipside of the magic and it lasts longer. You remember Wicked Witches better than Munchkins.

With *Bodies*, I wanted to come to grips with the fear, to bring it back with an adult subtext. Let's face it, you no longer have to worry about a bigger kid snatching your dinner money, but as you grow up the world gets more complicated. It was bad enough being afraid of losing your school custard, now you have to be afraid of losing your house, your job, your marriage. Scary, isn't it?'

Yes.

The boyish, balding genre journalist looked at his digital notepad. He was the only badly dressed person Allan had met in California.

'Where did *Where the Bodies Are Buried* come from?'

'A diseased little tumour inside my brain. Actually, I was thinking about the EC Philosophy of Cosmic Justice. You know the EC horror comics of the fifties?'

Mockridge nodded an 'of course'. Asking the Man From *Fango* that, was like asking a literature professor if he knew D.H. Lawrence.

'Most of their stories follow a simple format. It certainly wasn't original to William M. Gaines. Since *The Haunt of Fear* was before my time, I came to know the formula through the Amicus films of the early seventies. It was also common in *The Pan Book of Horror Stories*, not that a heathen American would know what that was, and *The Twilight Zone*. Essentially, you have a protagonist who goes around being a complete bastard until God drops a brick on his head. The subtext is that people who bring evil into the world but are beyond human law invoke a cosmic justice that allows for a horribly ironic fate.'

'Like the vivisectionist who is kidnapped by aliens and experimented on?'

'That was a famous one. Robert Bloch always used Cosmic Justice as an excuse for a bitter pun. You know, "cat got your tongue"?'

'You used the format in *Strange Segments*. In 'Off-Ground Touch', for instance, where the middle-aged guy goes back to the school where he was a bully and gets menaced by the adult-sized children. Isn't it limiting for a full-length film?'

'It would be. It's basically a lazy man's short story outline. What I've tried to do in *Where the Bodies Are Buried* is examine the metaphysical workings that would allow for that kind of plot. Rob Hackwill, as we learn in the flashback, was a typical EC protagonist, a scumbag blackmailer who was tortured, mutilated and murdered by his victims and buried by dead of night in the town graveyard. His punishment in the afterlife is to become the wholesale implement of Cosmic Justice. The Devil Princess, my version of the ruler of a malign but ordered universe, sends him back as a monster vigilante. Everybody in town was rotten in the first place, or Hackwill wouldn't have been able to blackmail them. He merely ups the stakes by forgetting money and extorting pain, fear and, ahem, hideous physical transformations.'

'Your work always comes down to a sense of order and justice?'

'That's a very astute insight, Turner. Indeed, Hackwill is all-powerful until he comes up against a truly innocent person, our heroine.'

Mockridge thought it over for a moment, digesting

what had been said. Allan, always delighted to dissect his own work, wondered if he had given away too many plot points.

'Now the question I am obliged by law to ask. What will your next film project be? Will it be horror?'

'*City Hammer* is science fiction action but it'll have monsters in it. I'm already perverting it in the rewrite. When I see an opening to scare people, I can't resist shouting "boo!"'

'Do you plan on continuing in the genre, as a writer and as a film-maker?'

'I can't see anywhere else to go. Writing about middle-class women who get cancer doesn't really appeal to me. I'd have the cancer be a living, thinking thing. Thus far, I've not had an idea which would take me beyond the boundaries of the genre continent into that cold clime they call the mainstream. I'm not one of those who'll say, you know, "This picture may be called *Werewolf Cheerleaders*, but it's not a horror movie, it's about relationships." I'd like it on the record that *Where the Bodies Are Buried* is a fuck of a horror film and I'd really like it to terrify people.'

By the premiere, Allan decided he could bear to watch *Where the Bodies Are Buried* again.

Sensing a chance for the kind of acclaim *Hacksaw Hookers* never had a hope of, Ray Calme had arranged a midnight matinee for celebrities from the world of horror. At first, response was disappointing: genre professionals had seen too many New Frontier pictures on tape to risk venturing out to the Century Pantheon to catch another *Cincinatti Flamethrower Holocaust* on the big screen. Allan's rep as a writer helped: the short story collection *Strange Segments*, while not the hot book it had been in England, had been well-received in America, and the novel *Busting a Gut* (which Stephen King said turned his hair white) brushed the lower end of the *New York Times* Best-Seller list. He had been profiled by *Cinéfantastique*. Word was out that, as films directed by writers go, *Where the Bodies Are Buried* was more like *Hellraiser* than *Maximum Overdrive*.

A lot more like Hellraiser, *eh, Mr Plagiarist? All those dangling chains . . .*

Mal Gariazzo, in full Hackwill drag, escorted Breeze Brasselle, the 'scream queen' who played the Devil Princess. They camped it up outside the Pantheon, posing with embarassed guests as a phalanx of photographers snapped like turtles. Forrest J Ackerman, Joe Bob Briggs and Elvira got into the spirit. Dennis Etchison looked as if he'd rather be somewhere else. Calme checked the guest-list: Alice Cooper, John Carpenter and David Schow had arrived; David Cronenberg, Ray Bradbury and Barbara Steele were no-shows so far. Mimes dressed as monsters mingled with the guests, offering trays of scary canapés: sugar tarantulas and sausage slugs.

A few people asked Lesley who she was and skittered away when she nodded at Allan and said 'I'm with the band'. Her only comment after the preview had been, 'Well, you can still surprise me.' The first time Whit had met Lesley, he'd told her she would have to watch Allan around all the starlets. Then, she had said she could handle it – her Deputy Head pay had supported them through years of his unsteady writing income – but now she might have changed her mind.

Breeze stuck her tongue down Allan 's throat for the photographers. Lesley looked up at the sky and shook her head the way Allan's mother used to.

City Hammer was in the can after four nightmare weeks in the desert with stunt-drivers and radioactive mutants, and Whit had meetings set up at Pyramid and Universal. The galleys of *Cornworld* were out at the studios, and the rights bidding started at $250,000. It was written into any deal that Allan would script and direct the film. An expansive fantasy with a New Age twist, *Cornworld* could very well be the Next Big Thing. He'd come a long way from St Louis. Sedgmoor, rather.

My-my, high muckety-muck, Mr Keyes. Next you'll be forgetting who got you where you are.

A nasty wind blew through the plaza outside the Pantheon, lifting the webby skirts of women at the *première*, scuttling discarded wrappers across the forecourt like crippled insects. This development was supposed to be litter-free, but – like the street people the Pantheon employed uniformed security men to exclude – rubbish had a way of creeping back in.

In the lobby, Allan sipped his New Frontier wine (ten cents a gallon, unless he misjudged Calme) and noticed how people he knew quite well avoided talking to him. After the film, that would be different, he hoped. It took a lot to scare professionals but he thought he had more than a lot.

It's just a question of knowing their secrets. That's what

*scares people, Allan . Knowing, heh heh heh, Where the
Bodies Are Buried.*

Everyone filed into the auditorium at midnight. Allan
and Lesley took their reserved seats in the back row,
and Lesley patted him on the arm, forgiving him for
the Scream Queen. Calme, who loved to strut about in
public and take credit, made a speech which was greeted
with sceptical laughter. Then the film played.

By the finale, Allan was in love with his baby again.
Months of post-production tinkering had made him hate
Where the Bodies Are Buried. As the soundtrack was laid
in (he wanted a harpsichord concerto; Calme insisted
on a 'hot band' named Putrid) and the effects scenes
were optically enhanced (why hadn't that eyeball burst
on cue?), he'd become intensely aware of the film's
deformities. The sets looked cheap, the acting was
variable at best, the exposition came in an unwieldy
lump near the end, Hackwill should never have come
out of the shadows and the good shots reminded him of
other, better films.

Isaac, the veteran editor, had helped with the delivery and made sure the child's head was on the right
way round. Cynthia Vanning, the twenty-eight-year-old
teenage heroine, had only three facial expressions; but
Isaac, who had valuable experience on Lassie movies,
manipulated off-cuts of film to jerk her strings to such
an extent that she actually seemed to be giving a
performance.

Even this audience reacted. They were scared.

Got them.

It wasn't 'A Trickle of Shame', but it was a film. With less money and fewer resources, he had done better than *Karnage*. On that alone, he could retire with dignity and write for the rest of his days.

Deep down, he liked it a little less than *Chitinous Splinters*.

Lesley's hand was around his upper arm, fingers biting like little snakes. He could feel her cringe at every superbly-orchestrated shock. Even second time through, it worked.

Rob Hackwill was dragged back to Hell and his victims tore him apart. Gobbets of fire were slung around. Gariazzo even managed to work a little sympathy in for the monster. In the end, like Kong and Karloff's Monster, he was a victim too.

One big scream and the ashes settled. Then came the scene Allan had never been able to love. He had written it, had filmed it, but could never *feel* it. After the end of Allan Keyes's *Where the Bodies Are Buried*, came the Ray Calme scene, the sequel hook.

It was all over but it was starting again. Tina, having survived, was in the school bathrooms, smoking and remembering. The faces of all her dead friends drifted by in the mirror.

Not a bad effect, he conceded, grudgingly.

Then came that godawful Heavy Metal and the monster exploded out of a toilet bowl, red-eyed and cackling. Everyone jumped and the Putrid music crashed over the credits.

The buzz was incredible. People who had avoided him all evening congratulated him. Whit had his pocket calculator out and estimated the opening weekend gross. Gariazzo took bows and did the laugh. Mockridge told Lesley he expected a sweep of the Chainsaw Awards. Calme puffed a cigar as if he were David O. Selznick the night *Gone With the Wind* came home with Oscar. Clive Barker didn't mention the familiar dangling chains.

Only Allan noticed the sequel hook. And his constant companion.

That ending, Allan. It's shit. It was a bad mistake. It'll come back to haunt you.

'. . . not since *Elm Street One* . . . *Carrie* . . . *Chain Saw* . . . *Psycho* . . .'

And if it doesn't, I will.

Cornworld was in turnaround for a rewrite (Pyramid wanted it *bigger*, plus the Green Man role written larger for Sean Connery) and *Pixie Patrol*, outlined well before *Where the Bodies Are Buried* and nearly forgotten, was suddenly a 'go' project. Pyramid said it was a good move to do a medium-budget studio film before taking on the herculean labour of *Cornworld*.

His writer-director fee on *Pixie Patrol* was close to the entire below-the-line budget of *Where the Bodies Are Buried*. The script was about a streetwise black cop, played by comedian Muldoon Pezz, partnered with an elfin warrior to reclaim Excalibur from a power-crazed televangelist played, with the most British accent imaginable, by Julian Sands. Mal Gariazzo was penciled in for the villain's sadistic sidekick, a heart-eating troll passing for human. For five minutes, it looked as if Allan would have to rewrite the lead for Whoopi Goldberg, then Pezz, needing a family hit to offset his drugs bust, committed. The deal fell in place overnight and shooting was due to start in three days.

Allan was by his pool, getting a massage, when Amaranth, his assistant, brought out a phone and asked him if he would take a call from Ray Calme. New Frontier had been trying to get to him all week, and he knew he would have to talk eventually.

He hadn't seen his old producer since *Where the Bodies Are Buried* pipped $40,000,000 in domestic box office. In a follow-up interview with Mockridge, Allan moaned about studio-imposed bad music and the cop-out ending. Calme sent *Fangoria* a letter about how artists didn't understand the real business of making movies.

'Allan, doll, how are you?' the tiny voice buzzed.

'Fine, Ray.'

'I saw *City Hammer*. Good picture.'

'That's one way of putting it.'

There are good things in it, Allan. They're just spaced pretty evenly among the crap things.

Allan gripped the phone tightly and the masseuse ran up against some knots.

'How are things at the Majors? See Oliver Stone much?'

Expert hands worked the aches around his neck. Sunlight shimmered on the waters of the pool. Prescription designer shades cut out the glare.

'Did you glom this week's *Hollywood Reporter*?'

'Yes.'

'What do you think?'

New Frontier had taken out a full-page ad, announcing

305

'Ray (*Hacksaw Hookers*) Calme Presents . . . Mal (*Rob Hackwill!!!*) Gariazzo in . . . Allan Keyes's *Where the Bodies Are Buried, Part II: Hackwill's Back!* (Credits Not Contractual).'

'I'd have changed a couple of words if you'd run it by me.'

'Which words?'

'"Allan Keyes's".'

'It's in your contract. Anything made from the *Bodies* premise, which New Frontier *owns*, has to be "An Allan Keyes Film". It's a good deal for you. You get your $15,000 all over again for *nada*.'

You made $15,000 before breakfast this morning. Once you get out here by the pool, money creeps in on autopilot.

'This Hackwill thing is big, Allan.'

The monster – *Allan's* monster – was being merchandised extensively by New Frontier. A *Where the Bodies Are Buried* comic book was forthcoming from Dark Horse and the Gore Store was marketing a Hackwill mask for Halloween. Every movie and monster magazine had done multiple covers with Gariazzo-as-Hackwill leering, looming, clutching, goggling or drooling. Allan's creation had become the Princess Di of the bizarro generation. Whit, soon to be Allan's former agent, hadn't negotiated a cut of any spin-off rights, though he had tied in compensations to the sequel clause.

'It's getting out of hand. I've had to take on an extra girl to handle all the Hackwill requests. Joe Bob has made him "Beast of the Year". Mal is doing the *Tonight Show* in character.'

Allan, of course, had followed his wayward child's

progress. The less scary Hackwill got, the less interested Allan was in him.

You're a bad parent. You should love me, however I turn out.

'I know we can't afford you to direct,' Calme said. 'We've got a line on the chick who did the Putrid videos.'

'Ellen Jeanette Sheridan?'

'That's her. Great talent. Like Walter Hill and Barbra Streisand in one package. She's hungry for a shot. She's comfortable with rubber. She's done a script.'

She's done a script?

'You'll love it. It's close to the first one. Mal's got more to do. It's more up-front about Hackwill. After all, he's who the kids pay to see. Frankenstein for the nineties. We've licensed the hobby kit.'

A cloud-shadow flitted over the sun, letting a wedge of cold fall briefly. Allan shivered and the masseuse soothed his gooseflesh away. His new $500 haircut itched.

'I'd like to work out an arrangement on *Bodies II*, Allan. If you'd just look at the script. Pencil out a few lines, scribble in a gag or two, dot some Ts and cross some Is.'

'I start shooting next week.'

'Yeah, yeah. Really, you don't have to read Ellen Jeanette's script. Just approve it. You'll get co-story credit, $50,000 loose cash, and a per cent of the gross. All for not doing anything.'

They'll make it anyway, whatever you do. They have the right. You gave me away, Dad. You sold me into slavery for a lousy fifteen grand. For ever.

'I really don't have time.'

'Allan, just do some pub when the film goes theatrical. We want you on board. You are the genius, the creator, the originator. Ellen Jeanette is in awe of you. Believe me, if you want a fast blow job at New Frontier, this girl is for you. She doesn't want to violate your vision. She sees herself as the channel through which you can work.'

You made me alone, master. Make me a bride, or I shall be with you on your wedding night . . .

'Shut yer neck,' Allan muttered.

'What was that?'

'Nothing, Ray. Look, I'll take it under advisement.'

'Just give us your blessing, just wish us well'

'Ray, make the film you want.'

The call was over.

I'm melting, meltiiiiing. They'll torture me, Dad. They'll do things you can't imagine. They're *the monsters, them, them, them.*

'So,' Mockridge asked, '*Pixie Patrol*, eh? That's doesn't sound like the Allan Keyes who gave us *Busting a Gut* and *Rob Hackwill*?'

'Wait until you've seen the movie, Turner,' Allan replied, 'I think you'll be surprised. I'm trying for a hard-edged fantasy. PG-13 sure, but we'll expand the ratings envelope. With a big sword macguffin, the temptation was to lop off heads and I've never been one to resist temptation.'

'But is it *horror*?'

'I think *Fango* won't be disappointed. Mal Gariazzo is aboard, eating some interesting new things.'

'What about the *Bodies* sequel? Are you involved?'

'I take a remote, paternal interest. But children have to leave home sometime. I hope Rob Hackwill is in good hands, because if mistreated he has a way of settling accounts that can be, as they say, final.'

'Allan,' Lesley said, 'this is nothing to do with you, but there's nothing for me here.'

She wasn't qualified to work in the US school system, and even if she started jumping through the hoops it would be decades before she could reach her former position.

West Somerset College said they would keep her Deputy Headship open for only six months and time was almost up.

'I have enough money for us both,' Allan said. 'Really, neither of us ever needs to work again.'

'It's not about money either.' Lesley shrugged, unable to explain. 'It's a quality of life decision.'

One thing about being where he was; he never *ever* had to be alone. Allan made Leech a gift of their old flat, paying off the mortgage with option money on a four-page story. After years of unwedded cohabitation, he'd been enjoying his bachelorhood. He specialised in the sort of girls who would have ignored him as a geeky teenager and who grew in clumps around the swimming pools out here.

Life was hectic. Going to a restaurant was a major operation, like invading France. At horror conventions, he was a top-of-the-bill guest. He turned down three-quarters of the TV and print interview requests.

Horror? No, I wouldn't really say I write horror. I'm a metaphysical romancer . . .

With *Cornworld* a Number One Best-Seller, he was an A-list Hollywood invitee; a *novelist* who could talk movies. Everyone he met had read the coverage, a few had even tried the book. In this town, he was glamorously intellectual, but he could play the game. When numbers were crunched, *Where the Bodies Are Buried* had a better cost-to-profit ratio than any major studio release of the last two years.

His new agency were pushing heavy for the *Cornworld* movie. It could be next summer's biggie. *Pixie Patrol* was nothing to be ashamed of, even if it faded after three weeks. After an opening weekend splash, it failed to grow legs.

He got back to the house and circumvented security. He dumped his keys in the tray on the hall table. The place sounded empty which, after the noise of the evening, was what he wanted. Sometimes it was blissful to be where nobody could hear you scream. By the tray was a package and a note from Amaranth.

He opened the package and found a cassette. It was an advance cut of *Where the Bodies Are Buried, Part II* with a scribbled compliments slip from Ray Calme. 'Ellen Jeanette is dying to know what you think.' Ellen Jeanette was well under five feet tall, had white hair down to her calves and suffered permanent hearing impairment from working with too many loud rock bands.

Busy on *Pixie Patrol*, even taking a trip back to Britain to do promotion and see Lesley installed in the West Country, he'd not kept up with *Hackwill's Back!* He'd read the script until the voice in his head yelled so loud he couldn't turn the pages and had reasoned that the whole thing had nothing to do with him.

Abandoner, betrayer, ravager!

Apart from the alcoholic police captain, the nympho-maniac French teacher and the perverted school janitor – and Hackwill, if he counted – all the characters in Ellen Jeanette Sheridan's screenplay were under eighteen. Allan thought the sequel would turn out like *Grange Hill* with tits 'n' gore. No, make that *Beverly Hills 90210* with tits 'n' gore. Back in Britain, with an 18 rating, nobody who would want to see *Hackwill's Back!* would legally be able to.

He might as well watch the thing now. If he fell asleep, he could always have the ending with his cornflakes tomorrow.

After making himself an Ovaltine in the bunker-like kitchen, he fired up the wall-sized projection video. Before settling down, he saluted the eighteen-inch Screamin' Rob Hackwill kit posed by the screen. Then he sprawled on the newly-installed, personalised divan, and tucked his legs under him. This was how he remembered watching Patrick Troughton as *Dr Who* in the sixties, when he was just learning the business of frightening people.

His parents had encouraged his interest in monsters, because somehow it made him less frightened. As a child, his problem had been nightmares. Often, he'd been kept back from school, which had its own horrors, through lack of sleep. The day he glued together his first glow-in-the-dark Aurora monster (the Wolf Man,

pumped-up plastic torso considerably more muscular than
the one sported by a hairy Lon Chaney Jr in the film) the
nightmares stopped. If there were monsters, then there
were monster-destroyers and the universe purged itself of
evil, at least until the sequel. Since then, he hadn't been
afraid. At school even, the horrors went away. When he
started telling stories about monsters, the other kids – one
of whom *had* been called Hackwill – stopped hitting and
started listening. He had discovered his power.

*Where is Robert Hackwill of Ash Grove Primary these
days? Do you suppose he's seen your little film?*

He zapped the remote. The screen was black. He
sipped Ovaltine. Red slashes appeared, making up a
stylised Rob face. Then the title, in letters of fire. *Where
the Bodies Are Buried, Part II: Hackwill's Back!*. Gariazzo-
as-Hackwill exploded snarling through the title, lipless
teeth chattering, red eye burning.

There was no story in the first ten minutes, just images.
Putrid struck power chords and pretty pictures stumbled
over the screen as if Ellen Jeanette had forgotten not
to make another rock video. So far as Allan could
understand, Hackwill was crawling back from Hell,
reassembling himself.

The film cut out and the screen became a black mirror.
Allan saw himself huddled, cooling cup in his hands,
goggling at the nothing.

All this expensive equipment, and it still doesn't work.

The image moved, as if the camera were circling. It
panned steadily, until it was no longer a reflection, but
a view from behind the divan. The screen showed the
back of Allan's head as he looked at a screen which

showed the back of Allan's head as he looked at a screen which showed the back of Allan's head . . . Smaller and smaller screen images zoomed to an infinite distance which tugged at him, threatening to pull the real Allan into the screen to fall for ever into the vortex.

He turned, but there was no camera behind him. Just the framed original Carson artwork for the *Cornworld* cover.

On screen, Allan was distracted by a sound. Ovaltine spilled as he jumped. A nanosecond later, unnerved by the fissure between real and reflected, Allan spilled his own drink. Warm stickiness spread across his thighs.

The film Allan got up and Ellen Jeanette cut to a close-up. Allan's heart began beating again. The man in the film wasn't his reflection, but an actor playing a character who happened to be dressed like him and in a set which was almost, but not quite, identical to the room he was sitting in. The actor, football player shoulders straining his jacket, didn't even look much like him.

Could this be some silly in-joke?

The actor made frightened faces as something scratched at the window. Allan couldn't remember any of this in the script. He couldn't help darting a look at his own unscratched windows. Outside, everything was dark. As he turned his head, the film showed a view of its windows. The shape of Hackwill was out there, unmistakable. The single red eye glowed.

'*I know everything, Kiss,*' Hackwill snarled nastily. '*About the girls, the parties, the pay-offs, the drugs . . .*'

The character – Kiss? – was horrorstruck.

As *Hackwill's Back!* played on, Allan got angry. The

313

high school story had been junked and the rewrite substituted a frankly libellous plot about a writer named, transparently, Adam Kiss. Instrumental in the original death of the blackmailer from Hell, Adam got rich on a trashy book about Hackwill which became a hit movie. Now the monster was persecuting him.

There was a scene where Adam argued with his girlfriend – Hedley! – and she walked out.

'Adam,' Hedley spat, 'this is nothing to do with you, but there's nothing for me here.'

Everything was twisted around. Really, Lesley left amicably, sadly confessing that she couldn't keep up. Her main reason for going was that her Mum was sick. They weren't definitely finished.

'It's not about money either,' Hedley snarled, throwing a bottle. 'It's a quality of life decision.'

In the film, Adam slapped Hedley around and tossed her out of the house, yelling abuse. The movie woman wasn't like Lesley; she was an older tramp who kept Adam in cocaine and got drunk in the daytime. Adam Kiss, a thoroughgoing bastard, wasn't like Allan Keyes.

A sad, complicated situation was turned into trite soap.

Hackwill made Hedley shrink while on a binge so she literally drowned in a gin bottle. After that, Adam got mixed up with Shelley, a Hollywood madame Allan recognised as the Devil Princess, and embarked on a crusade of degeneracy that allowed for edge-of-hardcore sex scenes interspersed with blubbering hysterical breakdowns. Hackwill stalked the feckless, worthless, useless Adam Kiss. Supporting characters died.

Allan looked from the screen to the Screamin' Rob and back again. He couldn't understand how New Frontier had allowed this to happen. His lawyers would take the company to pieces.

You didn't do anything. You're innocent. You're not Adam Kiss.

Covering all the sleaze bases, *Hackwill's Back!* stirred in elements from the Roman Polanski and Rob Lowe sex scandals. Adam was videotaped in an orgy with two extremely underaged girls. Allan found the scene deeply disturbing. As Ellen Jeanette's camera got excited and the Heavy Metal throbbed like a painful erection, the image went in and out of focus and Allan kept seeing his own features instead of the actor's. The speakers behind the screen shrieked.

Hackwill was looming. The monster stepped in, steel claws flashing, and he gutted the girls, covering the screaming Adam-Allan with insides. After the blood settled, a phone rang in the murder room, and Hackwill reached for it to make a joke.

The real phone rang, shocking Allan into action. He grabbed out for it, stabbing the pause button. Adam's face froze, dripping.

'*Enjoying the show?*' Hackwill croaked.

'Mal, you bastard, is this you? You didn't tell me about *Hackwill's Back!* I'll take Calme for everything.'

'*Silly Daddy, this isn't Mal-de-merde. This is Rob.*'

Allan froze, feeling the warm wetness on his own face. Numbed, he slipped into his own darkness.

He woke up in a wash of pain. Bloody pulses shot through

his brain. His sinuses were sandpapery and his gums hurt. He tasted rinds of whisky blood between his teeth.

Allan had got half-way out of the video room and was twisted in a static-crackly sheet. He was out of his clothes and sticky all over. He'd just lie here for a moment and hope he wasn't about to be sick.

The projection video buzzed.

He sat up, getting the door-jamb behind his back, and the sheet fell away from his chest. There was bruising around his right nipple. He touched the spot and it hurt. It was as if a powerful vacuum cleaner had been stuck to his tit.

His back was scratched and trickling. He thought he felt splinters of raw wood in there. Trying to remember, his head fogged.

Heavy night, Adam?

'That's not me,' he said, his voice ancient, 'that's the other fellow.'

He still wore his $15,000 watch. It was O8:22. At nine, Amaranth would be here. And Consuela, who cleaned. Looking into the video room, he saw Consuela would earn a bonus today. The place was almost wrecked. Furniture overturned, empty bottles broken and trodden into the rugs, clothes scattered. Even pictures hung crooked. The blinding white of the screen upon which light was still projecting was splashed with something that dried to brown-orange.

He remembered *Hackwill's Back!* and he remembered being angry. He must have cut loose.

I guess this is that Lifestyle of the Rich and Famous you always wanted.

Unwinding himself from the sheet, he found he was wearing a condom. As he slipped it off, it squelched.

Somebody had a good time last night.

It was as if he'd skipped a couple of days. He had come home, watched half a video, got angry, fallen asleep. Checking his watch again, he confirmed that it was the next morning.

He couldn't even remember a debauched dream. In his night thoughts, he'd been at school again naked, sitting an exam he hadn't prepared for, chased by bullies, trying to wrap a parcel that came apart in his hands. A wet dream would have been a relief.

In the bathroom, he dealt with the condom. Two others floated in the toilet. Like a persistent turd, one took three flushes to vanish.

Looking in the mirror, he was alarmed by red streaks around his mouth. Tasting, he realised it was lipstick. He washed the stuff off, easing grit out of his eyes, and extensively brushed his teeth. He wanted a shower but it was 08:33; he should check the rest of the house before Amaranth and Consuela arrived. He didn't want any more surprises.

He pulled on a bathrobe (a ratty Marks & Spencer garment that had come all the way from Somerset to Beverly Hills) and stalked back to the video room. Some of the clothes on the floor, and distributed around the furniture, were obviously not his.

A pair of diaphinous panties hung over the Screamin' Hackwill. Allan saw his monster's snarl through the thin material. He whipped them away. A cursory search found a single white ankle sock, a violently pink halter top and a studded leather item that was either a belt for a very thin person or a wristlet for a very fat one. In an ashtray, speckled with grey fluff, was a half-sucked lollipop. Also three cardboard-and-rizla-and-spit lumps he recognised from his film school days as roaches.

Outwardly, Allan Keyes is a normal, well-adjusted individual, not at all like the monsters he creates. But after dark, he turns into a raging party beast, a pervert who loves to be whipped with a pony-tail, a sad swinger with a taste for illegally young flesh . . .

08:47.

He would think about this later. Now, he needed a bin-liner for all the . . .

evidence?

. . . for all the alien articles. Something strange was happening, and he needed to re-establish control.

As he worked through the house (whatever happened had been confined to the downstairs rooms, it seemed) Allan became more aware of the memories of his body. He discovered interesting new aches and pains. He might have thrown his neck out.

08:56.

Done.

You have been.

One last look at the video room. Divan upright, cushions in order, stuff wiped off screen, pictures straightened, floor picked clear. Any suspicious stains were nothing more than Ovaltine.

09:01.

He didn't insist on exact time-keeping. But he heard the beeping of the security override and a bustle out in the hall that he associated with Consuela. She listened constantly to salsa on a walkman and unconsciously hummed along with it.

The video remote control lay on the divan. He picked it up and stabbed at EJECT but missed and hit PLAY.

It was the orgy scene from *Hackwill's Back!* Adam Kiss and the two underage girls. Body-parts pumped in close-up. He was sure the breasts came from a different film.

Consuela shrilled a 'good morning' from the next room.

The New Frontier quality was appalling. He could swear this was video, not film. The image was fixed, as if someone had dropped a camcorder and let the tape play on. From a skewed perspective, Adam Kiss entered a squealing girl from behind.

Is this supposed to be sexy? The MPAA will never let this through. She looks about twelve.

The image moved again, as if the other girl had picked up the camera, and then zoomed shakily towards Adam.

This isn't film, this is video.

And it wasn't Adam.

Knowing at last that something was definitely broken inside his head, Allan was unable to freeze the image. He was fascinated by his own distorted face. It *was* him but he wasn't like that.

He wasn't.

The screen Allan lost his stroke and grinned at the camera, then, biting his lips, started to thrust again. A girl said 'you're hurting me' and Allan said 'good'.

Consuela walked in.

'I no longer consider myself purely a horror writer,' Allan told Mockridge, 'I'm not sure I was ever really comfortable in the category. I mean, if you compare what I do to Steve King or Dean Koontz, you'll see . . .'

'That doesn't sound like the Man Who Made Rob Hackwill.'

'Turner, let's put it like this: the genre can be comfortable. Too comfortable. It's at once a cradle and a trap.'

'It's been a while since *Cornworld*. What will your next book project be? Will it be horror?'

'It's kind of a magical fantasia with a Gulf War subtext. I'm not quite sure of the direction it'll take at the moment.'

'What about *Hackwill's Back!*? What did *you* think?'

Allan's fixed grin must have been distinctly Hackwillian.

'Well, Ray Calme and I are *talking* again. We had a rough patch, but he's the first one to admit that the sequel strayed from the path somewhat.'

'Will there be a *Part III*?'

'*Hackwill's Back!*, without getting a single positive review, grossed $20,000,000 *more* than *Where the Bodies Are Buried* theatrically. The kids who saw the first one only on tape or cable bought tickets to the follow-up. With figures like that, there will certainly be a *Part III*. Nothing I can do will stop it.'

'And will you be involved?'

'There are business questions still unanswered. I doubt very much, with *Cornworld* on the go again, that I could schedule a gig, even if New Frontier offered it to me. But Ray always wants me to be involved.'

'And the *Hackwill's Horrors* TV show?'

'If there is one, it's news to me.'

Somehow, Allan kept a lid on things. He *still* didn't know what had happened that night (and, as it was, didn't want to know) but, though he had trouble hiring another domestic, he'd not gone down in a blaze of supermarket tabloids and morals clauses. Fleeing-the-country-at-midnight careericide had not taken place.

He had burned the cassette. Still labeled *Hackwill's Back!*, it'd been recorded over. Occasionally, he wondered if he shouldn't have kept it for further examination. It must have been faked. He knew technology existed to lay in his face on someone else's sex scene.

And your moles? Your appendix scar?

He tentatively investigated the possibility of a libel suit, taking a lawyer associated with his new agency to an advance screening of *Where the Bodies Are Buried, Part II*. The smart young woman politely thought he was crazy, and Allan had to agree with her.

The film they saw was nothing like the one on the tape, the one that had been wiped over. It was the high school story he'd read in the script, about Hackwill possessing a geeky teenager. It was also not very good. The for-one-night-only, special-for-Allan-Keyes *Hackwill's Back!* had been a better piece of film-making.

He did not return calls from Ellen Jeanette Sheridan.

The Hackwill Juggernaut rolled on. Martin H. Greenberg edited a shared-world paperback anthology in which leading horror writers from Karl Edward Wagner to Philip Nutman explored the 'Rob Hackwill Mythos'; Allan allowed the reprint of 'A Trickle of Shame' but refused to rewrite it to make it consistent with the film version. New Frontier *was* producing *Hackwill's Horrors*, a cable TV anthology hosted by Mal Gariazzo in monster make-up. Though TV rights had been signed away in the initial contract, New Frontier alotted fully two-thirds of the script budget for the show to buying the rights to a couple of stories from *Strange Segments*.

As weeks and months passed, he no longer expected a sudden eruption of furious parents, sobbing girls and vice cops. A hurricane had passed and would never return. *Cornworld* was put back and back.

'No more writer-directors,' Calme promised. 'Well, no more writer-directors who aren't Allan Keyes.'

Allan shrugged, non-committal. He was doing lunch as a favour to Mal Gariazzo. Like a child of divorce forever trying to manipulate his parents into a reconciliation, Gariazzo was constantly nagging Allan and Calme to get back together.

'The next *Bodies* has got to be a wow or the franchise is a bust,' Gariazzo insisted.

'I hear Ellen Jeanette has a three-picture deal,' Allan said.

'Positive discrimination will get you a long way in this town,' Calme suggested, waving away the memory of *Hackwill's Back!*

Their waiter brought drinks out to the terrace. Clogged with greenery, the restaurant annex was like a standing set from a Tarzan movie. To blend in, Calme wore a Banana Republic shirt of the type popular among moguls with paunches. Everyone in the room wore shades of pastel.

'When does *Cornworld* start?' Gariazzo asked.

Allan mumbled a harrumph but Calme saved his explanation by laying out his cards.

'Just give us a concept, Allan,' he said. 'We'll have it developed into a story, then machined into a script. You'll have approval at every stage. We have a line on a 3–D process that doesn't give you a headache. And we've got this incredible Icelander to direct.'

'*Icelander?*'

'Snordlij Svensson,' Gariazzo put in. 'He made an action movie, *American Atrocity*, out of nothing.'

Allan shrugged.

'We want you back, Allan,' Calme said. 'The fans want you. Breeze says she'll only do the Devil Princess for you. The East Coast needs your name.'

'*Rob Hackwill* wants you,' Gariazzo said, finally.

It was an insane situation. On the one hand, Allan was two rewrites away from a green light on *Cornworld*, a $45,000,000 and up Summer picture he thought guaranteed Huge. On the other, he could pick up $100,000 pocket change by grinding out three pages of notes for a *Part III in 3–D* that was almost certain to be an embarassment.

There was no reason he couldn't do both. But somehow, he wasn't doing either.

The new novel, *The Great Satan*, had come out of

a bidding war with a million *pound* advance from Real Press; but he was only three chapters in, and finding it heavier going than before. Reluctantly, he was on the point of conceding that he couldn't possibly meet his deadline and would have to make a research trip to Bagdhad as soon as the ruins stopped smoking. He couldn't believe that, six years ago, he'd written the 14,000 words of 'A Trickle of Shame' in a single day. On a manual typewriter.

The more you pull, the tighter the knot gets.

Finally, one night, late, he wrote a concept for *Part III in 3–D*. It had been there all the time, waiting. As he word-processed, he found himself chortling Gariazzo's Hackwill laugh. His concept, if he could call it 'his', was about Adam Kiss, a tabloid reporter who'd covered up the original murder of Rob Hackwill, then churned out a supermarket paperback about the dead blackmailer's crimes. Having developed a taste for perverse high life, Adam was open to exposure when Hackwill returned yet again from Hell to rip his life apart. Everyone around Adam died in gruesome ways; Allan didn't even bother to specify them, knowing New Frontier's effects bods probably had dozens of extra freak deaths they'd never been able to work into a film and would love to shove in here. Finally, Adam took the blame for the whole thing and was dragged off, protesting his worthless innocence, to death row where, in a last-scene kicker, the man who pulled the switch was Hackwill himself. There were no sympathetic characters, but that was a problem for whoever turned the concept into a story.

He felt entitled to the Adam Kiss Story; it was *his*

psychotic episode, he had the right to turn it into money.

With it out of his system, the words started flowing again. He turned around a *Cornworld* rewrite and had it in with Pyramid, then had a major breakthrough on *The Great Satan*. Once he stopped thinking of it, even subconsciously, as a horror novel, the whole thing took shape and developed its own forward momentum. Occasionally, he would try out new-coined category descriptions, seeing how comfortable he was with them: *Nouveau* Gothic, Mainstream *Guignol*, Slaughterpunk, Metaphysical Realism. This time, he was really reaching. Sometimes, he felt as if he were back in the coffee-and-pills rush of *Chitinous Splinters* or the *Strange Segments* stories, back before the career millstones had been tied around his neck. In idle moments, he pondered his Booker Prize acceptance speech. And his graceful thanks to the Academy of Motion Picture Arts and Sciences.

The day he got a start date for *Cornworld*, he insisted his credit on *Where the Bodies Are Buried, Part III in 3–D* be changed from 'original screen story by Allan Keyes' to 'based on concepts created by Allan Keyes'. Like a President, he wanted 'plausible deniability' if the Wizard of Rekjavik turned out a howling dog like *Hackwill's Back!* New Frontier went along with it.

In a letter to Lesley, he said that, for a while, he felt he had lost the reins of his career; now, he was back in charge. 'I write the stories,' he said, 'they don't write me.'

'I don't see why I should have to justify myself, Turner.

The Great Satan is not a horror novel. I've never written horror, I've always written *Allan Keyes*. There has been some overlap. This time, I want to go a different way. It's not like I've betrayed a religion. I just want to say something. There are people I can't reach with horror and I need them for this one. There is some major league ass that I have a burning compulsion to kick. Trust me, I've never broken my covenant with the fans yet.'

'And *Cornworld*?'

'What can I say? We lost the corn. We had fields lined up in Canada but Costner couldn't commit this summer and the harvest came along. I guess we'll be back again next year.'

'And you'll still direct?'

'There is no question of me not directing *Cornworld*, Turner. It's my baby.'

A sly light burned in Mockridge's pale eyes. He came to the next question.

'What *Fango* is really interested in, of course, is *Bodies III*. Will it really be in 3–D?'

'You'll have to ask New Frontier about that. I've not been in communication with them for a while. Whatever happens, it can't be worse than *Hackwill's Back!*'

'What do you mean, "insurance problems"?'

Allan had Everson Deeming, his new agent, on the speaker-phone. As he listened, his hands made fists.

'Allan, I've been delving. My informant at Pyramid tells me there's been a change in the climate. Since the buy-out, it's been musical chairs in the executive suite.'

Derek Leech, the multi-media magnate, had just

bought Pyramid. He already owned Real Press, so he was a majority shareholder in Allan Keyes.

'But *Cornworld* is still go?'

'Indubitably. But, in strictest confidence, they've been talking with Ellen Jeanette Sheridan.'

Ellen Jeanette had waltzed off the *Hackwill's Back!* fiasco into *Laughing Boy*, a medium-budget action romance about a housewife and a private eye. The film made a new male star, re-established a fading female one and passed the $100,000,000 mark in domestic gross.

'I'm pay-or-play, right?'

'Yes but they can pay you *not* to direct.'

'If they do, someone dies.'

'That's not a very helpful remark.'

The buzz was that Ellen Jeanette was close to signing with Allan's new agency.

You should have been good to me, Allan. People who are good to me get on in life . . .

The Great Satan was nearly finished. It *was* good, it *was* important. Real Press swallowed their objections and were gearing for a promotion massive enough to recoup their investment. Everybody knew there would be controversy; feelings about the war still ran high everywhere, and Allan Keyes had been no respecter of feelings.

He would not give up *Cornworld* without a fight. Loretta Grange, his new new agent, said she could fight his contract up to the Supreme Court. If he didn't direct, it didn't happen.

And Rob Hackwill was *everywhere*. Allan had daily

interview requests; always to talk about Hackwill, never the rest of his work. Critical articles claimed Hackwill represented the Dark Underside of the American Dream. Televangelists, who hadn't forgiven him for Julian Sands, preached that Hackwill led American teenagers into Satanism. New Frontier went into licensing frenzy: there were Hackwill action figures, make-up kits, pop-up books, video games, jokes, T-shirts, posters, lunchboxes, parade floats, novelty records, soundtrack CDs, stationery, soft toys, condoms.

Sometimes it seemed as if Rob Hackwill had made Allan Keyes.

But, without you, Allan, I'm not me! These merchants don't understand the real Rob Hackwill. You didn't mean me to be cuddly, you didn't mean me to be a comedian. When will I be a monster *again?*

He picked up the phone and heard the familiar chortle, echoing straight from Hell.

'Who is this?' he fairly shrieked. 'Why can't you leave me—'

'Relax, relax,' said Mal Gariazzo. 'It's just an actor.'

Allan made up an excuse about crank calls. Gariazzo had been to enough *Fangoria* conventions to understand. Some people were seriously sick out there.

'You free tonight?' Gariazzo asked.

'What's up?'

'The first answer print of *Where the Bodies Are Buried, Part III* in 3–D. I'm screening it at the house. Even Ray Calme hasn't seen it yet. And I've got an extra pair of 3–D glasses with your name on them.'

'I really don't know . . .'

Gariazzo did the voice again. '*What's the matter? Scared, are we?*'

The actor was identifying too closely with the part, Allan thought.

He'll have to be reminded who the real Rob Hackwill is.

'I think you'll be surprised,' Gariazzo said. 'Snordlij Svensson is a genius.'

'I'll be over.'

Gariazzo's mansion wasn't finished. Half the house was covered with plastic sheets, concealing exposed wooden bones that had yet to be fleshed with plaster. The backyard was an excavation site which would be turned into a pool.

Rob Hackwill had made Mal Gariazzo prosperous. When he signed for *Where the Bodies Are Buried*, he'd been living in a rooming house in Ventura and doing shopping channel voice-overs.

In the foyer, currently paved with yellow newspapers, a bigger-than-life Hackwill stood to greet visitors. Gariazzo posed beside it when Allan entered, as if ready for a publicity still.

Gariazzo was hyper, a couple of snorts into happyland. He showed Allan through the place, describing what would be where and how much it would cost. In one room, Gariazzo had more Hackwill merchandise than a Halloween sale. He had the phonecards from Japan, the Christmas tree ornaments, the velvet portraits, the stained glass windows, the cookie mixes.

I'm spread too thin, Daddy. I'm leaking away in cheap tat.

The basement 'romper room' was outfitted with a large bed and lots of strange devices Allan imagined were sexual implements. Gariazzo, with his choice of gothic groupies, no longer had a problem getting laid, and his priapic activities at conventions were becoming industry gossip. Allan heard Gariazzo had serviced Ellen Jeanette in order to get more close-ups on *Hackwill's Back!*

The screening room was finished. Gariazzo ran the projector himself. Allan settled, adjusting the 3–D glasses as the New Frontier logo thrust out from the screen. Hellish violet murk swirled and green letters formed.

'"All spirits are enslaved that serve things evil" – Shelley.'

Shelley! A bit high-fa-fuckin-lutin' for New Frontier!

The familiar *Where the Bodies Are Buried* title emerged from the murk, and then *Part III in 3–D* shot out like a clawed hand. Allan cringed in his seat. He heard Gariazzo chortling. There was no longer a difference between the actor's laugh and the monster's.

In the first scene, the camera crept through a cemetery to discover a dark figure violating an unmarked grave. This was where the town fathers had buried Hackwill after they tortured and killed him, and the site of the exorcism finale of *Hackwill's Back!* Gravestones loomed in 3–D, sheets of rain cut down. Svensson was certainly a good picture-maker. This had a richness, a quality far in excess of the first sequel. Objectively, *Part III in 3–D* looked better than *Where the Bodies Are Buried*.

The earth was removed from the grave and the rotted but still whole body of Hackwill was disclosed to the night. In a flash of lightning, the monster's distorted face flared with evil dead life. The make-up had been redesigned, to stand closer scrutiny. It was wetter, more complicated, more expressive than the simple mask Allan had worked around on the original.

'That's me,' Gariazzo giggled. 'I insisted on being buried, not the stuntman.'

The grave-robber picked Hackwill up by the shoulders and flipped him over, ramming his face into the wet earth. Lighting struck again, the effect paling from over use. The grave-robber produced a bayonet, slowly drawing it from a scabbard. This being 3–D, the weapon thrust obscenely at the camera, its point seeming to hover nine yards out of the screen. Allan's eyeballs tried to revolve.

Gariazzo whooed as if on a rollercoaster.

This clown is beginning to irritate me.

The grave-robber, face still in darkness, stripped Hackwill's corpse of dirt as if he were undressing a lover. Then he stabbed deep into the dead body, opening up a hole in the small of the monster's back. The gash seeped blood.

Then a reverse shot showed the violator's face. It was Allan. Not an actor playing Adam Kiss, but Allan himself. He looked at his own face in 3–D and wondered how – and why – the trick had been done.

The 3–D Allan unbuttoned his long coat and slipped it off. He was naked to the waist, with stereoscopic gooseflesh. Allan recognised his own scars, the patterns of his body hair. Again, the world was dizzyingly out of joint.

Allan pulled off his 3–D glasses and gripped his face.

An ache had set in behind the bridge of his nose. The polarised image was fuzzy and rainbowed. He looked at the screen and saw something different. A clothed actor he recognised. Brion James, the great B-picture villain. Even the scene was different.

He put the glasses back on and saw himself in the graveyard. His head buzzed, but he had to watch. The 3–D Allan made a fist and thrust it out of the screen. Allan cringed at the effect.

The film which seemed to be projected only in his head continued. Allan Keyes fell upon Hackwill and mightily thrust his fist into the aperture, burrowing up through the corpse's spine. The images were explicit, and disgusting. The film Allan reached in beyond his elbow, making a ghastly glove puppet of the monster. In close-ups, steel-clawed hands became rigid and razored. Allan was sure he would see himself gutted by his creation, but the monster eased himself gently out of the earth and was helped out of the grave. Hackwill's single red eye glowed with malign intelligence, Allan's hand lodged somewhere inside his head.

Allan lifted his glasses again. The real film was continuing, with Gariazzo-as-Hackwill stalking James-as-Kiss. It was stylish and it had a plot. Gariazzo had drifted into a happy baby daze.

The 3–D mind movie continued. The film Allan and the real Hackwill, under whose rotten face Mal Gariazzo did not lurk, left the graveyard and walked into town. It wasn't the Anywhere, USA, of *Where the Bodies Are Buried*, but the real West Country town where Allan had grown up, where he had set 'A Trickle of Shame'.

Creator and monster, joined by flesh and blood, made their way through familiar streets. There was the Corn Exchange, the Palace, Denbeigh Gardens, Brink's Cafe. A poster for the council elections cried 'Vote Hackwill'. Finally, the camera climbed familiar stairs up above a shop to a familiar flat. The film Allan had lost his keys, so he rapped on the door. After fumbling, Lesley answered and let him in. Her eyes literally bulged in surprise as the bayonet rammed into her stomach and she was lifted off her feet . . .

When consciousness returned, Allan found himself naked on bare bedsprings, smeared with something sticky and smelly. One arm was wrenched back behind his head, shoulder joint straining, and his wrist was circled. Craning, he saw upside-down that he was handcuffed to a knotched black wooden post above the bed. The image was fuzzily strange. He was still wearing his 3–D glasses. Concealed lighting flashed on and off, filling the room with lavalamp swirls.

Something heavy weighed on his midriff. His nose stung and his mouth was thick with a terrible taste.

Somewhere, Hackwill was laughing.

'Get off,' he said, bucking his hips to dislodge the person draped across him.

The body came free and, in strobing light, Allan saw Mal Gariazzo's staring face through plastic. A bag was fixed over his head and twist-tied at his neck. The actor wore only a black string vest. His torso was smeared with blood.

Allan shifted himself and found the handcuff loose

enough to slip out of. He got off the bed. The imprint of the springs must be on his back and bottom. He was covered in someone else's blood.

A bore-hole had been made in Mal Gariazzo's back, and used. It was quite shallow and had not displaced anything vital. It was the hood that had killed the actor.

There can be only one.

There were older marks on Gariazzo's body, where he had been cut before. Real scars looked nothing like the latex on Hackwill's face.

'I didn't do anything,' Allan said, aloud.

M'lud, while I concede that my client was found with the victim's blood generously plastered over his body and that Mr Gariazzo's wallet was in Mr Keyes's back pocket at the time of arrest, I'm sure his previous good character will be taken into account.

'Shut yer neck,' Allan shouted.

It ws 05:09. Allan looked at the mess. There was no question of cleaning any fingerprints he might have left. The room, probably the house, was liberally smeared with his dabs.

If you're serious about concealing evidence, your best bet would be to torch the place. Sure, in this weather, the fire might spread and other people might die, but they can't gas you twice . . .

Allan had never had his fingerprints taken. They weren't on file anywhere. He'd been alone in the house with Gariazzo. Nobody had seen him arrive. No one would see him leave. Nothing could put him at the scene.

'And, what's more, I'm innocent.'

He found his clothes neatly piled on a rack by the door, folded exactly as his mother taught him. He dressed, uncomfortably aware of filth between skin and underwear, and shoved his cardboard glasses into a pocket. He darted from the house to his car, which had been in the garage out of sight, and drove unobtrusively out of the neighbourhood. This being California, there were no pedestrians to remember him. Early morning light made everything look polarised.

Home and dry, killer?

Only as he neared his own house, red flakes of dried blood falling from his face and scalp like gory dandruff, did his insides relax. His worrying brain patterns kicked in again.

Someone was dead, someone was responsible. *And it wasn't Allan Keyes!*

He got back to his mansion and stripped for a shower. Warm jets washed him as clean as his conscience.

After *Hackwill's Back!*, no schoolgirls had come forward and testified to being in an orgy with him. After *Part III in 3–D*, no corpse would make him out to be a murderer.

If this was the same as the last time, the physical evidence would be misleading. Gariazzo probably wasn't dead. Allan had just lived through his own imaginary *Part III in 3–D*. In the real world, *Where the Bodies Are Buried, Part III in 3–D* was a story about Adam Kiss as played by Brion James. Mal Gariazzo would be happily taping his pun-filled links for *Hackwill's Horrors* and looking through his black book of starlet wannabes in search of a target for tonight.

The phone rang just as Allan got out of the shower.
Bad news.

It was too early. Even if it had happened, Gariazzo
wouldn't have been found yet. It must be something
else.

So few people have this number, though.

'Cut it out, or in the next sequel – which I'll personally
write – I'll reincarnate you as a fluffy pink bunny rabbit
and have you befriended by Macaulay Culkin.'

He got to the phone before the machine cut in. It was
his mother, with terrible, terrible news. About Lesley.

'I'm sorry, babe,' Loretta said, voice tinny from New
York, 'but publishing is a conservative business. The
chairman himself, Derek Leech, has ruled on *The Great
Satan*. Real Press will not publish, and I quote, "a love
letter to Saddam Hussein".'

'But that's ridiculous. Leech can't have read the book
properly. The hero is a *dissident* Iraqi, for heaven's sake.'

'We're not talking rational, babe, we're talking rich.'

It seemed horribly possible Allan would have to
return a million pounds. His contract was ambiguous
on the point.

'There are other publishers and there's lots of interest.
You're enough of a name to ensure that. In the long run,
this will help. Controversy sells books.'

Allan swallowed rage.

'It looks like Leech will become hands-on in Pyramid,'
Loretta continued. 'With the *Cornworld* situation so
delicate, it probably wasn't a good time for him to sour
on Allan Keyes.'

'I didn't do this on purpose. I just wrote an honest book.'

Like Salman Rushdie, eh?

'Contrary to what they told you in school, babe, honesty sometimes is not the best policy.'

The phlegmatic Los Angeles coroner ruled Mal Gariazzo's death as 'accidental, due to sexual experiment'. New Frontier launched a search for 'the new Rob Hackwill'. The West Somerset Constabulary were following several promising leads, but no suspects at this time were sought for questioning with regard to the murder of Lesley Conyers. One of the tackier supermarket papers asked him if he felt the violence in his books and films contributed to the moral climate which created monsters like the fiend who had killed his girlfriend. Allan had scared the reptile off with a Hackwill look.

Where the Bodies Are Buried, Part III in 3–D outgrossed both earlier *Bodies* films put together, and Snordlij Svensson was attached to several major projects. Sean Connery and Kevin Costner were keen to work with him. Sales of Mal Gariazzo Memorial Hackwill merchandise were heavier than could have been predicted.

Allan sat at home and didn't answer the telephone.

He watched *Chitinous Splinters* on video, over and over, and saw other paths he might have taken, leading into the world of art cinema rather than the bloodied fields of the horror genre. He reread *Strange Segments* over and over. Not just 'A Trickle of Shame', but all the other stories. Some of the prose was rough but he was surprised by their strength. He could see the seeds of *The Great Satan*, his unpublished (unpublishable?) masterpiece, already germinating. He regretted his over use of the Cosmic Justice formula, though.

Now, as each day drew a noose tighter, he felt he was *living* through an EC horror comic plot, and that he was the protagonist. But there was a difference, a cosmic injustice which he needed to appeal to the highest court.

He hadn't done anything wrong.

'I'd like to talk about rumours that you're working on a fourth *Bodies* script? The title that has been leaked is *The Redevelopment: Where the Bodies Are Buried IV.*'

'I'm sorry, Mockridge. I can't schedule an interview now.'

'But—'

'*Just fuck off and get a life you little anorak.*'

The dead line buzzed in his hand. He had sounded more than ever like Hackwill.

He was acting as his own agent. He could hardly do a worse job than the deadweights he'd been stuck with.

'If it were me, *I'd* have you direct, but you understand the East Coast Boys . . .'

Calme let that hang.

The new script was on on the desk. *The Redevelopment.* Allan might have to work with New Frontier's in-house rewrite man. He was getting a flat $15,000. That was more than he had earned for his first two books, five years of solid work, but now it felt like an insult.

'It's terrible about Mal, but fans don't care who's under the mask. Hackwill is the star of the *Bodies* franchise. And Hackwill can't die.'

Allan sat quietly. Writing *The Redevelopment* was like taking dictation. He listened to the voice and wrote it down.

'No jokes in this one,' Calme said. 'It'll be serious, scary. Like *Bodies One*. No French teacher in the hot tub. We've got away from your original concept and I'm glad you're back. Rob Hackwill without Allan Keyes is not the same monster. Things have been rough, but we will endure.'

The Redevelopment would be dedicated to Gariazzo. The fans would expect no less.

At first, Allan had not been interested in working on the sequel. He had other irons in the fire. He could get meetings at any of the Majors. But Calme told him he had talked with Gariazzo the night before he died and that the actor had told him he was expecting company. There was no question of anyone accusing Allan of anything. But it would be tidier if Calme kept secrets.

It'll be you and me, Allan. For ever.

Calme paged through the script. He came to the last scene. After the climax, in the graveyard, something stirred. A hook. The producer smiled, sequels yet unborn stirring in his eyes, and congratulated Allan on anticipating his needs.

Allan could feel the hook, in his own flesh. It was a tiny pinprick, among many tiny pinpricks. The hooks were endless. There would be further sequels. Next would be *Hackwill's End: The Last Body*, followed by *Where the*

Bodies Are Buried VI: The Next Degeneration, Where the Bodies Are Buried VII: Devil Bride of Rob Hackwill . . .

And Allan Keyes was yoked to the wheel that would grind on and on. He knew now he was enslaved and that his punishment was just. He had brought evil into the world and betrayed it. That evil was now his master. Hackwill was his responsibility, and everything else he had written, everything else he had filmed, everything else he had done, was a cosmic irrelevence.

Think of it, Allan, Hackwill X, Part XXXVI, Part MCMLIV . . ., *Spiral stories without beginning, without end, a ritual of retribution re-enacted as long as there are graves and corpses and secrets and sins . . .*

'If we play this right, Allan, it can run and run and run . . .'

Having written a story about franchise characters, it seemed an obvious move to write a sequel. There's something fascinating about the way story-tellers become the slaves of their stories. Probably the best way to get very rich in this business is to write something people like, and then rewrite it once or twice a year for the rest of your career. The bad news is that on the fifteenth or sixteenth go-round, you get very, very bored with what you're doing and start to resent the thing you are best known for: obvious examples of this syndrome are Arthur Conan Doyle and Arthur Sullivan, both of whom came bitterly to hate their successes, believing their important work was obscured. But I'd still take *The Hound of the Baskervilles* over *Sir Nigel* or *The Mikado* over *Ivanhoe*. I also happen to prefer Shakespeare's plays to the sonnets, *Fort Apache* to *The Quiet Man* and *The Books of Blood* to *Imajica*. I think that everybody who's written anything that was well-received feels like Allan Keyes sometimes. I also don't rule out writing another 'Where the Bodies Are Buried' story sometime.

The Pale Spirit People

It was a perfect circle, such as might be drawn in dirt with a stick and a length of twine. Less broad than the span of a man's hand, the spirit object was thin yet resilient, fashioned of stuff unknown to the True People. Hawk That Settles understood from one of Two Dogs Dying's followers that the object could sing, but he did not understand how this could be so. Since taken from its place of concealment, it had been silent.

Hawk That Settles had found it supple as a good bow; now, he watched Sky Buffalo tap, taste, shake, strike and scratch. The circle would not be hurt, though, in truth, neither the young man nor the shaman put it truly to the test, throwing it on a fire or hammering it with a rock. To destroy a spirit object was to invite ill fortune into the lodges of the People.

As Sky Buffalo turned the singing circle over to sniff its underside, the silver mirror caught light, holding rainbows to itself. The edge was sharp enough to draw blood. At the centre was a hole through which the shaman poked his forefinger to the first knuckle. On one side were tiny scrawls in black, scarring the almost beautiful surface.

'Two Dogs Dying found this in the burial ground?' the shaman asked. The lines about his mouth and eyes were grooves worn in old leather and he had fewer teeth than fingers.

'It must be so,' Hawk That Settles replied, 'for it was hidden near the lodge Two Dogs has built among the dead.'

'Hidden?'

'Two Dogs hides many objects, as one would hide a shameful thing.'

'Objects?'

It seemed to Hawk That Settles that to be a shaman mainly required the repetition of odd words with a questioning inflexion. He did not share his fathers' reverence for the storied wisdom of the aged. After forty-two summers, the song of Sky Buffalo was sung. The shaman had built his last lodge far from the encampment and refused to hunt, sustained in his dying days by the superstitious kindness of old women.

But here was Hawk That Settles – who argued that food left after young men and women had fed was better stored against winter than wasted on those grown old and useless – sitting at the last fire of Sky Buffalo, asking for help.

'There are other objects,' Hawk That Settles explained. 'Not like this one. Some have seen them, though Two Dogs and the others waste effort building invisible lodges for their concealment.'

'Invisible?'

The shaman was doing it again. Swallowing impatience along with smoke, Hawk That Settles continued, 'Lodges made to seem like solid stone or patches of ground, like traps made for men of the Other People. He has built many such in the burial ground.'

Sky Buffalo coughed wisely.

'Some of these spirit objects make noises like animals or men wounded in battle,' Hawk That Settles said, remembering with a spear-thrust of fear the horrible yammering he had heard.

'These things are troubling,' Sky Buffalo said, hardly great wisdom. 'There is a great disturbance in the Ghost Lands.'

That also was something Hawk That Settles could have told the shaman. Every child of the People knew the Ghost Lands met the World Around like one track crossing another, and that sometimes objects were found at the crossings of the paths. The more spirit objects migrated to the World Around, the more disturbance there was in the Ghost Lands.

'You must carry me to the burial ground, Hawk.'

The young man had been afraid of that. With no complaint, he turned his broad back so the shaman could climb upon it, arms around his neck, knees gripping his waist.

As he stood, Hawk That Settles grunted. The old man was surprisingly heavy, as if his breechclout were stuffed with stones.

'You have often thought of carrying me to the burial ground,' Sky Buffalo said, not chuckling. 'Those who make fervent wishes often regret them.'

Hunched over like an old man himself, Hawk That Settles walked towards the lodges of the People.

In seasons at the old encampment, the young men of the People hunted game and made war on the Other People. As brothers, they honoured the dead with the songs of their fathers.

Hawk That Settles and Two Dogs Dying were born of the same woman. In their time, they fathered babies for women of their generation. When Spotted Water birthed twins, one resembled Hawk That Settles, the other Two Dogs Dying. Among the People, such things were without strife. No man claimed ownership over a woman or a child, just as none thought to keep for himself a particularly sturdy spear or sharp knife. If there was water enough to quench the thirst of all or fire enough for the warmth of all, why should any hoard such things for his special comfort? 'We are not the Other People,' the fathers said as the sons learned, 'and that is the strength of our spirit. No thing or person is slave to us, as we are not slaves to any thing or person. This is the path of the True People and it is as it should be.'

Then they made the encampment by the river. It was a site with good game, plentiful water and many trees. Hawk That Settles wondered why the Other People had not claimed it in earlier seasons. There was no trace of past encampment; thick grass grew where no fires had ever been set, unscarred trees grew tall, deer did not flee the approach of a hunter. The land was fresh.

The People cut down trees and made lodges. Fires were

set and songs were sung. From that day, the place was the encampment of the People. If the Other People came for it, they would be met with arrows. The place by the river would be good for many seasons, maybe for all the seasons of Hawk That Settles and Two Dogs Dying. Maybe for all the seasons of the sons of Spotted Water.

That was before the trouble in the Ghost Lands.

From boyhood, Two Dogs Dying was drawn to the dead. He made himself a bonnet like that of Horn Knife, the Custodian of the old burial ground. He helped Horn Knife through his dying days, chosen by the old man to end his uselessness with a loving thrust. When Horn Knife joined those whose path to the Ghost Lands he had eased, Two Dogs Dying led the song.

When an encampment was built, a sacred area, somewhat removed from the lodges, was set aside for the dead. By tradition, it was first chosen and last prepared. During the days of building, a tree fell on Angry Bear. The crushed body was tethered in the fast-flowing waters until, after the day of dedication, Two Dogs Dying could sing the song of Angry Bear. He carried the cold corpse to a bier fashioned of branches and stones and laid Angry Bear out. The young man lay with a warbonnet on his head and an axe in his hand, lest he encounter the spirit of the murderous tree in the Ghost Lands.

It was a considerable thing to be Custodian of the burial ground. Hawk That Settles was glad his brother should rise to such a position and was less saddened now when one of his brothers was killed in battle or by sickness. Two Dogs Dying would see to the care of their spirits. The sign of a good Custodian was that he could open the throat of an unwanted girl baby or an old person whose song was sung with honour and respect. Never did any such cry out under the keen knife Two Dogs Dying wore on his belt, the knife passed to him by Horn Knife himself.

After a season marked by an outbreak of the coughing sickness and skirmishes with the Other People, the burial ground was properly settled and Angry Bear's spirit did not walk alone in the Ghost Lands.

Though it was difficult to talk under the weight of Sky Buffalo, Hawk That Settles, at the shaman's insistence, told again of Two Dogs Dying and the burial ground. He was ashamed to remember fear, certain the shaman must notice his prickling skin and chilled sweat. Hawk That Settles was brave in battle and the hunt but trouble in the Ghost Lands frightened him.

He first realised something was wrong when, after bringing two deer to the fires after a day's hunting, he had a yen to take pleasure with Spotted Water. She must be ready to swell with child again, having birthed three weeks ago - a girl, but these things happen – and Hawk That Settles always found her enthusiasm for coupling most stimulating.

With a leg of cooked deer, he called on the women's lodge and was told Spotted Water was in the burial ground with Two Dogs Dying. Not thinking to be disappointed, he presented the greasy meat to Red Doe. Only after they had coupled did Red Doe tell of the strange behaviour of Two Dogs Dying and Spotted Water.

It seemed that two days earlier, Two Dogs Dying visited the women's lodge and bore Spotted Water away. Hawk That Settles's first thought was to grin at his brother's appetite: any man who could couple for two days without tiring was worthy of his own song. Then Red Doe told him Two Dogs Dying had also taken Spotted Water's children, the twin sons and even the infant daughter. She said Two Dogs Dying had built his own little lodge, like the lodges of the dying, and lived there alone, with only Spotted Water and her children about him. As Red Doe said such an unthinkable thing, Hawk That Settles realised he had indeed not recently seen his brother in the men's lodge.

Among the People were men who chose to live in the women's lodge, offering themselves for the pleasure of other men. Hawk That Settles had, for the experience, pleasured with several and, while confirming his preference for women who might bear sons, had to concede such couplings were not unenjoyable. Hawk That Settles and Two Dogs Dying had shared pleasure of live goats and killed deer, for such was the right of the hunter.

Hawk That Settles thought himself untethered by the ways of the People; he accepted what was good of the wisdom of the fathers but did not let tradition bind him to stupidity. Yet, he could not but feel disgust at the perversion of which Red Doe accused his brother.

Unable to believe Red Doe more than a lying gossip, he took a green stick and beat her. To suggest Two Dogs Dying might hide Spotted Water away for himself, that he might wish to hoard her children as a bear hoards

349

food, was an obscenity he would not believe. If Red Doe repeated such lies, he would cut out her tongue.

Thinking of it made Hawk That Settles sick. One man, one woman, children! Yet, Two Dogs Dying and Spotted Water were gone from the lodges. And the children of Spotted Water too.

He must go to the burial ground and see his brother. Two Dogs Dying must be told of the lies before Red Doe spread them further.

Sky Buffalo clucked as if the story were familiar. To the fathers, no land was ever fresh. The warrior of the Other People killed in battle by Rock Garden was hardly as fearsome as a warrior of the days of the fathers' fathers. The bear bested by the young men was considerably less ferocious than the long-ago bear whose skin, visibly smaller than the fresh skin, decorated the lodge. The flock of pigeons which filled the skies for three days was a passing cloud set against the great mass of wings which brought darkness for a whole season in the days of the fathers of the fathers' fathers. This trouble in the Ghost Lands was meagre compared with the Great Trouble of many seasons gone. Each time the shaman clucked, Hawk That Settles had a yen to pitch him into the river, yet he continued with the story of Two Dogs Dying.

Red Doe had not lied about the lodge Two Dogs Dying had built. She had not even told the worst of it. The burial ground was covered with strange little lodges. All the biers were under lodges, the dead improperly covered from the skies. The spirit of Horn Knife must wail in the Ghost Lands. The lodges were identical boxes, arranged in a disturbingly regular pattern. Around the boxes were barriers, too low to keep away animals or enemies, interrupted by neat gaps and beaten paths. Lodges filled the burial ground; they seemed to spread across the world, crowding out everything else.

Hawk That Settles felt spirit presences. Not the natural spirits he had known all his life, but pale cloth-wrapped ghosts. If he shut his eyes, he saw their shadows moving awkwardly like wounded men. Alone in sunshine, he wanted to return to the men's lodge and speak no more of Two Dogs Dying. But the Custodian was his brother, as were all the young men of the People; it was his duty to watch his brothers' backs in battle, and there was a great spirit battle in this place.

He knew which was the lodge of Two Dogs Dying; it was more finished than the others, the thing itself rather than an image. The path was more elaborate, the barrier less flimsy. Enclosed grass was shaved as close to the earth as the men of the Other People shaved their hair to the skin. There was a doorway; wood hung over it, like the boards which kept out snows in winter or the Other People in attacks. He could not imagine why a man would make such a thing in summer at a time of peace. When he touched the wood, fixed to the doorway by strips of leather, it swung inward. The arrangement was ingenious if peculiarly repulsive.

Stepping into the lodge, he was assaulted by a horrible yammering. He drew a knife, prepared to fight the evil ghost that had maddened his brother.

No attack came, but the noise continued.

There was a box in one corner, making the noise. Bright lights burned on its face, hurting his eyes. The box sang the song of a young girl taking pleasure for the very first time. Knowing the object to be unnatural, Hawk That Settles killed it.

Another doorway was before him. He knew evil was here, for the inside of the lodge was much smaller than the outside. Pale spirits had lured him in, now walls were contracting to crush him. He began the song of his dying.

The situation was stranger even than that. The walls were not moving; inside the lodge were divisions, walls between poles, splitting space into smaller spaces. For a moment, such an arrangement made sense: young men need not be troubled by the night-noises of the old, food might be stored away from hungry animals. Then, laughing, Hawk That Settles realised how impractical this truly was. With no centre, the lodge could have no fire; without a fire, a lodge was just a cave of wood, not a fit place for People.

He shoved aside the barrier and passed into an area walled by stout, defensible barricades. It was a lodge with no roof. Above was unclouded sky. Two Dogs Dying stood by an unnatural fire, grinning as he manipulated hunks of cooking meat with a short spear, singing an unfamiliar song of yellow ribbons and old trees. Clearly an evil thing, it was an obscene chant. The fire was elevated in a dish of black stuff. There was too little smoke for the meat to be healthy.

Spotted Water was nearby, body indecently covered.

Confining hides were uncomfortably taut about her, as if she had been sewn into a wet leather shroud and left in the sun. She was tethered like a dog, a rope about her ankle fixed to a stake hammered into hard earth. Her children clung to her, too frightened to speak.

'Hawk,' Two Dogs Dying said, smiling, 'good to see you, brother. Just in time for food.'

Hawk That Settles cringed.

'Be-Be-Cue?' Two Dogs Dying asked, licking his lips and prodding meat.

The Custodian had mutilated and adorned himself. His hair was hacked short and the rings were gone from his nose and nipples. He wore a strange apparatus of twigs around his eyes, over his nose and hooked onto his ears. Instead of the breechclout and paint of the People, he wore skins sewn together, like those he had forced upon Spotted Water. His arms and legs were trapped in tubes of soft leather. His bonnet had a bill like a duck's and an evil totem: a grinning rat with black circular ears.

Spotted Water whimpered, fearing for her boys. Even the infant girl was too frightened to cry.

Hawk That Settles backed away. Two Dogs Dying's mad smile filled the sky. Behind twig circles, his eyes were large. Around him were pale spirit people, their faces like bone. They wore shirts of fire and rainbow. Their feet were trapped in thick white moccasins like fungus tied with twine.

His foot touched a patch of ground that snapped. He looked and saw a depression that had been covered over. It was full of objects that clinked and swished: sparkling thin round pebbles, flimsy oblong leaves. Trinkets suitable only for ornamenting young women.

'Get away,' Two Dogs Dying said. He advanced. In his hand was a spear upon which were impaled hunks of meat and chunks of vegetable.

'Two Dogs, you need help.'

'Get away,' his brother said, evenly. 'You who have pleasured with your mother . . .'

'Yes, of course, in the manhood ritual . . .'

'. . . stand away from my riches.'

Hawk That Settles moved away from the trap. Like a snake, Two Dogs Dying was on it, covering over his useless hoard.

He looked up at Hawk That Settles and, voice like death, spat 'This is *mine!*'

'Mine?' Sky Buffalo repeated.

'As if things were his alone, like a part of his spirit. As if he were the People all by himself, and all the things of the People were his . . . his *possessions*.'

The shaman clucked.

'The next day, Crow Foot and Rock Garden went out to the burial ground to see the madness of Two Dogs Dying for themselves. On his return, Crow Foot took White Cloud for himself and built his own lodge beside Two Dogs Dying's. Others have joined them.'

Sky Buffalo groaned.

'Each night, more leave the lodges of the People and join the madness of Two Dogs Dying.'

That night, as he slept in the men's lodge, Hawk That

Settles was visited by Angry Bear. The dead man spoke of the Pale Spirit People and of how they filled the Ghost Lands with Moving Lodges and Be-Be-Cues and Wide Stone Paths. Angry Bear told of hunting grounds like huge lodges where game was already killed and smoked, stacked for women – not hunters, *women!* – to pick like fruit from a tree. Of dark caves where children were fixed to boxes that buzzed and flashed lights and sapped their spirits in battles without honour. Of piles of oblong leaves for which the Pale Spirit People cut each other to pieces with knives that had moving edges. Of boxes that sang, that danced, that told stories, that held fires, that lied. If a man of the People were to take his pleasure with a woman of the Pale Spirits, her brothers would use moving knives on him for all that they were unable themselves to give pleasure. The spirits of the People were outnumbered by the Pale Spirits as trees outnumber deer.

When he woke, Hawk That Settles told his dream to Sky Buffalo, who nodded wisely, repeating the occasional word, clucking that things were as bad as he had feared.

The remaining men of the People listened as Sky Buffalo spoke, nodding at his wisdom. Some fathers muttered that things had not been as they should be since the shaman removed himself to the lodge of his dying, and that the young would do well to remember the strengths of the old. Hawk That Settles, remembering Two Dogs Dying's mad song, kept quiet.

'The Pale Spirits are insects,' the shaman said, holding

the singing circle like the hair of an enemy, 'once let into your lodge, they breed and infest. Worse even than the Other People, they are a sickness to be cut out. We must pity them, for they are mad, not truly evil, but we must not let our sorrow at their sad condition stay us from making war.'

'How can we make war on spirits?' Rock Garden asked.

'We can not,' Sky Buffalo said, 'for spirits are strong. But these are not true spirits, merely ghosts. Spirits endure, flowing like a river or the wind, but ghosts simply pretend things are as if they were alive. The strength of the True People is in our spirits, but the strength of the pale people is in their *things*.'

'Things?' Hawk That Settles asked, feeling like a shaman.

'The things they delude themselves are theirs. They waste strength on getting and keeping things which can not be got and kept. They try to swallow sunlight with their throats and keep water in their hands. Their men have only one father, their women only one man. They are many, but they do not act as the People but as many Other Peoples.'

Some of the young men laughed. Sky Buffalo smiled, showing his few teeth, his eyes sharp.

'This is one of their things,' he said, holding up the singing circle. 'See how pleasing it is to the eye. Yet it can not be eaten, it can not harm an enemy, it can not cut through the bark of a tree. This is not a true spirit object, this is merely a *thing*'

He threw the thing into the fire. It melted like ice,

colours joining the smoke and passing up through the hole in the roof.

'The Pale People have put their spirit in their things. Every time one of their things is destroyed, their spirit leaks away. And their things have no true existence. They are the ghosts of those who have never been born.'

'How can we save Two Dogs Dying and the others?'

'Find the objects they have hidden, the things found or made in imitation of the spirit objects, and destroy them. As they are broken, so the Pale Ghosts grow weak.'

Together, by night, the men went to the burial ground. Some were struck helpless with fear to see what had been made of it and could go no further, but Sky Buffalo was resolute. He decreed the sham lodges be torn down and burned, and the men of the People set to work with fire and spears.

Hawk That Settles saw the Pale Spirits, watching impassively. Most lodges were affairs of reed and sticks, flimsily built and already tattered by rains and winds. The men sang war songs as they destroyed things. The men who had joined Two Dogs Dying stood by and watched as their lodges came apart, some joining their brothers in pulling down the things they had made. There were shrill noises in the air, but Sky Buffalo told the People to take no notice of them. They were ghost noises and could harm no one.

Two Dogs Dying came out of his lodge and watched, making no effort to save the other lodges. He stood behind his barrier, a strange branch in his hands, singing a song of small dogs and windows and tails. He wrenched his branch, and fire exploded from one end, opening a red wound in Rock Garden's leg.

Sky Buffalo decreed the branch be taken from Two Dogs Dying and thrown into the river.

'You'll take my fire branch from me only by wrenching it from my cold, dead fingers,' Two Dogs Dying shouted as his fire branch was taken away from him and thrown in the river.

The men fell upon the lodge of the Custodian, hauling its timbers apart and scattering them.

Two Dogs Dying shouted strange words and was held down. 'Believers in communal property . . . poorly-educated men of dark skin colour . . .'

Hawk That Settles dug through the soft earth of the lodge and hauled out a white box with a grey ice face which sprang to life, containing tiny people and many fires. He looked into it as he would look into the eyes of a snake, fascinated but resolute, fearful yet aware of beauty. The box sang the song of an unskilled hunter unable to feed his people, whose arrow unloosed black water from the earth and whose new lodge was built in hills of plenitude. With a gathering of the strength of his arms and a scream that came from his stomach, he hurled the box high, between trees, and heard it splash into the waters of the river to be born away and dashed to pieces on the rocky bed.

They found many strange things – some that Angry Bear had spoken of in his dream – and all were destroyed by fire or water as Sky Buffalo sang the True Song of the People over them.

Two Dogs Dying cried like a baby as he was rescued from the constricting skins. Hawk That Settles used a knife-point to pick apart the stitches that fixed the torturous things to his brother's body, trying to draw as little blood as possible.

Spotted Water, torn from her leather and properly exposed, snatched the twigs from Two Dogs Dying's face and snapped them to fragments. When this was done, the Custodian lay exhausted.

The men of the People backed away from their fallen brother. Sky Buffalo stood over Two Dogs Dying, examining him. Hair would grow again, Hawk That Settles supposed, and a breechclout could easily be found. Two Dogs Dying tried to sit up, but collapsed. Dazed, he sang to himself. It was one of the songs of the People. His spirit had returned, dispelling the influence of the Pale Ghosts.

'There are things in the earth here,' Sky Buffalo said, 'like seeds. They come from the Ghost Lands. We must not trouble them, lest they sprout flowers of sickness. This was caused by tampering with spirit objects.'

'Must we find another burial ground?' Hawk That Settles asked.

The shaman rattled his medicine bag. 'No, we must fill this one up with our dead, sons upon sons. We must sing the songs of their dying so their spirits seed the earth, make this place a part of the Ghost Lands. Our spirits must stand here close as blades of grass on the plain. The Pale People are weak and can be driven from this place as we have thrown their things into the fire or the river. If we resist their madness, their seeds will never sprout.

This is the burial ground of the People and always has been so. Nothing else has ever been here and nothing must ever come here as long as the grass grows, the river runs and the sun crosses the sky.'

Hawk That Settles supposed that after this they would have to take Sky Buffalo back into the men's lodge.

The Indian Burial Ground, one of the most pernicious clichés in horror film and fiction, was popularised by *The Amityville Horror*, in which a modern house is built over a burial ground and something ancient and evil is disturbed. This has become so prevalent in the field that Ramsey Campbell (no less) edited for the Horror Writers of America a shared-world anthology set in an airport built over an Indian Burial Ground. It's called *Deathport*, but I thought it was funnier (surely, Ramsey isn't being serious) when called *Under the Tarmac*.

Implicit in the IBG cliché (also in many horror stories involving Ancient Egypt, African Voodoo or other non-Christian, non-white civilisations) is a suggestion that our way of life is the right one and that anything else is inherently evil. Obviously that's silly, so here's a story about an Indian tribe who put their burial ground over something ancient and evil.

Out of the Night,
When the Full Moon
Is Bright . . .

'Oppression – by its very nature – creates the power that crushes it. A champion arises – a champion of the oppressed.'

The Mark of Zorro (1920)

1

'Stuey,' Officer García began, 'how about this for *high concept!*'

The idea bulb above his cop cap practically turned the inside of the windscreen into a silver-black mirror.

'These two cops in East LA, man . . .'

García grinned at Officer Scotchman, who kept his eyes on the street, hands on the wheel.

'. . . and they're really *werewolves* . . .'

The Hispanic officer half turned in the patrol car's front passenger seat. Neck twisting, he looked back at Stuart with glittering, amused steel eyes.

'. . . and the title of the *cho* is . . .'

The cruiser eased over a speed-bump, unsettling Stuart's jet-lagged stomach.

'*Prowl Car*.'

Maybe it wasn't a speed-bump. Maybe it was something lying in the road.

García snickered at his high concept, repeating his projected title like a mantra. Stuart shrugged in the shadow of the rear compartment, blackly invisible to the cops up front. Scotchman's face, impassive in reflection, slid up the windscreen as they cruised under one of the rare functioning streetlights.

When García first introduced the other cop, Stuart assumed his name was Scotch, man. He sussed Scotchman thought his movie crazy partner was a prick.

'How d'ya like it, Stuey? Think it'll play in Peoria?'

Stuart shrugged again. Last night, García had come up with a dozen movie ideas. Cop movies.

'Take it to New Frontier, man,' García insisted. '*Prowl Car*, man. Will be *the* werewolf cop movie. Be boffo boxo. Can write it together. Like a *collaboration*, man. Split credit.'

García's eyes rolled like the comedy Chicano he pretended to be when he wasn't beating someone. He howled at the moon. It was nearly full tonight, a sliver away from a perfect circle.

The cop had a Cheech Marín moustache, but was skinnier in the body than the straighter half of Cheech and Chong. He had overdeveloped forearms like Popeye's. He would look proportioned if his torso were Schwarzeneggered out by kevlar body armour.

'Werewolf *cho*, man. Everybody loves *el hombre lobo*. Specially when he wrestle with *El Santo*. Those were great *chos*. *Santo contra Dracula y el Hombre Lobo*, man. Scotchman, you get yours when the moon is full and bright?'

Scotchman's eyes swiveled to one side and back again. Reflection cut in half by shadow, his eyes shone in the dark upper half of his face. He looked like Batman.

Or Zorro.

His hair was gathered at the back of his head into a Steven Seagal ponytail which seemed to pull his face flat into lizard-like impassivity. The officer worked at being scary. He had the kind of hardness and smarts they called 'onstreet' this year.

This was the second night of Stuart's three-week ridealong with García and Scotchman. The LAPD had good relations with New Frontier; Ray Calme, the so-called studio head, had been able to arrange this tour of duty with no hassle.

There was the usual jaw-drop when the Brit writer turned out to be black, but it passed. Most cops he'd met so far were black, Latino or Asian. The city had just appointed its first Japanese-American Police Chief, Yasujiro Ryu. Whites, actual *anglo* Angelinos, were a minority, barricaded in secure enclaves, hiding behind 'Armed Response' signs on their lawns.

They passed through dark streets. Stuart had the impression of people scurrying away from the cruiser's path. Every building was tattooed, each block with its own style of graffiti. The overlapping scrawls were an endless layering of tag upon tag. Some called it art, but the coloured chaos looked to him like a canvas signed so many times there was no room for a painting.

He was supposed to pick up background for the *Shadowstalk* script. The book (Soon To Be A Major Motion Picture) was set in a North London council estate, but the movie (the *cho*, García would say) was relocating to Any*barrio*, USA. He was now learning what an American hellhole looked like from the inside. He'd have been happy enough to spend a long weekend with tapes of *Boyz N the Hood*, *South Central* and a couple of PBS social problem documentaries, then make it all up. It was more or less how he had done the novel.

Scotchman slowed the cruiser as he turned a corner off Van Ness Avenue. Kids in highly-coloured windbreakers stood outside a barricaded liquor store, conversing with what looked like sign language. Even through armoured glass, Stuart heard savage scratchrap rhythms from boomboxes. García craned to clock faces, but Scotchman looked without seeming to look. The white cop had a billion dollar brain for mug shots and rap sheets.

Scotchman shook his eyes without moving his head. No one worth busting. The kids were black or somewhere thereabouts, and they all wore badges even Stuart could identify as gang colours. Back in Britain, he'd heard of the Crips and Bloods, but they were Old Hat, long split into other factions, superseded by newer waves of ethnicity and criminality. Last night's lecture on the nomenclature and uniforms of Los Angeles gangs had been about as intricate and dull as an account of the dissolution of the Austro-Hungarian Empire.

Stuart knew he should be writing another novel, not traipsing around the Big Car Park (which was what LA looked like from the air when he first saw it) with a cowboy film company trying to wring some sort of commercial movie out of *Shadowstalk* (Soon To Be A Minor Video Release).

This year, black writers were onstreet; even a company as low down on the Hollywood food chain as New Frontier needed to buy one. Black and Brit was a whole new spin; Ray Calme was congratulating himself on having hooked a live one in Stuart Finn.

Raymond Chandler, one of Stuart's idols, said: 'If my books had been any worse, I should not have been invited to Hollywood. If they had been any better, I should not have come.'

The roof was suddenly thumped. The interior of the patrol car rang like a bell.

'Bee-bee, man,' García laughed. 'Onstreet shot. Feel up there, Stuey.'

Stuart ran his hand over the roof. It was armour-plate covered with thinning and holed foam rubber.

'Can you find a bump?'

Stuart couldn't.

'What was that?' he asked.

365

'A steel ball-bearing,' Scotchman said. 'Kids fire them from pistol-grip catapults like miniature crossbows. They're for hunting birds. You can punch through a crash helmet if you aim at the visor. Go through a skull like a walnut through wet ricepaper.'

'Fockin' kids, man,' García said, tolerantly.

'Someone shot the car?'

'Don't call it a shot unless there's a dent. No time for paperwork.'

Neither of the cops seemed to care about the attack. Stuart was sure a London copper would mind very much if someone propelled a steel missile at him with killing force. This was a different culture; he had to keep notes until he knew it well enough to translate *Shadowstalk* into its language.

Scotchman scoped out the roofs of the single-storey buildings lining the street. The Catapult Kid was up there, somewhere. It might not be worth filing a report, but the cop was certainly filing a grudge. One night, he'd get his payback.

Thanks to jet lag, Stuart was perfectly adapted to the ridealong life. He was awake at night and sleepy in the day, just like the cops. Only he felt lousy about it.

'You got Projects back in England, man?' García asked.

Projects? Oh yes, housing estates. Council houses.

'We have Projects.'

'Like in your book?'

'Yeah.'

'Onstreet book, man.'

When he found out his ridealong was a writer,

366

García read *Shadowstalk*. Stuart, interviewed to death on publication, didn't have anything more to say about the novel, but García kept bringing it up.

'Must be heavy, man. What you say the name of that Project was, Bridgwater Farm?'

'Broadwater Farm.'

'Yeah, heavy.'

'Certainly is.'

Actually, Stuart had spent about four afternoons in his life trudging around Broadwater Farm, visiting his uncles with Mum and Dad. In Autumn, the place was boring rather than threatening. Kids made fun of his school uniform, but that was it. No guns, no knives, no ball-bearings. He had noticed all the concrete litter bins had had fires lit in them and been rained out, leaving streaks of sooty sludge. He'd used that in *Shadowstalk*.

'You like that, Scotchman? They got a *barrio* in Britain. Drive-bys, man. Gangstas, zonk houses, riots. Whole *enchilada*. It's in Stuey's book. Should read it, man.'

Scotchman, who only read rap sheets and law enforcement magazines, made no answer.

Shadowstalk was about killings on a North London Estate, and the young black policeman (a convenient author's stand-in, as everybody rightly said) who realises the murderer isn't just a psycho but the voodoo incarnation of all the social misery abroad in the land. It wasn't exactly a thriller, more a portrait of life in the dead end of the twentieth-century United Kingdom. Ray Calme saw it as about a younger (i.e. cheaper) Wesley Snipes or Denzel Washington tracking down and totalling a bad-ass monster motherfucker. It could certainly be read that way, Stuart admitted, but he hoped to keep some content in the screenplay.

'Where Stuey comes from is just as onstreet as the Jungle, man,' García said. 'Only with a different accent.'

Stuart didn't mention that his Dad was a doctor in Bath, and that he'd been a day boy at a private school. There were plenty of blacks and Asians at Sexey's (yes, that was the real name, by Damballah), members of Royal Families or the sons of coup-elevated Third World army officers.

No one could say it hadn't been tough, though. He always wished he had gone to an inner city comprehensive. At least, then, he might not now be a twenty-three year old virgin.

'Real riots in Britain, man. They kill cops just like here. Stuey, in the last LA riots, me and Scotchman got cut off in the Jungle. Crowd turned the car over, started kicking in the windows . . .'

He tapped the reinforced glass with his knuckles.

'. . . only they couldn't crack it. Tried to get in the gas tank to fry us up, only it's got a bullet-proof combination lock. The end, they just got bored and went away. Scotchman, though, he remember the faces.'

Stuart was a member of the Charlie Aziz Group, founded in memory of a Pakistani killed in police custody. They were still trying to get some lads who had been fitted up for assaulting police officers out of prison. He signed petitions and wrote letters to his MP but deplored direct action. When one of the CAG was suspected of throwing a petrol bomb at a police station, he personally made the resolution calling for his immediate expulsion and censure.

'We ran into some of those *cholos* from the riot. Scotchman, he make them strip naked and walk down a corridor, whistling the *Andy Griffith Show* theme while me and other officers beat on them with rubber flashlights, man. Was real payback.'

Stuart had heard similar stories about London police, who apparently made you whistle *Dixon of Dock Green*. That was a weird international police tradition.

'The Jungle out there, man,' García said, proudly. 'We're the *beasts*. We're the *kings* of the Jungle. Gotta be, to survive. Put that in your screenplay, man. Give the cop guy claws that cut like razors and a roar that chills the blood of evildoers. Like us.'

If he couldn't write for the movies, García would like to act in them. He said he became a cop because the first thing he could remember on TV was Erik Estrada in *CHiPS*. That was culture for you. For Stuart, it had been *Fawlty Towers* repeats.

The patrol car had its route marked out, but Scotchman put his own random spin on the detail. He had explained that it was important in the Jungle not to be predictable, so he superimposed his own course. They started out and finished up where they were supposed to be and hit certain points along the way, but there were any number of deviations he made sure to work into the schedule. Scotchman called it a *skedule*, of course.

They were covering the LA grid, taking as many cross-streets as possible. Names which sounded exotic in Bath (Sepulveda, Pico, Figueroa) had turned out to be nondescript thoroughfares stretching for miles, for all the world like Surbiton High Street with more palm trees and fewer pedestrians. This route was away from those names, threading from Downtown to the South-East, through the bitterly-contested territory called the Jungle. The neighbourhoods were mainly Chicano, most blacks having been driven out. A wave of Koreans was coming, García said. Stuart wondered where the people who were driven out went.

Most cross-streets were dark, streetlights shot out and businesses shuttered up behind graffiti-covered steel rollers. Scotchman drove slower, and Stuart felt the crunching caltrop-like obstructions under the armoured tyres. The roads were very poorly maintained, far worse than in Britain.

To the left, a shutter rolled up like a broken blind, and light flooded out of a garage. Stuart flinched: the shutter reminded him of flaps going up over a pirate ship's gunports as the cannons delivered a broadside.

A sleek black van slid swiftly out, crossing a forecourt in a liquid instant like a panther. The van *nudged* the patrol car's nose as it took possession of the street. Stuart felt the impact in his teeth as Scotchman braked.

García swore in rapid Spanish.

The van slipped into the night, at once beyond sight. With its one-way black windows and reflective paint job, it could be swallowed by shadow. Stuart had seen no visible licence plate.

'Shouldn't we go after that?' he suggested.

Neither cop said anything. Light from the garage still filled the car.

'Should check for damage,' García said, at last.

Scotchman nodded. He unlocked his driver's side door, and stepped out, hand easy on his gun.

'Stay here, Stuey,' García said, also leaving the car.

Stuart bridled. He couldn't pick up much from sitting in the back while the world went on outside. Then again, he wasn't sure how much he wanted to pick up.

The cops examined the hood, where the van had side-swiped. They talked intensely, maybe argued, but Stuart couldn't lip-read. He looked at the garage. It seemed floodlit, and yellow light poured down the forecourt. In the yellow were trickles of red that gave him a bad turn. Knowing he'd regret it, he opened the door and got out.

2

From the *Corrido* of Diego

'I was born within a day's ride, as distances were measured then, from *El Pueblo de Nuestra Senora de la Reyna de los Angeles de Rio Porciunculo*. My mother was an Indian, my father was a Jesuit. They were, of course, not married. Such arrangements were common in our neglected corner of the Empire.

'My father baptised me Diego, and finally, grudgingly, left me his family name. My mother birth-named me Fox, for her totem animal. You may know me by the Spanish form of my Indian name, *Zorro*.

'This was 1805; five years before the *Grito de Dolores*,

Father Hidalgo y Costilla's call for revolt against Spain; sixteen years before the end of the rule of Madrid over Mexico; forty-three years before California was ceded to the United States by the Treaty of Guadalupe Hidalgo; forty-five years before the territory attained statehood . . .

'Had I merely lived out my expected years, I should have experienced history enough for any man. As things happened, history and I have become intertwined until we are each inseperable from the other.

'Mine is not a story, as an *anglo* would have it, but a *corrida*, a song. What is true and what is not have long ceased to matter. From the very beginning, I have been a legend as much as a living creature. Often, I lose myself inside the legend.

'Sometimes, I am Diego, masked as Fox; sometimes, I am Fox, hiding inside Diego. This, what you know from motion pictures and television, is true. Little else is.

'I was born Hispanic if not a Spaniard, and I shall die an American if not an *anglo*. Stories represent me as of the *ricos*, strutting around a *hacienda* in absurdly embroidered finery, galloping over peon-tilled land on a pure-bred Castilian steed, elegantly duelling with a Toledo blade. Such men were fewer than stories would like, and rarely made themselves evident. I was of the *pobres*, the nameless thousands who were born, dug out goods from the ground with their hands, and, in the normal course, died.

'The *ricos* left behind their names (the streets of this city bear them still), but the *pobres* passed utterly from the land, leaving not even a memory.

'Except mine.'

'The *viejo* had changed me. That I knew from his last touch, which struck like lightning. I thought myself dead but trapped in my body. I felt the weight of my limbs but could not make them move. Then I realised my body merely had an unfamiliar shape. With a little concentration, I could move.

'I was different.

'Since early childhood, my back had been bent in field labour, my hands had fought earth and rock. Pain was as much a part of my body as the taste of spit in my mouth. Now the pain was gone. For the first time, I had pleasure in movement. Simply raising my hand to my face was an exhilaration.

'Against sky, I saw my long-fingered, sharp-nailed hand. It was dark and thinly furred. The knuckle of my forefinger burned with pain. My finger lengthened, joints popping. See, my forefingers are as long as my middle fingers. That is part of the old stories.

'I no longer felt the cold of the night. My clothes were stretched in some places and loose in others, and confined me intolerably. I looked at the full moon and saw not the familiar silver disc, but a ball of light brighter than the sun, containing all colours of the rainbow.

'As I looked about, the dark was banished. Each rock, each plant, was as plain as if under a frozen streak of lightning. Bright, moving forms were animals. I saw movement as well as colour, and could discern a grey rabbit which would by day have been hidden in similarly-coloured scrub.

'I rent apart my shirt, my thick pelt bristling as I let night air at my rough skin, and brought down the rabbit. The animal moved slowly as a muddy stream and I was swift as a hawk.

'Swift as a fox.

'The rabbit's blood was like a pepper exploding on my tongue, like *peyote* blazing in my brain. My powerful jaws, lined with sharp teeth, could crunch through bone; my mouth was wide enough to finish the rabbit in three bites.

'Sights and smells and tastes blossomed. I was lost in a new world. I could stand straight-backed, as never by day; and I could run swiftly on all fours, my claws striking sparks from stone.

'The *viejo* lay in the moonlight, body dry, limbs like black sticks. The Indian, whom my mother said was of the People Before Our People, might have been buried in the desert and unearthed after ages. His face had turned from leather to parchment. Dead for only a few moments, it seemed life had fled from him many years ago.

'As he died, something had passed from the tired old man to me. I, Diego, ran under the moon and fought beasts for my food. Soon, I would fight beasts for my people.'

3

Thin blue smoke swirled hypnotically under the strip-lights. A thick smell stung his nose and eyes like teargas.

A pedantic copy-editor at Real Press had told him not

to call it cordite (the stuff wasn't used any more), but couldn't suggest an up-to-date alternative term for the afterstench of discharged guns. Something Stuart had never smelled before, it was unmistakable.

The garage was filled with people. There was no doubt about how dead they were. The far wall was pocked with bullet-holes and splashed with bright blood. A line of young men slumped where the skirting board would have been, limp arms overlapping, surprised heads lolling on chests. It was his Dad's usual suggested solution to industrial disputes; they'd been put against the wall and shot.

The predictable thing to do was bend over double and bring up his doughnuts and coffee. Stuart, in this case, was highly predictable.

García and Scotchman found him on his knees, coughing into a pool of chyne. Clear, bitter fluid hung in ropes from his mouth. His head was whirling.

Scotchman whistled and García swore.

Stuart shut his eyes, but his mind's instamatic developed polaroids in his head. Gouting wounds in colourful jackets, puckered out and leaking meat stuffing. Crisscross trails of blood like rafia strands on a concrete floor. One man, a boy, hanging from chains, stripped not only to the waist but almost to muscle and bone.

'This fool got special treatment,' Scotchman said.

The hanging boy had been chubby; pockets of fat stood out in his flayed torso. Stuart was carrying around about half a stone more than he should have been.

His gut twisted again, but there was nothing left inside.

'Stuey, man,' García said, not unkindly, 'clean yourself.'

He found a handkerchief and wiped his wet face. He tried to lick the ghastly taste out of his mouth.

Now he had stopped being sick, he had time to get scared.

When he opened his eyes, it wasn't so bad. He told himself it was special effects. In movies, he had seen worse.

The hanging boy's arms were wrenched upwards, probably out of his shoulder sockets to judge by the stretched tendons, and fastened to the chain above his head. His wrists were cinched together like beer cans by once-piece plastic cuffs. Whoever had worked on him had known what they were doing.

Scotchman whispered a report into his wafer-phone, glancing over each of the dead. He mentioned that all the boys had been given a just-to-make sure head shot. That was where a lot of the mess came from. García rooted around on a work-surface. He found some car mechanic tools, and a large chemistry set.

'Looks to be a zonk house, man.'

Zonk was the latest packaging of the product, cocaine. It came in squeezable plastic bulbs, like tomato-shaped ketchup containers. A single oily drop on the tongue was a force ten hit. Conoisseur zonkbrains preferred to drip it into their nostrils or on to their corneas. Chief Ryu had declared war on Zonk.

As well as taking out the zonk krew, the killers had raked their equipment with gunfire. The chemistry set was smashed and odorous. Pools of different coloured liquids mixed and steamed on the bench-top.

'Party favours,' García commented, flipping open a

deep Samsonite to reveal densely-packed zonk squeezers. 'Couple of hundred K, easy.'

Scotchman had made his report. He folded up his wafer-phone and slipped it back into his top pocket.

'Gang activity,' he diagnosed. 'These are Caldiarres. They've been warring over turf with the Eyes.'

All the dead people flew colours. Scarves and symbols and jackets and headbands. The Caldiarres' badge was a red, angry demon face. From the tribalism, you'd have sworn the Indians had won in the Americas.

'Wouldn't another gang take the drugs?' Stuart asked.

García looked into the face of the hanging boy and said 'Think I recognise this fool. Esquiverra, Escalante, Esca-something . . .'

Scotchman looked around, crossing names off his mental wanted list.

García picked out a squeezer and felt the weight of it. A single hundred dollar pellet of zonk was inside, diluting in liquid.

'Feels like a tit, man. Really does.'

Zonkbrains called their poison Mother's Milk, and talked about 'sucking Diablo's Teat'.

García gave an experimental squeeze and a tiny gusher of whitish fluid dribbled from the nipple.

'Ever wonder what it's like, Stuey?'

Stuart had a particular horror of drugs. When his sister was fourteen and Stuart eleven, Dad had caught Brenda with a joint and gave them both a scarifying tour of a rehab clinic. Neither of the Finn kids so much as smoked cigarettes; Stuart worried about the amount of coffee he drank.

'Let's post the Crime Scene: Keep Out notice and be on the road,' Scotchman said. 'The clean-up will be here in minutes.'

'You just leave these people?' Stuart said, astonished.

'They're not going anywhere. And nobody is going to mess with them.'

Scotchman took a last look around the garage. The smoke had dissipated.

'A message has been delivered,' he said. 'Let's hope it gets to the right people.'

4

From the *Corrido* of Diego

'My mother had fourteen babies that I know of, at least five with my father. By my twenty-fifth year, I alone still lived. My brothers and sisters were taken by illness and the land.

'My father wished to give me work at the mission. Don Esteban would not hear of a peon being taught to read and write. I was in all but name a slave of the *patrón*. Under the Spanish statutes of California, I was prohibited from tilling earth or raising livestock for my own table. I was paid six *reales* (twelve cents, American money) a day. Obliged by law to buy food from Don Esteban, I never saw a coin. Like all peons, I inherited the debt of my family. The debts of my dead brothers and sisters, which fell upon my shoulders, were numbered in thousands of *reales*.

'This was the way things had been under Spain; this was the way things were under Mexico; this was the way things would be in the United States.

'The mission collected its tithe from Don Esteban, who deducted it from the earnings of the peons. My father taught us to be devout and dutiful, for we would receive our reward in Heaven.'

'One night of the full moon, soon after the change, I hunted down and killed Don Esteban.

'In the stories, Don Esteban might be a tyrant, lashing about with a whip, striping the backs of the peons. Perhaps one of my sisters survived to young girlhood and became beautiful. Or maybe one of the daughters of my neighbours was comely and promised to me in marriage. From his steed, the *patrón* espied beauty under dust and carried her back to his *hacienda* to be abused. Or the priest might raise gentle protest against the lot of the peons and be turned away roughly by Don Esteban, falling dead in the dirt with a throwing knife buried to its hilt in his godly back. One night, Don Esteban and his men might become distracted with wine and, as a sport, ride through the village, pulling down the one-room *jacales* in which we lived, emptying one-shot pistols at random at any human shadow.

'None of these things were the case. By his own lights, Don Esteban was a pious man. He treated his peons as he treated other beasts that he owned, strictly but with care. His wealth was founded upon our work, and you do not slaughter a good horse or ox until it is too old to work.

'Killing Don Esteban was something that came to my animal mind. He was not the first man to feed my night hungers, but he was the first whom I sought out.

'If the *patrón*'s home was a *hacienda*, it was a modest one. It was made of stone but its floors were beaten earth. My feet made no sound as I entered. Don Esteban was reading his Bible by firelight. As I stalked towards him, he gripped a rosary tight and stared.

'At the first sight of me, Don Esteban fouled himself. To my snout, the smell was intense and exciting.

'With my long fingers, I gripped the *patrón*'s head firmly as I tore out his throat. I chewed through the fine lace of his collar. My teeth hurt as I bit down on a silver button. His muttered prayer cut off sharply.

'When finished, I found my hooked thumbnail had cut a zig-zag-zig into Don Esteban's cheek as he struggled. A red letter stood out in the brown skin above his beard. The letter Z.

'A servant found me squatting over Don Esteban. As often after tasting human blood, I had fallen into a reverie, distracted by patterns in the flames of the hearth. The servant gave the alarm and I was chased into the hills.'

'Next morning, when I returned exhausted to my *jacale*, the peons mourned the passing of the *patrón*. Many loved Don Esteban as a dog loves its master. The mission bells tolled for his death. By this time, my father was dead of fever and a young Jesuit, Fray Molina, had taken his place.

'A cousin of Don Esteban sold his lands, and we had

a new *patrón*, Don Luis. He was much like the old *patrón* and, after some years had passed, I took the opportunity to kill him also. Of course, there would always be *patrónes*. This was understood. I could not exterminate the breed. Also, I killed Fray Molina, whom I knew troubled the young boys of the village. And I killed *Capitan* Cordoba, who hanged Tío Pancho for speaking against the Church. I killed many. Still, I kill many.

'With my long finger, I took to leaving my zig-zag-zig on my kills. Others took to using my mark. Often, I saw it cut into the bark of trees or the adobe of a wall.

'By now, there was much talk of a curse and a demon. The old women, more Indian than Spanish, said the curse was always upon the land. In the times before the *conquistadores*, when the Apache preyed upon the Pueblos, the demon fought the raiders. It was a fox, a wolf, a bear, a wild man . . .

'Some said the demon was an angel, that only the unjust were struck down by its hand. I *was* drawn to certain men: cruel officers, venal priests, murderous bandits, harsh overseers. If I chanced upon one such by daylight in the period just before the full moon, their flesh seemed to glow like the moon through my altered eyes. I would be certain our paths would cross by night.

'By day, I took a wife, Dolores Lolita. She grew old and died in short years. I did not grow old and die. My sons seemed to me like my brothers, then like grandfathers, then they too died. Few remarked upon my situation, but other peons kept their distance from me. After I buried my Lolita, I could find no other to wed me. My grandchildren avoided me. I was no longer welcome at the mission.

'Eventually, I would have been driven from the land. Those who sang of the Fox of the Night wished to deny the Diego of the Day. I became as a phantom, entirely invisible to those among whom I lived. If I did not work the land, no overseer reprimanded me. If I found my sustenance by night, no one questioned my well-fed appearance. My *jacale* fell into disrepair, but that did not trouble me.

'Each month, the Fox had five or six nights, immediately before, during and after the full moon. Only then did I live. I hunted, I found lovers, I struck. Sometimes I wished Diego would disappear forever into the Fox. Then I could depart for the hills, there to live away from the cares of man.'

5

'Be a blue moon tomorrow, man,' García said, thumbing up at the sky.

Stuart looked up through the wide window, puzzled. The moon above was silver, as usual.

'A moon can be called blue when it's full twice in a month,' Scotchman explained. 'It was full on the first and we've a couple of days to go till September.'

So that was what 'once in a blue moon' meant. Stuart guessed you got a better education on the streets of LA than at Sexey's School for Boys. Maybe night patrol was so boring, you picked up all this trivia.

Of course, tonight hadn't been boring.

García and Scotchman were known at the Coffee Stop. An eighty–year-old counter girl with a jet-black beehive served them without being asked. She might have been eighteen when the sun set and aged through a long graveyard shift. No greeting, no conversation.

They didn't talk about the zonk house. Stuart, stomach empty, was hungry but found the idea of food repulsive. He dunked a doughnut, then sucked coffee out of it.

He felt gimlet eyes on his back. Now he knew what it was like to be with the Heat. Even at 4:30 am, the Stop was crowded. Thin old people and restless young ones. Night people. One or two teenagers wore discreet colours, almost as quiet as AIDS remembrance ribbons. Scotchman was the only *anglo* in the room. Stuart wasn't quite the only black guy, but he was the only one who felt as though he were from outer space.

He could tell the night people knew he wasn't a cop. He sensed eyes searching for a gun bulge under his pullover. Not being a cop wouldn't be any protection if that black van cruised down the street and someone rolled down one of the reflective black windows to spray automatic gunfire at the Coffee Stop, shattering the window and perforating García and Scotchman as inconvenient semi-witnesses. Stuart would get just as many bullets.

A screen-fronted sphere above the counter gave out a smog forecast in Spanish. The golden-skinned weathergirl was one of the CGI simulacra so popular this season. It had only taken America fifteen years to catch up with

Max Headroom. Traffic and crime stats stuttered across the image, those with an immediate effect highlighted in pulsing red.

A young Chicano walked over to the cops. He wore silver-tipped cowboy boots and tight black jeans. His hair was covered by a tied-at-the-back black bandana. If he slipped the bandana over his eyes, he would look like a masked avenger. Though clean-shaven, his eyebrows were slicked and teased like a Douglas Fairbanks moustache.

'*Buenas noches*, Vega,' Scotchman said quietly. No doubt Vega merited his own file card.

The kid said something to Officer García and the cop inclined his head to think. Remembering GCSE Spanish, Stuart gathered the cops were invited to talk with someone called the Alcalde. 'Alcalde' meant 'Mayor', but Stuart guessed Vega didn't mean Krystina Jute, the controversial Mayor who wanted to change the city's name to Las Angelas.

'The Alcalde is concerned about what went down this night with the Carriares,' Vega explained, diplomatic but forceful like an ambassador of an overconfident superpower. 'He would like to discuss this matter.'

García looked at Scotchman, who gave no signal. As one, the cops stood.

'Who is this Alcalde?' Stuart asked.

'Could call him a community leader,' García said.

As they all walked across the checkerboard floor, people at the tables cringed to give them air-space. The cops had a special saunter, probably from lugging all the iron around on their belts. The Colt Police Python on one hip was balanced by the multi-use stunstick on the other. Stuart, taller than García and within an inch of Scotchman, felt he was trotting in their wake like a tolerated younger brother.

At a table in the farthest alcove, the Alcalde held court. He was a white-haired man whose unlined face was adorned with a neatly-trimmed goatee beard, black but undyed. He wore a white jacket over a sparkly black shirt, and had a necklace with an animal-tooth fetish. Clustered around him were serious-looking kids like Vega, sharply dressed but without obvious gang colours. All were Latino, save a girl with oriental eyes and a braided queue who might have been half-Korean or Vietnamese.

If the Alcalde's party had eaten or drunk anything, the waitresses had long ago cleared away the washing-up. The Alcalde smoked a thin cigar. He smiled at the cops and, speaking Spanish so slowly Stuart could follow with no trouble, invited them to sit with him.

Stuart found himself crammed on a squeaky seat between Scotchman and the half-oriental. He was aware of the cop's holstered gun, pressing into his thigh as he was crowded against the girl.

'This is a bad thing that has happened,' the Alcalde declared. 'Blood spilled, lives wasted . . .'

Stuart expected Scotchman to comment on the occupation of the dead kids, but the cop said nothing.

'The Eyes are evil fools,' García said. 'This was coming for months.'

The Alcalde waved the comment away. 'This was not the work of the Eyes. They themselves suffered a similar attack three nights ago. A black van was seen.'

'We saw—' Stuart began, then halted as Scotchman tapped his knee.

'The Caldiarres and the Eyes have made cases to me,' the Alcalde continued. 'They say there will be no war.'

'As long as they're in the zonk business, there's war,' Scotchman said.

The Alcalde shook his head. 'This is regrettable. This zonk is a poison, the Devil's Milk. It is right that your Chief Ryu should wish it vanished from our streets.'

Vega nodded, eyes on the Alcalde. The kid reminded Stuart of Deal, the boy in *Shadowstalk*. The boy who shows the policeman where the evil comes from.

'But there are other poisons.'

Dawn seeped into the Coffee Stop, dispelling the grubby corpse light of crackling ceiling panels. Shadows appeared on the Alcalde's face. Back in Britain, it was getting near bed-time. Stuart was exhausted to the point of dropping.

García and Scotchman stood, ending the audience. Stuart, reluctant to unbend from the soft seat, got up too. Formal farewells were exchanged. The cops walked to the door and the patrol car outside.

For an odd instant, Stuart stayed behind, looking at the faces of the Alcalde's entourage. Vega, the oriental girl, others. He saw an intensity that touched a chord. Something he could use for the script.

Throughout the audience, the Alcalde had not seemed to notice Stuart. His followers, though, took turns to stare at him until he had nowhere to look away. Now

the Alcalde looked straight at him and said, in precise
English, 'Take care, black man. This is a jungle.'

6

From the *Corrido* of Diego

'On February the 2nd, 1848, at the end of the Mexican-
American War, the Treaty of Guadalupe Hidalgo was
executed. Mexico ceded to the United States territory
greater in size than Germany and France combined.
Aside from giving up claim to the Republic of Texas,
which was taken promptly into the Union, Mexico
yielded New Mexico, Arizona and California.

'By that time, I had walked away from my village. Runaway peons were traditionally hunted down
and punished, returned in chains like the slaves of
the Southern States. But the *patrón*, like everyone
else, had come to regard me as invisible. I left the
graves of my family and the ruin of my *jacale* to the
dust and wind and followed the paths of the beasts.
I drifted from place to place, never settling. Diego
lived long months of hunger for the nights of the
moon.

'I was greeted with suspicion by those I chanced
across. I still saw the strange glow and I made my kills.
Bandits, mostly; *renegados*, bad men. Some understood
my situation; I was given shelter and food in the homes of
the *pobres*, but never for long. For some years, I was with
the Pueblo Indians, my mother's people. They were less

unsettled by my presence. A few even commented upon my situation with humour.

'Fox was known to them of old.

'Some moon nights, young girls would couple with Fox. With Diego, these girls were respectful and obedient, as if with the father or elder brother of a lover, but with Fox, they were passionate, enthusiastic, delighted. They wore zig-zag-zig scratches like badges of honour. I noticed some old women wore similar, long-healed marks, and thought occasionally of the *viejo*.

'In giving away California, Mexican negotiators believed they were disposing of an Indian-plagued wilderness inhabited by only 7,000 Christian souls and an indeterminate number of savages. They were unaware that *nine days earlier* an *anglo* by the name of James Marshall had struck gold in the Sacramento Valley. Within three years, 200,000 people had flooded into the territory. Not all the newcomers were *anglos* from the States; many were *gambussinos*, experienced Mexican prospectors who headed North from Sonora to swell the population of the gold-fevered land.

'The *anglo* story has Marshall rushing into Fort Sutter shouting "gold, gold, gold!" In truth, the word he used was "*chispa*", Spanish for "bright speck". In everything concerning gold, the *anglos* followed the Spanish. *Conquistadores* named California for the gold they believed they would find, and Mexicans were prizing precious poisons from dirt long before Marshall got on his mule. In Nevada, the *anglo* Comstock was about to abandon an unsuccessful gold strike when a passing Mexican miner told him the bluish stuff he'd been discarding signalled that he'd hit upon the richest silver mine in the world.

'Gold and silver are poisons. This I know; once, much later, an Americano named Reid put a silver bullet in Fox. Sometimes, I limp still, after more than a century.

'Like a sudden wind rising, the empty lands were crowded. Rarely was I alone on the trails. I fell in with *gambussinos*, and, from boredom rather than need, took to prospecting.

'Many speak proudly of their "Spanish heritage", as if their ancestors were *ricos*, born on silk sheets in Madrid and sent to the colonies to win fortunes. It is a fact that when California became a state in 1850, over half of the Spanish-speaking population had arrived within the previous two years, *gambussinos* in search of gold. To be Chicano has nothing to do with the Dons of Aragon and Castile; it is to be the sons of miners and peons and Indians.

'I have been a miner, a peon and an Indian.

'With gold came guns. The rich flow of metal attracted men and women whose business was to dig their goods out of the purses of the men who had dug it from the ground. Mining camps bristled with vice and violence, then turned to ghost towns as a strike petered out. Cities were founded and abandoned. Deserts were littered with possessions cast away when they became too heavy.

'Eventually, there were more miners than could be supported by the wealth of the earth. At many strikes, *gambussinos* were more successful than *anglos* who had left Philadelphia or Kentucky for fabulous riches without troubling to discover, for instance, what fresh-mined gold actually looked like. Many expected to unearth shining bricks, brush off a little dirt and take them to the bank.

'It was from these men that I first heard the expression "greaser". It was to these men that I first applied the expression "*gringo*". Both words cannot be said without a snarl of hate.

'The new-born State Legislature, flexing *anglo*-dominated muscle, passed laws with official names like the Greaser Act of 1851, which limited the rights of the *pobres* to stake mining claims, raise livestock or buy land. Of course, laws only applied selectively. *Rico* and *anglo* embraced like long-lost cousins, each searching for the other's purse. Don *Patrón* was never a greaser to his face.

'It was to be expected that ill-educated *anglos* would be unable to comprehend the finer points of our new laws. Documents subtly worded to weight a balance in their favour were interpreted in the field as bestowing the legal right to murder Mexicans and steal their goods. Towns appointed Sheriffs and Vigilance Committees to do the murdering and thieving.

'Under the light of the full moon, gold shines pale like silver, like the faces of those I must kill. Fox was almost blinded by shining silver-white faces in an ocean of *gringos*. Diego learned quickly that he could not visit all who deserved the zig-zag-zig on their cheek.

'But I still had to try.'

• • •

'There was a man, surnamed Murieta, called Joaquin. He lived, he died, he did few of the things ascribed to him. He was a miner, then he was a bandit. Driven from his claim by *anglos*, he raided the makeshift banks of the mining camps for the gold he was no longer allowed to dig with his hands. There were very many like him. Sheriffs put up posters offering a reward for anyone by the name of Joaquin. There were many Joaquins, and many were bandits. When the *gringos* said Joaquin, they meant upwards of five men who were called by that name.

'I was myself a notorious Joaquin.

'Another man, named Salomon Maria Pico, was a bandit also. Often, it could not be decided whether a thing had been done by a Joaquin or by Pico. To the *gringos*, we were all one. When they pickled the head of Joaquin Murieta, they were satisfied. He had come to stand for us all, a legend more than a man. The head of "the renowned bandit" was exhibited at various places throughout California. As an added attraction, the hand of another "notorious robber and murderer", Three Fingered Jack, was also exhibited.

'But a legend cannot be killed like a man. This I know. Many were convinced that Joaquin Murieta lived still. And there were many called Joaquin, ready to take his place.'

7

It was hard to believe Millennium Plaza, a cross between a high-tone shopping mall and a Japanese Garden, was part of the same city as the Jungle. It was impossible to believe the hanging dead boy was in the same California demographic as the ornamental creatures grazing all around.

Everything was new in this Pastel Inferno. Men and women wore *chinoiserie* robes over swimming costumes and ambled with remote, beatific smiles. A few retro sharpies in shoulderpad suits moved faster than the herd. Discreet public speakers, inside statuettes of Buddha and the Tasmanian Devil, broadcast whale songs and purred reminders that smoking was illegal outside the red-marked areas.

After less than three hours of hotel sleep, Stuart was in a headachy fug. The Plaza's air of reassurance and safety was subtly aggravating. He was sure the security guards registered his black face and typed him as a zonkbrain, marking him for a back-clap with a palm-pad stun-gun.

High above the walkways, sun-screens stretched across sky, a parasol for the Plaza. *Parasol*, that was another one. Stuart was noticing the number of Spanish loan-words in California English. Millennium Plaza was a controlled environment, with musical fountains and an artificial, rose-scented breeze. Finally, a Californian dream was achieved: outdoor air conditioning.

The smiling security guards were bulked out in white *Star Wars* armour. A young black goon with a gold nostril-plug played with bejewelled kids, lumbering like

Frosty the Snowman. Tan mothers in wide hats with scarf bands exchanged bleeping business cards by an *espresso* robot. Their children dressed like mini-adults, with child-sized Rolexes, Rodeo Drive harem outfits and thousand-dollar Nikes.

A street market for millionaires, Millennium Plaza was a subliminal laxative for the bank account. Tasteful products were displayed on stands, like art objects in an exhibition. A card in a slot and a tapped-in code number could make payment in a second. The purchase would automatically be delivered to your upscale address.

All buildings were identical, so Stuart couldn't find New Frontier. He was twenty-five minutes late for the meeting and wasn't one of the personnel in whom tardiness was permitted. He was to be kept waiting, not to keep others waiting.

He queued by a free-standing mapscreen. A console listed companies, individuals and institutions he might wish to visit. If you pressed a stud next to the name, a pathway lit up from this spot to the address. A father and son team were taking advantage of the mapscreen's general function to decide which film to see. Pressing 'Movie Theaters', they made the grid light like an electrified web. There were over a hundred screens at six locations in Millennium Plaza, offering upwards of forty movies. The map could access information on films by classification (automatically excluding NC-17), start time, finish time, genre category (teenage zombie comedy), box office gross, and star rating averaged from a poll of ninety nationally-syndicated critics. Stuart felt as if he were in a Post Office with one small parcel, stuck behind a pensioner who hadn't talked to anyone since last week and needed a full half-hour of therapy with the bewildered counter clerk.

The family unit (a divorcé spending court-ordered quality time with his son) finally opted for the film which had made the most money: if so many others had seen it, they must know something the crix didn't. Stuart, trying not to be desperate, returned the father's shrug-and-grin combo and stepped casually up to the console, then ran his eyes up and down columns. There were dozens of companies called New Something; he found New Frontier between New Front and New Fruitz. A tiny squiggle appeared by the pulsing You Are Here dot. The New Frontier offices were just across the Square.

Alerted, he could see the NF logo on a building's shield-like marker-plate. The quickest path was through the crowded grass-and-pool area.

As he force-walked, Stuart saw a lot of white armour. Goons gathered around a group of chanting women in black. Old and young, the women didn't fit with Millennium Plaza: their clothes were not only an unfashionable colour but shapeless. Bodies deviated from the emaciated ideal: some had light moustache furrings, others wore unsubtle face paint. Thick ankles, barrel-waists, angry faces. They chanted in sing-song Spanish. A young woman, hooded like an agonised nun, held a placard which listed, in micro-letters, hundreds of names, almost all obviously Latino.

The guards were antsy, armour plates shifting in insectile clicking. A young man with a rank insignia on his breastplate argued reasonably with an emotional spokeswoman. Stuart didn't have time to find out what it was about, but a wide woman blocked the walkway and chattered at him in rapid Spanish he couldn't follow, presenting a clipboard and a pen. On the board was a sheet half-covered with signatures.

This was all to do with *Los Disaparidos*, the Disappeared Ones. That usually meant political dissidents 'vanished' by the apparatus of a police state. He knew about these women: mothers, wives, sisters, sweethearts, daughters. This must be some Latin American protest. He looked about for an Argentine Consulate or a Paraguayan Trade Commission.

The woman would not let him by, so he scribbled his name on the petition. The goon he'd seen earler, with the gold in his nose, glared as if he were giving succour to the enemy. Once Stuart had signed, he became the large woman's best friend. He was embraced and passed on to the other women.

A banner was held up. *Comité de los Disaparidos de los Angeles*, Committee of the Disappeared of the Angels. No, Committee of the Disappeared of *Los Angeles*.

He was uncomfortable. The chanting was louder, the goons' smiles set in concrete. The black guard forced his gauntlet palms close together and an arc crackled between them. The spokeswoman gave up arguing with the ranking guard and joined her voice with the chant.

Stuart managed to get out from between the factions. The officer spoke into a throat-mike which amplified his voice to a Crack of Doom, instructing the women to 'kindly disperse and clear the square'. One woman fell on him and stabbed his armoured chest with something black and stubby, a marker-pen. In a swift movement, she scarred the officer with a thick black streak. It looked like the Mark of Zorro, a zig-zag-zig . . .

The officer made a pass by the woman's scarved head with his open hand, as if to cuff her ear. There was a crackle, and the woman fell, twisting and spasming, to the ceramic tiles.

'Will you *please* kindly disperse and clear the square!'

Shaking and queasy, Stuart got away from the action. The building recognised his temporary tag and automatically opened for him. The doors were tinted, soundproof glass. When they hissed shut, he saw white guards, ungainly like marooned spacemen, tussling with crow-black protestors, but could not hear the kerfuffle.

Tansey, a tiny girl introduced days ago as a 'personal expediter', greeted him in the foyer. She was eye-candy, a knock-out blonde who decorated New Frontier as a bikini extra decorates a beach party movie. She put a paper cup of decaf in his hand and escorted him to the elevator. She ordered him to have a good time and sent him up to the conference suite.

There was no table in the conference suite, and few items of furniture recognisable as chairs. Stuart was invited to loll on an inflated beanbag. Electronic equipment towers rose between the cushions, like hookahs in a cyberpunk Arabian Nights. A spherescreen revolved, quietly playing a video clip whose images stuttered along with scratchrap vocals.

Ray Calme, President of New Frontier, knelt on a

karate mat, white robe tented about him. Its thong-laced neckline disclosed a scrub of grey chest hair and a tan, corded throat. On his chest, a penphone, a slimline tabulator and other gizmos hung like a *generalissimo*'s medal cluster. The company fortune was founded on pictures like *Gross* and *The Cincinatti Flamethrower Holocaust*, but New Frontier had climbed to mini-major status with franchises: the *Where the Bodies Are Buried* horror films and the *Raptylz* urban youth comedies. Nestled securely in a portfolio of media interests, New Frontier was shooting its wad on hard-edged genre merchandise, to wit: *Shadowstalk*.

There were two others: the haggard bikette with an enormous troll-cloud of bleached hair was Ellen Jeanette Sheridan, soon to sign as director of *Shadowstalk*; the fat boy in the one-piece orange skinsuit was Brontis Machulski, the richest teenager Stuart had met since school. Ellen Jeanette had gone from Metalhead promos to a *Where the Bodies Are Buried* sequel to A-list star vehicles, working with hot comedy and action names. Machulski designed interactive software and had invested his obscene profits by buying into New Frontier (in effect, he was Calme's boss), developing movie projects to tie in with computer games. Synergy was the watchword: a movie might bomb, but the ancillaries (games, merchandising, spin-off, cable, laser) could turn over major money.

While Calme talked script ideas, Machulski tapped keys on a personal note-pad. He could have been making a shopping list or zapping flying saucers for all Stuart knew. Ellen Jeanette sniffled badly as if she had flu coming. On being introduced to Stuart, she'd offered him a demi-squeeze and told him it was important to stay onstreet if he was to keep his creative *cojones* pumping story sperm. García had told him Beverly Hills zonk was so diluted as to be barely illegal.

Machulski had brought *Shadowstalk* to New Frontier. Though Stuart had never got up the nerve to raise it, he was sure the kid was also the only person involved who'd *read* the book rather than glanced at coverage. Ellen Jeanette refused to read anything: scripts, treatments, contracts and even personal mail had to be recorded on microcassettes she could play back through helmetphones while tooling around the Secure Zones on her 'hundred thousand dollar hog', a vintage Harley motorcycle.

Calme had word of last night's escapade from his LAPD fixer. When he commiserated with Stuart, Ellen Jeanette perked interest. Stuart haltingly went through the story, trying to balance the onstreet callousness they expected from the author of *Shadowstalk* with his genuinely conflicted feelings about patrols through the heart of darkness. Much as he hated to say it, he felt it was equipping him to write better, if not this script then the next book.

'Hung up like meat?' Ellen Jeanette squirmed. '*Guh-ross!*'

'I saw that footage on *CrimiNews*, Channel 187,' Machulski said. 'The kid looked like he'd been crucified, with his arms stuck out.'

Machulski's arms rose as if he were pretending to be an aeroplane.

'We should get *Zonk War* shooting soon, Ray,' Ellen

Jeanette told Calme, 'before we're eclipsed by events. The script is nearly whipped. A few more tweaks, and Muldoon will commit.'

Muldoon Pezz was a black comedian looking for a serious role. *Zonk War* was a project Ellen Jeanette was more enthusiastic about than *Shadowstalk*.

Calme showed the ad that was going in *Daily Variety* and the *Hollywood Reporter*, announcing that the project was in development. Stuart thought they'd taken artwork from an old *Where the Bodies Are Buried* and retouched it to fit his story. Maybe they would retouch his story to fit the art.

Stuart, almost bursting, asked if anyone had notes on his four page treatment, which they'd all had for three days. Ellen Jeanette pinched her nose and looked out of the panoramic window. Calme admitted his reader hadn't finished going through the document yet. Machulski pressed a button on his gadget and a tickertape chittered out in a coil. His comments were about the game, which demanded a multiplicity of scenarios, rather than the film, which needed a single plot. One thing about the game business was that no script draft was ever discarded, it simply became another path the player could take through the maze of the story.

'Know this,' Calme began, 'English is a minority language in the Los Angeles school system. I've had to send my kids to some rich brat academy so they don't come home spieling Spanish. I mean, it's snazz they can talk to the maid, but it's getting so they can't talk to me. Sometimes I feel like the last white man in my neighbourhood.'

Calme realised what he had said and swallowed. Stuart was fed up with having to speak for an entire race, anyway. The British reviewers had gone on about his blackness, and his publishers tried to make him seem a lot more onstreet than he actually felt. Whenever he was profiled in the press, his parents would chide him for trying to come on like a tough kid from a broken home, battering a word-processor because it was either that or push zonk.

'It's what *Shadowstalk* should have,' Calme continued, recovering. 'The sense of *threat* of the *barrio*, the way it swallows the city, dragging it down. Like a monster, like a disease. You know now why they call it the Jungle, Stuart. It's a great image, the jungle getting thicker, growing over everything, everyone. That's what I love about this project, the chance to say something about the way the city is going. We're not after Academy Awards, but maybe we can make a difference.'

'Look,' Ellen Jeanette said, suddenly, 'isn't that pretty.'

Columns of pink and blue smoke jetted towards the sun-screens and swooped down again like the exhaust trails of an invisible jet. Calme was aghast. He talked into a gizmo.

'Tansey, shut off the a-c and seal the building. They're gassing again.'

Stuart looked out of the window, down at the Square. Everything was blurry and silent. The goons wore snout-like masks now and were spreading coloured smoke over the protesters, who shook and fell as if speaking in tongues. Millennium people fled, or produced mouth-and-nose breathers from inside robes. Some of the protesters were hauled out, twitching but manageable, and piled on to an electric cart like an old-fashioned milkfloat. The large woman with the petition could hold her breath long enough to fight back and had to be stunned with a palm-touch, then have her wrists plastic-noosed behind her back. The petition clipboard probably got lost in the melée.

'I wish they'd find the goddamned Disappeared and get those harpies off our necks,' Calme said. 'It's the third time this month. There ought to be a law.'

Stuart's eyes followed the smoke as it pooled around the writhing protesters, layering pastel over black.

8

From the *Corrido* of Diego

'Chispa del Oro was like any other mining camp. It was strung out along the banks of a creek, where men, women and children panned for sparkles among the sands.

'It was an hour before true sun-down. I was at the creek, circling the grit in water, holding my *batea* up to the light, hoping the last red rays would coax a gleam my eyes had missed. As the moon neared the underside of the horizon, my sight changed. The water swirled heavily, like quicksilver.

'Fox crept up on Diego. At first, there had been pain with the moon-change. Now I could pull on Fox as easily as one pulls on a cloak. If I concentrated, Diego could resist Fox and pass a moon night in human form, if with considerable discomfort.

'I had a woman and children, then. At least one of the children, the youngest, was mine. The baby boy's elder brothers were fathered by a man who had been killed, one of numberless Joaquins. The woman, Julietta, was part-Indian, like almost all of us. She loved Fox but lived with Diego, even became fond of him. She came to me because I killed the men who murdered her true husband. I marked them with my zig-zag-zig.

'A trickle of gold was coming in and I fed my family. In evenings when there was no moon, I would listen to Julietta play the flute with another woman who played the guitar. This was all a man could want; I wished to grow old and die like others, mourned by my children . . .

'Diego could almost pretend Fox had fled. Except on moon nights. Mostly, then, I hunted rabbits.

'One of my son's brothers pulled at my sleeve and pointed. The creek ran through a valley, washing gold down from the mountains. Up on the lip of the valley were seven white men, five on horses. Chispa del Oro had no problems with *anglos*. We were too removed from the big strikes, our yield was too meagre. We panned mainly for placer, the thin sand from which gold could be distilled only with more patience and skill than most *anglos* could summon.

'With the red of the dying sun behind them, the seven men were shadow figures. But I saw their faces as blobs of gloomy light. I told the boy to fetch a gun. He was barely ten yards from me when a bloody gobbet exploded in the back of his neck. One man had a long rifle, and was a fine shot with it.

'I stood, howling my rage and felt a *push* in my chest, the force spinning me off my feet. I dropped my *batea* and fell backwards into the creek. Water ran all around me, soaking through my clothes, trailing my hair away from my face.

'The horsemen passed me, cold shadows washing across my face.

'"Greaser ain't kilt," one said.

'"I allus has to finish your leavin's," another replied, voice close.

'A man knelt over me, face upside-down over mine. The glow on his skin was so bright I couldn't make out his features. A shining blade passed below my chin, cutting. I choked blood out through the hole in my neck.

'"A clean job, Hendrik," the rifleman said. "Crick'll bleed him dry 'fore sun-down."

'"Clean and quiet," said Hendrik.

'I lay still, hearing and feeling, unable to move. The current kept open the throat wound. Water streamed in as if through the gills of a fish, gulping out of my mouth.

'Hendrik stood up and doffed his wide hat. From inside his placket shirt, he produced a hood which he slipped over his head. Ragged scarecrow eyeholes shone like candleflames in the night. All were hooded now, night-riders.

'"Gotta run them greasers off," someone said. "They dirty up the crick. Dang Meskins."

'The night-riders moved on. In time, I heard more shots, and whoops, and the slow crackle of fire.'

•   •   •

'The moon rose, and the hole in my throat closed. Fox slipped out of Diego's wet clothes and padded towards Chispa del Oro.

'The shacks were ablaze, casting a circle of light. The dead lay in heaps. Fray Juniperro, our *gambussino* priest, was slumped dead on his knees, bleeding from the gashes in the side of his head. His ears had been cut off. Juan Ochoa, who had fled North from Santa Anna's soldiers, was several times gutshot and dying slowly. The night-riders had staked out my Julietta and torn her clothes. They took turns to violate her.

'Fox leaped from the dark and closed daggered fingers in the throat of a man who was holding a firebrand. I threw him at the feet of the others. With a clawed swipe, I stripped a zig-zag-zig of skin from the side of one of the horses, exposing ribs and vitals. The beast neighed and collapsed, gore gouting around my ankles.

'Pistols were discharged into my chest and I felt mosquito stings. I tore the hooded head off the man who knelt between Julietta's legs, working with his bowie knife. My woman had been dead for minutes. I crushed the head like a rotten grapefruit.

'"Well, if it ain't a weirdwoof," Hendrik said, calm.

'I killed two others and howled, the blood of my kills bubbling in my throat. I had meat scraps between my teeth.

'One of the night-riders was down on his knees praying and sobbing and tearing at his hood. I grasped his chest with my feet, crushing ribs with my barbs, and I ate out his eyes, chewing through the cloth of his hood.

'"Look at him *feed*," said Hendrik.

'Only Hendrik and the man with the rifle still stood. The rifleman was tamping powder in the barrel. His hood was up over his nose, a powderhorn dangling by a string from his mouth. I stood up, flexing my limbs and growling.

'The rifleman was a cool hand. He got a ball into his weapon and packed it down, then brought the gun up and pointed it at me. I laid a hand on the barrel and held its aperture to my forehead. With my animal's snarling mouth, I called him an accursed *gringo*, a killer of women and children, a man with no honour . . .

'He fired and the ball flattened against my skull. I smelled the singe of my furred face, but felt no pain.

'The rainbow ecstasy of killing was on me.

'I made a hole in his head with my thumb, then jammed his powder-horn into the hole and held his head in one of the fires. The explosion was satisfying, scenting the air with burned powder and blood.

'I dropped the rifleman's body and looked at Hendrik. He was clapping, slowly.

'"Savage critter, ain't ye?"

'As I bounded towards him, he slipped off his hood. His eyes still glowed, but his skin was rough and dark, angry fur swarming across his face.

'I must have frozen in the air.

'"What be matter, fox. Ain't ye never met a wolf afore?"

'Hendrik's mouth was misshaping as teeth crowded out of it. As his body expanded, his clothes split along their seams. Bony knives burst through the fingers of his gloves. I howled and threw myself at him, tearing and gouging and rending. Powerful claws ripped my hide.

'We fought to the death, only neither of us could die.

'Hendrik chewed clean through my shoulder until one arm was hanging off on a thread of gristle. I wrestled his jaw free of the skull, yanking it to one side. We both healed within minutes, struggling still.

'Hendrik was a bigger beast than I, and master of the creature he became. Finally, he bested and humiliated me. He ground my face into dirt soaked with the blood of my woman, and sprayed me with a jet of thick piss. I smelled him on me for years.

'At sun-up, we both changed. The killing frenzy was gone from me, though daylight disclosed more atrocities done to my family and my people. My baby son hung from a post by his ankle.

'Hendrik and I didn't talk, but we sat opposite each other in the burned village. I heard the rushing of the stream and the settling of the embers.

'"I'm sorry for ye, greaser, that I am," Hendrik said, before leaving. "I've got what I've got and it's my way, but you've got the *curse* . . ."

'Still, I didn't understand.'

9

'And this baby is the Leveller,' said Muldoon Pezz. 'State-of-the-art all-in-one burpgun, grenade launcher and flamethrower. An ideal Riot Weapon.'

The comedian, whose sculpted hair made his head

look like a sugarloaf mountain, hefted the Leveller and posed with it. His arm disappeared entirely inside the weapon. He might be auditioning for *Black Terminator*.

Stuart looked into his half-coconut of fruit-filled exotic alcohol as guests oohed and ahhed over the array of gleaming steel deathware. He had thought the guns and knives mounted on the display wall were movie props, but Pezz was eager to explain how real they were.

'Is that loaded?' gasped Leitizia Six, the coffee-skin starlet. She was stapled into a brief flame-red dress.

'What the use of a gun that ain't loaded, child?'

Pezz shimmie-jerked with his metal partner, hip-thrusting at the girl. He wore a leather codpiece, decorated with a sequinned roaring lion, over a pair of the baggily diaphinous harem pants popular (and costly) this year. He made a dakka-dakka-dakka sound and raked imaginary death at his laughing guests.

Welcome to the Black Pack, Stuart thought.

This was the Ethnic Elite: scratchrappers, foulmouth comics, Spike Lee or Wesley Snipes gottabes, colour-coded execs, MC-DJ alpha beta soupers, lower echelon politicos, transvestite TV anchors. Instead of eye candy, the party had chocolate drops, like Leitizia Six. It was impossible not to imagine five earlier Leitizias who hadn't worked out so well.

Stuart wandered out of the gun room into a sunken area where a jacuzzi full of young black writer-directors waiting for their first credits passed around a smoky crystal ball. They sucked the ball's nipples and described projects, competing yarns of how onstreet the hoods they'd left behind were.

The wri-dies wore nothing but gold: necklaces, bracelets, armlets, cock-rings, nose-plugs, belts. Extras from a black porn *Cleopatra*.

'Homes,' shouted the wri-die of *Mama Was a Crack Ho*, 'get in on the bubbles, man. Anyone can write *Shudderslash* and get out of the hood has earned bubbles.'

Stuart wasn't sure whether the bubbles were in the jacuzzi or the crystal ball. He certainly wouldn't be comfortable stripping to his Marks & Sparks boxers and hanging with this crowd. His worst teenage experiences had been on a rugby pitch.

'I'll take a rain check,' Stuart said, using an expression from his English-American phrase book.

'Don't know what yo missing, my man.'

Back in the gun room (which was where people ended up chatting at this party, rather than the kitchen) Pezz was ranting. When 'the next time' came, he'd be onstreet with the Leveller, 'protectin my home, my people.'

Having missed the set-up, Stuart didn't know whether Pezz would be protecting his people from rioters or cops. One of the wri-dies, who had read a synopsis of *Shadowstalk*, shoved him in a corner and preached at him for quarter of an hour: Stuart had to change his hero from a cop to a gangsta. 'The cop is the natural-born enemy of the black man, Finn. We gotta stop makin' cops heroes.'

The wri-die got sidetracked by a diatribe against all the performers who had sold out to the man by playing cop heroes: Poitier, Whoopi, Murphy, Washington. The wri-die was rapping along to 'Cop Killer' when someone reminded him Ice-T played a cop in *New Jack City*.

Pezz was weighed down with more weapons. Chocolate drops draped him with guns as if he were a terrorist Christmas Tree. Stuart had seen *Pixie Patrol*, Pezz's last hit, and not thought much of it. His catch-phrase was '*bitch, fuck that shit!*', also the title of his best-selling comedy CD and scratchrap single. Pezz had played a cop in *Pixie Patrol*; he maliciously thought of mentioning it to the wri-die on the next pass around.

Now that Pezz was completely tooled up – his display case was empty, and he was *wearing* all his weapons – he wanted to party. One of the girlies, a bald freeway shaved through her hair, climbed up on a stool with an eye-dropper and squeezed fluid-smidgens into both his eyes.

Stuart didn't think zonking up a walking armoury was too clever. Pezz yelled encouragement and jiggled his guns, clanking like a junk-cart. Sooner or later, he was going to go off. If he wasn't too zonked, he'd do it in the yard because this was his house; if he *was* too zonked, he could afford to replace a ceiling or a wall. Maybe even a guest.

'Yez hear about the time Muldoon dropped a frag grenade in Mike Ovitz's swimming pool?' Leitizia asked.

Leitizia was very friendly whenever Stuart got near. She was the star of the *Velvet* series of 'erotic thrillers', rated NC-17 on the top shelf at a video store near you. In his blazer pocket, Stuart had Leitizia's card: it was plastic with a chip set into it that breathed her name and number when caressed.

Last night: a garage full of dead kids. Now: swimming pools, movie stars. Los Angeles was disorienting. Mood Change City.

'Stuart Finn?' said a young man with goldwire-rimmed glasses.

As they shook hands, Stuart realised the young man wore surgeon's gloves. He'd seen that in the last few days. It was a health fad, ANSC: Absolutely No Skin Contact.

'Ouesmene Collins,' he said.

Leitizia's scarlet-tipped fingers slipped up and down Stuart's shirt buttons. He had the idea she *believed* in skin contact.

'I'm with Reality Programming, Channel 187. *Crimi-News*. We understand you were at the Obregon Street Crimescene?'

'Obregon Street?'

'The garage.'

Stuart knew where Collins meant.

'We're doing a follow-up newsbite, and would like to schedule an interview.'

Collins spoke in a monotone and had no expression. Stuart thought he was squirmy.

'I'm afraid I signed a contract with LAPD,' Stuart shrugged. 'One of the conditions of my ridealong is that I do not discuss anything with the media.'

'Indeed. But there are ways around contracts.'

'I've another five nights to go,' he said, looking at his watch. 'In fact, I should be leaving. The patrol starts at midnight.'

'There are serious questions about Obregon Street,' Collins continued, intent. 'Ryu has stated that there are no concrete suspicions.'

Something warm and wet slipped into Stuart's ear. Leitizia's tongue. He'd waited twenty-three years for this and now had to skip out. Would the Velvet Vulva, as she introduced *herself*, 'take a rain check'?

'It was the van, surely,' Stuart said. 'The men in the van.'

'What van?'

'The black van leaving the garage.'

'There's no van in the reports.'

'Ouesmene,' Leitizia purred out of the side of her mouth, 'disappear, would you?'

Collins, still thinking *van*, vanished.

'You British guys,' Leitizia said, 'you've just got *it*.'

A tiny thought (shouldn't have mentioned the van: *contract violation*) shriveled in his mind. Other thoughts loomed larger, more pressing.

'Yo,' shouted Pezz, 'Velvet Vulva, all the waayyyy!'

One of his smaller guns went off, putting a thumb-hole dent in the wall. Everybody laughed.

Stuart made excuses.

10

From the *Corrido* of Diego

'If I could change, others must too. I was not greatly surprised to learn I was not the only creature of my kind. The old stories had come from somewhere. But what Hendrik said about a *curse* disturbed me greatly. I realised I did not understand my condition. Then again, who among us can say he fully understands his condition?

'Maybe ten years later, I crossed trails with a wagon

train. Its cargo was women: mail order brides for California miners, paid-for wombs to yield a harvest of *anglo* babies. Many were from far corners of Europe. Irish, German, Dutch, Hungarian. Gypsy, even. Few spoke English, let alone Spanish.

'For a while, I rode with the wagon-master. It was a harsh trail, across a desert that burned by day and froze by night. There was disease and hardship and privation and accident. As a month passed, I saw a glow growing in the face of one of the trail-hands, who took to what he called "breaking in" the brides. If the wagon-master hadn't hanged him, I would have killed him.

'Among the women was a Serbian girl who was also a cat, a big cat. From the first I saw her, I knew she could change. Her monthly cycle and mine did not jibe, so Fox never met Cat. In her centuries, Milena had learned languages; this skill made her special, not her ability to change. She was the interpreter, between the women and the trail-hands, and with whoever we chanced across.

'I asked Milena what Hendrik had meant by my *curse*, but she could not help me understand, though she thought she understood herself. I knew it was something quite apart from the moon-change, something that marked me as different from the rest of the changing kind.

'"Men call us the creatures of darkness," Milena explained, "and they have good reason. Many, perhaps most, of us are like this Hendrik, animals in human skin. Our place is the dark, our strength is the night. But your strength is the moon. The light of the moon is the light of a sun shining back from a silver mirror.

You are a creature of the light, perhaps even a prisoner of the light. I hunt where I will, for cats know no rules. The path you walk is narrow and lonely, for you must always hunt the evil in men, must always protect your people. Yet you can never be truly with your people, for you change. I do not envy you, Diego, and yet I accept that you are better than I, perhaps better than us all."

'Soon after, I killed a German woman without knowing why. Her face had glowed like a ghost-flame, as sickly and bright as the face of the worst ravager or tyrant I had ever slaughtered. It turned out the woman had stifled two of her children and taken their water rations for herself. During the desert crossing, a dozen women died who might have been saved by a few drops of water.

'The wagon-master said the woman must have been mauled to death by a mountain lion or a coyote. Gypsies and Hungarians muttered that they knew better. I left the next night, racing off as Fox.

'Later I heard a tall tale about a wagon train who turned on one of their womenfolk and skinned her alive to prove her hide was furred on the inside.'

11

'Got another high concept, man,' García said. 'This cop becomes a Mexican wrestling star, *El Demonio Azul*, and goes undercover . . .'

A whining shriek cut through García's movie idea, the public address system's way of saying 'Listen Up'. The cops in the locker room all looked to the wall-screen.

Like all public buildings in LA, the police station had its own interactive TV station, narrowcasting from a top floor studio suite. There were commercials: cop insurance and pension schemes, special bilingual coaching for promotion boards, holiday-camp descriptions of faraway stations that needed personnel to transfer in, new brands of body armour. Then the sergeant of the watch, outlined in frizzy blue against a blurry slo-mo explosion, gave a cop news round-up.

Mug-shots flashed by. Scotchman paid attention, nodding slightly at each face he recognised. The sergeant downloaded new charges to his patrol teams: some players were climbing, from rape to armed robbery to murder one; others were slipping down the leagues, narco beefs diminishing as they lost territory to the comers.

'As a result of last night's Obregon Street incident, the Caldiarres are Off The Board,' the sergeant announced, to general cheers. What looked like home video footage of the garage came on, the camera circling around the hanging boy. Arms outstretched and head hung, he did look as if he had been crucified. A crude computer graphic represented the angry face Stuart had seen on the dead boys' jackets, and a big black X crossed through it. 'This investigation is closed. Chief Ryu has commended the officers on the scene for the speedy mop-up.'

ID photos of García and Scotchman appeared in an iris, and cops gathered to josh the patrol team.

'They found the van?' Stuart asked.

'What van?' García said, fighting off a hug-happy *hermano*.

'The black van,' Stuart insisted, feeling dumb. Something about Obregon Street was nagging the edge of his mind. 'From last night, remember?'

'Didn't see no van, man,' García said, eyes swiveling towards an angling security camera. Its directional mikes could pick up what he was saying, but his face was out of shot. García shook his eyes from side to side.

Stuart gathered he should drop the subject.

Plenty of people wore sunglasses at night, especially those who also carried white canes. But this blind girl was waving a snub-nosed pistol. Far less aesthetically stimulating than anything on Muldoon Pezz's wall, it could still put a dent in a person. García yanked the gun out of her paw and whipped the heavy glasses from the suspect's eyes. They were red marbles, with tiny yellow irises like pus in pimples.

This one was far gone, a tertiary zonkbrain.

The girl's friends backed off and let the officers make an arrest. They were piling out of a club in the Jungle, having made enough trouble to prompt a call to the cops. Probably, they'd just run out of money and the management dropped the dime to bring round the garbage collectors.

Through windows as thin as arrow-slits, strobe-lights pulsed. A band named Dire Tribe did a scratchrap take on 'Heart Attack and Vine'. A sumo wrestler in combat armour barred the door, watching García and Scotchman take care of business.

When Scotchman shoved the zonkbrain against the patrol car and pulled disposable cuffs from his belt, the penny dropped. Stuart realised what bothered him about Obregon Street.

The zonkbrain, mad eyes leaking blood, twisted and kicked out blindly. She wore a ra-ra skirt and combat boots. Scotchman got out of the way of the kick and jabbed his stun-stick into her side. There was a crackle and the smell of ozone. She was so zonked she didn't feel the charge.

'The Caldiarre in the garage was cuffed,' Stuart said aloud, recalling the horror-flash image. 'His arms were fixed over his head. In the news footage, his arms are loose, stuck out like a scarecrow's. Someone uncuffed him.'

'Case closed,' García said. 'Don't think on it, man.'

García waded in and pummeled the zonkbrain. He took her head by a beaded scalplock and slammed it against the hood of the car. The fight went out of her. Scotchman got his ratcheted plastic noose around the perp's wrists and pulled tight. It would have to be clipped off with special shears.

Some clean-up cop must have cut the cuffs in Obregon Street. They were disposable, so they'd been disposed of.

The zonkbrain's boyfriend stood back, astonished but not appalled. He seemed to find it all quite entertaining. Struggling with the cuffs, she fell in a fetal ball, leaking foam. The sidewalk where she twitched was patterned with overlapped and faded spray-paint body outlines.

'Too far gone for detox,' García said as she rolled into a gutter clogged with concaved zonk squeezers, take-out food McLitter, and empty shell cases. Scotchman helped the girl stand and wiped off her mouth.

The boyfriend laughed and left at a run, taking off with his buddies for the next club. Some night, it would be him dribbling strawberry froth on the sidewalk.

Why would cops cut the cuffs? Because *cuffs* meant *cops*?

Cops covered cops, that was the first thing Stuart had seen onstreet: Scotchman distracting him while García popped pills. García was right: he shouldn't think about it, he'd only get his brain hurt.

A combat ambulance arrived. Zonkbrains fell between offender and casualty, and rated secure hospital facilities. A Paramedic, a Chinese guy in dark coveralls, hit the street.

'Why the camouflage?' Stuart asked.

'Whites make too good a target,' the Paramedic said.

García helped the Paramedic sling the zonkbrain in the back. Scotchman threw her white cane and dark glasses in after her.

As the ambulance turned a corner, Stuart noticed it was the same model vehicle as the van on Obregon Street, jungle-striped rather than dead black.

The sumo guardian looked up at the sky, weary shoulders weighted down by armourpads.

'It's always like this in the Jungle when the moon is full,' he said. 'It gets to their rotted brains. Moonlight is like a drug.'

'Gone quiet back there, Stuey? What's going down?'

Stuart was thinking hard. He couldn't help it; in his

mind, he was putting together a jigsaw. The picture that emerged was scary, but he couldn't stop himself from fitting in the pieces.

They were driving down a well-lit strip. There were clubs and all-night shops. Pedestrians wandered onstreet, drifting between cars.

The banner with the names of the Disappeared of Los Angeles. Cop-issue cuffs on the Caldiarre kid. A garage full of dead zonk dealers. The closed investigation. A van so black it fades into the night.

There were shots in the night. García sighed.

Every time Stuart turned on the television in his hotel, Chief Ryu was talking about the War on Zonk. Ryu reminded him of Gomez Addams, a shark-smiling little man in pinstripes. Mayor Jute was always behind the Chief, voting more funds to special Zonk Task Forces.

Stuart wasn't thinking Task Force. He was thinking *Death Squad*.

'Fuckin' Jungle,' Scotchman said, hitting the brakes.

A car was overturned in the street. A couple of kids with guns crouched behind it, dodging and returning fire from a low rooftop.

A slug spanged against the windscreen, but didn't shatter the armoured glass. The shot came from the roof faction.

'Shoot 'em in the brain,' Scotchman muttered, un-slinging a pump-action shotgun. He got out of the car, bent low, and ran across the street. García radioed for back-up.

Scotchman straightened and fired at the roof, not apparently aiming at anything in particular.

García finished his call-in.

'This time, man, stay here. Hollywood can't afford to lose you. Needs all the talent it can get.'

García drew his Colt Python and slipped out of the side door.

García and Scotchman didn't come back. Stuart heard gunfire, shouts and sirens. The patrol car's radio crackled, but no messages came through. He shifted on the squeaky seats and thought of the Disappeared, remembering crowd control smoke settling on the protesters in Millennium Plaza.

If, for some reason Stuart couldn't fathom, you *wanted* Millennium Plaza, you had to have the Jungle as well. It was how the city worked. All the folks at Muldoon Pezz's party were standing on the backs and heads of the onstreet scavengers who scuttled away when the shooting started. If Pezz stepped out into a riot, even toting his precious Leveller, he would last about seven seconds before someone drew a bead on his unprotected hairstyle and pre-empted his last punchline. And Stuart Finn didn't kid himself he was any fitter to survive out in Darwin City.

The street was clear now, as if cordoned off to be a movie set. The skirmish had shifted. García and Scotchman must be in pursuit. Everyone else had made a policy decision to get out of the way.

Stuart had enough background for his script now, and wanted to go home. He could work in Bath and fax the pages to New Frontier. The council might complain about the spare change brigade, but even the rabid

Right didn't suggest rounding them up and putting bullets through their eyes.

A pebble-tap hit the window near his head, startling him. He looked out and saw a black-uniformed cop chest. A gauntleted hand made a beckoning motion.

Stuart was puzzled, then realised he was invited to get out of the car. He nodded, and pushed the door. It wouldn't give. There was a green light on the inside handle. Like a London taxi, the rear doors could be locked from the dashboard. To prevent prisoners making a break. Last night, in Obregon Street, the lock hadn't been on; that was how he had been able to wander into the garage and see what he shouldn't have seen.

He shrugged an apology at the uniform. The green light cut out and the door pulled open. The lock was overriden by remote control. Stuart stepped out and looked into a silver-visored crash helmet. His own face was fish-eye reflected. Other uniforms, García's back-up, stood about. They wore no insignia, just black jump-suits and crash helmets. Stuart could tell they were cops by the gizmo-weighted belts. And the walk, the stand, the attitude. Actors couldn't fake that.

Stuart pointed in the direction that García and Scotchman had taken off. The uniform shook his helmet and laid a gauntlet on Stuart's shoulder, then spun him around to face the patrol car.

Something bit Stuart's right wrist, like the jaws of a dog, and he heard a familiar rasp. He was being cuffed.

Over the top of the car he saw the black van the uniforms had come in and his knees became water. He fell down before the uniform could cuff his other wrist, and realised he was yelping.

He was a writer, not some hero. He was not going to survive. He would be one of the Disappeared.

Still squealing, he shrank and writhed under the car. He shut his eyes, but nothing changed. He saw boots. Other boots joined them. There was a buzz of communication.

They were being cautious, Stuart realised. He hadn't been searched so no one wanted to lie down and take a shot in case he was nestling his own gun, ready to hole a visor. The patrol car weighed a few tons, so they couldn't lift it. By accident or instinct, he had gone to ground.

Something small and white had fallen out of his pocket and lay on the gritty asphalt next to his cheek. It was Leitizia Six's card. It recited Leitizia's name, address, phone and fax, representation and major credits.

He raised his head and banged it against the underside of the car. Pain jammed through his skull.

Those cop bastards had set him up for this. García and Scotchman. How was that for high concept? That wri-die was right: the cop was the natural enemy of the black man, even a black man who'd been to public school and wasn't in the least onstreet or zonkbrained or even bloody American.

Boots shifted, heels clicking on the street. He heard the car door opening. The floor was armoured, so they couldn't shoot through it. This moment, he was turtle safe. It wouldn't last. They could pour petrol in the street and drop a match.

Maybe his Dad would be like Jack Lemmon in *Missing*,

and bust the LA Death Squad story in a fit of grief-stricken political outrage. It didn't seem likely, though.

The engine engaged, loud near his head. They were going to drive a few yards and expose him to the air, like lifting a rock off a worm. He twisted to look at his feet. Moonlight fell on them as the car moved. He pulled in his hand so his fingers wouldn't be squashed under a wheel and banged his elbow on armour-plate.

Lying like an animal, extremities tucked in, he waited for bullets. The boots stood around, in a circle, examining him. He looked up black-clad legs, past weapon-heavy belts to flak-armoured chests and expressionless silver screens.

He remembered the boy in Obregon Street, who had seemed crucified. Suddenly, he prayed for a bullet. The alternative was to be hung up and worked on.

One of the squad popped a stud in his helmet and pulled it off. He was young, of indeterminate race, with long hair tyed back.

'I always like to be face to face,' he said.

12

From the *Corrido* of Diego

'This city grew, encompassing the village of my birth, spreading fingers across the state. Wherever I wandered, I would find myself back in Los Angeles.

'In 1919, my *corrido* caught up with me.

'I was fighting still, striking owners of canning factories

and fruit orchards who treated my people as cruelly as any of the *patrónes* of old. Indeed, many were far worse: with a superfluity of labour, wastage was acceptable. If a union organiser was whipped or an overworked family starved, there were many in line for the job vacancies.

'It was the year of the Great Influenza Epidemic. In a few months, a disease cut down more of my people than the worst sweatshop tyrant could in a lifetime. And what could I do? I could not kill a disease.

'For ninety years, I killed the enemies of my people. But I was alone. The tide of death swept around me, rushing faster. I recognised how little I could do, but each moon night I fought harder, killed more.

'That year, I left my zig-zag-zig in scores of hides.'

'As grapes ripened, itinerant pickers gathered and were signed up for work. I was among their number. We moved into shanty towns near the vineyards, dormitory shacks.

'During the harvest, I found a magazine under my cot at the dormitory, left by one of the few *anglos* who worked the vineyards. It was *All Story Weekly*, and it contained the third instalment of "The Curse of Capistrano", a serial by Johnston McCulley.

'The action was laid in an Old California that never was, a scramble of different times: the time of the mission, the time of Mexican rule, the time of the Gold Rush. The hero of this idiotic fiction was Don Diego de la Vega, a young noble who masked himself and rode as a renegade. This defender of maidenly virtue and justice called himself Zorro, the Fox. In this Zorro, I heard echoes of Joaquin Murieta and Salomon Pico. But in his mark, carved elegantly with the point of a blade rather than slashed with a claw, I saw myself.

'As a people, we tell stories and sing songs. Nothing happens which does not become a story or a song. I had plainly crept into these legends, and in retelling they had seeped through to this *anglo* writer. I do not know where McCulley heard of the zig-zag-zig.

'I was shocked for a moment, but assumed this obscure story would pass and be forgotten. It was, as even I could judge, not very good.'

'The next year, I was running. For the first time, the night-work of Fox was not written off as that of an animal. The name of Diego came up in police investigations, and my description circulated to Pinkertons in the pay of those I killed. The science of the century nipped at my heels.

'I took shelter in the centre of the growing city, in the old district around the fresh, new railroad station. Many thronged to California, looking for work in motion pictures. Cowboys and beauty queens paraded the streets, hoping to be discovered. Thousands had been employed by D.W. Griffith for *Intolerance*, whose sets still dominated a backlot.

'In a mission (at last, I had returned to the world of my father), I heard a film company was looking for men of my people. They paid up to fifty cents a day.

'Between moons I need to eat as anyone else, so I turned up at the United Artists studio. A crowd of red-headed Irishmen and cornfed Swedes were all shouting *caramba* and *arriba* at the tops of their voices. With many others, I was picked as an "extra" in the new Douglas Fairbanks picture.

'On my first day, I was singled out as a "type" by an assistant director in knickerbockers and a knit cap. A costume was found for me, a carnival parody of the dress of the *ricos*, and a moustache gummed to my lip. I was given a hat and a sword and sent to the set.

'These films are now called silent pictures, but the studio was noisier than a factory or battlefield. The air rang with the din of construction, the rattle of cameras, the shouting of directors, the chatter of extras and the boom of powder-puff explosions. Instrumental combos competed and clashed, supplying "mood music" for scenes of love, violence, tragedy and comedy.

'The Fairbanks set represented an Old California *hacienda* or some such nonsense. Doug, as he was called by all, appeared – a notably diminutive hero, which explained why many taller men as qualified by looks as myself were unable to secure employment on his set. He was dressed in black, with a mask and a broad hat.

'Short and tubby as he was, Doug Fairbanks was a hero who looked like a hero. His face, I was relieved to say, did not glow unnaturally. I have never killed anyone famous, which may account for my longevity.

'In the scene being shot under the blazing arc-lights, Doug fought a villainous officer (a type I remembered too well) to a stand-still, humiliating his defeated opponent by leaving a sword-mark on the man's neck.

'After the fight was filmed several times, a make-up

man came on set and worked on the actor who played the dastardly officer. I stood nearby, momentarily fascinated as the make-up man drew in and elaborated a fresh scar. He stood back to admire his handiwork. Doug came over and grinned famously at the wound he was supposed to have inflicted.

'It was a zig-zag-zig. My zig-zag-zig.

'"What's the name of this picture?" I asked another "extra".

'"*The Mark of Zorro*," I was told.'

13

The breath was forced out of Stuart's lungs as the killer cop knelt on his chest, padded knee coming down hard. He slipped a knife from a sheath on his utility belt. Its serrated blade shone silver in moonlight.

The knife would be the last thing Stuart ever saw.

He had published a novel. That was something. A year ago, he'd have said he could die happy after the achievement.

The cop raised the knife for a backhand slash. At the top of the arc, he paused for the briefest instant.

He would have liked to have had sex.

Stuart forced himself to look not at the blade but into the eyes of his murderer. He saw nothing.

'Any last thoughts, nigger?'

This was one time he wouldn't think of the right thing to say twenty minutes after the moment passed.

Then, in a rush, the weight was off him. An animal

– a big dog? – barrelled out of nowhere and struck the cop in the side, wrenching him off Stuart, carrying him across the street and sidewalk. They crashed against the chain-link shutters of a pawnshop.

Under the three ball sign, the animal dropped the cop and trampled with barbed feet. There were scatters of blood.

Stuart sat up, too astonished to hurt. The Death Squad stood about, stunned. The animal moved too swiftly for the mind to develop the eye's photographs. It wasn't a dog, it wasn't a man.

It picked up the cop by the throat and rammed him against the pawnshop shutter. The cop's boots dangled inches above the sidewalk. A sharp thumb gored into his neck. Blood squirted like juice from an orange.

With its free hand – it was more hand than paw, long fingers tipped with horny razors – the animal tore its prey's flak-jacket out through his uniform, exposing a white torso, hairless and untattooed. With three passes of its hand, it left a mark.

Zig-zag-zig.

The animal squeezed harder, and the cop's head popped off his spine. The animal dropped its kill.

The Death Squad brought up firearms and emptied them into the animal. It jitter-slammed against the shutter, explosions bursting against stiff, red fur. Stuart's ears were assaulted by the intolerable blurt of close-up gunfire. Forgotten, he pulled himself to his feet.

He should run.

. . . but he needed to see what happened next.

After a continuous burst of co-ordinated fire, the Death Squad shut off the bullet-spray to examine their kill.

Hey man, should've seen the beast we brought down last night. Freak must've got loose from a zoo or something . . .

The animal still stood, scorched and smoking. Its ragged clothes were holed and afire. But it wasn't dead, didn't seem even to be hurt.

Stuart looked at its eyes. It was not an animal, not entirely.

'Take a head-shot,' someone ordered.

A rifle came up, and a red dot wavered against the beast-man's forehead. There was a bone-snap as the rifle discharged.

'On the button.'

There was a blackened patch above the thatch of darker eyebrow fur, but the eyes were still alive.

'Mother . . .'

The hunter pushed away from the pawnshop, and attacked. Besides the dead killer, there were seven men in the squad. Within twenty seconds, they were all dead or dying.

Stuart couldn't look away. The hunter was fast and sure, a graceful yet deadly dancer. Smooth muscle shifted under a thick pelt. Eyes, teeth and claws shone silver. A red veil splattered across silver.

Several cops got off more shots. Others tried to get away. It was all useless. Uniforms came apart. Screams bubbled through cracked helmets. Limbs wrenched from trunks like twigs from branches, ropy coils of gut pulled through claw-holes.

All the dead were marked with the zig-zag-zig.

It was over so quickly Stuart's ears still ached from the gunfire. He had not got used to the fact that he was saved from the descent of the knife.

Saved, but for how long?

The beast-man who had executed the Death Squad rooted on all-fours among his kill, shutting off voices that still moaned. Satisfied, mouth stuffed with flesh, he stood erect and bipedal. Surrounded by dead, this was the ruler of the Jungle. A broad chest inflated and the hunter howled at the moon.

The howl was an animal sound, but the song of a man was mixed in. Stuart knew eyes were looking, from behind shutters, through windows, from alleys. In the Jungle, they knew about the hunter. They just hadn't told the Man.

The hunter's song ended. With sharp nyctalopic eyes, he glanced about the street. Somewhere above, a helicopter's muffled blades cut through thick air. More back-up coming down.

Stuart was against the abandoned patrol car. The hunter looked at him, full mouth curving wickedly, more and more teeth exposed.

Having fought for it, the hunter was entitled to this scrap of food. This time, Stuart was calm before death.

The hunter's mouth grew wider still. The shark-grin was a smile. The whole snouted head shook as the hunter swallowed what he was chewing. He padded towards Stuart, interest in his intelligent eyes.

The eyes were familiar.

Stuart knew the beast-man wasn't going to kill him.

This hunter bore down only on those who deserved death.

The hunter was close now. Stuart saw a human face buried under the animal's skin, and just failed to recognise it. The beast-man breathed heavily through his snout. He reached out to touch Stuart's face. Stuart saw a leathery, hairless palm; short, ruffled bristles running down each finger; polished, sharp oval knife-nails.

The hunter laid his hand against Stuart's face. Stuart tried not to flinch. They looked at each other, each seeing something.

The beast-man pulled away, almost whirling in the air. He extended a long, clawed forefinger and etched a swift zig-zag-zig into the roof of the patrol car, then bounded away.

Stuart was alone on the street with eight torn and bleeding corpses.

A wave of people appeared and swept across the street, descending on the dead squad like vultures. The black van was hot-wired and driven off. Bodies were stripped of guns, knives, radios, flak-jackets, boots, belts, everything. Stuart was manhandled away from the patrol car, and five young men with gang colours and power tools got to work on it, disassembling the vehicle like a factory team in reverse motion.

He stumbled through the carrion-stripping crowd, thinking of the eyes of the beast-man. For him, the world had changed; he shared the earth with creatures of wonder and moonlight.

A helicopter lowered, and light brighter than the sun

raked across the street. Stuart's eyes stung as if he stared into a nuclear fireball. A call-to-attention signal whined.

Someone fired single shots at the huey, which responded with a rain of strafing. Holes pocked in the asphalt, puncturing legs and vehicles, as a chaingun raked the crowd.

Stuart remembered Muldoon Pezz's apocalypse talk. And the negro spiritual quoted by James Baldwin.

> 'God gave Noah the rainbow sign,
> No more water, the fire next time . . .'

Things were moving too fast to keep up.

'LAPD,' announced a robocop voice from the huey. 'Cease and desist . . .'

The helicopter touched down daintily between bodies. Cops hit the street, firing indiscriminately . . .

'Cease and desist . . .'

This time, Stuart ran.

14

From the Corrido of Diego

'"Hoy, pachuco," I was greeted outside the bar.

'Miguel Ynostrosa whirled down the boulevard, dancing as much as walking, pleated pants flapping. He wore "drapes": high-waisted pants with loose legs and tight cuffs; wide-brimmed hat with a velvet band; jacket a yard across at the shoulders, cinched tight in the middle; a loop of watch-chain; pointed toes and highly polished shoes.

'My outfit was no less outlandish. We were both zoot-suiters. I raised my hand to receive the slap of greeting.

'"Papers come through, Diego," he said. "You lookin at a private, first class."

'Everybody was enlisting. I wondered if there was a way round my lack of birth papers. Throats in Berlin and Tokyo would be the better for Fox's attention. I had always been a lone predator. It was probable I could not survive unnoticed in the services.

'"Maybe soon you're lookin at a *serjente*," Ynostrosa grinned.

'He was a good kid, an epitome of *pachucismo* but with a streak of the political. We'd met collecting for the Sleepy Lagoon Defence Fund.

'To be young and have a Spanish surname in the early forties was to be branded a gangster by the yellow press. When a murder was committed near a swimming hole the Hearst papers tagged "the Sleepy Lagoon", seventeen youths were convicted. The "evidence" consisted of confessions beaten out of the defendants. The case was fought through appeal after appeal. What the Scottsboro Boys were to blacks and Sacco and Vanzetti to union men, Sleepy Lagoon was to the *chicano*.

'Roosevelt promised to be a "Good Neighbour" to Latin Americans abroad, but his policies had no influence with the Los Angeles police, courts and city council.

'We strolled down the boulevard. The bars were full of sailors, in town on leave from the Chavez Ravine

Armory. Everyone was waiting to go overseas. The city was bustling to a swing beat. Panicky citizens had been known to imagine Japanese subs in the municipial plunges and bombers over the LaBrea Tar Pits.

'Ynostrosa suggested we go to the movie theatre. There was a re-release double bill: *The Mark of Zorro*, with Tyrone Power, and *The Wolf Man*, with Lon Chaney. I'd seen both, but there were always people at the theatre, zoot-sooters and their girls. Afterwards, we could get a crowd together and go to one of the night-clubs that admited coloureds and "Mexicans".

'It was early June, a clear night. The breeze smelled of oranges. The moon was past full.

'A sailor slouched at the corner of an alley, dragging on a Lucky, looking up and down the street. I could tell he was look-out. His buddies were probably among the garbage cans with a whore.

'As the sailor saw us, he tossed his butt and looked over his shoulder. There was a faint glow on his face, which shocked me. At this time of the month, my strange sight was at its weakest.

'In the alley, someone was being beaten up. We stopped by the sailor and looked past him. Five of his comrades, caps askew, were beating and kicking a boy who wore a zoot-suit.

'The sailor called; his shipmates left off work and rushed out. We were surrounded by a white wall.

'"Fuckin' zooters," the smallest sailor spat.

'"Zooter" was the 1943 synonym for "greaser".

'A zoot-suit was seen by *anglo* servicemen as a challenge to uniformed manhood. Unjustifiably, zoot-suiters were reckoned draft-dodgers, seducers of left-behind sweethearts, sons of fascist Spain, black marketeers.

'"Strip your drapes," a sailor said, shoving me hard in the chest.

'I snarled, Fox struggling inside me. The moon-time was just past.

'"Fuckin' animals. Look at the hair-oil on this nance, Costigan."

'"Strip your drapes," Costigan repeated.

'The sailors began to rip our clothes. We fought, but there were reinforcements. Word got into the bars that the Navy was giving zoot-suit hoodlums a lesson. More sailors, plus soldiers and marines, rushed to join in.

'Ynostrosa fought harder than I. For so long, I had relied on Fox; now, there was only Diego. Fox was a month away.

'We were stripped to our skivvies, bloodied and battered and left in the street. Then the police came and arrested us. As we were man-handled into a paddy wagon, I saw the uniformed mob roll down the boulevard, siezing another young zoot-suiter. Four were required to hold back a girl as twenty or thirty heroes trampled her beau. As she spat and kicked, hair coming loose from her high pompadour, soldiers made jokes about Mexican spitfires.

'An *anglo* rushed up to the wagon, protesting. He was a bar-owner, and his place had been smashed up by sailors. A zoot-suiter had been thrown through a window.

'"It's a matter for the Shore Patrol," a cop told him, turning away.'

•   •   •

'That night, and for about a week afterwards, hordes of servicemen charged into town, hired fleets of taxicabs, and cruised the streets in search of zooters. Girls were raped, boys were killed, but only *pachucos* were arrested. No sailor, soldier, or marine was charged with any crime. The police adopted a policy of driving meekly in the wake of the mobs and arresting their battered victims. Newspaper editorials praised servicemen who took action against "lawlessness". Many openly lamented that the raids were stopped, on orders from on high, before "the zoot-suit problem" was subjected to a final solution.

'Miguel Ynostrosa never went into the army; he lost the use of his legs.

'In the lock-up, I healed fast and was at least safe from further brutality. Enraged, I heard of the cripples and mothers beaten by the cops when they protested arrests. The Los Angeles City Council adopted a resolution which made the wearing of a zoot-suit a crime.

'I sweated out a long month, knowing the moon nights were approaching. The bars of my cell seemed strong, maybe strong enough to hold Fox. The faces of men around me began to glow. I knew I would have to resist the change.

'I remembered the sailors in the alley. Some faces had glowed, some hadn't. Some believed they were doing the right thing; perhaps they were worse than the men who relished the chance to go out and beat someone up without suffering consequences.

'I was released after three weeks, no charges laid against me. During the moon-nights, I prowled the streets, searching for glowing faces and sailor suits. I found prey, but never saw any of the men who crippled Ynostrosa. I killed drunken servicemen, whom I found alone. Once, I found two Military Policemen raping a girl, and exulted in killing them. The girl saw me up close, but never told.

'At the end of the full moon, I was exhausted. I had done nothing, though the press screamed at the police for failing to catch the "Zorro Killer" who left the zig-zag-zig on his victims. Those who had attacked the zoot-suiters were mainly overseas, directing aggression against the Japanese; within a few years, most would probably be dead. It was not up to me which would live through Guadalcanal or Midway; just and unjust, good and bad, all would fall in this war.'

'I was tired and I knew what Hendrik had meant by my *curse*. No matter how I fought and killed for my people, no matter how many zig-zag-zigs I left, I could do nothing.

'I was one creature, alone and unaided. Evil was too vast, a mob with no true leaders. I couldn't even protect friends like Ynostrosa, let alone an entire race, an entire country. But still I saw the glow in the faces of those who deserved to die, still I changed on moon-nights and left my zig-zag-zig.

'I got into the war, working in a defence plant. In October, 1944, the convictions of the Sleepy Lagoon defendants were reversed by the Court of Appeals. By then, they had served two years in jail. When released, several youths of previous good character turned in bitterness to crime and were swiftly returned to prison.

'When men with Spanish names came back from the Just War minus limbs or with medal ribbons and insisted they be served in "No Mexicans" bars and restaurants, things began to change a little, on the surface.

'I began to feel old.'

15

Firefights lit up the Jungle. The War on Zonk had just passed DefCon 4. A row of window-fronts exploded as fire raked across them. Next to tonight's police action, the Rodney King beating was a misfiled parking ticket.

Stuart jogged through the pre-emptive riot reprisal, running with the fox as hounds made steady progress down wide streets. No arrests were being made, but instant sentences were carried out.

If he had a gun, he would shoot back.

There'd be nothing worth looting in the burning stores. People were too busy fleeing to take advantage of excellent terms offered on electrical goods.

This all couldn't be some crazy scheme to trap the beast-man. This was way too big, way too organised. Even for a wonder like the hunter Stuart had seen, there was no need to send in an army. This had the feel of something long in the planning.

From helicopters, soothing voices assured those on the ground that they should lay down their arms and surrender.

'You will not be harmed.'

Nobody believed that. There were no innocent by-standers any more. If you got shot: sorry, but you must have been guilty.

What the hell was this all about?

Stuart made a bad decision, and took a left into a cross-street that turned out to be a blind alley. A wire-topped wall came up in front. He could never get over it.

He turned and pain caught up with him. His lungs and knees hurt. He was seven years away from his last rugby match; the only exercise he had taken since was climbing stairs.

'Shit,' he breathed.

A cop came into the alley, a flash-light fixed to his helmet like a miner's lamp. That gave him both hands free to hold his gun.

Stuart reached into his jacket pocket and pulled out his passport.

'British citizen,' he said. 'Diplomatic Immunity,' he lied. '*Civius romanus sum*,' he tried, desperately.

'Who ya got?' someone shouted from outside the alley.

'Nigger on zonk,' the cop said over his shoulder.

As the someone advised 'waste him', Stuart pushed himself away from the wall and at the cop.

He felt the gunbarrel slam against his shoulder, and was sure he'd been shot. The cop, surprised, collapsed backwards. His gun skittered away into garbage.

Stuart felt his wound. The barrel had just gouged at him, not even ripping his clothes.

Angry, he dug into the cop's chest with his knees and

wrestled off the lamp-helmet. A face appeared. Young, white, freckles. Stuart made a fist and smashed the cop's nose, over and over.

Policemen Are Your Friends, he'd been taught in infants' school. Cop is the natural-born enemy of the black man, he'd been told at a party.

Something animal inside made it necessary for Stuart to break this killer cop's skull. He was becoming acclimatised to the Jungle.

A slim shadow fell on Stuart and the cop. Stuart looked up.

'Stop fuckin' around and ice the pig,' a girl said.

Anger froze.

Ice, waste, *kill* . . .

'Pussy,' the girl said, kneeling. In the lamp-circle, Stuart recognised the half-Oriental who had been with the Alcalde. She had a little silver gun, which she fired into the cop's forehead.

Stuart felt the cop die, the last writhe of his body like a hobby-horse between his legs.

He stood up, shuddering, cold.

'Come on, gangsta,' the girl said, 'let's get offstreet.'

She led him out of the alley and along the sidewalk to a door. Mop-up crews were proceeding ruthlessly down the boulevard.

The girl got the door open and shoved Stuart through. They were in a hallway, lit only by scarchbeam passes over a skylight.

'Esperanza,' said a weak voice. 'That you?'

Stuart looked at her. She shrugged and said, 'Esperanza Nguyen. Some call me Warchild, but that's kidshit.'

The girl shouted back, identifying herself.

A door was opened and Esperanza marched Stuart into a room. Computers and desk-top publishing equipment on desks, framed covers of Spanish language periodicals on the walls.

One of the boys from the Coffee Stop, side soaked with blood, jittered around.

'How is he?' Esperanza asked.

'Bad, man, *muy* bad.'

In a baggy leather chair slumped the Alcalde, face drained white. He looked as if he'd been beaten extensively. On a desk by him was an old-style square TV set, with news coverage. There were aerial views of the burning Jungle.

Irises showed ID photos of García and Scotchman.

'What is this about?' Stuart asked.

'You, gangsta,' Esperanza said.

The iris showed Stuart's passport shot. He hated it; he was wearing his old school tie.

'They say you've been taken out by a zonk gang,' she said, translating the garble of the newscast. 'Two cops are dead, you just missing. There's an "orgy of cop killing" going down, and Chief Ryu is sending in Special Tactical Groups.'

The TV cut to Mayor Jute, improbably well-groomed for someone hauled out of bed in the middle of the night.

'Genfems of the press,' she said, 'the officers who've fallen will be honoured. The sympathies of the city are for the significant partners and offspring of the law enforcement casualties.'

'What about the ridealong?' a non-CGI journo asked.

'Every effort is being exerted to recover Stuart Finn. I have just interfaced with Prime Minister Heseltine and assured him our best non-gender specific operatives are onstreet . . .'

'I didn't vote for *him*,' Stuart blurted.

'At this temporal juncture, it seems decreasingly likely that Mr Finn is still living. The Zonk Gangs have demonstrated in the past their savage ruthlessness.'

Back in the studio, the news-anchor summed up. 'Following an unprovoked attack by gangs, two LAPD officers are confirmed dead . . .'

Grainy homevideo footage showed two burned bodies hanging from cuffed wrists. The camera focused on a boiled face. It was García.

'. . . and a British writer on a ridealong is missing . . .'

García and Scotchman had set Stuart up, then been set up themselves. This was a stage-managed riot.

But why?

'Chief Ryu has vowed . . .'

The Alcalde spasmed with coughing. Stuart thought the man had a couple of broken ribs, at least.

'They're coming down like a hard rain,' the boy said. 'Soon as this shit started, they got the Alcalde. It was deliberate, man. On radio, I got word others have been taken out. Not just gangstas, man. Others like the Alcalde. That commie priest, he's dead. And a couple of women from the Committee for the Disappeared. It was a surgical strike. Shut up the trouble-makers, man.'

Esperanza was thoughtful.

'All this community spirit garbage is over,' the boy

waved around. There were anti-zonk posters, schedules for educational drives, portraits of positive ethnic role models. 'The Caldiarres were right, Warchild. We should just've fought back.'

The Alcalde died.

Esperanza thought it over. The boy hefted a machine pistol, itching to get onstreet and take out some cop butt. Finally, the girl nodded agreement.

'Gangsta,' she said, pointing at Stuart, 'we dead by dawn, dead or disappeared. You, you have to live, live to show the lie. You a writer, right? Tell this story. Tell them all how it went down.'

It seemed a fair bet to say Stuart would not be working on the *Shadowstalk* script any more.

'You a hero, man,' the boy said. 'I can see it on you.'

He was alone. The explosions had died down, though there were still bursts of gunfire. The TV chattered quiet lies, and repeated shock footage of edited truth. There was talk of arrested zonk gangstas, but not of slain communtiy leaders.

The Alcalde was under a dust-sheet. Stuart gathered he had tried to give his people an example, tried to keep them out of the gangs, off the drugs. Something about the waste of effort chilled Stuart to despair. There were kids out onstreet who had hung with the Alcalde, studied hard and tried their best; they were just as dead as the zonkbrains and gangstas.

He wondered where the beast-man was in this fight. Lost, probably. In a city-wide battle, one small impossible wonder counted for little.

The office door opened.

'Fuck shit death,' Stuart said.

A young man staggered in. It was Vega, one of the Alcalde's boys. His clothes were a ruin. He had been in a fight.

'Black man,' he said, looking at Stuart. 'I'm spent.'

His eyes shone. Stuart recognised them and staggered back against a desk.

Vega smiled; the smile became a snarl. The hunter's snout surfaced in Vega's face and receded again.

Now Stuart knew Vega's secret, could the beast-man let him live? The whole of Los Angeles had reasons for finding it more convenient if Stuart Finn were dead.

'What did I do?' he said. 'I wrote a book? Hollywood called, I took the money. Do I deserve to die for it?'

'Depends on the movie,' Vega said, grinning.

16

From the *Corrido* of Diego

'So, black man, that is what I am, what I have done, what I have been, what I have learned.

'Some call me monster, some call me hero. They will call you the same things. I know truly I am neither. I am merely a fool. I know I can make no difference, can change nothing but myself, but I have been compelled to try. Many are deservedly dead by my hand, but many more equally as deserving never crossed my path. I have felled tiny trees in an ever-expanding jungle.

'That poor dead man, the Alcalde, was better than I. He was a man of peace, of learning, of love. His way was best. And yet he has been killed. Others, men and women of good will, are slaughtered. This is as bad a time as I have known and it wearies me more than I can tell. I am near the end of my days and I am not sorry.

'At first, I understood that I killed for my *people*. I was wrong, I killed for my *kind*. Chicano, black, white, whatever. My kind is all colours. I am of the *pobres*, the poor, the oppressed, the neglected, the inconvenient. I am the cry of the sad, the true *grito de dolores*. My task has been futile, but I have not abandoned it until now.

'You are different from me. You will understand the *curse*. You will tilt at windmills, for you have no choice. You will stand knee-deep in the sea and cry "go back, waves". I am truly sorry for you, but I have no choice, as I have never had a choice. Your face shines, not as the faces of those I kill shine, but with a rainbow brilliance. The *viejo* must have seen that rainbow in my own face.

'Live long with your legend, black man . . .'

17

'What do you mean?' Stuart asked.

'This,' Diego Vega said, holding out a frail hand. Pain passed across his face. His eyes were ancient.

Diego struck out, and touched Stuart's face.

It was an electric jolt. Stuart convulsed and fell,

banging his head against a desk-leg. His body throbbed as something coursed through his flesh.

After a time, his mind came back together. He did not know how long he had been space-voyaging inside his skull. The *corrido* Diego Vega had told him was imprinted in his brain, as if the man's memories had passed from his mind to Stuart's at the moment of the jolt.

Scrambling across the floor, he found a body. Diego Vega was dead; an old man, withered to a husk. There was no particular expression of peace on his face. Nobody was home.

Stuart stood, wondering how he was changed.

As Diego had spoken, the noise from the Jungle had changed. Fewer shots and explosions, more sirens and helicopters. They had ignored the TV as the flickering images of violence became pacified. Onstreet, the Tactical Squads were taking control.

Stuart knew he should get out of the office. People were looking for him. He had to find the right way of coming out of the Jungle. It had to be public, preferably televised. Mayor Jute had said he was probably dead, and many of her subordinates wouldn't hesitate to turn her supposition into a statement of fact.

The door was kicked open and three cops with shotguns piled in, levelling gleaming barrels.

Stuart, in the throes of a change he couldn't understand, was still going to die. He would die before he had achieved his potential.

'It's him,' a cop said. 'Finn, the Brit.'

They paraded him, half-captive and half-trophy. An officer made a comprehensive report into a wafer-phone,

The Jungle was tamed. The dead had been disappeared. Now things were being cleaned up. Teams shifted the burned-out cars, searched for survivors and culprits, even picked up empty shell-cases like litter collectors.

Stuart was still too high on the jolt he had taken to be tired. Last night, several times, he'd thought he was a changed man. Now, he truly was. He remembered Diego's voice, at once urgent and discursive, and the *corrido* that had been an education and a preparation.

Small businessmen sighed outside smoking wrecks. Crying mothers searched for missing sons. Floral tributes lay on corpse outlines. Cops stood around with paper cups of coffee. Newsteams scavenged for interviews with firefighters and cops.

Everyone would want Stuart's story.

He was hustled to an intersection where a tangle of newsies pointed cameras and mikes at a knot of officials. There were uniform cops, faces grimed from the action, and serious, smiling dignitaries. He recognised Chief Ryu and Mayor Jute.

Their faces glowed like moonlight.

The gleam made Stuart sick. He clenched fists, and felt his sharp, strong nails breaking his skin. His forefingers were lengthening, strange aches in their knuckles. The pain was not unpleasant, and made him aware of the growing reconfigurations of his nerves and senses.

The crowds parted and Stuart was welcomed. Hundreds of questions were asked, but a suit Stuart had never seen explained, 'Mr Finn is exhausted from his gruelling ordeal, but will answer all serious inquiries later.'

Stuart knew he'd rate a debriefing before he was allowed to say anything.

Chief Ryu and the Mayor competed to shake his hand. The Mayor, a head taller, won. Dazed by the almost-opaque wasp's nest of light around her head, Stuart accepted Mayor Jute's grip.

He left her palm bloody, and smiled.

'I'm sorry,' he apologised.

'This atrocious situation will not be repeated,' Chief Ryu insisted to the media. 'When the moon comes out tonight, things will be different.'

'That's true,' Stuart said. Reaching out as if dazed, he wiped his bloody hand on the hood of a police armoured car. It was warm in August sunlight.

Diego Vega had talked most of the day away, invisibly dying all the while, something inside him gathering to make a *leap*. Now, evening was rushing on, and night was creeping after.

As Stuart's smile stretched, he ran his tongue over his teeth and felt an unfamiliar sharpness.

'Regardless of the bleats of the bleeding heart bunch,' Ryu said, arms extended, 'there is Evil all around us. And Evil must be suppressed. Wrong-doers must be punished.'

'I couldn't agree more,' Stuart said.

He looked at the car he had smeared. His mark was drying. His mark in blood.

Zig-zag-zig.

Having done an intricate vampire story in *Anno Dracula*, which originated as a piece for Stephen Jones's *Mammoth Book of Vampires*, I was hunting around for an idea to work up into a similarly large-scale piece for Steve's follow-up *Mammoth Book of Werewolves* when I hit upon the immediate inspiration for this story, the Chordettes' record of the 'Zorro' theme song, from which the title comes. I must also credit three invaluable books for crystalising my feelings about Los Angeles, California history and Zorro: Mike Davis's *City of Quartz: Excavating the Future in Los Angeles*, Carey McWilliams's *North From Mexico: The Spanish Speaking People of the United states* and Bill Yenne's *The Legend of Zorro*.